BOUND IN BLUE

The Narvan · Book Three

Jean Davis

All characters, places and events portrayed in this novel are fictional. No resemblance to any specific person, place or event is intended.

BOUND IN BLUE: Book Three of The Narvan

www.jeandavisauthor.com

Edited by Joan Young

ISBN-13:   978-1-7345701-6-8 (print)
                978-1-7345701-7-5 (ebook)

First Edition: February 2021

Published by StreamlineDesign LLC

Also by Jean Davis

The Last God
Sahmara
A Broken Race
Destiny Pills and Space Wizards
Dreams of Stars and Lies
Everyone Dies
Not Another Bard's Tale
Spindelkin
Frayed
19

The Narvan

One Shot at the Sphinx
Trust
The Minor Years
Chain of Gray
Bound in Blue
Seeker
Tears of the Tyrant

I adjusted my son's stance yet again within the small arena bordered by furniture that we'd shoved aside. "You need to keep your eyes on me. Watch what I'm doing. Be aware."

"I am." Daniel shoved his shaggy hair out of his face. "You're way bigger than me."

"There are a lot of people bigger than me. That doesn't mean I can't take them down."

Instead of coming at me again, he stood up straight and turned away, heading for one of the chairs at the edge of our makeshift training space in the middle of the common room. I brushed over Neko's link, making sure he was still with Stassia in her lab. She wouldn't be happy to come home to this mess or to find me working with Daniel, but he needed to burn off some energy and I needed something to keep me busy.

No amount of credits had swayed the local shipping companies to let me buy in. The human colony of Pentares had no use for a large scarred, obviously modified, Artorian who attracted a herd of enforcers every time he left the apartment. Other than adopting the High Council's practice of wearing a hooded cloak, there wasn't much I could do to hide my distinctive appearance.

Life here was boring as all hells, but considering the unholy surplus of vastly unpleasant excitement I'd endured prior to my arrival on Pentares, I wasn't complaining. Very much.

"I hate it here." Daniel flopped into the chair, folding his arms over his chest.

"I know."

"So do you. Ikeri said so. Why can't we go live somewhere else? Why do you pretend to like this place?"

I really needed to do something about my daughter reading my mind and sharing her discoveries. The only sure way to keep her out of my head would be to shut down our connection like I had when I'd left them before my imprisonment, but I wasn't willing to do that again. Her calming presence was one of the few things keeping me sane when the hellish visions hit at all hours of the day and night.

"Your mother likes it. She has a career here."

And I liked seeing her happy. Anastassia thrived on being in control, and since the High Council had screwed her over, she'd been trying to find her way back to a position like this. Supervising her lab was a far cry from advising a star system, but she found the job satisfying. I refused to take that from her.

Using the knowledge she'd garnered in her early years of working with her father, and later from overseeing Merkief and the Artorian University as they carried out experiments for the High Council and for the betterment of the Narvan, Anastassia had made quite a name for herself here. It wasn't necessarily that she was brilliant, at least not in a scientific mind kind of way, but she'd observed a lot of things and had a knack for at least generally understanding them. It also helped that old or common knowledge from the Narvan was seen as a downright cutting edge discovery in this corner of the known universe.

The pay wasn't half bad either.

Her lab had taken over most of the building where I'd found her after Merkief, Jey, and I had eradicated the High Council, allowing me to escape after years of punishment at the Council's hands. Her staff kept growing, and though Raphael, the human who had hoped to replace me, was still one of them, they all treated her with the utmost respect.

That might have been because they knew I could appear there at any time without warning. I made her employees more nervous than the local enforcers.

"I want to see Artor," said Daniel.

"I want you to see it, too."

He'd never been to my homeworld. Maybe he'd find his place there, surrounded by people the same size as us, who looked like us. Or at least, like him. Thankfully for everyone in the known universe, there weren't many people as damaged as dealing with the Council had left me. Ikeri, favoring her mother, fit in among the humans quite well and was doing fine attending school with them. Daniel did not.

I'd taken pity on him shortly after my arrival, and in an effort to occupy my days while Anastassia was working, had taken over educating him at home. My way.

"Then let's go," Daniel said. "Your link has been working for what, a year and a half now? We can Jump there and back before mom comes home." He gave me a challenging stare. "I won't tell if you won't."

I shook my head and pointed him to the ancient terminal by the table. "You have work to do."

If I set one foot on Artor I wouldn't want to leave again. Maybe Stassia was that distracted with her job, or my time with the Council had finally honed my ability to lie to her, but I'd gotten a lot of shit by her since my arrival on Pentares. Visiting home would be too big to hide.

The last time I'd given an inch to my ambition, I'd ended up a slave to the Council. I liked to think I might have learned a lesson.

I'd already caved and contacted Jey a year ago through our linked connection to start consulting on Narvan business. But I'd told Stassia about that after a couple days. I'd assured her that I had no plans to go there in person, that it was just something to do, helping a friend.

From time to time, she asked me how it was going, but neither of us gave the endeavor much voice. It was almost as if we were both avoiding that particular temptation.

Daniel heaved a great sigh as he pried himself out of the chair and meandered toward the terminal. I put the furniture back with practiced efficiency. We'd been doing this for almost as long as my link had been fully operational.

Anastassia had been adamant that our kids have normal lives here, like we'd had on Veria Minor before Jey and Merkeif had screwed things up. The kind of lives that didn't require learning to use weapons or fighting. That all sounded well and good, but Daniel had found his own trouble here in my absence. He needed a constructive outlet before he got into something worse than fighting kids from school. I let Ikeri have Anastassia's normal, but my son was going to get the kind of education he would have received on Artor, had we been able to go home.

Whether Anastassia noticed I was going against her wishes or was merely pretending not to, I didn't dare guess. There were enough things that I lied about on a daily basis—like why I couldn't sleep for more than a couple hours at a time, or why I couldn't remember people or events that she referred to. I was grateful that our training sessions weren't on the list.

"When is Uncle Isnar coming home?" asked Daniel.

"He assured me he'd be back in time to help make dinner."

Daniel nodded, sitting up straighter in his chair and at least appearing to focus on his assignments.

My return had allowed for a dramatic increase in free time for our two guards. While Neko enjoyed spending off shifts with the locals, Fa'yet preferred quiet and the female company of our own kind. Now that he didn't have to worry about the Council hunting him down, he'd chosen to return to his home on Karin, only Jumping back to Pentares to fulfill his obligatory shifts so Neko could sleep and I could pretend to.

Once I was sure Daniel had settled in, I touched the natural connection I shared with Ikeri. She was enjoying some time outside with her classmates before they returned to their studies. She made friends easily. Likely because she had a bad habit of slipping into their minds and knowing exactly what to say.

I kept dropping hints to Stassia that we needed to get her into some sort of training for that. Veria Prime or Minor seemed the best choice. Stassia had connections there, and we were all familiar with the culture, having lived on Minor when the kids were little. We could find a Seeker there to help Ikeri learn to control the hybrid telepathy created by mixing Stassia's abilities with mine. Artor had never smiled on hybrids, but that was my backup option. Not that it mattered. Stassia avoided my hints as though I'd never given voice to them. She continued to work with Ikeri on her own.

I spent the next couple hours on the couch, half-watching Daniel and answering his occasional questions while looking over the latest batch of reports that Jey had sent me. Daniel's sporadic tapping on the keyboard and the soft squeaks of his chair as he shifted his position slowly faded into the background. The words on my eyelids began to blur.

When I became aware again, a harsh yellow light beat down from above. Hot and humid air filled the tall domed room. The acrid smell of digestive fluids lingered from Arpex's last meal. I wiped my face on the sleeve of my grey suit, but the fabric came away bloody. The side of my face throbbed. Arpex had been snacking on my memories again, but I'd fooled it, giving it something other than what it had asked for. I didn't need a mirror to know that Arpex's fury had caused me to shred the side of my face.

Arin, the Council's spy and my cellmate, was suddenly there, looming over me with a wet cloth. He dabbed at my face while casting worried glances at the platform high above us where Arpex rested.

"Why am I here?" I asked. "This base is gone. Destroyed. Arpex is dead. You're dead."

Arin smiled sadly, his scars puckering alongside his face. "Vayen, you're not important, remember? This is our life now. Rest."

I tasted blood. My ribs ached where Arpex was fond of kicking me.

Doubt crept in. Was this real?

"This is a dream," I told him. "The Council is gone. I'm on Pentares with my family."

Arin held me down. "Pentares is a dream. Your family is a dream. This is real. Go back to sleep and dream if you want to. It's all we have left."

I had to get up, to get out of there. But I was weak, sluggish, and slow. I couldn't shake Arin's heavy weight. Panic took hold. I had to get out of the domed room.

I couldn't be there again, not another day. Another hour. I couldn't lose anything else.

Thought-rending pain seared my wrist. Arpex's claw sawed through flesh and tendons, shattering bone. My hand dropped to the floor beside me, blackened with decay, the skin shriveled. The putrid stench of rotten flesh overwhelmed me. Gasping for air, I beat at Arin with the one hand I had left, reaching for his face, but never getting close enough.

And then I was awake on the couch, sweating and terrified. I sat there, listening, but the terminal was quiet. Slowly, still catching my breath, I got to my feet to find I was alone.

"Daniel?"

"I'm in here," he called from his room. "Thought I'd let you sleep. Mom says you don't sleep enough."

"Thanks." But it would have been far kinder to wake me than leaving me to all the shit that haunted my dreams.

The only way I managed more than a couple hours in a row was a serious workout with Neko or a workout of a different sort with Stassia. Or drinking heavily. But that wasn't something I could get away with regularly without gaining notice.

It was bad enough that I'd uprooted my family from our relatively normal life on Veria Minor in my attempt to take back the Narvan, only to have that go tragically sideways. Then I'd stranded them out here in the middle of relative nowhere to make a new life for themselves—which ended up being without me for nearly three and half years. They didn't need to be weighed down by any more of my shit. I'd get by. I would make this work for their sakes.

I sat down at the terminal to check over Daniel's work but ended up staring out the window. From up on our floor, the jungle was visible beyond the city. It would have been nice to be closer to it, to something green and natural, away from the perpetual noise of traffic and the smell of too many people and vehicles in close proximity. But this was the home they'd chosen without me.

Arin's voice echoed in my head, as it often did, still trying to convince me that this reality was the dream. Running my hands over the worn surface of the desk, the textured weave of my pants, and the smooth clearplaz of the window, I assured myself that this was real.

But I still tasted blood. My tongue sought out the truth, finding a sore spot where I must have bitten the inside of my cheek in my sleep. I was awake.

I was pretty sure.

Either way, this version of reality beat the hells out of the other one.

My concentration was shot. I gave up on Jey's reports and Daniel's work and spent the rest of the afternoon cleaning up the apartment. The bots here were junk, outdated like everything else, worse than even the cheap bot my parents had owned. Neko said he'd tweaked it to the best of his ability, but it still didn't reach Stassia's standards of cleanliness and order. I had plenty of time, and it was more efficient if I did most of the work myself. Besides, the physical activity helped keep my mind off things.

As he had before my arrival, Neko split his day between Stassia's lab and Ikeri's school, monitoring the other through vid feeds from cameras he'd set up in both locations. He and Fa'yet had set up a networked interface that they both accessed through their links, allowing everyone some personal space.

Maybe they didn't have to worry about threats here. They might have all gone about having regular boring lives instead of being guards and guarded. But they hadn't. It may have been habit or perhaps they couldn't kick the feeling something bad was waiting right around the corner any more than I could. They'd continued the roles they'd left the Narvan with, even in this relatively safe and uncomplicated corner of the known universe.

Neko let me know the three of them would be home soon. He'd left Stassia's lab and now they were heading over to get Ikeri.

I'd picked her up once. Due to the level of panic that had caused among the young kids and the barrage of questions Ikeri had had to answer for weeks afterward, we'd all agreed that it would be best if I avoided that task.

Fa'yet arrived with supplies for dinner in hand. Daniel burst from his room upon hearing bags rustling on the counter. The two of them struck up an animated conversation punctuated with the clanking of utensils and pans.

Anastassia, Neko, and Ikeri came in shortly after the tantalizing scent of baked fish filled the apartment. Not only did Fa'yet staying in his own house give us all more room, but it also allowed plenty of time for him to come up with veritable feasts for dinner nearly every night. And the majority of the food came from Artor. My stomach appreciated that greatly. Between the good food and spending my mornings in the local gym with Neko or, on occasion, Stassia, I'd recovered the mass and muscle that had melted away during my incarceration and then some. Not that it mattered. I wasn't doing a damned thing that required speed, agility, or strength, but I did feel more like myself. More like Shoulders or anyone else wasn't going to be able to beat me down ever again.

While I'd been gone, Daniel had worked himself into a kitchen assistant position, cooking alongside his honorary uncle with great enthusiasm. Seeing the two of them together made me angry about the years I'd missed. Daniel had been in good hands, but even having been back as long as I had, there still seemed to be a distance between us. We didn't have the easy-going camaraderie we'd once had, that he now had with Fa'yet and Neko. Maybe it was because he was into his moody adolescent years and neither of them was his father. Or maybe he was still resentful over me being gone as long as I had been. Whatever his issue was, he had no interest in talking about it.

Ikeri gave me a quick hug and promised to tell me about her day later. Neko nodded my way and went to his room to disarm. Fa'yet was technically on duty once everyone was home.

Anastassia sat down beside me, chattering about her staff. She took out her braid and shook out her hair, her signal that she was done working for the day. Neko had confided that she'd often brought work home with her before I'd returned, but now she left it all in the lab. He claimed it was an improvement. I wished she was more distracted some evenings. Like this one, when echoes of Arin's voice were still in my head. But she carried on without giving me any grief about my general silence.

Was it because she understood? She'd done time with the Council too. Sure, she'd been weak, half-starved, dealing with the damage to her brain and link, and they'd convinced her I was dead, but once we got past that, she'd seemed all right. I never noticed her waking in a cold sweat to the degree I did, and in a quick analysis of her behavior after her incarceration, I couldn't pinpoint anything that made me suspect she was covering for memory loss, certainly not on the scale I was. Maybe she was just really good at faking it, or Arpex had taken memories of her past before she'd met me. But she talked of her father and brother in passing and, when we were alone, sometimes of her friends she'd left behind on the Verian station. She remembered Chesser. I couldn't think of any other memories the Arpex might have found particularly tasty. She didn't talk about the time she'd served, and I hadn't pried. Perhaps she was simply returning the favor.

We made it through an uneventful but enjoyable dinner, during which everyone provided the requisite answers to how their day had gone. Once that was over, Neko went to bed. Daniel cleaned the dishes. Fa'yet took the chair at the terminal. His glazed look told me that his attention was focused on his link where he could access the security system. Ikeri settled in at the table with Stassia to continue whatever therapy or lessons the two of them were on these days. With all the chaos in my head, I didn't need Ikeri in there more than she already was. I left them to it and poured my Stassia-approved single drink for the night. I did manage to make it the strongest liquor Pentares had to offer without any of my housemates questioning my choice. The size of my one glass had grown over time, also without open comment. It took the edge off the chaos in my head just enough to help me begin to relax.

Settling back onto the couch, I turned on the local vid so I could feign caring about what was going on in the world of people who had no use for me. I mostly ignored the words, the majority of which I didn't understand, nor did I have any inclination to make the effort to learn. Instead, I attempted to focus on the pictures because they kept the visions of glaring yellow light and fiery explosions at bay. The news also gave me something to time my drinking by, making me stretch out my one large glass over a whole hour rather than just gulping it down. More civilized, as it were. I was trying.

In the midst of contemplating what Neko and I could work on in the gym in the morning that might wear me out enough to allow me a few more hours of real sleep after everyone went about their day, something like a hardened bubble nudged my internal awareness. It brought with it a familiarity that appeased my sudden panic that a surviving High Council member was nearby and reestablishing a very unwelcome contact.

A long-disused natural connection came to life. At first, it was a whisper, too quiet to make out. Then Stassia's presence was there.

She'd undergone surgery again on Minor after our arrival due to further complications from the damage the Council had caused. That had helped improve our bonded connection, but this was almost as if the Council's damage had been erased. Stassia was back.

I whipped around to see her grinning. Ikeri beamed beside her. The whispers of emotion that had sustained her end of our bonded connection for years were washed away by the tidal wave of excitement that rushed at me clear as day.

"It worked," said a voice in my head that I'd deeply missed.

Natural speech, one mind to another, was far more intimate than the vocal variety we'd been relegated to for too long. Though I wanted to reply in kind, a hundred questions begged to be asked simultaneously. My brain and tongue warred for the opportunity, rendering me speechless on both fronts.

I nodded. Finally my tongue won. "What did you do?"

"I fixed her. Sort of," said Ikeri. "It took a long time, but now I know how."

"You fixed her?" I wanted to run over and hug them both, but I was too stunned to move. "How? What do you mean, sort of?"

Stassia jumped out of her chair and ran over to me, her entire face aglow. "Do you think this means I might be able to host a link again?"

My heart began to race. If her natural speech had returned, we could talk to one another at a distance. Link or not, we might be able to work together like we had before. We could leave this fucking colony and get back to doing what we both loved.

I grabbed her and pulled her onto my lap, spilling my half-full glass of costly mind-numbing liquor all over the cushion and my pants. I didn't care.

"We'd have to have the LEs at the University take a look at you," I said, barely holding my own excitement in cautious check.

She kissed my cheek and scrambled off me, tugging at my hand like an exuberant kid. "Well, what are you waiting for? Let's go."

ONE

"I hate to complain boss, but it's been eleven days since anyone has tried to kill you. No one's even threatened. I'm getting bored," said Neko. He'd been my ever-present shadow since Stassia and I had decided to bring our family back to the Narvan six months ago.

"Sorry, I doubt the Premier is going to make things any more exciting for you." Granted, he was five minutes late for our meeting, but I wasn't going to get aggravated over that quite yet.

The door opened, allowing the Artorian Premier's secretary to bustle in. "Please accept our most sincere apologies for the delay, Advisor Ta'set."

He bowed and sat in the chair to the left of the Premier's desk. The Premier joined us a moment later, his usually crisp and pressed shirt appeared rumpled and his thick silver chain of office hung askew. He wiped at a stray grey hair on his lined forehead and gave me a tight nod.

"Do we have a problem?" I asked.

"We need more funding. All this scrambling and juggling is going to fall apart any day. Work will grind to a halt and protests will spring up. It's all downhill from there." He shook his head and took his seat. "Your designated replacement drained us dry."

"He has been dealt with."

Merkief. The stench of burnt flesh made me gag. I took a deep breath and let it out slowly.

"And I appreciate your advice on recovering our losses, truly, but it's not enough." His hands fidgeted on the desk. He licked his lips. "We're going to need a loan."

"A loan is only a bandage. We need to address long-term solutions."

And I had no credits to loan, not after financing Jey's reclaiming of the Narvan from Kess and then relocating my family during my imprisonment. Stassia's income on Pentares had given us a little cushion upon our return, but on a good day, with a couple years worth of Kryon payouts thoroughly and wisely invested, I would have been hard-pressed to hand over the amount that it would take to bail out an entire planet's financial problems.

"We've already addressed those solutions. Progress is being made, however, it's not working fast enough." He licked his lips again.

I rested my oversized grey replacement hand on the desk, mere inches away from his. His gaze darted to the ugly black nails protruding from the thick grey fingers. Stassia had suggested that I get a more fitting replacement now that we were back home, but I'd grown used to this mismatched one. It fit the rest of me.

"You've enjoyed a long term of office," I said.

He sat back in his chair, nostrils flaring. "This isn't my fault. We did what was asked of us. We've always given what you and your people ask for. Always. Because you've treated us well. You've helped us recover and grow and expand faster than we'd thought possible. I'm asking this one thing, this one time, for your people. We need this loan."

Damn all the High Council manipulation and infighting between Merkief, Jey, and Kess. They'd created a hellish mess of the tidy and productive package I'd left behind. Jey had been making strides to set things right during my long absence, but there was a lot of damage to recover from. The Premier was right. It wasn't his fault, and my people shouldn't have to suffer for it.

I sighed. "I'll need details, where the credits will go, what you'll lose if you don't get them. On each and every damn program potentially affected. Got it?"

Hopefully, Stassia could help me figure out how to pull credits out of nowhere. When we'd destroyed the High Council, we also destroyed our source of lucrative income. Jey and I had been strategizing for over a year before I'd returned to the Narvan, trying to figure out how we could generate the income we were used to having at our disposal. Neither of us had come up with a sustainable answer.

The Premier nodded and then gave me a look like a man about to ask how I meant to kill him. "And the terms of the loan?"

"Will be discussed when I give you my answer."

He stared at the desktop. "And when—"

"When I get to it. This might be my homeworld, but it's not the only planet in the Narvan."

He stiffened. "Thank you for your kind offer, Advisor Ta'set. I'll get that information to you shortly."

I stood.

"Where to next?" asked Neko through our linked connection.

"Home."

Hopefully no one would want to kill me there either. Neko might be bored, but I'd had enough of dodging bullets for several lifetimes.

When he'd hired on with us, our lives had been a chaotic mess, we'd all been scrambling to survive. He'd been dependable from day one, but the years on Pentares with Fa'yet and Stassia had fine-tuned-his training and allowed him time to get comfortable and confident in his duties. Being back in the Narvan now, he thrived on all the action, reminding me a bit too much of myself when I'd simply served as a bodyguard for Stassia. I hoped it didn't take him as long to learn to appreciate the eventless days as it had taken me.

We Jumped to the foyer of the home I'd purchased on Artor upon our return. The large sprawling estate had belonged to the previous Premier. It was even more opulent than the mansion Stassia had owned on Merchess and had the price tag to show for it. Not that I cared about the grand estate quite so much as the space it offered, both inside—we'd all lived in cramped quarters for too long—and out, where the large parcel of property kept us away from the general public.

Still more credits had gone into a bribe so that the public security satellites avoided our house. I'd also bought a new wardrobe of comfortable Artorian clothes, including new high-end armored coats for Stassia and me.

The last of my dwindling stash had gone to the substantial bribe I'd offered the government to acknowledge that Stassia and I were joined, yet kept us both listed as deceased and any records of our new interactions listed under aliases to keep the threat level as low as possible. I also wanted Ikeri and Daniel acknowledged as legal citizens should they choose to remain on Artor as adults or need to obtain the correction procedure in case either of them had inherited that reproductive issue from their Artorian side.

Artor had received a great deal of my credits of late, just not in the places that the Premier felt they were needed.

Stassia's boots echoed on the polished tiles as she came down the hall to greet us. Light poured in through the high windows, lending her streaming hair a golden glow.

"You'll need to have a talk with your son before you consider sitting down."

Angry Stassia was a danger Neko was not suited to protect me from. I waved him off. He escaped the way she'd come.

"What now?"

"Daniel got himself thrown out of the academy today."

"Again?"

"Yes, again." She thrust her hands onto her hips and exhaled loudly. "This is your fault, you know, always making light of the situation. This isn't an adventure. Vayen, his future is at stake, and he needs to start taking it seriously."

"I'll talk to him."

Her hair might have been loose, her body free of weapons, and her armor hanging on a hook by the door, but she again carried herself like she was in command. I couldn't get enough of it. I pulled her close and kissed her.

Her annoyance subdued, she took my hand. We walked past our offices to the spacious common room filled with the furniture she had left behind on Merchess long ago. Jey had surprised her with it upon our return. He'd held onto it in our absence.

She'd spent the first two weeks here with a calculating look in her eye and a datapad in her hand, ordering what she wanted to make the estate our home. As with every house she'd touched in our past, it bore a minimalist and tidy appearance, though this one was colored as it had been before we'd arrived, the walls varying shades of browns and amber. That suited me just fine. I had dealt with securing our fortress and let her have her way with the rest.

"How was your day?" she asked.

"Good. Eleven in a row."

"That's a record."

"Progress, certainly. I think we're finally weeding our way through the disgruntled Council contacts and surviving Kryon."

They had mostly left Jey alone. He'd appeared just as much a victim as the rest of them, but there had been plenty of Kryon that hadn't been in residence during our attack on the Council bases. Upon my reemergence in certain circles, they'd worked out who was responsible for destroying their source of income. Jey and I weren't the only ones struggling without the Council's financing.

The former Kryon were quite adamant in expressing their

displeasure in various deadly ways. Thank Geva Jey had gotten the tank back in full working order long before our return.

My stomach rumbled. "Daniel or Fa'yet?"

"Vayen, seriously, I don't care who's turn to cook it is, that boy needs consequences, punishment, to suffer from his actions. You of all people should be great at this. Don't go easy on him. Not today."

Maybe we were bad parents. Or we had really difficult kids. Probably both. I certainly hadn't helped matters with moving them between several planets and thrusting them into entirely different cultures. It wasn't their fault that they'd had a hard time of it all.

I hung up my coat in the bedroom, removed most of my weapons, and went upstairs to see how much of a bad guy I needed to be.

The door stood open. I went in. Daniel sat in the middle of his large room, his back to me. His bed was a mess, as was the floor. The poor kid took after me in that regard. I wondered if it was the state of his room or the issue at school that had set Stassia off more.

His academy uniform lay in a rumpled pile by my feet. From the glow in front of him, I gathered he was enraptured in something on his datapad.

"You better get this uniform hung up or you'll get detention tomorrow."

Daniel jumped to his feet, fumbling with the datapad. He spun around to face me, hair flopping into his face. "I don't need the stupid uniform."

"Is that so?"

"I'm not Jalvian, and I'm not going back there."

"You had a choice, tech or military. You demanded military. That's what you got."

"But we're Artorian. Why can't I go to school here?"

"Because your uncle offered to place you in the best academy in the entire system free of charge. How do you think he feels about your constant insubordination?"

Daniel shrugged his already broadening shoulders. He stood nearly as tall as Stassia but was all arms and legs. I distinctly remembered hating that awkward stage when I was his age. And now we were home, living on the planet he'd been begging to see, and we were making him try to fit in on Jal with yet more people who weren't Artorian. I'd cut him slack the first time he'd been kicked out of the academy because of it. I'd even briefly considered teaching him myself as I'd done on Pentares, but I was too busy now. Besides, there was far more at stake with his appearance at that academy than getting an education.

Jey and I had been making efforts toward unifying our people, trying to heal the rift between Jal and Artor so there would never be another war to tear the system apart. That included getting Artorian kids into Jalvian academies and showing they could do just as well as the Jalvian students. Jalvians were also attending training here on Artor. The whole exchange program was going well so far, at least overall.

When Daniel had begged to go into military training, I couldn't have been happier, but now I regretted the depth of my enthusiasm. I should have kept him here on Artor. I should have known better. But I'd hoped this time, now living in my home system, he would have fit in better, found his stride. Instead, it seemed like he picked up right where he'd left off on Pentares. He kept getting into arguments, two of which had gotten physical, though he swore Jalvian students were at fault. While I didn't think he was lying, I knew first-hand how obstinate he could be and that the idea of backing down for the sake of diplomacy was entirely lost on him. A point he made painfully clear according to the report I accessed regarding today's dismissal. During a class discussion about the last Fragian conflict, he'd proclaimed that the Artorian academies produced better-rounded soldiers, citing that I'd come from one of them and it was thanks to me that Fragians weren't running the Narvan.

What he didn't seem to grasp was that I couldn't have done what I had without Jey or the Jalvian fleets. Then again, from the derogatory faculty statement highlighting that I was superfluous in that effort, I could see why Daniel had felt compelled to speak up.

We were like Jalvians. They knew us. Sure, there was a long-running enmity, but the war had ended twenty-two years ago. I'd expected more compliance in following our objectives from a high-standing academy, especially in their teaching of recent history.

I'd also expected more from my own son. He knew how much this exchange mattered. I was sure of it because both Stassia and I had told him, loudly, to his face. Several times.

I gathered my resolve and put on a stern expression. "Perhaps you'd like to explain to Jey why you think the same academy where he sends his daughter isn't good enough for you?"

Daniel rapidly shook his head.

I contacted Jey through our linked connection. *"Might I borrow your formidable self for a moment?"*

"Does this concern your delinquent son?"

"Watch it."

"I'll take that as a yes. I'll be right there."

I nodded to the pile on the floor. "You may want to hang up that uniform now."

Downstairs, I could hear Stassia's surprised greeting as Jey strode in. Seconds later, his boots were on the stairs.

Daniel's slightly contrite act turned frantic as he raced to the uniform and scrambled for a hanger. Jey walked in just as Daniel was attempting to put the two together.

"She said to let him have it," I said.

"Then you might want to leave the room." Jey closed in on my now terrified kid.

I knew Jey wouldn't lay a hand on him, but Daniel didn't. He'd only met Jey upon our return to the Narvan. All Daniel knew from before that was that Jey and Merkief had dragged me away from my family on Veria Minor and I'd returned home years later, covered in scars and missing a hand and an eye.

While the two of us might be partners now, Jey was a big man with a few scars of his own and a whole lot of decoration on the Jalvian military uniform he wore. He'd cut his blonde hair back above his collar, which did nothing to hide the anger crackling in his blue gaze as he bent down to get right in Daniel's face.

I didn't want to desert him, but I did retreat to the doorway to give Jey space to work. Daniel getting kicked out of a Jalvian academy with Jey as his sponsor was personal.

I'd had a similar, but less intense talk with Jey's adopted daughter two months ago after learning that she was one of those talking shit about Artorian students. Being the Prime's granddaughter lent her a high level of popularity. We discussed the importance of setting a good example at the academy when it came to dealing with Artorian students and the political reasons why she'd better play along. Jey's wife, the daughter of the Jalvian Prime—a political marriage but also a civil one from what I could tell—had been attending a charity party at the time. She was blissfully unaware of our tactics at sowing political accord with our children.

Whatever Jey said left Daniel quaking. "This is your last chance," Jey said loud enough for both of us to hear. "If you screw this up, I'll make sure you never get back into another Jalvian academy. Any of them. Do you understand?"

Daniel nodded.

"I mean it," he said to me. *"Once more and I won't pull any more strings for him."*

"Understood. Thanks."

Jey vanished into the void, leaving Daniel staring at me like I was a horrible person for letting Jey have at him, like I'd betrayed his trust that I would protect him. It hurt.

I worked hard to keep my voice flat. "You heard him. Last chance. Don't waste it."

"I won't." He sounded so defeated and alone. I wanted to hug him, but Stassia was right, one of us had to have a spine or he was going to narrow his chances for a promising future.

"You're confined to your room until further notice."

He let out a pathetic gasp. "But Uncle Isnar is going to show me how to roast peppers."

"He'll have to show you another night."

Tears shown in his eyes. "But we bought them at the market together yesterday."

Calling off cooking lessons with Fa'yet was an even worse punishment than facing Jey? I hadn't intended to make him more miserable, only to keep him out of Stassia's iron glare. Now I couldn't back down. "Perhaps you should have considered the possible repercussions of your actions earlier."

His lips began to tremble. I walked out the door before my resolve crumbled.

"I hate you," he whispered over our natural connection.

I made my way down the stairs only to find Stassia waiting at the bottom.

"Well?"

"Make sure someone brings him dinner."

"You aren't staying?" she asked as I passed by.

"I'm not hungry."

I walked down the long hallway that led past a massive bathroom, two cavernous but mostly empty closets, and a sitting room, before passing through the door to our private space. Keeping the room dark, I slipped inside.

I'd just stretched out on the bed to consider what to say to Daniel when Stassia came in. She turned on the lights.

"What did he say?" she asked.

"Nothing."

"Vayen." She sat on the edge of the bed beside me.

"Those Jalvian kids are antagonizing him. You know they are. This time, I really don't blame him. He was merely correcting a skewed recounting on the Fragian conflict. They said I was superfluous."

She winced. "Do we need to have a talk with the academy administration? We could have Jey sit in too. Maybe that would straighten them out."

"Stepping in to correct their history lessons every time we disagree with them isn't a viable option. We can't expect Daniel to stay quiet either. Maybe we should pull him and send him to an Artorian school."

"Jey would love that after all the time he spent convincing the academy to accept Daniel in the first place."

"This isn't about Jey."

"No." She straightened herself. "It's about proving that your people and his can get along in more than a symbiotic supply and protection relationship. Daniel isn't the only Artorian student there. If we pull him, what message does that send to the others?"

I rubbed my hands over my face, ready to be done with the day. Decades of hate weren't easy to overcome with a few gestures of goodwill. Even Jey and I had devolved into several heated arguments since our return. I could easily see how he and Merkief had ended up as they had. This was going to take time.

She patted my leg. "Whatever Daniel said to you, don't take it too seriously. Keeping him on Jal is the right move. He just needs some time to figure out the whole diplomacy thing."

Though I didn't believe her, I nodded so she'd drop it. "I have some things I need to figure out." That was sort of the truth.

"What things would those be?"

"Funding for Artor."

"Oh." She cringed.

"Any ideas on how to make a lot of credits fast when there's no one to pay us but ourselves?"

Years ago, we would have just taken a High Council contract, unfortunately, in this one regard, I'd nullified that option. For far less pay, I would have sunk to taking a slew of assassination contracts, but Kess had a corner on that market, and even if I could stomach doing work for that viscu, he was just as likely to set me up for a fatal accident. That left us with less deadly and more legitimate options, none of which paid as well or as quickly.

"Sales." Stassia poked me in the arm. "It's what you're good at, Warehouse Overlord."

"I don't have a warehouse anymore, and that would hardly make a dent."

"You have obscure control of all the warehouses on three planets. Use your old Kryon contacts, if there are any friendly ones left. Hunt down some of the other system advisors. Set up some deals to make the most out of your cut."

"Taxes. That's what we're supposed to call them now."

She shrugged. "I'm sure you'll figure something out. I'm still working on tracking down the remainder of my old accounts. How much do you need?"

"I don't know yet."

"Then don't worry about it. We'll figure it out when you know."

She made it sound so easy, like the impossible debt shouldn't be looming over me, and my son didn't really hate me. But I couldn't shake the feeling that she was wrong.

"Isnar will be back from Prime with Ikeri any minute. I'll let him know about the change of plans with cooking." She leaned over to plant a quick kiss on my forehead. "I'm going to get some work done, but why don't you take a short nap? You seem to have forgotten how to sleep. I'll save you some dinner." She turned out the light and closed the door behind her.

Despite the University telling Stassia that she couldn't host another link, the allure of finally entering the partnership we'd both wanted was too big for either of us to pass up. She couldn't Jump on her own, but she could talk to me again and our bonded connection was back in full force, as much as it ever had been, given that she wasn't Artorian. She didn't have a link to access information, but her time on Pentares had made her a master user of datapads. She'd agreed to play it safe and work from home for the most part. We were both back in top physical form, though our use of that asset was more of a defensive nature rather than causing trouble beyond the occasional need to present a physical threat.

Jey was overjoyed to have us both back, even if we were acting behind the scenes as we had previously, leaving him to be the public face of the Narvan Advisory position.

The diplomacy end of things wasn't easy for me either, but I was working on it.

I'd hoped that getting back to work, being home again, would either help put me at ease or at least offer the level of exhaustion required for me to sleep through the night, but it hadn't. If anything, being back in the Narvan was worse.

There were reminders of Merkief on the planets I'd agreed to help Jey with. Signs of the chaos the Council had created by pitting Kess against Jey and Merkief were everywhere. There were also constant references and encounters that further illustrated just how many of my memories Arpex had consumed. As much as I enjoyed working with Anastassia again and being home with my people, it was all a continuous affirmation that there were as many scars inside me as out.

Every day was a challenge to covertly bridge the holes in my memory, to shut out the voices of Arin, Merkief, and Arpex. All of them whispered, and sometimes, outright yelled in my head. I had the nagging feeling that for every moment I appeared to hold myself together like I was doing fine, moving forward and enjoying myself, I was actually taking another step toward losing my shit for good.

I was staring at the ceiling with my artificial eye that could see in the dark, assuring myself that the clicking I kept hearing was the air cooling system and not Arpex's claws, when the door flew open. Stassia propelled herself onto the bed next to me. The lights came on, blinding me for a moment as she grabbed my arm and pulled it over herself. She was shaking. And sobbing.

My mind flying to a handful of situations awful enough to make her cry, I braced myself. "What's wrong?"

"I just received a message from Cragtek. Gemmen is dead."

It was clear this was terrible news, but I was at a complete loss. As I did with most newly discovered memory gaps, I dove into my link to try to figure out what I'd lost, to cover myself. It worked best with Jey because I had an excuse to ask him for current information or more details. Stassia required more delicacy. I often used a good deal of cautious conversation and prayed she gave me enough hints so I could employ my link to fill in what I was missing. In this case, the local network yielded little beyond a reference to Cragtek. It was a shipping and trading company on Rok. Though it seemed like a valuable resource, Stassia had strongly suggested we keep our distance for Kess-related reasons.

If she was this upset, surely I should know who Gemmen was. Stroking her hair, I held her tightly.

"I can't believe we didn't get a chance to see him again. Damn Kess and the mess he created." She sniffed. "What are we going to tell the kids?"

Two years of covering the vast number of Arpex eaten memories unraveled in a handful of tear-filled minutes. I desperately wanted to comfort her, but that would require exposing just how broken I was. My mind spun, seeking some solution, some tidbit of information, any hint that might spare me this indignity.

Stassia went quiet. "Vayen?"

Dammit, there was no way out of this. Not this time. I loosened my grip on her and sunk back into the pillow, wishing I could disappear.

"Who's Gemmen?"

TWO

"Who's Gemmen?" Stassia pulled away and looked at me like I'd turned Fragian. "Vayen, Gemmen is dead."

I nodded. "I understand that."

She smacked me in the chest, and she didn't hold back either. This wasn't going to go well.

Arin started to whisper, telling me to wake up now, warning me that the dream was going to turn unpleasant. They all did, but as long as Stassia was still in it, even if she was pissed off, it couldn't be as bad as the others.

"This isn't the time for your terrible sense of humor," she said. "Gamnock sent the message, so maybe he's forgiven us."

"I wasn't joking."

"What the hell is wrong with you?" She sat back farther.

"A lot of things."

I hated that when she needed me most, my screwed up head forced her to put distance between us. I ran my hands over my face, cursing every scar and wanting to hide, to leave, to escape. But she'd sensed a weakness. There was no way in all nine hells she was going to let it go.

"You have a grand total of five seconds to expound on that, or you can go pretend to sleep on the couch."

Fuck, now she was calling me out on that too?

She'd mentioned Gamnock and that he was pissed at us. It was something to do with Kess going on a killing spree while after us at the Cragtek complex and me hiring Neko out from under him. We were avoiding him. That's all I'd been able to piece together from scattered memories and inferences from passing conversation with Stassia.

Scrambling for some way to pull out of this mess, I dove into my link, tearing through public records associated with Cragtek.

Gamnock Mackenon owned the company. I found a still frame of him, a typical Jalvian, short blonde hair, angry blue eyes, and a face that said he'd never heard of a sense of humor. Digging deeper, I found mention of the previous owner, Gemmen. From the resemblance, they had to be related.

"He's Gamnock's father?"

"Are you guessing?" Her brows furrowed. "You honestly have no idea who I'm talking about?"

Not good enough.

There suddenly wasn't enough air in the room. My skin prickled all over. I had to get out.

Rolling out of bed, I got to my feet and headed toward my coat. There had to be a valid excuse to leave, to put her off long enough to figure out who this man was, why she was so upset, and how the kids might know him. I could do this, I chanted to myself while fighting to inhale enough air to fill my lungs. My fingertips went numb.

She didn't need to deal with all the holes inside me. Not while we were getting along so well. Everything outside my head was falling into place. I just needed more time.

The bed and Stassia seemed to rush away, creating a vacuum that I couldn't escape. I couldn't move. Arin laughed. Arpex chittered and hissed. I squeezed my eyes shut and shook my head, willing them both to silence.

"I need to—"

"Oh no." She grabbed my arm. "You're staying right here."

"Stassia, I need to go."

The room was too warm, too small, the walls too close. I tried to shake her off but she held on.

"I don't think you do," she said.

The white light of our bedroom blossomed to a sickly yellow. Somewhere up above, Arpex sat on its platform, waiting for me to bring its next meal. I tried to scratch the scars on the side of my face with my stump, but it throbbed. Blood dripped from the open wound, staining my grey suit and spilling onto the floor.

So much blood on the floor.

The pressure on my arm grew until I saw Arpex's claw wrapped around it, slicing, cutting. The pain was unbearable. I couldn't lose more of myself. Shoving with all my might, I wrenched my arm away.

I turned to run but found myself wrapped in its wing-jaws. Its barbs driving into my back and shoulders. Pressure built in my head.

It was going to steal something else from me. I couldn't let that happen. I couldn't end up like Arin, not even remembering my full name. Tearing at the wings, I dug my fingers into the fleshy membranes and braced for the acid to burn my flesh.

The pressure vanished.

Somewhere in the distance, a voice screamed my name. A long burst of electric current jolted through my body. I lost control of my legs and toppled to the floor. Instead of landing in the bloody mess, a thick rug cushioned my fall.

Stassia sat on the floor across the room, pale and shaken. She rubbed the back of her head.

Fa'yet stood by the open door, his sleeves torn. Long scratches ran down his arms. He held a stunner in one hand.

Stassia's voice shook. "Vayen?"

I tried to get up but discovered my legs were entirely uncooperative. Had he drained the damn thing on me? "What the hells?"

Fa'yet didn't move other than to throw the empty stunner at my shoulder. "That's a very good question."

"Go on, Isnar. I've got this. Thank you." Bracing herself on the wall, she got to her feet.

"Are you sure, Ana?"

"He's back to himself now," she said, but she made no move to help me up either. In fact, she kept her distance. From the way she was standing, she'd taken a hard hit and maybe even had the breath knocked out of her.

"I'll be close by if you need me." He closed the door.

I glanced around, seeking out who might have attacked her, but we were alone. There was blood under my fingernails. I swallowed hard.

"This happen often?" she asked.

"What?"

She rubbed the back of her head again and rolled her shoulders. "Hallucinating. Does that happen often?"

Uncertainty tugged at me, making my stomach roil. I was pretty sure I'd kept the flashbacks relegated to when I was sleeping. I'd never acted on them. At least I didn't think I had.

"Did I—"

"Throw me across the room and about tear Isnar's arms off? Yes. Care to explain?"

"No, this hasn't happened before," I declared.

"And the rest?"

"I don't want to talk about it."

"That's too damn bad." She stalked closer. "Why don't you remember Gemmen?"

No getting out of it now.

"Arpex took memories from me, quite entirely, like whatever or whoever it was never existed. I tried to keep a list, but it got too hard. I don't know what I've lost until it comes up. Like Gemmen."

She came closer, but less like stalking and more like she might want to hug me but was too afraid to get that close.

"So whenever I've mentioned Cragtek, you've been faking your way through the conversation?"

"I know the company, well mostly. Somewhat." I shook my head. "The details are hazy."

"What else have you been faking?" she asked.

"Nothing important." At least, I didn't think so, but now I was second-guessing several things I'd faked my way through.

"And that outburst just now?"

"I don't know. It won't happen again. I promise." I tried to reach for her, but she stayed out of range. "Did I hurt you?"

"Yeah, you did. The wall over there isn't soft."

"I'm sorry. It won't happen again. Really." If I could figure out what had happened. It had all seemed so real. I stared at the blood on my fingers. Thank Geva it wasn't hers, but knowing it was Fa'yet's didn't make me feel much better.

"Damn right it won't. You haven't been sleeping, and it's making you crazy. I can deal with your usual level of crazy, but not this. What if one of the kids had seen you? What if you had hurt them?"

Not having any answers, I let her continue her tirade.

"You're going to take some time off."

"I can't do that. Artor needs credits now more than ever. You said it yourself, I need to pull in Kryon contacts and establish new trade routes. I've got warehouses to inventory and cargo loads to figure out." My legs began to tingle as feeling came back.

"This isn't open to discussion. When we decided to come back, you swore to me that we were going to do this together."

"We are."

She often attended meetings with me and working remotely, had resumed many of her projects throughout Artor, Moriek, and Syless, as well as on a few of Jey's planets with his permission.

She shook her head. "You're in this too deep. The Council isn't pushing us anymore. Step back and advise. Let the planetary heads do the heavy lifting. That's what they're there for."

Stassia stared at me like I was a bomb she wasn't sure had been diffused. I reached out to her. She finally took my hand and hauled me to my feet so I could stumble toward the bed. I sat on the edge.

"You'll take a few days off and catch up on sleep. Get your bearings back," she said firmly, sitting next to me.

With her close, I wrapped my arms around her. "Do you need to go to the tank? Stassia, I didn't mean to hurt you."

"I'll take the bruises over gel and a long nap. I don't think I should leave the kids—"

"Alone with me? Fa'yet is here. Neko too. Please, if you want to go, tell me and I'll bring you."

"Isnar couldn't reach you. Neither could I. You were gone in there." She rested her forehead on mine. "You were running on autopilot."

If that was true, I was closer to becoming Arin than I'd thought. I couldn't let that happen. Artor would have to wait.

"So where are we going for these days off?" I asked.

The tension in her back eased a fraction under my hands. "Frique. The kids like it there."

Under the circumstances, I wasn't going to argue even though it was the last place in the Narvan I wanted to be with her. Too much had happened in that house. We'd said goodbye there, she'd nearly left me, shut the door in my face. Would she do that again if she learned the depth of how damaged I really was?

"Great, when do we leave?"

She softened more, her body resting against me, melting in my arms as the tension between us dissolved. "I'd say now, but the kids are already settled in for the night. So, tomorrow. Maybe you'll sleep better there."

I highly doubted it. "Sounds good."

"Gemmen's service is in the morning. We should go alone, in case—"

"I have another...episode?"

She nodded. "I don't want the kids to see that. And well, Gamnock probably won't be thrilled to see us, but he sent the notice, and it explicitly said he was following his father's wishes by inviting us. So we're going."

"Should we take Neko then?"

"Even Isnar was of little help except to use the stunner. I can do that. We don't need either of them thinking you've lost it." She kissed my neck. "You just need some sleep. No stims. Get some real rest for a few days. You'll be fine."

Fine. I resisted the urge to laugh. If she knew I wasn't sleeping, that my head was full of holes... I'd just hit her, for Geva's sake. She knew damned well that *fine* had nothing to do with it. But I was also thankful that she wasn't shoving some Seeker therapy shit in my face. If she was willing to gloss this over in favor of focusing on Gemmen's death, at least for now, I'd gratefully accept the reprieve.

"I'll lay off the stims, but I'd rather not have you stun me in the middle of a memorial service in front of hundreds of people I may or may not know."

"Then tell me if you feel something coming on and we'll leave. I won't stop you this time." She sat up and looked me in the eye. "That's what you were trying to do, wasn't it? Get out of here before it happened?"

"Yes."

Sort of. Maybe. Geva help me, I wasn't even in that much control. Now every time I felt anxious, I needed to worry about slipping into a violent hallucination? This was a whole new level of stress I didn't need.

"All right then. You and me tomorrow at the service. Neko can watch the kids and get them to the house on Frique when they've finished their classes for the day. I'll let Israr know to meet us there. That will give you some downtime without worrying about not spending time with them."

She went on, in her organized glory, rattling off what to bring, who would Jump who and what, and what she could work on while we were there so I could rest easy knowing the Narvan wasn't running amok without my attention. She finished with, "I'll leave Jey a message so he lets you relax too. Now come get something to eat and then back to bed with you."

I was half inclined to quip about her acting like my mother, but I realized I had no idea what my mother was like. From the foggy spots surrounding my father and brother and most of my early childhood, I gathered she'd also become a meal for Arpex. Nausea crept over me. How many people had I lost?

Keeping my dismal revelation to myself, I followed her out of the bedroom to wash Fa'yet's blood off my hands.

Stassia might have been used to getting knocked around, but not by me. I wished she'd let me take her to the tank. It would have appeased my guilt a tiny fraction. But she assured me again that she didn't want to go.

Dinner consisted of a variety of colorful peppers with thin strips of hot spiced prantha eaten alone while Stassia went upstairs to inform the kids that the man they'd called grandfather had died. Ikeri's distress fluttered through our natural connection. Daniel seemed to be ignoring me, and Neko was sound asleep. Fa'yet happened through the kitchen. He took the seat across from me.

He'd changed his shirt but held his arms awkwardly as he sat. I pushed my empty plate aside and figured I might as well get on with it.

"Sorry I tried to rip your arms off."

"Not sorry I drained a stunner on you."

I shrugged. "Understandable, given the circumstances."

"Which were what exactly? Are the two of you having problems?"

"As if I'd throw her around if we were." I glared at him.

"That's not out of the question. We did once have a conversation about you killing her. It's still quite vivid in my mind." He faced my glare with an unblinking gaze.

"And I didn't. I didn't kill you either, as you'll recall."

He offered the slightest concessional nod.

"I've been ordered to take a vacation. Overworked and under-rested seems to make me a little off these days. I'm sure you'll be getting your packing orders shortly." I pointed toward the floor above.

"This have to do with what they did to you?"

And I'd now had enough of this conversation. I stood. "Yes, and before you ask, I don't want to talk about it."

"Well, talk to someone," he said before I'd taken a step. "I'd hate to see you do something you'll regret the next time one of us isn't around to stop you."

"I will." No one needed to hear what the Council put me through. They'd be up all night too.

"Good. Then you can make it up to me by watching your own ass for a few hours while I take a dip in your tank of wonder."

"By all means."

We'd shared the tank and its jump point with Neko and Fa'yet upon our return to the Narvan. The kids had profiles too. Everyone had been instructed how to operate it in case of an emergency. Stassia might have been content to keep it a secret from us when we were newly hired guards, but Fa'yet and Neko weren't newly hired anymore. They'd both proven themselves trustworthy. Good help was hard to come by, and the Narvan, until eleven days ago, had been full of threats.

Grateful Fa'yet had let me off so easy, I made a hasty retreat to the bedroom but then realized no one was on watch with him gone. I walked back out and planted myself at the security station.

Stassia found me there an hour later. "Where's Isnar?"

"Tank."

"Ah." She sidled up beside me, resting her chin on my shoulder. "Well, that's done."

"How are they?"

"Upset, but it's been years since they've seen him. I guess that's good in their case, softened the blow a little.

I wrapped one arm around her. "And you?"

She winced and shifted her weight away from my arm.

"Stassia, I'm sorry."

"I know. I'm sorry I made you stay." She squeezed my hand. "I'll be fine. Not the first time I've been thrown around."

"That doesn't make it right."

"Get to bed." She nudged me out of the seat with her hip. "I've got this for a while. Besides, one of us should speak at the memorial, and considering your memory issue, it's going to be me." She pointed me toward the other half of the house. "Go on, I've got a speech to prepare."

Knowing she'd check on me, I undressed and got into bed, but not before popping a stim, despite telling her I'd lay off them. If I sunk deep enough into my link, it really would appear that I was in a deep sleep. Normally I didn't like to do that in case Stassia or the kids needed me, but she expected me to be exhausted. Content in knowing I had an excuse to go deep this one time, I passed the night on my link, reestablishing contacts with other system advisors and becoming familiar with the contents in various warehouses on the planets in my charge.

Geva only knew what I'd do if I actually slept. I wasn't about to hurt anyone again.

THREE

They'd dressed the elderly Jalvian in a green shirt that puddled over the withered form beneath it. The thin skin on his hands revealed every vein and tendon where they lay crossed over his chest. His face was most perplexing, hollow and empty, just like my memory of this man who Stassia claimed had been like a father to me.

Had he spoken words of wisdom that had shaped me at some point in my life? Perhaps provided training or a shoulder to lean on in trying times? I wished I knew.

After being cleared by Cragtek security, we worked our way past the viewing table. The line behind us trailed out of the room and down the hall. There seemed to be an array of attendees. A good half wore Cragtek uniforms, and a surprising number wore armor. The rest were in regular clothes of Jalvian or Artorian make with the random foreigner here and there.

Gamnock's steely glare settled on me, a solid affirmation of why we hadn't been here in person since our return to the Narvan. His blue uniform, clean and pressed, highlighted his broad Jalvian build. A single black rectangle broken with two gold vertical bars adorned his left sleeve. His hair was so short I could see his scalp beneath the blond fuzz.

He greeted us with, "What the fuck are you doing here?"

Stassia took a step forward, forcing him to take a step back. She'd always been good at making people back down.

"I would assume your secretary carried out your father's wishes to invite us since it clearly wasn't you," she said.

Gamnock jabbed a finger toward his father and then brought his focus back to me. "And see where his wishes got him, an early death. He would have had years in him yet if not for you."

No matter how deeply I searched the brief memory fragments of past interactions with Gamnock, the man on the table wasn't in any of them. Arpex had been quite thorough.

"He wanted you to have all the shit you left in your office." He smirked. "I burned it, just like you burned my compound when we gave you shelter."

Stassia took another step forward. People stared in our direction. Most of them were armed, being security, employees of Cragtek, or members of Gamnock's family. I appreciated Stassia telling me to put my nice clothes back in the closet and to wear my armored coat.

Gamnock didn't appear to be armed, but he may well have been hiding a weapon somewhere. I kept my hands empty and at my sides.

"That wasn't our fault," she said. "And you damned well know it. You were also given ample compensation for that incident. How dare you destroy Vayen's property?"

"Anastassia."

She glanced at me, but her attention remained on Gamnock.

"Let it go," I said.

"Are you serious? Those were your things." She added over our natural connection, *"Your office."*

Great, another memory lost in the holes. A significant one, by the emphasis she put on those two words.

I'd worked here, or run the business behind Cragtek, advised it? I couldn't remember. The buildings were familiar, and I seemed to know my way around well enough. I even recognized some of the employees. But the more I tried to think about what the company was to me, of my time here, the more blank spaces I fell into.

"He doesn't care." Gamnock snorted, shaking his head and turning to me. "I burn your shit, and you don't even care. You don't give a damn about anything, do you?"

"Maybe it's not that important in light of the situation." I gestured to where his father lay and tried to conjure up some of the emotion I'd felt when my father had been killed. But it had been so long ago. All that had transpired in my life since then had muted that tragic experience to nothing but a vague sense of loss.

I took Stassia's arm before she started trouble. "Let's find a seat. The service is about to start."

The muscles on Gamnock's jawline twitched. "You're staying?"

I smiled calmly for the benefit of the woman beside me who's deep sorrow bled freely through our bonded connection. "He wanted us here."

Stassia resisted my urging toward the chairs for a second, then conceded. We made our way to two empty seats in the front of the left wing of seating. Gamnock remained by his father's side, his gaze locked on mine as if he could incinerate me on the spot.

"I really pissed him off."

"Kess's attack on the compound was a tragedy, but that wasn't our fault," she reiterated forcefully. "I don't think he liked you much before that either, but you never said why, so I can't help you there. I can't believe you're not more pissed about your office though."

With a sigh, I admitted, "I don't remember my office either."

She rested her hand on mine but avoided my gaze. That was just as well since I couldn't give her any reassurances that I would be fine or that there wouldn't be anything else seemingly big or significant that I might be missing.

The others took their places. Stragglers made their way into the service, filling the few empty seats, and then they packed the rear. Everyone looked to the old man with misty eyes. Gemmen hadn't only been important to us, he'd meant a great deal to all these people.

Gamnock finally let me out of his sight as his gaze drifted over the now quiet and waiting crowd. He stepped up to the podium beside the table.

"Friends and family of Gemmen Mackenon, I welcome you. Today we gather to remember this great man, my father."

As he spoke, going into detail of seemingly every accomplishment in Gemmen's life in full Jalvian fashion, my attention drifted to the three elderly women sitting in the front and center. Those would be his wives. The three rows directly behind them were filled with men and women ranging from Gamnock's age to those just out of their teens. His children and grandchildren. So damned many. How had the man stayed sane?

Most disconcerting was that I knew some of their names, their faces, their personalities, but for no apparent reason. As if their snippet of memory was isolated in a bubble, the important part of how and why I knew these things was lost. The more familiar faces I found throughout the room, the more the feeling of disassociation hit me. So many holes, hundreds of them. They had all once held the memories that connected me to this man who lay dead on the table.

Being here, now, surrounded by people who knew this stranger like I should have, hurt like all nine hells, providing the devastating feeling of loss I'd sought earlier.

Had I lost Gemmen before I'd learned to cheat Arpex or after? And if I'd given him up in exchange for someone else, who had that been: Stassia, my children, Jey, my father or brother, maybe Fa'yet? I couldn't think of anyone else central to my life that I'd give him up for. The more I thought about it, the more loops I did in my head, always circling back to the hazy edges of too many voids. I'd never know. I hoped that damned Arpex was rotting in whatever hell their dead inhabited.

"Are you all right?" Stassia whispered, squeezing my hand.

"I'm fine," I said automatically, knowing a second later that it was a lie, and she'd know it too.

Her hand stayed on mine until Gamnock had finished half a glass of water and the list of accomplishments that summed up Gemmen Mackenon's life.

Gamnock surveyed the crowd. "Is there anyone here who would like to speak?"

"Stay right here and don't move," she said.

Stassia shot to her feet, her armored coat rasping over the seat as she did so. She stormed the podium, driving Gamnock aside before he had a chance to do anything but retreat.

For a moment, I forgot the things I'd lost and just loved her. It was times like this, when glimpses of Kazan came out, that I got chills.

She began to speak of the man behind her, of how he'd been a dear friend, a mentor, a confidant. Gemmen had been a grandfather to our children, a man we could rely on even when the Narvan was in turmoil. He'd begun the business as a young man, and later, had grown it first with her, then further with my help and guidance, to become the sprawling and profitable company that it was today. When she spoke, she addressed everyone, even Gamnock. Now and then her gaze would rest on me as if begging me to remember, as if telling me who Gemmen had been would trigger some miraculous recovery.

There were too many people focused on me as she spoke, their eyes accusing, wondering why I wasn't the one up there, why I wasn't speaking of the dead stranger with the same respect and fondness that Stassia was. They didn't know her like they knew me. I'd been here, a lot it would seem, and had an office here. Maybe even hired some of them.

I owed them. I started to get up.

"Stay," Stassia said in my head.

"I'm not a damned dog to be commanded." I'd seen plenty of them on Pentares. Sad little creatures, always trying to please their masters. The kids had wanted one. I'd refused.

Her face stayed calm, but her presence in my head bristled. *"Great, now they're all staring at you."*

"They already were."

I knew what they saw, a scarred man, his hair threaded with grey before his time, his cold artificial eye judging them all, and his giant ugly grey hand protruding from an armored sleeve. I'd changed, and now I wasn't doing what they expected.

Already on my feet and under intense scrutiny by everyone present, I made my way to Stassia's side, all the while wondering what I was going to say. Was he a good man? If he was close to me, most likely not. He was a Jalvian, like Jey, and we got along. That made at least two Jalvians that enjoyed my company, but that didn't seem fitting to share. I looked down at the shell of a man who had accomplished so much, who had also aged far faster than his natural years, and I wondered what had been the cause.

Lightly touching his exposed hand, I held out hope that physical contact would trigger something, but it didn't. He was only a cold, dead stranger.

As I turned to face the crowd, I went with how I'd learned to lie to Stassia, a version of the truth. "Gemmen was a dear friend. I miss him very much."

There, I'd said something. They all appeared to expect more, waiting patiently for me to expound on my grief. I looked at Stassia.

She gave me a patronizing smile. "We both do."

With a nod that both signaled that I should shut the fuck up and that we were done here, she took my arm and forcibly guided me back to our seats. As the next speaker took to the podium, I tried to block out the stares, the smell of too many bodies crammed into a single room, and how, ironically, it wasn't the dead man who smelled the worst.

Murmurs and whispers wafted through the rows of seats as the speaker sat down and one of his daughters took her turn. Were they speculating about what was wrong with me? I strained to hear, but their voices were too distant, too hushed.

Stassia was either too focused on the service or annoyed to distract me with silent conversation like she usually did when we were out socially. It didn't seem like a good idea to initiate a conversation myself given that I'd snapped at her.

After the first hour of additional speakers, my back started to hurt. The metal chairs were not meant for long-term use. By the second hour, my legs began to cramp.

While I knew that I was immensely fortunate to have had the regen tank to repair my injuries during the time I'd been in the Narvan, my fortune had taken a turn for the worse during my years of servitude and the massive injuries I'd incurred when taking out the Council. Now I had constant aches. Even though I'd used the tank many times since our return to the Narvan, it couldn't undo what had healed naturally while I'd been away. I shifted every few minutes, trying to find relief.

"Will you sit still? What's wrong with you?"

"Everything, and my ass is numb."

She shot me a look. *"Do we need to leave?"*

"No." I tried to keep my search for comfort to a minimum.

When Gamnock finally returned to the podium, it took a lot of control to keep my relieved sigh to myself.

"Thank you all for coming. If you will please adjourn to the next room, lunch will be served, and afterwards, ashes will be made available."

I didn't belong here with all the weeping and teary eyes, with men and women who continued trading stories as we went into the adjoining room and took our plates of pre-portioned food to our tables and ate. Stassia spoke with the eight Jalvians with which we shared a table. I pushed food around on my plate and wished I was anywhere else, preferably somewhere I wasn't constantly hit with gaping holes. Somewhere that I knew everything about the people around me. A place far from the room two floors below, where they were incinerating the dead man who had been a central part of my life.

But we stayed, Stassia chatting, and me lost in my head, until Gamnock approached our table with a fraction less disdain than he'd directed at us previously.

"Might I speak with you privately for a moment?" he asked me.

"Don't kill him," said Stassia.

I gave her a dry stare before following Gamnock over to a recently vacated table in the corner. Without a word, we went around opposite sides of the table and took two chairs next to each other in the corner, both of us facing outward. We sat in silence for a moment before he spoke.

"I can see my father's death has hit you hard. I've never seen you so subdued."

I stuck to a nod, wondering where this was going.

He fiddled with his hands on the table in front of him. "Look, I'm sorry I burned your stuff."

"All right." I probably should have acted as though I were more affected by his apology, but I didn't dare say much more for fear that I'd say something wrong. Then he'd begin to realize that my brain was like the rest of me: not what it used to be.

Gamnock tapped his fingertips softly on the table. "My father spoke of you like the son he wished I was, always comparing me to you, pointing out how I could do better and think of everything like you did. But I didn't have your connections, your wife, your funds—" He shook his head. "I hated you, and I don't know as we'd ever spoke until you returned from the dead."

"Sorry about that." Had we met before the time he'd mentioned? I didn't remember. My pulse began to race and my palms started to sweat.

"After hearing your wife speak...well, I'm...sorry I threw in with Kess Atta and kept both of you away from my father. It says a lot, despite how close you all were, that you stayed away when I told you to."

I stared at my hand, the one that had touched Gemmen, still feeling his cold papery skin. "Did he avoid us in keeping with your demands too?"

Gamnock swallowed and watched the funeral guests as more of them began to disperse. "Family was important to him, but you were his family too, I suppose." He shook his head. "He argued about it when we were alone. I did my best to not be alone with him. All the way up to the end."

If I said the wrong thing, he'd know. He'd know I was totally faking my way through this utterly important day to him, to Stassia, to all these people, people who respected me. And here he was offering this apology. I didn't want to make a mockery of that either. My mouth went dry, and I couldn't quite breathe fast enough to keep up with what my body required.

"He wanted peace between us," Gamnock said quietly.

He was watching me with those too bright Jalvian blue eyes, taking in every detail. He'd been trained well. He had to be to take charge of a business that focused on reappropriating goods and altering them to sell to the highest bidder.

Even though we were out of earshot from everyone else, his voice dropped to a whisper. "Are you all right?"

"No, not really." Again with my truth that wasn't his truth.

"He said the same thing to me when I caught him sitting alone in his office one night after word had come in that the two of you had been killed. Don't let it do to you what it did to him."

Grief had aged the man who was important to all these people. Grief over my death, while I'd been alive and well on Veria Minor, playing warehouse baron and raising children with Stassia. The few bites I had eaten swirled around in my stomach, pitching to and fro until they made their way up my throat and into the back of my mouth.

I swallowed the sourness and took a deep breath. I hated Arpex, and even more, I hated myself for giving up this man and everything attached to him, because it was a whole damn lot of my life.

"Don't kill me for saying so, but you don't look so good," Gamnock said.

"I say that every morning."

He chuckled nervously. "I don't mean to pry, but what did—"

"Don't."

"Right." He cleared his throat. "I just wanted to say that I do appreciate all the business you've been sending my way, especially that deep spacer with connections to the trading route out to the fringe."

"Figured I owed you." That, I did remember.

He got to his feet. "I should get back to it."

"Nice talking to you without all the hostility."

Gamnock nodded and headed over to another table, stopping to say a few words to those he passed along the way.

I took a few deep breaths in and out in an effort to get my shit together before getting back to Stassia, but it was a lost cause. She arrived at my side before I could stand.

"What was that all about?"

"He apologized for being an asshole."

She swore under her breath. "How badly did you threaten him?"

"No threats."

"You're much better at diplomacy than I gave you credit for." She looked me up and down, her brows lowering and drawing together. "What's wrong?"

"We're at a funeral service. I'm allowed to be a little off."

She tapped my shoulder. "Let's get out of here before you get further off and ruin your progress with Gamnock."

We made our way out, back through the room where the service had been held and into the relative quiet of the hall. Tables had been set up with memory sticks. I took one. A pinch of grey fluttered inside the thin clearplaz tube.

The rod came alive in my hand, projecting the image of a middle-aged Gemmen. He stood, hovering in the air just above my hand, an able-bodied man, full of life. My heart broke for what had been taken from me and what I had taken from him.

Stassia pushed my coat aside and wrapped her arms around me. "You remember now?"

"No, but I very much wish I did."

"What about the tank, would that help?"

I lifted my hair to reveal the missing top half of my ear. "Even the tank can't regrow parts that are entirely missing, not even immediately after the fact. It didn't make my hand grow back, take these scars away, or fix any-fucking-thing-else either. My head is no different."

"Maybe it is."

"Think about it, Stassia. How many times have I been in the tank since we came back? It can't fix what's wrong with me."

She held on tighter. "We'll figure something out."

I Jumped us to the clearing outside the house on Frique. We went inside to find we were alone and took our coats off, hanging them by the door. Stassia led me to the couch overlooking the woods. She curled up beside me, her mind opening to mine as we shared comfort with one another.

"How are your sessions with Ikeri going?" I asked after a while.

"Great. I never thought I'd get my telepathy back, and now we're working beyond that. We made quite an amazing child."

"We did." I kissed her forehead.

While I was relieved Ikeri was finally getting some professional training for her gifts, it scared me that she was barely ten. If she was already this powerful, would she soon be like Tomias's acolyte, Etara, able to ransack my mind with no effort at all?

A tingle in my head alerted me to an invasive presence bumping against my defenses.

"What are you doing?" I slid away, putting space between us on the couch. Anything resembling a probe felt far too much like Arpex touching me. It made my skin crawl and my stomach knot.

Stassia sighed. "Trying to do, you mean. We're working on it."

"You think you can bust into my head and make me all better?"

"Would that be so bad? I get that you don't want Ikeri in there, but why not me?" The sincerity and pleading in her voice filled me with guilt.

"I don't want anyone in here. Not even you. It's not a good place."

She stayed where she was but her drive to help me was thick through our bonded connection, smothering.

"But it's you," she said. "I know it's not good. I don't care. Please, let us try to help."

"You can't, not even if you were a full Seeker with robes and a bald head full of tattoos."

She sat forward, looking like she was ready to get up and start her pacing routine. The determined set to her jaw didn't bode well.

"How do you know? You won't even let us try."

"Stassia, please. It's been a rough day."

"All right, not today, but only because you said please. Which I'm recording for posterity by the way."

I tried to smile, but I just didn't have it in me.

"Stay here." She got up. "You need to start this relaxing thing so you can get some sleep and feel better. Sleep *will* help, right?"

Her face begged me to say yes, so I did. It was when my eyes closed that I was at my worst, but I couldn't tell her that, not when she wanted to help so badly.

She came around behind me. Her fingers ran through my hair, her chin resting on the top of my head. "I'm going to go find us something to drink. We could both use it."

Her footsteps faded into the kitchen. I pulled the memory stick from my pocket and watched Gemmen watching me. The more I searched, the more I found I didn't know, not only about him, but how I came to be involved in Cragtek, let alone control it. How had we evaded everyone in order to slip away to Veria Minor while the poor man had thought us dead? Stassia was in many of the fragments, but the deeper I dug, I realized I was missing bits of her too.

My memories were peppered with more holes than a well-used target at a gun range. I put the stick away and tried to disappear into the couch before she returned. Stassia trusted me to have my shit together, to watch both our backs, and over our family. If she knew how close I was to becoming Arin, she'd demand I go see a Seeker because they'd helped her. And they had, through Ikeri, I couldn't deny that.

However, I wasn't convinced that she knew what power they truly had. She'd mocked me once for fearing a little girl invading my head. It hadn't been the drugs I'd been on, Etara had been that powerful. So was Tomais, and now he was training our daughter, who already slipped into my head far more than she should. I didn't want to be scared of my little girl, but I was terrified that she'd find out who I really was.

Behind me in the kitchen, doors opened and closed. Ice clinked into glasses. Bottles scraped around in the cupboard as she searched for whatever she was looking for.

I didn't want to come to the point where Stassia would make demands I wasn't willing to fulfill. That wasn't a fight I looked forward to in the least.

As long as she was beside me, I'd be all right. I could piece my memories back together, sew the holes shut, knowing what had been there, even if I had lost my own experience of those things. She could help me that way.

Her footsteps came back to my side. Ice crackled softly. She held out a glass full of rich amber liquid. The smell of highly potent alcohol made my mouth water. This was exactly what I needed, to forget how much I'd forgotten.

"Thanks."

She sat beside me, sipping from her glass. It wasn't filled with the same liquor as mine. I cast her a questioning glance.

"One of us has to stay alert until Neko and Isnar get here."

I nodded, savoring the burn twisting down my throat and the blossom of warmth in my gut that followed shortly thereafter. It went down far too easy. She didn't even blink when I set the empty glass down in less than ten minutes.

"Another?"

I just might sleep after all. Or pass out if I kept this up. That counted, didn't it? "Sure."

Her green-eyed gaze was soft as she set her glass down and went to refill mine. Geva only knew what chaos she was picking up over our connection.

Cupboard doors opened again and bottles knocked together. Then she was back at the couch with a full glass and a bottle that she left on the table beside me.

"I shouldn't. What if someone needs me?"

"You're on vacation, remember? Don't argue. Just drink."

"Seems like you said that once before and we both ended up drunk and in bed." While I'd meant to be lighthearted, it came out hollow and tired.

"Actually, we ended up on the floor, but you're going to bed all right." She smiled, raising her barely touched wine.

I took a sip, wondering what I could ask her that would start filling the gaps without revealing how many there were. "How many times were you in my office at Cragtek?"

She eased back on the couch, leaning against me. "Once."

"Why only once?"

"It was your private place. I owed you that."

"When?"

"You brought me and the kids there." Her voice wavered. She cleared her throat. "It was where we returned to life after Merkief and Jey found us on Minor. I'd never seen Gemmen so happy."

"Should I have been angrier that Gamnock destroyed my things?"

"Should you? Your lack of anger worked greatly in our favor today, so I suppose the official answer is no. Your response caught him off guard. Me too. I fully expected to have to pull you off him."

"For a moment there, I thought you were going to take him on for me."

Stassia gave me a guilty smile.

I took a long drink, savoring the ease that it brought to my muscles. "I wish I remembered Gemmen."

She nodded. "I wish you did too."

"He touched a lot of places in my life. Now they're all empty." I drained the rest of the glass and refilled it.

She eyed the bottle with disapproval but didn't say anything. Hells, if she didn't want me to drink more, she shouldn't have left the bottle in reach.

We sat in silence, watching the wind dance in the leaves and the wildlife scurry about. Birds swooped in and out of the branches calling after one another. She'd finished a second glass by the time I'd tried to pour my...whatever number I was on and the bottle came up empty.

She took the bottle and the glass from me, setting them aside. "They'll be here with the kids any minute. Why don't we get you to bed before that happens?"

I embraced the hazy drunkenness wholeheartedly, not at all concerned with the vague knowledge that I was stumbling toward our room. No one was here to care and she'd encouraged me.

Stassia helped me get undressed and then draped a thin blanket over me. "I'd tell you that I'll try to keep them quiet, but by the look in your eyes, I don't think you'll care." She leaned over and kissed me. "Sleep. You'll feel better soon."

FOUR

"Vayen," said a slurry voice. "Frique is under attack."

There was nothing I could do about that, trapped in Arpex's lair, scrubbing the blood and stringy remains of its last meal off the floor. The stump ached where my hand had been. I held it close to my chest, trying to keep it elevated so it wouldn't start bleeding again. High above, Arpex's barbed wings clicked together as though it were ready to swoop down to command me to retrieve another hapless victim for it to gorge on.

Something slammed into my shoulder, but when I glanced around the room, there was nothing there.

"Vayen." Stassia's voice.

And there she was in front of me. Arpex plummeted toward the floor, stopping short just over her head. It dropped to its feet behind her, its wings wide open.

How did she get here? She was supposed to be safe, far away from the Narvan and the reaches of the High Council. But there she was, calling my name, begging me to save her. There was nothing I could do.

"Tell me about this woman," Arpex commanded, its probing mind already in my head, gobbling up memories of the two of us together, of our children, of everything that kept me sane.

Its wing-jaws snapped around Stassia, this woman I shouldn't know after my memories had been eaten, but I still did. We were bonded and joined and had two children, we loved and we fought each other and repeated those two in a not always equal cycle. I watched as Arpex devoured her, numb on my knees in a puddle of blood and digestive fluids.

"What the hells is wrong with him?" asked a slurry voice.

It sounded like someone was next to me, but I couldn't see anyone there. My eye. One of my eyes had been destroyed when Merkief had bombed the High Council's bases. The stench of his burning flesh flooded my nostrils. I tried to see with my natural eye but there was only darkness. Darkness and that smell. And voices. Arin led a host of grey suits, screaming that I'd killed them all, that they were innocent, slaves just like me. I'd killed them all. Murdered them. Ripped them apart with bombs.

Maybe I could save some of them. Or save Merkief. I needed to find him and get him to the tank. He didn't have to die here, not with the High Council bastards. I bumped into body after mangled body in the dim flickering light, turning each of them over to see their face, but none of them were Merkief. I kept searching.

Stassia's voice curled around me, offering distant comfort as I waded through the wreckage of the base. "I may have added a little something to his drink."

"Brilliant idea, Ana. With a mate like you, he doesn't need enemies." Less slurry now, I recognized it was Fa'yet.

"Shut up, and help me wake him."

The base shook. There must be more bombs still going off. I had to get out before the whole place came down. Every stairway was destroyed. The lift doors were all jammed. Everyone here was dead. Everyone but me. I looked down at my skin, covered in blood and embedded with debris from Merkief's bomb. Red soaked through the thin cloth of the yellow robe I wore. Maybe I was dead too.

"That was too close. We have to go. I'll come back for him."

My whole body shook violently. I tried to move toward the voices but they were so far away, on a different planet, far from the base and Arpex's lair.

"Get the kids to the ship. I'll stay with him," she said.

I shook again.

"Dammit, Vayen. I promise I will never drug you again if you wake up right now."

Everything shook around me. A loud crack, like wood shattering, glass breaking. There was nothing left in the base to make those sounds. It had to come from somewhere else. Somewhere where she was. Where Stassia was. But Arpex had devoured her. Yet her voice was yelling in my ear, begging me to save her.

No, begging me to wake up. Which one was the dream?

Arin laughed in the shadows. "They're both dreams. You're in a coma, remember?"

Suddenly I found myself back in the Council clinic with Deep Voice's cloaked form standing beside my bed. "You'll never be on the High Council now," he said.

"Ana, we have to go. Neko will be here to get him in a minute. Vayen would want you safe."

"Of course he would, but that's too damn bad. Tell Jey to get over here, now."

"Jey's busy trying to form a line of defense against whomever is attacking the Narvan."

The Narvan. My home. Someone was attacking my home.

Knocking Deep Voice aside, I got up and ran through the base. There had to be a way out. I needed to protect my family, my people.

And then I felt her hands on me, shoving my shoulder into the mattress. My eyes sprang open to see her frantic face. Fa'yet loomed over her shoulder.

"Welcome back," he said in a hushed voice that sounded like a relieved sigh.

The thick haze in my head made talking too much of an effort. I sat up, grabbed Stassia's hand, and Jumped her to the ship. We spilled out of the void and onto the metal floor. My stomach heaved as the mother of all unholy hangovers descended upon me. Stassia rolled away, avoiding the mess. She got to her feet.

Fa'yet arrived seconds behind us, standing in the shadow of the tank with both of our children in hand. Getting to my feet, I staggered toward the terminal, lightheaded. The lone chair caught me before I met the floor again. Fa'yet rushed the kids out of the room while Stassia handed me the bucket we used for cleaning up the room. I proceeded to fill it.

She gripped my bare shoulder. "I'm sorry. I was trying to help."

"By drugging me."

"In your own words, yesterday was rough. You weren't supposed to drain the whole bottle."

I turned from the bucket to glare at her. The room spun. "You could have stopped me."

"You needed sleep, the good deep kind. I figured a little more wouldn't hurt you. Besides, you would have slept through the worst of the hangover."

Closing my eyes, I tried to block out the bright lights, Fa'yet's thundering footsteps as he came back in, and the sour stench coming from the bucket between my legs. My head slipped into my hands, trying to find a steady place while the rest of me swayed in the chair.

Stassia came around to stand in front of me, pulling my hair out of my face. I swatted her away and tried to focus on Fa'yet.

"What's going on up there?" I asked him.

"Frique is under attack. The house got hit, not directly. By a tree, I think."

"Why would anyone attack our little backwoods sauna of a planet?"

"I don't know. Jey might, but he's in the middle of scrambling defenses together for the entire system."

I held out a shaking hand. "Give me a stim."

"Is that safe?" he asked.

Stassia grimaced. "I'd rather you didn't, but it won't kill him."

"We need him on his feet." Fa'yet dropped the tiny savior onto my open palm.

Tossing it back, I hovered over the bucket, swallowing the excess saliva that kept pooling in my mouth. "Where's Neko?"

"Still above," said Fa'yet. "Locking down the house systems."

"Someone hand me some damned clothes."

Stassia dashed off to my bedroom.

"Shall I get my stunner out in case this gets out of hand again?" Fa'yet asked.

I couldn't tell if he was joking or genuinely asking. "Stay out of this."

The stim stilled the nausea but only pushed the fog back a few steps and did little to offer any energy. Whatever she'd slipped me was counteracting the effects, particularly the ones I needed most.

By the time Stassia returned with my clothes, the room had stopped spinning. She set the stack on the table and unfolded the shirt, shaking it out like she was going to dress one of the kids. I yanked it out of her hands and pulled it over my head. She backed away.

"Stay here," I told Fa'yet as I finished getting dressed.

"You," I grabbed Stassia's arm, "are coming with me." I Jumped us both to the house above. "Armor and weapons. Now."

"You don't have to yell."

"Shut up."

Arming up took longer than usual thanks to my shaking hands and the general feeling of wanting nothing more than to fall back into bed.

"Are we taking Neko?" she asked.

"Yes. How long until this shit wears off?"

She had the grace to look guilty for once. "Probably another seven or eight hours if you were sleeping."

The shaking got worse the angrier I got. "I'm not sleeping, am I?"

"I don't know with the stim. Five to ten?"

"Stassia!"

"I said I was sorry, all right?" She tried to put her hands on my arms, but I knocked them away. "Your nightmares are getting worse. Knocking you out was all I could come up with to get past that. You needed the rest."

"Nightmares are something little kids have. I'm fine. Other than you drugging me."

"Vayen, you're not fine, and you damned well know it."

"I should have known something was up when you were encouraging me to drink."

She scowled. "It should have helped prevent the nightmares."

"For the last time, I do not—"

"Fine, you have past traumatic life experiences that manifest themselves into disruptive sleep experiences."

"Don't you dare try anything like that again."

Her scowl didn't lessen one bit, and while regret flowed through our bonded connection, so did determination. It seemed neither of us was getting off easy.

Stassia followed as I marched out of the bedroom to find Neko standing at the security station. His gaze was everywhere but on either of us.

"I'll need you to Jump Anastassia in a moment. I'll give you the location. Then it's watching both backs, hers being the priority. Got it?"

"Yes, boss." He waited patiently while I took a deep breath and centered myself. It wasn't easy with the fluttering in my chest and the sludge in my brain, like I was at the end of a three-day stim-binge with no sleep, drained and scattered.

Mostly confident that I would stay on my feet after another Jump, I reached out along my link to Jey. *"You got a location for me?"*

He flashed me a corner of what appeared to be a bunker, probably on Jal. I relayed the point to Neko and we Jumped.

Jey stormed over. "Where the fuck have you been?"

"Someone drugged me." I glared at Stassia over my shoulder.

He held up his hands and shook his head. "I'm staying out of that one."

"Wise choice. What are we dealing with?" I approached the projection map floating in the middle of the room. A handful of ships, fairly small, more the size to test defenses or survey the system, dodged in and out around each of the populated planets within the Narvan.

The defenses on Artor were dealing with their attackers efficiently, only one of which was still intact. The other planets were also faring well, including Jal, which showed no sign of enemies, and a quick scan of their news feeds revealed nothing had reached the surface. Frique was a different matter entirely. Because they shunned the idea of housing a military force, the nearest defenses had to be launched from Artor and Rok.

The fact that I chose to house my family there part-time seemed to give the Friquen government enough confidence that I'd protect them, and that was all they asked. Well, that and that I kept technology to a minimum, trade set at a pace they liked, and my hands out of their treasury since they asked so little of me. But it was hard to defend people who didn't want to see a defense, and so they were encountering losses while the enemy ships lit up the morning sky with destruction from above.

"Jey?" Stassia prompted, not liking his pause in answering any more than I did.

"We don't know who they are. The ship we were able to capture was unmanned. The rest were either blown to bits or self-destructed."

"Nothing about the ship gives us any clues?" she asked.

"They're nothing we've seen before. Remember when the Fragians first hit the Narvan and everyone was at a loss?"

I nodded.

"We're back at that again. And before you ask, no, it's not Fragia. I've already been in contact with their liaison and have been assured they have no part in it."

"Would they tell you if they did?" Stassia asked.

He nodded. "They've been upholding their end of the treaty, and my agents haven't seen anything suspicious. Unfortunately, these ships are also nothing we've encountered on any of the not-so-peaceful explorations the High and Mighties sent us on while you two were off making babies."

If I'd had more energy, I might have punched him, but I figured it wiser to focus on remaining vertical. "Did you piss anyone off with those explorations? Maybe people who convinced someone else to test our defenses?"

"That's always possible," he admitted.

"Any ideas?" I looked at Neko, trusting my gut, which told me he might have some insight because he'd worked at Cragtek, though my hole-filled mind wasn't sure about the specifics.

Neko shook his head. "Nothing I've seen either."

"I'd like to see the captured ship."

"I figured you might. It's on the way to the station over Moriek. I'll let you know when it arrives."

I nodded, watching as Jey's well-trained forces earned their pay. The skies over Artor, Moriek, and Karin were now clear, as were the Jalvian worlds. Three of the six over Frique had been dealt with.

Jey passed along orders to the generals in attendance while we stood aside, observing our little corner of the known universe. Neko stood patiently beside Stassia and me, scanning the room and probably the local networks too.

I touched base with contacts on each of my planets, seeking assurance that all was well and any significant damage had been avoided. Only Frique had sustained losses. Next, I contacted the planetary heads, praising them for their efforts, except for Frique. I'd have to deal with them in person later.

Once the threat had been eliminated, we went over the recordings. The ships had come through a jump gate and left no trace beyond the one we'd captured. At a loss and with my eyes drooping, the three of us Jumped back to the ship. It took everything I had left.

Before I fell into bed, I figured I'd better check in with the kids. I found Daniel in Jey's room, sharpening his knife.

He looked up. "So what was that all about?"

"Something was testing the Narvan's defenses."

"You mean someone?"

"I don't know that yet."

"What do you know?" he asked.

"Not a whole lot in this particular matter. However, I do know that you've got class in about an hour. Your uncle would probably like a break. I'll have Neko take you."

"The Narvan is under attack, and you're still making me go to the academy?"

I shrugged. "The threat has been eliminated."

At least for now. That we knew of. Daniel needed consistency, to be assured things were normal. He needed to get his ass to school before he lost that option entirely.

"Dallaryan is going. So are you. Jal is clear and no attacks even hit the ground there. You'll be just fine, Neko will be nearby."

His face wavered, losing its defiant edge. "Are you sure they're all gone? Maybe you should keep Neko with you."

He was concerned for me? Maybe Stassia had been right.

"Your mother will be with me."

He returned his gaze to his knife, the one Fa'yet had given him on their journey to Pentares. "You should take him then."

"We'd feel better if Neko was near you."

"Maybe I'd feel better if he was near you."

Despite my exhaustion, I chuckled. "We'll cut him in half. You want the upper or lower body?"

"Upper please."

"Deal."

He smiled. I missed seeing him as a happy kid. Of course, I supposed most happy kids didn't joke about cutting people in half. Only mine.

"I need my uniform then."

I nudged Neko over the link. He showed up with Daniel's uniform in hand, tossed it at him, and went out to wait in the hallway.

"I take it I'm getting the whole Neko then?" Daniel said.

"Unless you can convince your mother she needs a bodyguard more than you do."

He snorted. "Right."

"Exactly."

"You'll be home for dinner?"

"Are you cooking?" I asked.

He gave me a challenging look. "Am I?"

"Yes. I'll let your uncle know."

His smile turned into a full beaming grin. I wished it didn't take an attack on Frique to give us an enjoyable conversation.

"And which kitchen am I supposed to use?"

With the roof damage on Frique, we'd be better off on Artor. But I had a feeling Stassia wasn't going to let her vacation decree go despite this interruption.

"Plan on here. I'll let you know if that changes."

"You mean you'll let Neko know." His smile faded.

I knew he resented that we kept him out of the loop, and I tried to remember to include him when I could, but I was used to relaying instructions to Neko. Relaying to both of them took additional time. That was a luxury I often didn't have.

"I'll let both of you know."

"We'll see about that."

A challenge, that's how this was going to be. "Get changed. You're going to be late."

I left him to Neko and went to check on Ikeri.

Fa'yet lurked in the doorway while Ikeri sat on the chair next to Stassia in her room, deep in thought. Or maybe in Stassia's thoughts. It was hard to tell with her, she was so subtle. Though, she had solemnly promised never to dig around in our heads without permission.

"There," Stassia said.

Ikeri frowned. "I'm trying."

"You're doing fine. I'm probably more sensitive than most people."

"That's why I'm practicing with you." Ikeri pouted.

"I'd like you to go up to the house with your uncle," I told her. "I'll send over someone to do the repairs. Your mother and I have to work."

Ikeri rose from the chair in a singularly graceful motion that reminded me of Stassia. I held out my arm. She gave me a quick hug before going to stand beside Fa'yet, waiting patiently by his side until he'd finished what he was doing through his link.

"The house then?" Fa'yet asked.

I nodded.

"I'll take care of the repairs. I'm sure you two have plenty to discuss," he said in that same dry tone that could have been humor or annoyance. "Watch your back. I won't be there to do it for you."

"Thanks. Now get out of here." I waved them off.

With his hand on Ikeri's shoulder, the two of them vanished.

"So just us?" Stassia asked.

"No, just you. I'm using the tank to flush out whatever shit you put in my system. Then we'll need to deal with the enraged government up top and see about that captured ship."

With the promise of dreamless sleep only moments away, I made quick work of dropping everything I had on my body into a pile in the middle of the floor. I also knew the mess would aggravate her.

"Vayen."

I got onto the platform.

She sighed. "I'm sorry."

"I know." Not that it made me any less angry. She had to know that I'd figure out what she'd done, but she'd drugged me anyway.

She seemed to be waiting for more from me. I didn't have more to give. "Just start the damned cycle already. We have work to do."

FIVE

I woke in my bed on the ship with Stassia beside me. As I had anticipated, my coat hung by the door and all of my weapons had been laid out neatly next to a clean pile of folded clothes.

"Did I miss anything?"

She shook her head and set her datapad aside. "How are you feeling?"

"Better." Which wasn't an outright lie with my system washed clean of drugs and alcohol. I was at least back to my usual level of shitty before she'd tried to help.

"Good." She tentatively leaned over to kiss me.

I didn't stop her. We had bigger and more immediate issues to deal with.

A wave of warmth washed over me as our bonded connection flared, bringing with it an utter peace that soothed my resentment. If I could stay here, like this, I would be infinitely better.

She pulled away slowly. "I let the city leaders know we would be there shortly. We should get moving."

"Probably." But I made no effort to leave the bed.

Her eyes twinkled as she reached back to grab my clothes. She handed them to me. "Shall I wait outside?"

"Why?"

She smiled. "You seem a little distracted."

"Maybe I like being distracted."

"We'll make time for distractions later."

I sighed and got dressed. "I'm holding you to that."

"I'm looking forward to being held." She pushed my boots toward me with her foot.

I slid my weapons into place and slipped into my coat.

She ran her hands over her armor and stood beside me.

This was the partnership I'd wanted from the start, equals togeth-er. I took her hand. The bond flared again.

She cast me a sideways glance. "We don't have time for that right now."

"What?"

"Don't even attempt to play innocent with me."

I snorted. "Since when was I innocent?"

"I suppose it's been a while," she conceded. "But seriously, we don't have time for this."

"You never have time."

She bumped her hip against mine. "Please, you're the one who's always busy."

"I could be busy with you."

She rolled her eyes, giving me an expectant look.

"Fine." I Jumped us to one of the buildings near the city center, the back room of a store where I'd once bought a tree for Stassia.

The owner nodded as we walked out of her back room. She went about her business as if we hadn't just appeared out of thin air.

Stassia paused. "Weren't you supposed to avoid wearing your armor to meetings here?"

"Yes, well, today, I'm wearing it."

"Feels like a good choice, given the day so far."

We made our way up the street. I didn't enjoy the leisurely walk as much as I normally would have. There was no time to stop to talk to the vendors or shop owners. Stassia stuck right next to me, keeping an eye on everyone.

They all watched us warily too. This was the only large city on the continent, as far as those terms could be used here. We spent time on Frique fairly often and as such, we endeavored to fit in and be a part of their society. The city council knew us as system advisors. The rest knew only that we were a wealthy off-world family that sat in on the city meetings from time to time. However, today we were walking among them in armor.

One of the shops had burned. Just one, for all the explosions we'd felt. However, the ground was charred in some areas and a wide swath of trees had been knocked down in the distance. A haze of smoke hung in the air. One of the nearby towns had not been so fortunate.

We entered the meeting hall. The hostility was palpable as we took our seats at the head of the long wooden table at the front of the room. As I'd expected, the public gallery was vacant. None of us wanted an audience for this conversation.

"We'll need an explanation," said their leader, marked by his red sash worn over the same pale orange tunic they all wore. This year's elected official was just like all the rest of them, as though they hatched from the same drab mold. Since Frique insisted on this group council ruling body, with each of them taking turns leading it, I'd long since given up trying to remember all of their names.

"I'd love to provide you with more details, but I don't have much information at the moment. It was an attack by an unknown force, unmanned from what we can tell, spread throughout the Narvan."

He returned to his seat, but his accusing stare remained focused on me. "Why were there no precautions against attacks? Our world suffered losses of a large magnitude. Seventeen people were killed. Four fields were set ablaze, large swathes of timber have been felled, two prantha herds were decimated and twenty-four buildings razed."

That was his idea of large? Maybe he should have focused a bit more energy on defense rather than facilitating a means of accurate damage reports. I tried to think of an audible response that would be productive but came up empty.

"Had this been any other planet, the losses would have been much higher under the same circumstances," said Stassia in her most level tone. "However, any other planet has defenses. Those worlds dealt with the attackers quickly. They suffered minimal to no losses. You chose not to have any defenses, even though we've offered them to you at no cost many times."

"We do not wish for a military presence on Frique," said the frowning leader.

"Then you will suffer losses while you wait for our military presence to reach you," I said.

Two of the councilmen leaned close to one another, talking quietly for a moment. One of them said, "We would like for you to provide a space station to house a defensive presence."

"I'm sure they would," Stassia said.

"We can't afford that."

Stassia nodded.

"I'll look into it," I told them.

"Unless you can guarantee that this won't happen again, we would like an answer right now," said their leader.

Stassia's voice rose in my head. *"What the hell are we supposed* to do, tell people we don't know to not attack again?"

"Can I just kill him?"

She glared at me. *"Not funny."*

I stood. "Perhaps you don't fully understand this situation. Even if we were to finance a space station to house a defensive force, it would take time to build and staff. Not to mention, who do you think is going to pay for those forces, feed them, and fuel their ships?"

The leader huffed. "You offered."

"I most certainly did not. I offered to provide men and ships. You, as a city, would need to provide for them, not me. I am happy to facilitate this for you, but I can't finance the entire system out of my own pocket."

The Councilman who had spoken up before did so again. "We've told you, we don't want your ships contaminating our air or your soldiers invading our towns with their expectations of what we owe them."

I wanted to slam my grey fist on the table or maybe his face, but that wouldn't get me anywhere, not with these people. "That's not how this works."

The leader's eyes narrowed and his jaw grew tight. "Then perhaps you could again explain, Advisor Ta'set, how your presence benefits us?"

Stassia understood their ideals better than I did, or had more patience for them anyway. And she owed me. *"You want to take this?"*

"Not really, but perhaps the discussion would be more productive if you left the room."

"As long as you're not going to kill them either."

She offered me a tight-lipped smile. *"I'm not making any promises."*

"I'll be right outside then." I addressed the men around the table, "Excuse me while I attend to people who aren't making absurd demands."

I went out to the lobby where I could listen to the conversation without actually having to pay attention to it. Just enough of their voices carried to let me know she was doing her best to balance their demands with our lack of finances while everyone remained seated and alive. With plenty to do through my link, I devoted half of my attention to various reports from contacts and officials.

My attention wavered as I noticed people gathering outside the hall. The voices outside began to rise, drowning out the council drone from inside. In the midst of debating whether I should take it upon myself to quell the little uprising or let the local leaders subdue their citizens, a rock hit the window. It did not immediately occur to me that Frique was unlike every other civilized planet that used clear-plaz on their government buildings—not until the rock shattered the fragile glass, filling the lobby with flying shards. Another followed right behind and hit me in the face just below my new eye.

"We've got a bit of a riot going on out here," I said to Stassia. *"Keep the council inside and yell if you need me."*

"Will do. Be safe."

"You too."

Like a one-man enforcer squad, I threw the door open and confronted the crowd. "What's the meaning of this?"

Angry chanting drowned out my voice. I grabbed a gun from under my coat and fired a shot into the air. The chanting faltered. A few people ran off. Most remained, muttering. No one brandished any sort of weapons so I put my gun away.

"Listen, your damages are being assessed. Repairs will begin in short order. There's nothing you can do here. Go home and see to your families, crops, and livestock."

"You did this," a woman said, pointing her dirt-stained finger at me. "You brought them here."

"I assure you, I did not. We don't even know who *they* are."

Shouts again filled the street. Another rock flew, shattering the remaining window. Then a bullet hit my coat.

I searched the crowd but didn't find anyone who looked out of place. Bullets on Frique were unexpected. Hardly anyone carried even a stunner here and the types that did carry anything more didn't blend well. I scanned the buildings.

Two heavy pulse waves blasted through the crowd from opposite directions, shredding them, tearing what had been people into bits of bone and flesh, limbs flying. Dropping to the dirt, I curled into my coat and buried my head under my arms just as the waves blasted over me. The pressure from the intense pulses drove the air from my lungs, and even under my armor, my bones screamed with what seemed to be a hundred fractures.

I sent Stassia a silent warning just as a third wave hit hard from yet another direction. After absorbing most of that, my armor would be useless for days. I clenched my teeth and tried to form a Jump. The wall behind me shattered. So did my concentration.

Something large and heavy toppled onto my back with a sickening snap. The sky turned grey with fuzzy black edges.

I couldn't feel my arms or legs and the crushing weight wouldn't allow me to take a full breath. The front half of the damned solid stone building had shattered. Rubble lay scattered around me. Most of the debris would be behind me, having flown into the building, propelled like tiny bullets through the air. Seeking out soft targets like Stassia and the unarmored councilmen in the room beyond.

Each breath came harder. Too much effort.

Another presence slipped into my head, softly, without the pressure of a probe or the terror of Arpex. Ikeri, comforting, telling me to hang on.

Fa'yet's boots appeared in front of my face. He dropped down beside me, and then we were on the ship.

Rough hands yanked off my coat and my clothes and manhandled me onto the platform. Even without the stone on my back, I couldn't move. My hands, even the ugly one, hung limp at my sides.

"Stassia?"

She didn't answer.

"Daddy?" Ikeri sat beside me in my little room on the ship.

While I was happy to see her, I couldn't shake the feeling that something terrible had happened. "Your mother?"

"She's safe," Ikeri assured me. She handed me a cup of water.

"You think of everything."

She smiled. "We've done this before."

Sadly we had, her being beside me when I'd woken from the tank. "How did I get here?"

"I felt you." She tapped her temple. "I got the picture of where you were from your head and sent Uncle Isnar to get you."

"Oh." I had no idea she could do that, that she knew what was needed to perform a Jump. She'd been in my head more than I'd thought. Or she was really damn perceptive, but more likely the former.

"You were broken. Everywhere." She grimaced. It wasn't an expression I wanted to see on her sweet face.

"Great," I said, trying to make light of the dire injuries to put her at ease.

The feeling that I couldn't move stuck with me. Usually, after a dip in the tank, I could shake off whatever had put me in there and get on with what needed to be done next. The sensation of being crushed, of an impossible weight holding me down, lingered. Even here, safe and healed on the ship, it was as though only a hairs-width of air protected me from the pressure that was waiting to hit me again. I breathed in and out slowly through my nose, hoping to keep at bay whatever insanity had caused me to hurl Anastassia across the room and attack Fa'yet.

I couldn't harm Ikeri.

"Have you been hurt like that before?" she asked.

Her soft voice gave me something to focus on. The impending weight eased from my chest.

"Can't say as I have. I guess I can check that off my injury wish list."

"Daddy." She sounded just like an exasperated Stassia.

I sat up to give her a hug, to assure her I was fine, but barely made it a few inches off the bed. I knew that feeling and it made my heart sink.

"He took me out to get her in, didn't he?"

"Yes." For once she sounded her age.

Ikeri had seen us in the tank before. She'd gotten over being alarmed pretty quickly. Her tone now made me worry.

"How badly was she hurt?" I asked, trying to keep my voice calm.

"We kept her stable as long as possible to give you as much time in the tank as we could," she said as though she were reciting words she'd memorized.

"That's not an answer."

Ikeri fiddled with her hands on her lap. She glanced up at me through her curls. "It's the one Uncle Isnar told me to give you."

I closed my eyes and tried to find Stassia, but she was nothing more than a distant presence. Alive but unreachable.

"Can you send your uncle in, please?"

She nodded and got to her feet.

Fa'yet came in before she'd taken three steps. It was almost as if she were more comfortable talking mind to mind than aloud. The two of them had grown quite close while I'd been away, and now that I was back, that hadn't changed. Thankfully, unlike Daniel, Ikeri had accepted me without penalty for my absence.

Fa'yet patted her shoulder as they passed. Ikeri was out the door before he reached the foot of my bed. His usual sardonic half-smile was missing which did nothing to ease my nerves.

"I don't like the look on your face," I said.

"I'm not fond of yours either, but I thought it rude to say so."

I glared at him. "How is she?"

"Much better now. She put herself in front of the councilmen, threw a table at them, I think. Or the blast did that. Either way, only one suffered serious injury. I'm sure he'll be angry when he wakes."

"Where is he?"

"Wherever they take their own for treatment. I left them to it. Ana was the priority."

"Thank you."

He looked me over. "I thought I told you to watch your back."

"I was busy watching my front."

Fa'yet scowled. "You did a fine job of that too."

"Could you leave the shit-giving to my mate?"

He leaned against the foot of the bed, arms across his chest. "She's busy."

"Why did I ask you to come in here again?"

Fa'yet shifted his weight, trying to ease his perpetually aching leg and muttered something to himself before saying, "The rest of the Narvan seems to be fine. Jey has a specialist team from the Artorian University going over the ship he seized. The Friquen people are going about their lives knee-deep in prantha shit as they usually do, and you're both alive."

"Well, there's that."

Jey's voice interrupted my moment of being up to date with a clear head. *"Slight problem."*

"Of course there is. What now?"

"That ship we had?"

"The one that you had the brains from the University going over?"

"Yeah, about that... The self destruct just kicked in. The explosion took out half the station. With the life support systems destroyed and the internal fires eating up what little oxygen was left, it's a dead zone. Total loss."

I was glad I was already flat on my back. I consulted my link, and after only a few seconds, shut out the flood of reports, complaints, and requests for compensation that were already being funneled my way.

"Can the day get any worse?" I said.

"Do not ask that."

"Please tell me you're kidding." But there was only silence. I groaned. *"What else?"*

"I went to consult with the Jalvian Prime, and he didn't

recognize me."

Fa'yet cleared his throat. I held up a hand and waved him to the chair Ikeri had vacated. He shook his head.

"Did we have an election I didn't know about?" I asked Jey.

"No. He. Did. Not. Know. Me."

"Yeah, that's what you said."

"Vayen, this is the man I've been working with for years. I'm in a marriage contract with his daughter for fuck's sake."

"Is he ill?"

"Not that I can tell. He knows Dayana. He knows everyone else in the family. Everyone but me. We showed him the still frame from the signing of the marriage contract. He had no recollection of that and threw me out of his house. He claims I've kidnapped his daughter and brainwashed her."

The selective memory loss sounded too familiar. My gut twisted into a knot and for a second, my brain refused to work, every thought scrambling to hide from the supposition.

Jey's voice went on while I tried to cling to reason. The Prime couldn't have been the victim of an Arpex. That would mean they were on Jal. We would have seen other signs of their presence if that were the case. And besides, Jal wasn't their target. They wanted defenseless Frique. This couldn't be Arpex. The memory wipe had to be something else, maybe hypnosis or some kind of specialized probe attack—something by a disgruntled Artorian group set on screwing with our integration plans. Yes, that made more sense.

The tightness holding me captive in my own body began to ease. I took a deep breath. Fa'yet was here. Ikeri and Stassia were close by. We were safe here on the ship. There were no Arpex in the Narvan. My thoughts began to flow freely again.

"And how is Dayana taking this?" I asked Jey.

Fa'yet looked more annoyed by the second. He crossed his arms over his chest and took up glaring at me intently.

"Give me a fucking minute. We have a situation. Several of them."

"Indeed you do," he said without sympathy. "Let me know when you have five minutes to discuss a couple more." He spun around and left.

"She's not taking it well. Vayen, I need her family's backing."

"We both need it. We'll figure it out."

"If what Fa'yet says is true, you can't even get out of bed," Jey grumbled.

Fa'yet apparently had a lot to say. With all the fires already burning around me, I wasn't looking forward to whatever it was that had him so agitated.

"I'll figure that out, too," I assured Jey.

"And Anastassia?"

"Still in the tank. So if you could remain uninjured at least until she is done, I would appreciate it. One of us half-baked is enough."

"You're going back in?" he asked.

"Considering how I currently feel, it may take days to recover otherwise. I'll deal with the University on the team loss while I wait."

"Good luck with that."

"Thanks." I cut contact.

With Jey out of my head, I pondered what I would say to the University officials. The loss of their people was tragic, their collective knowledge irreplaceable. They'd been selected for a reason: they were the best. And now they were ashes. A sour taste filled my mouth. I didn't want to do this through my link. The University deserved an in-person visit. I needed to stay on good terms with them. Without endless credits to buy their cooperation, that required more diplomatic methods.

Fa'yet and his impending barrage of shit could wait. He would have led with whatever it was if it was important. He'd be focused on Anastassia's recovery and watching over Ikeri for a while. Neko had Daniel under control or he'd have left me a message. The tragedy with the University staff took priority until Stassia had fully recovered so I could get back in the tank.

I popped two stims, gave them half an hour to get my system going to the point where I couldn't stand to be in bed because my blood was itching, and got up.

After getting dressed, which included my very degraded armor and a host of weaponry, I Jumped to the current point I had set within the University. A quick check of the location of the executive board members led me to one of the meeting rooms on the lower floor.

Since the University was responsible for the link implants that allowed us to Jump in and out of wherever we had a point set, they followed the same practice Stassia and I did. Furnishings and wall decor were kept to a bare minimum, offering little to provide a distinctive point of reference that was required for Jumping. They also did regular sweeps for handmade patterns such as what we used and removed them if they weren't authorized.

The air here was clean but sterile, a testament to the filtration system that isolated the hundreds of experiments and tests that were happening throughout the sprawling building. I stopped before the secretary's desk, the top of which was empty, merely a station for a person to be in case he was needed. The young man had watched me come down the hall with a face that said he knew exactly who I was and was merely deciding whether I would stop to talk to him or burst through the door to interrupt the meeting taking place inside.

When he spoke, his tone was surprisingly even. The University did hire good staff. "Can I help you, sir?"

"I'm afraid I must interrupt the meeting for a brief announcement."

"I see." He nodded. "Allow me just one moment, please."

He dropped his gaze to the blue surface of the desk while he spoke naturally with someone inside. When he looked back up, his face had taken on a pinched look.

"They're ready for you."

"Thank you."

It was hard to remember to be polite. That wasn't the way I was used to operating, and the people I'd dealt with before my absence seemed more disturbed by my change of tactics than if I dropped an ominous threat or shoved a gun in their face like they were used to.

I opened one side of the double door, rather than both as I would have preferred—that would have created more open space for movement should I need it in case of attacking or being attacked. But this was a room full of executives, unarmed and about to hear that their prized team had been obliterated. I figured a quiet entrance was more in order.

My tactful entrance didn't seem to matter. They all still stared at me as if I was here to announce the end of the known universe or mow them all down in a spray of bullets. Being locked in their rapt attention didn't help the skin-crawling sensations from the double shot of stims on top of the half-healed state where the tank had left me. I'd hoped to slip in quietly and wait for a lull in the discussion. No such luck.

There were no empty chairs at the long rectangular table. Not that I could have sat in one for more than twenty seconds without my knees starting to bounce.

I opted for standing at the head of the table. The two men nearest that spot spun to face me. They all waited expectantly.

"We greatly appreciate your cooperation in expediently sending a team to Moriek to investigate the newly discovered ship from these recent attacks. Unfortunately, something in this unknown vessel caused a self-destruct sequence to activate. I regret to inform you that the entire team was lost along with any research they may have begun."

My announcement was met with silence that stretched out until I hoped one of them stood up and took a shot at me so I'd have an outlet for the energy careening through my body. Sadly, everyone remained in their seats, their expressions quickly going from shock to processing the data I'd delivered.

"We have procedures in place to prevent self-destruct triggers. Our team could not have been at fault," said one of the men who had moved and now sat a few feet to my left.

"We do not assume your team was at fault. It was a tragic accident."

"Ships don't just explode," sputtered one of the others.

"Was anyone else hurt?" asked a woman with her hair pulled back from her face, making her high cheekbones stand out like a bare skull. My jittery brain supplied her name: Vivina Sa'cota.

"Unfortunately, yes. We estimate losses upwards of a thousand. There was significant damage to the entire station where the ship was docked. All lives were lost."

The man to my right shot to his feet. "How could you miss such an obvious ploy to harm our people? You took their ship in and filled it with our brightest minds. You docked it at a major port station."

"I didn't personally dock it there. Advisor Te offered. The station over Moriek provided a safe zone for studying the ship. The station population is minimal, and the station there is far more isolated than any over Artor. Granted, the loss will be an issue for Moriek's imports and exports for some time, but we'll do our best to facilitate a quick rebuild."

"But why not send it to a Jalvian station?" asked one of the accusing faces glaring at me. "Did it occur to you that Advisor Te could have easily rigged this ship to take out one of our stations? That his intent may have been to kill as many Artorians as possible, including our team?"

"Advisor Te should be held accountable for this loss of Artorian lives," one of them suggested.

Yet another of them chimed in, "I would suggest, Advisor Ta'set, as we suggested to your predecessor, that the Artorian worlds again be unified under a single Advisor. Let the Jalvians fend for themselves."

My hands twitched at my sides. "This isn't about Artor and Jal.

Advisor Te did not act with malicious intention. This new threat involves the entire Narvan. We're working together to keep you all as safe as possible. Keep your damned conspiracy theories and political suggestions to yourselves." I gave them all a stern look. "We certainly didn't expect that a ship that didn't self-destruct like all the others, would suddenly terminate itself without any provocation or warning. We would have never docked the ship or sent a team in if we suspected any such thing."

I took a moment to attempt to center myself, forcing my electrified nerves back into a feigned semi-calm state. "We don't know who we are dealing with. We had hoped that the investigation of the abandoned ship would yield clues as to the origin and threat level, but instead, we're back to guessing. We would appreciate any thoughts your staff may have on this matter, as the threat directly impacts us all."

"As our esteemed system advisor, we rely on *you* to assess and deal with threats of this nature," said the man on my left.

"And furthermore," added another. "We will be expecting remuneration for damages to our staff members."

"You have got to be kidding." I couldn't hold back any longer. With the stims singing in my veins and on top of the stupidity from the Friquen government, my limited patience expired.

Stassia would possibly have been able to deal with them more effectively, but these were my people and she'd vanished on them before, unleashing the chaos of her safety net. Now they didn't trust her. I'd at least left them in Artorian hands, even if those hands were more inept than anticipated.

"You will not be receiving restitution of any sort. You will provide me with any helpful information you may have or gather in the near future so that I can do my best to prevent another incident. There will be no arguments or bribes. You will do as I ask so that our people will not suffer again. Do you understand?"

Their faces were a mix of shock and expectation. My outburst had not surprised the older men and women. The younger ones were cowering nicely.

"If you think you can force our hands with threats, Advisor Ta'set, you are mistaken," said Sa'cota. "You will find your favors revoked if you continue this line of bullish behavior."

"Is that so." I stalked toward her. "Would you like to find your projects defunded and your research put in other hands? You are my people and as such, I prefer to patronize your services, but make no mistake, there are other options."

They weren't great options, but I did have connections from Kryon contacts. However, she didn't need to know that.

Sa'cota stared me down. "You wouldn't dare."

"Really?" I laughed ruefully.

Her pinched disdain remained.

I held her gaze in a stranglehold. "Think very carefully before you speak another word."

The chairman cleared his throat. "I think our meeting is suitably concluded. We will be in touch should any epiphanies arise, Advisor Ta'set."

Sa'cota broke away, glancing at the chairman with blatant disapproval. I remained beside her, hoping that she'd do something stupid.

Instead, she remained primly in her seat, pretending I wasn't there, which only pissed me off more.

The look I gave the chairman made him blanch. The threat I wanted to form to conclude the meeting tumbled through my mind. The words became incoherent before they reached my tongue. Sweat broke out from every pore, and my hands started to shake. My heart thudded erratically, leaving me lightheaded. The stims were wreaking havoc on my half-healed system. I settled for a nod and Jumped back to the ship before I killed anyone or collapsed.

SIX

Stripping off my coat, weapons, and clothes, I ran to the shower. Even knowing I'd be back in the tank before too long, it was the only place I could think of to find any relief. Standing naked under the water, the steam flowed over me. I breathed the hot moist air until I got my heartbeat under control. Slowly backing off the hot water, I stayed there until goosebumps rose over my entire body. Chilled, I dried off and crawled back under the blankets on my bed. Even with the residual effects of the stims, my eyes drifted closed. My body was too damaged for the miracle pills to last very long.

I woke to find hours had passed and still no one had come to switch me out for Stassia. Neko and the kids were asleep, likely in the house because there wasn't enough room for them all here. Stassia was still distant, hopefully also asleep and not still in the tank. Fa'yet was on duty, but other than brushing over his link enough to sense that he was awake, I avoided any further contact.

I'd missed dinner and, more importantly, failed Daniel's challenge. Mid-curse, I realized there was also an insistent contact through my link. After a silent plea to Geva to please not have one more fucking thing go wrong, I allowed the unfamiliar connection.

A female voice I didn't immediately recognize cautiously said, *"Vayen?"*

"Who?" I rubbed my face, trying to wake up enough to assign a name to the voice.

"Dayana." Jey's wife sounded scared.

We'd established contact when Jey had insisted she get a link implant in case of an emergency. I wondered if she'd ever really used it before now. She wasn't that kind of woman, she was pleasant and competent, but not like us.

"What is it?"

"There's someone here, insisting to speak with Jey."

No one should be showing up on his doorstep. And if it had her worried enough to contact me... I cursed Geva as I sat up. Once I had my bearings, I got dressed even though my hands were uncooperative. I could barely keep my eyes open. Habit put me on autopilot.

"I don't know who it is, but they're very persistent. I haven't opened the door, but they know I'm here. It's like they're in my head," she whispered as if she were afraid this person could hear her speaking to me.

"Where's Jey?"

I leaned against the bed and put on my coat, sliding whatever weapons were in arm's reach into the appropriate places. Sweat rolled down my face from even that little effort. I tossed back my last two stims and put the empty tin away. I rarely doubled up on them, but I couldn't stay on my feet without them in this condition. Stassia would no doubt be yelling at me. She'd filled the tin only a few days ago.

"He's trying to work things out with my father. As you probably understand, his selective amnesia is causing quite an issue, both with our family and the government. Jey was very firm about not interrupting him."

"I'll be right there." I made my shaky-legged way down the hall to see Stassia sound asleep on the platform. I covered her with a sheet and checked the terminal. Her cycle showed it had successfully completed. Thank Geva she was fully healed because I couldn't take much more of this.

A deep breath later and with a gun in my hand, I arrived in Jey's foyer on Jal.

"Over here," she whispered from the far corner of the common room. My artificial eye spotted her in the dark, huddled in the corner, knees drawn up in front of her.

"Stay there. Your daughter?"

"Asleep in her room."

Hopefully, she stayed that way. I wasn't up for Jumping anyone other than myself, and barely that.

The security station seemed a good place to start with minimal physical effort on my part. I slid onto the stool and brought up the vids, which cast a soft light over the room. The view from the front of the house revealed a bulky form standing there, cloaked from head to foot.

The last time I'd seen a cloak like that, it had been on a High Council member. But they were gone. We'd destroyed their bases. All of them. Jey had confirmed Sere was obliterated, and I'd verified the destruction of the other bases before agreeing to return to the Narvan. Even if a few of the High and Mighties might have Jumped to safety, surely they would have made their presence known long before now. This couldn't be one of them. It couldn't.

The gun in my hand shook so badly that I'd be just as likely to shoot myself or Dayana. I put it away.

"Who's out there?" she asked from her corner.

"Contact Jey. Whether he likes it or not, I'll deal with him." I couldn't do this alone, not in the shape I was in.

I considered calling Neko in, but if this was the Council, he wouldn't be much better off than I currently was. He'd never worked for them. He didn't know their games, and I wasn't prepared to lose him. Neither could I lose Fa'yet. Better to take on whatever it was myself and know that the two of them, who were whole in both mind and body, would be there to watch over Stassia and the kids.

A familiar pressure built in my head, and for a second, I assumed it was Jey, but it felt wrong. Very wrong. I was powerless to prevent it from diving in. A voice full of hisses stomped into my brain, clacking underlying its words.

Oh Geva no. This couldn't be happening. Not in the Narvan. Not one of *them*. My thoughts shattered. Pain seized my chest and shot through my arms. I couldn't breathe.

"Tell me about your wife," the voice commanded.

The room faded in and out of focus as I slipped off the stool and fell to the floor. My heart kicked and screamed against bone, trying to rip its way out of my body.

"Your wife," the Arpex repeated, its grip on my brain growing tighter.

I knew the rules of this game and how to break them. And the cost. My eyes and mind focused on Dayana crouched in the shadows, devoting every thought to her.

She was a decent looking woman for a Jalvian, a good mother to her daughter. She treated Jey well within their political union, maybe genuinely loved him. I had no complaints or concerns about her. She made him happy, even made him laugh.

And then I couldn't remember what I'd been thinking, like the lights had flickered out and I was left in the dark, fumbling to find a candle.

A candle would be nice, they reminded me of Stassia.

From my vantage point on the floor, I looked around, fighting to get my bearings within my spinning head. Who was the strange woman hiding in the corner, watching me with wide, terrified eyes?

"You were going to tell me about your wife?" Arpex asked, doing its usual gloating after a meal, letting me know that it held all the power.

As much as I'd tried before, and even now, I'd yet to simulate the correct level of loss and terror after swapping its meal. Like the others, this Arpex knew what I'd done in seconds. It wasn't pleased. Every nerve in my head exploded.

Somewhere, far from the pain wracking my body, Jey's panicked voice registered as a distant whisper. "Why is he here? What's going on? He's ripping himself apart!"

The woman screamed.

SEVEN

Light crept between my lashes as someone pried one of my eyes open. I caught a blurry glimpse of Stassia's face. I tried to swat her away but my arm was so heavy I don't think it moved. Why couldn't they let me be? She was always after me to rest.

A conversation drifted in and out, distorted and distant, then clear, like waves disturbing my silent beach of sleep.

"Why is it taking so damn long for him to wake up? I'm going to kill him."

"Maybe that's why he's in no hurry," said Jey. "For someone who played a healer for years on Minor, your bedside manner is atrocious."

Feet scuffled over the floor. There was a heavy thud of a fist hitting armor.

"His stupidity doesn't deserve any sympathy."

The more I listened, the clearer their voices became, and though I didn't want to wake up just yet, I forced my eyes open a crack.

"Let me go." Stassia squirmed in Jey's arms. She pounded on his chest. He let her continue, even though every blow brought a wince.

"Anastassia, he'll be all right. Just give him time."

"This is all your fault, you and your stupid wife. I should kill—"

"I suggest you don't finish that sentence."

"Quiet." I meant to yell, but it came out barely a whisper.

They were both at my side in an instant.

"You idiot!" She slapped me in the face.

Jey grabbed her hand before she could do it again.

As much as I wanted to tell them both to shut up and leave me alone, speaking took too much effort. I let their voices drift away and sank back down into the warm sand.

Neko sat beside me the next time I opened my eyes, feeling far more alert. His tall form was hunched in the chair, his eyes closed. How damn long had I been out?

I checked my link to find I had messages from two days ago. Three tank visits ago. That was far too much time in the tank for my liking. Stassia's too, as I recalled from her slap. Neither she nor Jey was in sight, and the ship was quiet except for Neko's soft breathing.

Relieved that I wasn't going to be slapped or screamed at, I sat up and reached for some clothes.

"Hey boss, I'm going to have to ask you to put those back," said Neko.

I should have known he'd wake at the slightest movement. "Hey yourself. Why?"

"The other boss's orders."

"Ah."

So I *was* going to get slapped and screamed at. "Can I take a shower first?"

Neko yawned and rolled his head in a slow orbit around his neck. "I might be convinced to sleep a few more minutes if you can offer protection from her wrath when she sees that I didn't retrieve her immediately."

"Given that information, I can't offer the level of protection you'd need."

"That's what I thought. I'll be right back." He stood, and quite sincerely said, "Please don't move."

"She's got you trained good," I said, returning the barb he often threw at me.

He laughed nervously and vanished into the void.

I contemplated running to the bathroom and making her wait, but decided that I couldn't do that to Neko. He returned with Anastassia, offering me one of his standard apologetic nods behind her back.

"I'll be at the house if you need me," he said to me just before Jumping to safety far from Stassia.

She wasn't wearing her armor, and as far as I could tell, she wasn't armed either. Her plain black shirt was rumpled like she'd been sleeping in it, and her braid had loosened to the extent of nearly coming undone. Disarray was a look she rarely wore.

Bracing for her attack on all fronts, I was totally caught off guard when she threw herself onto the bed and wrapped her arms around me. She stayed there, head pressed against my chest until I relaxed enough to hold her.

"You're not allowed to leave this bed ever again," she said quietly.

"That's kind of impossible considering that I have—"

"I don't care." Her whole body trembled.

"Well, all right then, you've convinced me."

She sat up, straddling me. I expected to see her smiling, but she wasn't. Her face had drawn tight.

"There will be no more stims. If you're tired, you sleep. I don't care what the crisis is, someone else can deal with it or it can wait," she declared.

"That's not very realistic in our line of work."

"You want realistic? Do you?"

She was definitely going to slap me again. I braced for it and waited, but her hand didn't rise.

"You died. You fucking died! You took so damned many stims that your heart gave out."

On a distant level, it scared me that relief at still being alive wasn't the first thing that came to mind. Instead, I was cursing Geva for kicking me back into this mess. More memories gone, Stassia beyond stressed over me again. Fucking Arpex in the Narvan.

My heart faltered for a second and my body went cold.

Stassia pulled the sheets back and ran her warm hands over my chest and then my face as if to assure herself that I was healed. "Whatever happened while you were serving the Council damaged your heart. We found the fault in your profile." She gave me a pointed look. "We had plenty of time to sift through the details since the tank took so damn long to heal you."

I felt awful, putting her through that, but it wasn't like it was the first time one of us had been touch and go on whether the tank was going to pull off it's magic or not. However, she was more shaken than I'd ever seen her before.

"I'm sorry. I'm fine now."

She shook her head, hands on my face again, stroking the scars on either side as though she could smooth them away.

"You're not. The tank can't heal the underlying damage." Her voice hitched. "I'm serious. No stims, and you're not going to overtax yourself."

"I wasn't overtaxing anything. There was an Arpex. It was at Jey's house. That's what—"

Her fingers dug into my shoulders. "Then you should have called

Jey. It's his damned house. His helpless-ass, ill-prepared, political snit of a wife should learn to take care of her own fucking self. And you did not need to run off to meet with the University. I agree that the delay would not have been ideal, but it could have waited."

Had she not heard me? "Stassia, I—"

"No excuses. You're killing yourself. Quite literally. Who do you think will benefit from that?"

"The damned Arpex that was standing outside Jey's door. It was in my head. It wanted something from me. It took...wait, Jey has a wife?"

Her tirade evaporated but her grip on my shoulders remained. "Are you sure? Really sure it was an Arpex? It wasn't your mind playing tricks on you?"

Arin laughed in my head. *Still liking this dream better? Look at what you're doing to her. Wake up and let her be safe wherever she is.*

"I am awake."

I shoved him back down into the shadows of my mind. But there shouldn't be Arpex here. Not if this was real. Chills ran over my skin. I had to be awake. Focusing on Stassia's warm hands and our bonded connection, I tried to pull myself together.

Had I slipped off the deep end? Had it all been a trick of my over-stimmed mind? I contacted Jey.

"Why was I at your house?"

"Glad to hear your voice. We thought we'd lost you there for a while. As quickly as the gel fixed something, another part of you stopped working."

That explained Stassia's unnerved demeanor. I pulled her back down so I could hug her. She molded to me. A perfect fit.

"Thanks for getting me to the tank, by the way."

"She would have killed me if I hadn't."

Stassia's threats and Jey holding her came back to me. Her hair tickled my neck. I smoothed it back into what remained of her braid and filled our bonded connection with the reassurance that I was all right.

"You know she doesn't mean that half the time, right?"

"It's the other half that worries me." Jey paused. *"In case you weren't aware, Anastassia is quite attached to you, and I'm talking on a deep and enviable level. You might want to lay off anything that might put you in the tank for a while."*

As if life was that easy. He knew better than that. But he didn't make a habit of friendly admonitions. The last one he'd given me was after we'd destroyed the Council and I'd awoken with him beside me to learn I'd lost an eye and would be covered in scars for the rest of my life.

"I'll try."

"Good. As to your original question, Dayana thought there was someone outside. She shouldn't have bothered you with that, it won't happen again. I appreciate that you came even in the condition you were in."

"Was someone out there?" I asked, near begging him to tell me I hadn't imagined the Arpex, and yet, at the same time, hoping that I had. Better to be crazy than have Arpex in the Narvan.

"Are you on the ship?"

"Yes."

And then so was Jey, in my bedroom, with Stassia laying on top of my naked gel-covered self. He took one step forward, mouth open as if ready to continue our conversation, then spun around.

"You could have said something," he said standing with his back to us.

"I wasn't expecting company." I pulled at the sheet but Stassia was on most of it.

Stassia sat up. "I assure you, I'm fully clothed."

"Does he often have conversations in the middle of head sex? That's an impressive level of multitasking."

"We were certainly not..." She sputtered as she climbed off me and sat in the chair, brushing gel flakes off of her shirt and face.

"I suppose you're allowed to shower and get dressed," she said.

Jey snickered. "So *that's* how it is between the two of you."

"I might have died yesterday, but I can kick your ass today," I informed him, getting the sheet around myself now that Stassia was out of the way.

"There will be no ass-kicking." She pointed me toward the door. "Go and then get back here and sit down if you insist on being out of bed."

I grabbed my clean clothes and made a break for it before Jey had time to say anything else.

When I came out of the bathroom, I found we'd adjourned to the small office. Jey spun the vid around so we could all view it.

"This is the feed from the front of the house."

The cloaked figure stood there outside the door. Something moved under the cloth, causing a clacking noise.

I could see its thin arms hanging, claws snapping beneath the fall of fabric, the slight ridge under the cloak where the black box was strapped to its shell. The tips of its blue shelled feet with their serrated edges created vague points below the hem of the heavy cloak.

The figure stayed there, still, for a total of thirty-six minutes before turning around to leave.

"It doesn't say anything, doesn't appear to be armed, just stands there," said Jey.

"It was an Arpex," I said with utter certainty.

"The thing that chopped off your hand?" he asked, eyeing my large grey replacement.

I nodded.

"How can you know? It could be anything beneath that cloak. Though I agree, it does look an awful lot like they use the same clothing supplier as the Council."

"It was in my head. My face, was I clawing at it?"

He nodded and then glanced at the feed where he'd stopped it, the cloaked figure a blur as it turned around. "You were in the middle of cardiac arrest when I got there. You probably felt Dayana in your head. She was scared. Maybe you had a reaction to the stim overload."

Stassia also stared at the vid feed. Her hand slid over mine. "He doesn't know Dayana."

Jey's mouth dropped open. "How can you not? Then why were you there?"

Admitting my memory issue to Stassia was one thing, but with both of them watching me intently, I couldn't find a way out of it. "I don't know."

"They know you're broken," whispered Arin.

"So you wake up here, still half-baked, pop a couple of stims for no particular reason, and Jump to my house to rip your face to bits and have a heart attack on my floor?"

"This was the last one, the one that will make you unravel," Arin said.

I looked to Stassia, silently begging for help, but her face only reflected mine. "I don't know."

Jey slammed a fist down on the desktop. "I don't need this. I really don't. Two of you now? What the fuck is going on?"

Visions of vid screens on the office walls flashed in and out of focus. I could smell Arin's sweat, hear the scattered conversations of distant Kryon members from the feeds. My clothes were grey, and then they weren't.

"We're the same, you and me," said Arin.

Leaning back in my chair, I closed my eyes and suddenly didn't disagree with Stassia's decree that I remain in bed. I craved the dark silence and the safety of the warm heavy blankets.

The words of the Arpex I'd served when I'd been a prisoner came back to me. They'd wanted the Narvan for their own purposes, but the High and Mighties had stood in their way, not allowing the few Arpex to out rule the majority who wanted our resources dedicated to expansion. But we destroyed the Council, and with it, our protection.

Logic put me on autopilot, blocking out Arin and snapping my brain into focus. "Those ships weren't empty."

Jey looked at me like I'd lost my mind. "Really? Because none of them had bodies inside."

"Not anymore. They'd already deposited their weapons. The attacks were an extra bonus, a distraction."

"And those weapons would be what?" he asked.

"Arpex. They eat selective memories. Ask your Prime if he had any visitors before he forgot you. I bet he did."

"Why would they care if you remembered Dayana?"

Stassia gripped my hand tighter. Thank Geva I still knew it was her.

"It thought I was you," I explained. "They're trying to drive us mad, make it so we can't operate, lose our supporters because they won't know us. The system will be in utter chaos unless we find them and kill them before this gets out of hand."

"How would they know who to target?" Jey asked.

A hollow pit formed in my gut. "There were Arpex on the High Council. They observed you. The one I served was in my head. Constantly. Either one survived, or they passed on the information."

"This is your fault," whispered Arin.

"How many Arpex would they send?" asked Stassia.

I swallowed hard, trying to block out Arin's truth. "No more than two or three would fit per ship, so maybe up to a dozen per planet? They wouldn't need more as long as they strike the right targets before they're found. Once their madness unfolds, we'll destroy ourselves and the rest will swoop in to feed off the survivors from the comfort of their Friquen nesting ground."

The words coming from my mouth made me ill. I couldn't believe how calm they sounded compared to the chaos in my head.

"Could it be that simple? That they could take us out with so few?" Jey sped through the feed in reverse. "They just stand there."

"You tell me. How much of a problem is it that the Prime won't recognize you as Advisor?"

"We risk losing our hold on the fleets," Jey said.

Stassia nodded. "Which would leave the Artorian worlds largely unprotected and your own not on a united front."

"Yes," I said. "And what's the one thing tying you to the Prime that you're relying on to fix the problem?"

"Dayana."

"If you didn't remember her?" Stassia asked.

Jey scrubbed his face with both hands. "I'd have a big mess to deal with and wouldn't be doing a damn thing to prevent them from causing more of a problem."

"Exactly. Worse, what if the Prime happened to forget his treaty with Artor? What if Fragia and Kess forgot about theirs?"

"I don't like this at all," Jey said. "Give me ships or troops to take down, not this devious mind game shit. How do we defeat them?"

"Bullets bounce off." The smell of the dirty bodies of the offerings filled my nose. "Heavy pulses, grenades, or explosives work."

The stench of burnt hair and flesh filled the air around me as Merkief exploded over and over in my mind. I swallowed hard, forcing the words to keep coming, trying to ignore the memories I wished an Arpex had taken.

"If they get in your head, answer their question with someone else," I said. "Give them someone else. They can be tricked."

I felt the pressure, the insistent force commanding that I think of my wife, that I think of Stassia. "It wanted my wife. I gave it yours."

The walls of the small office drew closer. Jey's fear smelled sour and Stassia's concerned gaze burned. I needed air. My stomach heaved.

Scrambling to my feet, I ran down the hall to the bathroom and promptly emptied the meager watery contents of my stomach into the toilet.

Stassia came in behind me. "Vayen?" She sounded small, uncertain, and scared. It crushed me that I was the cause.

"I'm fine. I'll be there in a bit." I waved her back toward the door.

"What's wrong, is it your heart again?" She ignored my protests and knelt beside me, her hands rubbing over my back. "You didn't take anything, did you? No stims? Nothing else? Have you eaten anything? You haven't. It's been two days. I should have made you eat something. Are you thirsty? Can I get you something? Anything?"

I'd never heard her ramble on so badly. I'd almost lost her to the Arpex. So close. Too damn close.

"Is he all right?" Jey called from outside the door.

"Vayen, talk to me. Do we need to get you back in the tank?"

I shook my head, trying to breathe in through my nose and out through my mouth as I focused on a single speckled tile on the floor.

She got up and went to the door. They whispered back and forth and then she stood beside me again. "He's gone. Please don't keel over on me."

"I won't."

Thank Geva, he was gone. Jey lurking outside the door was far too much pressure. It was bad enough that she was in the room.

"You can go, too."

"Like hell. You're a mess." A hint of hysteria edged her voice. She needed me to be strong, but I couldn't, not knowing those blue bastards were traipsing about in my system, standing outside doors and invading the minds of anyone inside. They could be standing outside our door on Frique right now, making Fa'yet and Neko think that I didn't exist.

If we were going to keep the Narvan out of their hands, I was going to have to face them again. I shuddered. There weren't enough stims and alcohol in the entire system to prepare me for that.

"I can't do this." I hated myself for speaking those words, out loud, to her.

"You can." She knelt in front of me, resting her forehead on mine. "We can."

"You don't understand." Whose voice was this squeak, this pathetic whine? It certainly wasn't mine.

I wanted to crawl into a dark corner far from her. No one should see me like this. This wasn't the system advisor, the man who'd taken down the High Council, the partner she worked with every day, the father to her children. I didn't even know who this was. But I hated him. I hated that he showed his face to her, that he couldn't rise above the weakness eating him nibble by nibble every day. I hated that he was sitting on the damned bathroom floor with vomit on his breath, doing nothing to reassure his totally unnerved mate.

I felt her then, nudging her way along our natural connection, trying to find something she could work with. And then Ikeri was there too. I wanted to vanish, to simply evaporate and cease being. It was one thing for Stassia to see me fall apart, but not my little girl. She should never see this. How was I supposed to keep her safe when I couldn't even form words to explain the terror in my head? Could I curl up next to the toilet, close my eyes, and wish them both away somewhere safe and far from me?

"Daddy, it's all right," Ikeri said so softly that I thought I'd imagined it. Her touch was so light that I found I didn't mind her there as much as I should have. She wrapped me in safety and light even from far away on Veria Prime. My scarily strong little girl.

Stassia's arms were around me too, her cheek against mine. "We have you," she whispered in my ear.

Tears rolled down one cheek. At least my artificial eye had the decency to keep its emotions on the inside. Ikeri faded away. I held Stassia tight, thinking of how close I had come to forgetting her.

"I can't lose you," I told her in that pathetic voice I hated.

Thank Geva I hadn't tried to let her go off alone when I'd first thought to fake her death and keep the Narvan. If this was what I would be reduced to, I would have been dead in a matter of hours.

"You won't."

"They can make me forget. I almost did, but I gave them Dayana instead. They may have tried to make me forget you before, but I gave them someone else. I gave them so much. These scars," I rubbed the sides of my face, "are for every time I tricked the Arpex. I don't even know who I gave them Gemmen for. Or my mother. I don't even know all the things I've lost."

I sounded like Arin, unhinged, and knowing it. His whispers, imagined or real, weren't wrong.

I tried to look at her, to make her see the holes inside me, to make her understand, but it was impossible to meet her gaze.

There was no use hiding anything now. She knew how weak I was. Too weak to even look her in the eye.

"If I don't know you, don't remember us, too much of me will be missing," I said. Even just giving voice to the possibility utterly terrified me. "I don't know what would be left. There are so many holes where Gemmen is supposed to be that I can't imagine the void you'd leave behind. You've been at the center of everything for so long that the parts that would be left..." I shook my head, unable to find the words.

She just held me, let me weep like a fucking idiot.

When there was nothing left inside, I wanted her gone, wanted the memory of the past hour erased from her mind. Why couldn't an Arpex help me with that? They fucking owed me.

Did they take requests? I imagined myself asking one for a favor and it eating me instead.

Maybe I really was crazy. Maybe Arin was right about that too. Losing Dayana was the one hole that tipped the ratio of gaps to memories out of my favor.

My son picked that moment to contact me, which he didn't do often on his own. I was hesitant to put him off even in the condition I was in.

"Are you and mom all right? We haven't seen you in days. Ikeri is worried."

Had she nudged him to contact me?

"You feel weird," he said.

"I know." I didn't trust myself to say much for fear I might start either laughing uncontrollably or crying again.

"Will you be home soon? Uncle Isnar and Neko won't tell us anything. I've been going to school. I haven't even gotten in trouble."

"That's good to hear. I'll be there soon."

I started to shut him out but he quickly asked, *"Is mom staying with you?"*

"Yes."

"We're not cutting her in half, but it feels like you need her, so you can keep her for now."

As much as I appreciated his attempt at humor, I couldn't muster the effort to even fake a laugh.

"Thanks, I will."

Dammit, even he could see through me. I cut contact before he got a full sense of what a mess his father was.

"Daniel?" Stassia asked.

I nodded.

"Isnar has been keeping me posted. They're both fine."

"We should be there," I said, pushing her gently away. "You go."

She shook her head. "I should be here. They'll get by for a while longer."

Stassia took my hands and stood up. "Come on. You'll be more comfortable in bed." She tugged at me until I was on my feet.

I didn't want to be anywhere. I wanted all the things that were wrong with me, the things that made me weak like this, to be gone, to go back to the dark recesses of my mind where I'd kept them locked away.

But I let her lead me back to my bedroom.

Stassia lifted the blankets and waited while I got under them. Once I was settled in, she wedged herself in between me and the edge of the bed, covering us both.

She turned out the light. Silence filled the tiny ship where I'd first awakened to learn the truth of who Anastassia Kazan was, of who I would need to be to stand beside her. I'd had a similar overwhelmed feeling then, though it had been her and the threats against her that had elicited those, not missing memories and flesh-eating Arpex.

Stassia lay there, her heart beating against my arm, her arm draped over my chest, head on my shoulder, breathing calmly.

"Tell me what happened when you went back to Sere to confront the High Council."

"I can't," I said adamantly.

"You can. I let you have your silence on the matter for far too long. You need to let it out."

I shook my head.

"You survived unbroken. You obliterated them. They are no longer, and you are in this bed beside me. Don't let them win. Tell me what happened."

"The Council stood against the Arpex, at least with the Narvan. They were allowed to take others. I observed deals for worlds— punishments or rewards, depending on which side was doing the accounting. I went to a world they were given." I shuddered remembering the ruined world I'd fetched offerings from. "But you're right, I obliterated the Council. I rid the Narvan of the one shield it had. Now fucking Arpex are here, and I'm lying in a bed doing nothing."

She expanded our bonded connection until I could see what she felt. None of it said I was weak. The peace of our bond soothed me enough to take the edge off now that I had a slight semblance of sanity.

"You're lying here in a bed with me. Does that still sound like a waste of time?"

"That's not what I meant."

"Then take the time to get whatever is haunting you off your chest, and then we'll both go out there and kick their asses."

I did laugh then, a single burst that burned my thick throat. "You know I love you."

She nuzzled my shoulder. "Uh huh. Now talk."

"Are you interrogating me now?"

"I'd rather not. I'm quite comfortable here." Her hand brushed across my chest, swirling back and forth.

"I really don't want to do this."

"I know, but talking about what happened isn't going to make it any more real than it was. You lived through it. Don't forget that."

"But I don't want to live it again."

"You do every time you close your eyes."

She had me there. In fact, I didn't even have to close them most of the time.

I couldn't keep everything locked away when I let down my guard. It spilled out in my sleep every damn night. If she was going to hound me about stims, and I couldn't blame her for that, then I needed to be able to sleep.

She'd already seen the worst of me.

I drew a deep shuddering breath and steeled myself. "Just this once then."

Even with the lights out, I squeezed my eyes shut, not wanting to see the images already playing in my head as I spoke. I told her how I'd gone to Sere to try and meet with the Council, how they'd laughed at me, and put me in grey. How they'd dragged me low and what I'd done to serve Arpex. I told her how it had cut off my hand and made me dispose of it as if it were nothing more than table scraps, and of Arin who spied on me and yet was my only companion.

Sharing that I'd been promoted and of my meeting with Deep voice, how he'd promised me a spot on the Council itself, was a little easier.

She gasped but didn't interrupt.

"But he took too long. I gave up. You're wrong, they did break me. I spent everything I had. Everything." I placed her hand on my scarred face. "To get Merkief a message, to show him where to Jump the bombs, knowing I would never get out. I wasn't coming back to you. I shouldn't be here."

"But you are," she whispered in my ear.

"You're not hearing me. Even if I hadn't given Merkief the locations for the bombs, and if he hadn't taken out the Council, I had agreed to join them. I wasn't coming back to you. I'm not supposed to be here."

She filled our connection with comforting warmth and kissed my cheek. "You are, or you wouldn't be lying next to me right now."

"That was an accident. A fucking lucky one."

"Maybe it was about time your Geva did something in your favor."

I listened to her breathing in the darkness and opened my eyes. "You're not mad?"

"You're here." She kissed me. "You were making the best of a desperate situation. Had you not devoted everything to your plan to obliterate them, you would have protected us from under a cloak. Either way, you were doing what you could for us. How could I be mad about that?"

I didn't have an answer, but I let her hold me again and didn't feel quite so guilty about it this time. We stayed like that in the darkness while I'd briefly told her some of what I'd endured. There was a lot more and she didn't need to hear about it, no matter how much she might think she could handle. I refused to give voice to the terrors of Merkief's death, of the screams of those I'd fed to Arpex, or the pain I'd endured every time Arpex snacked on my memories.

With her here, the stench of charred bodies and the heat of the explosions couldn't touch me. The darkness stayed dark. The warmth from her body soaked into me, soothing and calming. Moments like this were what I'd dreamed about while on my mat with Arin close by and the perpetual light of the vid screens or the Arpex dome pelting through my eyelids.

This wasn't a dream. This was real.

"If you say so," said Arin.

"Shut up. Just shut up!"

I tried to send him back into the shadows, but he just smiled sadly and shook his head.

"Vayen," she said softly, drawing me back to her. "What happened to Merkief?"

My entire body rebelled against giving life to the words she asked for, every muscle at once going stiff, shattering the modicum of peace I'd gained. She remained where she was, and even when the silence stretched long and tight, she didn't retract the question. I had to give her something.

After a futile attempt to clear my thick throat and another two minutes of silence in case she decided to mercifully back down, I began to formulate an answer.

"Would it be easier to show me?" she asked as though she was offering me a lifeline.

"No." Fuck no. To all the nine hells, no.

I breathed in the clean air and let it out slowly. "When Merkief saw me in grey, he wasn't the same man we'd known, not the one before we left, or the one who dragged us back into all this. He was different. He said to tell you he was sorry. He'd lost everything, there was nothing left inside him."

"Suicidal," she whispered.

"Yes." And he hadn't been the only one.

Clearing my throat again, I forced myself to continue. "He knew exactly what he was doing. Losing his family was the final straw, according to Jey. It's what put him on the path to eventual self-destruction."

I told her how he'd died in as few words as I could, all the while reliving it in vivid detail in my head. Hot tears ran down her face and onto my shoulder.

I'd shed enough tears for him. Now I just wanted him to quit haunting me, to quit reminding me of what I would become if I lost Stassia.

Recalling my initial anger at Geva upon waking from the tank, I was dismayed to admit I wasn't far from being like Merkief already. Even with Stassia right here.

"You're afraid you'd be the same way if you forget me," she said.

Goosebumps rose over my body. She wasn't in my head. I'd feel her. It wasn't often I cursed the return of our full-bonded connection, but I did then. I was too wide open, my thoughts too scattered to attempt to mute them.

"You wouldn't," she assured me.

"How can you know that? You've seen me when I'm only working. You don't like it. You're scared of me."

She went quiet for a few minutes, but I didn't sense that she was scrambling or concocting a lie. "I don't like it, and you're right, but that doesn't mean you'd be a terrible person. You're still you. It's just that your focus becomes very singular. Jey told me how you were when I was serving my time, but you did great things for the Narvan."

"Because I knew you were coming back."

She shifted on the bed, lifting her head and propping it up on her arm. Her other hand spun lazy swirls on my shoulder. I imagined they were like the pattern on the bands that signified our joining.

After a couple minutes, she said, "You're a rational person, Vayen. Whether I'm around or not, you still have the same goals for your people, for the Narvan, for our kids."

"Don't talk like that."

Her words gave me chills and lit a wave of panic. If I wanted to avoid slipping into another hallucination, I needed to change the mood fast. She'd had enough truth for one day. Or all of them, at least on those particular topics.

"If I'd never agreed to join with you, and we lived apart, knowing what you do about me, would you think I was a terrible person?" she asked.

"Only because you didn't agree to join with me."

She swatted my arm. "I'm serious. My point is, we're not automatically crazed lunatics if one of us ceases to exist. There was a lot more at play there than just Merkief losing his family, horrific as that was for him, I'm sure. You're not him. Even if you forgot me, you'd be yourself, just alone."

I rolled over and wiggled my arm under her, pulling her closer. "I don't want to be alone."

"And neither do I, but we would deal with it and continue to be who we are with or without the other."

"But I have the bond," I said.

"You wouldn't if you didn't know me."

If she was trying to alleviate my biggest fear, she was doing a terrible job. The emptiness I would return to without her and the peace she offered in my head was a horrifying thought. One I'd given into during my imprisonment. One that had led me to suicidal actions.

Again the silence stretched out. Was a little hope too much to ask for?

"If I did forget you, do you think we'd bond again? Naturally, I mean?" I asked.

She ran her fingers through my hair along my temple, a rhythmic motion that eased the tension from my neck. "I'd like to think so."

"Really? You weren't exactly on board with it the first time around."

Her lips curled into a smile against my neck. "Neither were you. I distinctly recall you quite harshly declaring that you had absolutely no intention of bonding with me while we ate a very tense meal in a very expensive restaurant."

"We were barely speaking to one another, and Geva, the secrets we were both keeping." I snorted. "I knew it would never work out between us."

"Shows what you know." She chuckled.

I turned toward her and kissed her forehead. "I suppose it does."

"And if you need further proof of how wrong you were—" She leaned over further and kissed me.

I couldn't have asked for a more pleasurable distraction from the chaos in my head or a better method of keeping her away from it. We spent the next half hour trying not to fall out of the narrow bed while enjoying the fact that no one was around to hear us.

EIGHT

"Do you think there's anything to eat at home?" Stassia asked.

"The way that boy cooks? The cold storage is overflowing with leftovers, I'm sure." My vacant stomach cried out for sustenance.

Stassia would never cook again if Daniel had his way. I wasn't sure where he got his culinary motivation from; it certainly wasn't from his mother.

We Jumped to the Friquen house to find the roof repaired, Neko at the security station, Fa'yet in bed, Ikeri watching me from under her long lashes, and Daniel grinning.

"I told you they'd be back soon," Daniel said to Neko.

"You all right, boss?" He gave me a cursory once over.

"It's been a rough couple of days."

"I see she didn't kill you. Congratulations." Neko grinned and then returned his attention to the feeds.

"Are you hungry?" asked Daniel. "I made extra last night."

"Yes, very," Stassia said. "But first, I'm going to change."

Uncomfortable under too many gazes, I followed. Sitting on the bed, I stared at the floor, listening to Stassia strip off her clothes and put clean ones on. The quiet safety of our bedroom offered a welcome reprieve that I was reluctant to leave no matter how much my stomach grumbled.

Finished, she started for the door, but then turned back to me. "Are you coming?"

"Go ahead. I'll get something later."

She shook her head, coming back to stand in front of me. "You need to eat. Come on."

Taking my hand, she pulled me back out to the kitchen. "Sit." She nudged me toward a chair at the table, then poured us two glasses of water and sat beside me. Daniel dashed into the kitchen and began heating leftovers.

"You're going to keep this up for a while, aren't you?" I asked.

"Oh yes." She squeezed my hand and said quietly, "I'm not losing you again."

"Sounds like you would go on an extensive killing spree if that were the case."

She cracked a smile but didn't let go. I didn't mind.

We ate a meal of baked squash and thick brown bread covered with warm cheese. I didn't know how good it had been the first time around, but it was damned good right then. And I didn't think so just because I was starving. I made sure to let Daniel know of my appreciation of his skills, which made him blush. Though he diverted his attention to the dishes, I caught him smiling several times.

After we'd finished, Stassia gave me a questioning look. I nodded. She went off to our room.

I noticed Ikeri hovering near Neko, but I stayed to help Daniel finish cleaning up in the kitchen, mostly to reassure him that I was all right.

"Mom helped?" he asked.

I nodded.

"Good." He gave me a quick, unexpected hug and darted off to his room.

That was just as well, because I knew Ikeri was not about to let me off so easily.

She left Neko and gave me her old woman stare, the one that told me I was going to have to explain myself to some degree because a simple, 'I'm better now', wasn't going to cut it with her. And I wasn't all better. I was only slightly less shitty.

Talking to Stassia had eased my mind a little. She'd suffered at the hands of the High and Mighties too. She knew how nasty they could be.

"Shall we sit?" Ikeri asked in a very adult voice, her gaze steady. It was unnerving to see my little girl this way. She was good at it. Very good. And while that made me proud, it also made me sad. I wanted her round cheeks and giggles back.

"They teach you that at Seeker school?" That came out sharper than I intended. I took her hand and led her over to the couch where we sat, looking out at the stars between the trees.

"I wish you would let me help you. I've helped Mother," she said, sounding frustrated.

I didn't remember exactly when Stassia had gone from Mommy to Mother, but it might have been around the time that Ikeri had truly started therapy with her. She was growing up too fast, even for my people.

"You've done an amazing job with your mother, and I do appreciate how much you've helped her, but this is different."

She dropped her gaze to her lap. "She's not going to get much better. I've done what I can, but there was a lot of damage."

"We knew that." I rubbed her shoulder, pulling her closer so we didn't have this professional divide between us. "You've brought her closer to her old self than we'd ever dreamed possible."

"Really?" Her eyes were bright as she looked up at me through her brown curls.

"Yes, really."

She grinned. And when she grinned, I couldn't help but do the same.

Then her joy dimmed and faded. "But you won't let me help you."

"The damage I have is different. There are holes in my memory and that's not something you can replace."

"Maybe I can."

I gave her a skeptical stare.

"Well, I can't know until I try," she said firmly.

"While I normally agree with that mantra, this isn't one of those times. There are too many things in here," I tapped my temple, "that you should never have to see. And I don't care how old you are, that will still hold true."

She sighed. "You were not in a good place today."

"Agreed." There was no use hiding it. She'd seen.

Outside the window, the trees rocked in a gentle breeze, no doubt a warm one, knowing Frique. A night bird called in the distance. One close by answered.

"Did Mother help you? You're not afraid of sharing what is in your head with her, are you?"

"Not anymore." Watered down versions of it, anyway.

She nodded.

It occurred to me that she'd been in Stassia's head. Really in it. Ikeri had to be to do what she'd done.

"Have you seen things in your mother's memories? The sort of things you shouldn't, I mean?"

"Yes, but I don't focus on that. We're taught not to. Discretion."

"That's good."

Though, for all I knew, she meant she was being told to say she wasn't focusing on anything specific, and the discretion bit was about knowing when to say what you saw and when not to.

"You haven't told her what you've seen, have you?"

"She knows, Daddy. She trained too, remember?"

That made me pause. Surely Anastassia wouldn't let Ikeri have free run of her mind. She'd done just as many unconscionable things as I had.

"She knows, and she still lets you continue your therapy?"

Ikeri chewed on her lower lip and finally looked up at me. "She said it was worth it because she really wanted to work with you again."

I wanted to hug Stassia and scream at her at the same time. Yes, I dearly wanted to work with her again too, but was that worth polluting Ikeri's mind with murder, blackmail, and Geva knows what else she'd seen us do while in Stassia's head?

I fought to keep my voice calm. "Ikeri, what you've seen..."

"I told you, I don't focus on it."

"But still, those things..."

I couldn't help pointing out that I knew she'd seen her mother hurting people, killing people, even while I wanted to deny that we both had done that. Many times. Especially in our past.

Since our return, without the High Council dictating our actions, the only people we'd had to take care of were the ones out to kill us first. I felt better about that, but still, it wasn't the sort of thing I wanted either of my children aware of. They shouldn't have to worry about people trying to kill their parents. That was the main reason we'd opted to stay dead on public record, to keep the attacks to a minimum.

"Daddy, stop." Her face flushed. "I don't want to talk about what I've seen. I don't want to know more about it. You're my parents, and there's nothing I can do about who or what you are." She slid off the couch and all but ran to her room.

I sat there, mouth gaping, until I realized I needed to breathe again. Was she ashamed of us?

Everything we were, had been, and even still were, went against all Verian teachings. The relief I'd felt after talking to Stassia fizzled, and the pit of blackness again beckoned me.

At least I was in control of myself this time and Arin stayed quiet.

My mind was my own and my emotions were in check. So the usual—turmoil on the inside, smiling or scowling on the outside.

I fondly remembered the days when I used to have my shit together. Sure, there had been bad days. The work I did for Stassia and the Council were to blame for most of those, but they were nothing a good night's sleep, some strong liquor, or a dip in the tank couldn't fix. Now it seemed like I was permanently broken.

Neko was either pretending to look busy or extremely focused on the nighttime view of trees blowing in the wind, because he didn't look at me as I passed by him and went to the bedroom. Not that I was sure he'd overheard us, but Ikeri's rapid exit would have been hard to miss.

"Everything all right?" Stassia asked as I entered.

"As well as can be at the moment." Which wasn't saying much.

"Any news from Jey?"

"No. Nothing from the University either."

She patted the open space on the bed beside her. "Want to get some sleep while you're at a loss for emergencies to tend to?"

"Probably would be a wise choice." I sat down on my half of the bed and took off my boots.

She quirked an eyebrow. "And since when are you wise?"

"Since you outlawed stims." I stripped off my clothes and left them in a pile close by in case one of the emergencies she'd referred to cropped up.

Her fear leaked through our bonded connection. I wasn't sure if she'd left the connection open that far because she was keeping tabs on how off I was at any given minute or if she was still so shaken that she wasn't in control of it. I had plenty to think about, and faking sleep wasn't anything new. It would make her feel better. I settled into bed.

"I have a few projects to check on. The light won't bother you?" She nodded toward the datapad sitting on her side of the bed and picked it up to turn off the lights.

"That's fine."

Though her not having her own link had its drawbacks, I did appreciate that I knew when she was working now, because she had to use a datapad. It was far easier to tell when I had her relative full attention and when I didn't.

I arranged the blanket over me and closed my eyes for a few moments, but my conversation with Ikeri kept replaying in my head. I gave in to my urge to dig a little. "So how are things going with

Ikeri?" I asked.

"Really well. Tomias and her other instructors are doing a fabulous job. She can do far more already than I ever could. And she's only ten. It's downright depressing."

"Or she's gifted, and you were doing the best you could with the half-training they offered you."

She kissed my cheek. "Or that."

"Has she said anything to you about what she sees during your therapy?" That was the nicest way I could think of to broach the topic without sounding accusatory.

"Not really? Why?"

"Remember how Thomas despised me?"

"And me, after he found out the full truth," she muttered.

I still felt guilty about that, and I didn't appreciate her bringing it up in light of the day I'd had.

"Do you think Ikeri feels the same way?" I asked.

She put the datapad down, the glow lighting the room and casting shadows on her face. "She's our daughter. She doesn't despise us."

"Yeah, I suppose you're right." But she was wrong. I knew what I'd picked up from Ikeri and it was far from the adoring girl who used to chide me for not wearing my armor. We were her parents, and she had no choice but to deal with us as we were until she was old enough to walk away.

Not having any further fight left in me, I let her be. With my eyes shut, I sank into my link, checking in with contacts until my focus began to fade. I drifted into real sleep with the sound of Stassia's fingertips lightly tapping beside me.

When I woke it wasn't light yet and no one else was up, but I couldn't get back to sleep. Amazed that I hadn't woken in a cold sweat even once, I slipped out of bed, pulled on some pants, and went to see who was at the security station. It was still Fa'yet. I'd only been out a few hours.

"Anything exciting going on?" I asked.

"Not a thing. Couldn't sleep?"

"Last time I did that, my mate drugged me."

He turned away from the vids to scowl at me. "Gave her all nine hells for that, did you?"

"I'm not about to forget it anytime soon."

"She did have your best interests at heart, you know."

"Poor choice of tactics."

Fa'yet shook his head, his usual signal for bowing out of the conversation.

"You don't think I have a right to be pissed?"

"I didn't say a word."

"You didn't have to. Why don't you take a break? I've got this for a couple hours."

His mouth went tight and his face twisted up, but then he glanced at the closed bedroom doors. "I'll be back in two hours then." He left a second later.

Spending time at the security station I'd so despised earlier in my life was a welcome reprieve from the thoughts swirling in my head. I'd spent long hours here, waiting for something to happen in those trees, in the leaves swirling lazily underneath them, in the empty skies up above. But unless more Arpex were about to attack, I had a feeling that, as usual, nothing happened on Frique. Ironic, that now, because of that, I was glad to be here.

While I kept an eye on the vids, I also wandered through the public networks, looking for clues as to what the Arpex were up to. I sent messages to each of the planetary heads, warning them of the Arpex and how to defend against them, noting that I'd follow up in person as time allowed.

I found myself, yet again, regretting taking out the Council, but this time, because I wished I'd been able to save one of the inhibitor fields they'd created while ruining Stassia's link. If we had access to even one of those, I could take it to the University and they might be able to replicate it. If we couldn't use links or telepathy, it stood to reason that Arpex abilities would also be nullified. Not that we could produce enough to shield everyone from Arpex, nor could I imagine most Artorians willing to give up their natural speech to take advantage of the field, but dammit, it would be an option. Sighing, I shoved my thoughts back on track.

The Jalvian Prime wanted an audience with me as soon as possible to discuss the issue of the impostor who insisted he was in control of Jal. I set up a meeting for first thing in the morning. Best to tell him the truth and see if we could get some sort of resolution worked out that I could apply elsewhere. There were sure to be other people who would suffer the whims of the Arpex.

As the sun came up, Fa'yet returned. His disgruntled expression had grown even darker than it had been when he'd left.

"It's time we continue the conversation you were too busy for after your third tank dip in two days," he declared, keeping his voice low. "Do you realize you spent more time in gel, or sleeping it off, than you did on your feet?"

"If you're going to preach at me to take better care of myself, Anastassia already did that."

He cocked his head and his eyes narrowed. "Maybe you don't realize how hard those three years of waiting for you, of thinking you were dead, were on your family, on all of us. I know you were bored out of your mind on Pentares. I get that; really I do. But now that you're back here, you're throwing yourself at everything in the hopes that something will take you out and end whatever shit you've got going on in your head. So either do it or get over it."

How dare he? I launched myself out of the chair. "*Get over it?* You have no idea—"

Fa'yet gave me a challenging glare, his former Kryon-self making an appearance. "Maybe I don't, but the rest of us are tired of dragging you back from the dead. It's hard as all hells to watch all of them go through that again."

"What the fuck do you want from me?"

"I think I made that quite clear. But I'll also take a few days off. I'm exploring my retirement options now that the Council isn't around to terminate me."

His damned deadpan delivery made it hard to tell if he was seriously threatening to leave or if he was just dropping a hint. Either way, I didn't need his aggravation. I was supposed to be relaxing. Hells, I was supposed to be in bed with Anastassia, enjoying a vacation. I didn't ask for Arpex to show up in the Narvan or to be pulsed by disgruntled Kryon or whoever the hells else had taken issue with me this week.

"Take your few days but don't think I'm paying you for them."

He made a mockery of a bow and Jumped.

I sat down just as Anastassia emerged from our bedroom to find me staring at where Fa'yet had just been standing. I was in the midst of deciding whether I wanted to Jump to his house to continue the conversation in a less friendly tone or give him his few days to reconsider his fucking employment status when she waved her hand in front of my face.

"We pay people to sit there, you know. Though, this is a view I could get used to every morning. You do make for a fine piece of eye candy, especially after all that time in the gym on Pentares."

It annoyed me when she used phrases she'd picked up in the years she'd lived with her people without me. I was never quite sure what they meant. When our bonded connection flared, her intention was clear enough.

"That big hand of yours doesn't look out of proportion anymore." She slipped behind me to run her hands over my bare back and shoulders. "So what's the occasion? You've been a quick-change-in-to-clothes-and-keep-the-bedroom-dark kind of guy since Pentares."

"I didn't want to wake you and it's damn hot in here, in case you hadn't noticed."

Stassia laughed against my neck as she nipped at my ear. "Oh, I noticed."

She came around, and after glancing at the other doors and finding them closed, slipped onto my lap. "We've got what, ten minutes before Neko is on? Did Isnar leave already?"

"Yes, and Isnar will be taking a few days off."

"*Isnar*, is it?" Her eyebrows rose. "Is there something we need to talk about?"

"Other than he's looking into retiring, or getting fired if he talks to me like that again, no. And no, I don't want you to talk to him for me."

Her playful attention in my head abruptly ended. She got up and backed away. "I take it from your lovely mood that you slept well."

"For a couple hours. We need to go meet with the Jalvian Prime."

"All right, we will, but when we're done, I've made an appointment for you on Veria Prime. You can take Ikeri to her lessons and then get your massage."

"I don't want anyone touching me." My skin crawled just thinking about it.

"Vayen, they have the same training I do," she said calmly.

"Then you do it if you're dead set on me needing a massage."

She shook her head. "One of us needs to be working so the other one can relax, knowing everything is taken care of. Now, I've already briefed them on your preferences for lighting and they are aware of your condition."

"*Condition?* And what is that exactly?"

"Your scars, Mister Prickly." She gave me a reproachful glare. "I set you up with two women. I thought that you'd prefer that over men."

"I'd prefer if you'd—"

She smiled tightly. "You're a big man with more tight muscles than one little Verian woman has the energy to untangle. You'll enjoy it, trust me."

I might have been fairly fresh from the tank, but all the reasons that put me there had indeed turned my back and neck into hard knots again. Maybe she was right, but I still didn't want anyone else to touch me.

"Vayen, you're going," she said in her most commanding tone.

"Fine."

She nodded. "You should probably get dressed before we leave. The Jalvian Prime won't be near as appreciative of your current lack of clothing as I am."

"I'd planned on it," I grumbled as I dodged around her to go to our room.

Once I was fully clothed, moderately armed, and wearing my coat, I found Stassia briefing Neko in the kitchen while the kids ate breakfast. She joined me without further nagging. Placing her hand on mine, she waited patiently for me to Jump the two of us.

We arrived in the office Jey and I shared in the Jalvian capitol building. A guard stood there watching us as we stepped out of the void. He communicated our arrival to his superior and waved us out of the room.

"What's this all about?" While I appreciated the extra security, I would have preferred that it was one of my contacts rather than one of the government's.

"The Prime is waiting for you," he said woodenly.

"I'm well aware of that. What are you doing in my office?"

"Sorry, sir, I'm supposed to watch for Advisor Te. There's some confusion over his role in our government."

"I'm hoping to clear that up."

"That would be most appreciated." He nodded and backed away.

We'd barely left the office when I got a notice that the relatively new Premier of Karin had requested a personal visit. Not having been in office long, I was already spending an inordinate amount of time overseeing him through my link. If he wanted to meet in person, there had to be a damned good reason.

"He better not want more funding," I muttered.

"Who?" asked Stassia.

"Karin's Premier. We've got a meeting there next."

"No, you have an appointment. He can wait," she stated firmly.

"If you want me to relax, then let me get all the stressful shit taken care of first."

Stassia pursed her lips and gave me a sideways glance. "As long as you'll promise me that you are going to go. I'm serious, I don't think I can go through seeing you like that again."

Fa'yet's admonishments hit me anew, but with Stassia beside me, I took them far more to heart. "I will. I promise."

"How long until we're on Karin?" She pulled out her datapad.

"I figure we can wrap this up in an hour."

She gave me a doubtful look.

"In fact," I patted her shoulder, "You're here. It should only take us half that."

She laughed and knocked her hip into me. After quickly typing for a moment, she put the pad away. "You're rescheduled for later today. I let Neko know to get Ikeri to her classes."

The aide at the door of the Prime's office let us through with a hasty bob of the head and a nervous smile. We entered the elaborate box of treasures. Even after being in the office many times, I still spotted something new on each visit. It seemed as though each Prime spent his time in power trying to take up more wall and display case space than the last. There were medals, ribbons, flags, emblems, and framed proclamations of victories on nearly every surface in the room.

The grey-haired Prime stood at his desk. "Ah, Advisor Ta'set, so nice of you to come. And your lovely wife too."

Stassia sent me the sensation of rolling her eyes. I didn't exactly blame her. At one time she'd forced the previous Prime to end his war with Artor, bringing peace to the entire system. Unfortunately, this Prime knew me in the dominant role. With our return, she found herself relegated to my lovely wife—with armor, weapons, and a wicked temper.

"Would you two prefer to sit?"

In the interest of being friendly, we sat.

I wasn't the only one feeling prickly. Stassia bypassed the usual requisite small talk and got right to the point.

"Did you have an unscheduled appointment or visitor before losing your memory of Advisor Te?"

The Prime addressed me rather than her, which only inflamed her further. It also annoyed me.

"The man who is dead set on convincing me that I've lost my mind as well as my daughter and grandchild?" he asked.

"He's confused and being an ass," I said before she took further offense. *"Let me handle it and you can have at the Karinian Premier. I don't like him much anyway."*

Stassia smiled in my head and sat back.

"That would be the one in question, yes," I said.

"I don't recall the details of my schedule. You'd have to check with my secretary. Now, what are we going to do about getting my daughter back from this man?"

"Why don't you go check with the secretary?" I asked Stassia.

She nodded and left the room. Once she was gone, I stood. I worked better on my feet.

"Here's the thing. You're not crazy, but Advisor Te is my partner, and he has a legal marriage contract with your daughter."

His well-manicured brows puckered. "But how can that be?"

"The message I sent you last night, about Arpex on your world?"

He nodded.

"You were the victim of one."

I wondered if this was what Arin had felt like when he watched over me those first few days, relieved for the fellowship, yet irritated at having to talk about Arpex. Giving life to the words made its terror all the more real.

"Like you, I have also suffered its singularly aggravating assault. It eats memories."

His mouth hung open, not a flattering look on a grown man in uniform. "So how do I get my memories back? If we kill the one who attacked me, will they return?"

"If you're killed, do a herd of pranthas return to the fields?"

He frowned. "This is an attack of a most personal nature, it's a matter of state, of planetary security and wellbeing. I need to know the truth of my relationship to that man."

"I told you the truth."

The Prime scowled and sputtered, peering about the room as if answers were hidden there. "But I have no sense of it one way or the other."

"You were there at the contract signing with your daughter and granddaughter. I know the memory is probably hazy, but you should remember that. There's a still frame of all of you together at the ceremony on the wall in their house."

His brow furrowed. "Yes, but I don't remember the man. All I have is your word."

"And your daughter's. What does she say about all this?"

He ran his hands over his face, his shoulders slumping. "She doesn't understand why I'm questioning what she claims is true."

"Jey knows about Arpex and what they do. He'll explain it to her. If you still doubt me, Jey has security footage of an Arpex at their house. I'm sure he'll be happy to show it to you. I was there. I can vouch for its validity."

He seemed to ponder me, staring intently, gaze locked on my face. "Who did they take from you?"

I picked the safest and most relatable answer. "My mother."

He scoffed. "Of everything in that head, that's what they went after?"

His amusement did not amuse me. Thinking of Stassia outside the office, I did my best to keep my temper under control.

"It's one of their typical fishing lines. Get's them an easy meal, and usually a big one too, lots of memories attached to them. Parents are sacred to most people."

"Yes, true, but to you?" He shook his head.

I flexed my fingers, keeping loose at my sides instead of doing something that would end all goodwill I had with this man. "As I stated last night, you will need to advise your people to avoid contact with cloaked strangers. If one is spotted, notify me immediately and then destroy it. On second thought, I don't care about the order in which those two things happen."

"And what about Advisor Te?"

"Let him do his job. He's damn good at it."

The Prime nodded slowly. When he spoke again, his voice had lost its authoritative edge. "It feels like so many things are missing."

That wasn't surprising. He and Jey had been working together for years and now they also had a personal relationship.

"I know. I'd say you'll get used to it, but you won't. Try not to focus on the voids, they'll drive you crazy."

"Is that what they're trying to do? Make us lose our minds?"

"It would soften us up nicely to become a subservient food source, yes."

Disgust colored his voice, "We're not talking killing, but consuming?"

"Yes, and all the medals and commendations in the Narvan won't improve your flavor. We need to make sure this attack never gets to that stage. I've been to a planet they've conquered. It made Frique look advanced. The people had forgotten who they were, and they served their own up for a monthly buffet."

"I'd rather be facing Fragians," he said. "At least we knew what we were dealing with."

"And they didn't eat us."

"There is that." He swallowed. "I'll mobilize ground forces to hunt down any Arpex on the surface."

"Send a force to maintain a watch over Frique. I had it firsthand from an Arpex that Frique is their main objective in the Narvan."

He nodded and made a note on one of the datapads in front of him. "What's so desirable about Frique?"

"Prime nesting climates."

"Nesting." The Prime sighed and shook his head again. "Simply wonderful, an entirely foreign enemy."

"Indeed. Which reminds me, I need to get to the University to see if we can't make the inner workings of the Arpex a little less of an unknown. If we can figure out how they do what they do, we can get to work on a viable defense."

"Don't you need a specimen for that?"

"That would be extremely helpful." I gave him a meaningful look.

"We'll get on it."

"I'd appreciate that." With our meeting concluded, I contacted Jey to let him know they were back on at least tolerable terms, then went to collect Stassia.

The secretary bore a dazed expression, while Stassia seemed intent. She held her hand up before I could say anything. A moment later, she turned away, rubbing her temples.

"Thank you for your assistance," I told the secretary who was now watching us with confusion. He nodded.

We walked back to the office we'd used as a jump point. "Did you have to probe him? We're supposed to be establishing goodwill with the Jalvians, not cementing stereotypes."

"I can barely manage a half-assed mindjack." She scowled, using the Jalvian slang for a probe. "He's fine. Besides, he said he didn't remember anything about the meeting."

"And?"

"And there was an unscheduled meeting before his memory loss occurred, and the Prime's." She blinked rapidly and winced. "Remind me not to do that again. It hurt like hell."

"You shouldn't push yourself. I could have talked to him."

"You were busy talking to the Prime. I had to be useful somehow."

I knocked into her lightly. "You're always useful."

She gave me a skeptical glance. "It doesn't always feel that way."

"You know, I used to work for this woman..."

She chuckled and held up her hands. "All right, yeah, fair enough."

"I need to have a talk with the University before we head to Karin. Do we have time?"

"I suppose we can squeeze that in. You're going to put this massage off as long as you can, aren't you?"

"I promised, didn't I?" I held out my hand.

She shook her head and took it. I Jumped us to the Artorian University.

I called an emergency meeting of the University board and went to the room in which we'd met previously to wait. They arrived one by one and in short order, all taking a seat and watching me.

"Wow, you put them on edge with your last visit," Stassia said.

"They're always this way. Especially that one." I nodded toward Vivina Sa'cota.

"We'll see about that." Stassia smiled sweetly, which was disconcerting anytime, but especially when she was dressed for business.

She went to lurk in the annoying woman's peripheral vision. Sa'cota scowled, her gaze wavering every few seconds to her left where Stassia stood.

With everyone in attendance, I began. "The enemy we face is called Arpex. I've encountered them before. They are evil in ways that make the Fragians seem no worse than Jalvians."

"What kind of dealings did you have with these Arpex?" asked the man to my right.

"Not the good kind." I held up my grey hand.

They eyed my hand with varying degrees of pity and distaste.

While I had sent my University contact the same briefing I'd conveyed to the planetary leaders earlier, I again conveyed what little I had, for what it was worth, to the board. Even though it made my skin crawl to talk about Arpex in detail, the more people that knew what we were up against, especially those that might be able to help us figure out how to stop them, the better. I explained their physical characteristics, feeding habits, their memory sucking attacks, how they could drive themselves into a mind with more force than the most invasive probe, and, based on the attacks I knew of in the Narvan, their probable goals.

Having Stassia there helped keep the flashbacks at bay. She might have been openly enjoying intimidating Sa'cota, but a steady flow of soothing energy flowed through our bonded connection.

"If you have firsthand accounts of dealing with these Arpex, would you consent to share those memories with one of us so we can better understand what we are dealing with?" asked the man to my right.

Had I been there alone, my answer would have been a strong 'fuck no'. But I wasn't, and logic told me that the more I could give them, the faster we would be able to form a defense.

I did not envy those two Verian women Stassia had roped into dealing with me. She'd thought I'd needed to relax before? My knotted muscles were going to have their own knots by the time I got through this meeting.

"I'll be right here," Stassia said in the same soft assuring tone she'd used when we'd had our talk in the dark.

I took a deep breath and forced a "Yes," out of my mouth while my brain screamed no at full volume.

The whole time I went about syncing my mind with the man sitting beside me, my nerves sang. My foot threatened to tap itself right through the floor.

"You can do this," Stassia said.

At least she thought so. I wasn't so sure.

I shut my eyes in an effort to convince myself that we were alone in my room on the ship.

The receiving mind on the other end of the transfer waited anxiously, as if he were bracing himself for whatever I was going to share.

I started with the all too familiar dome where I'd first served Arpex, the heat, the lighting, how it fed. The screams almost knocked me out of the memory transfer. As did the smell of the digestive fluids dripping onto the floor. Dripping into its plate.

Needing to focus on something else before I lost it and started hallucinating all over the boardroom, I switched to the world where I'd retrieved the offerings. There, my hold on the transfer started to waver. Memories began to rush out of my control. The Arpex arriving in Arin's body, it taking over mine and forcing me to shoot my own foot, how it made me forget...someone. And then the nerve-flaying pain when I tricked it by forgetting someone other than who it had asked for.

And then Stassia's hands were on my face. "Vayen, that's enough."

I gasped as the connection of the memory transfer snapped shut.

The room came into focus with its bright white light and morbidly curious board members craning forward in their seats.

The man who was now clearly regretting volunteering, sat back in his chair with his hands clenched on his lap. After several moments of silence, he swallowed loudly and again faced the others. "After the meeting, I will share this with any of you who wish to see."

Sa'cota nodded enthusiastically, the others less so. Knowing that my traumatic memories would soon be common knowledge made me vastly uncomfortable. I hoped that these people would do something useful with them. And quickly.

Stassia left my side to resume her post. I stood, needing to move before Arin made an appearance or charred Merkief showed up. I was due for a visit from either of them given what I'd just relived.

"And why are the Arpex here? What do they want from us?" asked one of the others.

"Frique has the ideal climate for Arpex nesting grounds. And from what I was told, directly from an Arpex, they have little use for the rest of the Narvan. We'd become nothing but a food source."

The room was silent for a moment before one of the others got up the nerve to ask, "And what kind of forces do they have?"

"We don't know," I said.

The man now holding some of my memories brought up a map on a datapad. "Where do they come from?" he asked.

"We don't know that either."

"How did they find us?" asked Sa'cota.

I couldn't exactly answer that. Even with the Council gone, Stassia, Jey, and I had all agreed to keep their existence quiet. Knowing that a secret organization had pulled everyone's strings would not inspire the confidence we were looking for.

"They've known about us for a long time," I said.

"So why attack now? Is this because of those exploratory missions?" she asked, her eyes narrowed.

"No." Then I wished I'd said yes. But those missions were Jey's call. I didn't want the University to have a reason to hold a grudge against him. That would refuel the distrust of all Jalvians and have us back in the midst of a war. However, no meant I had to give them a different reason, maybe even the truth.

Sa'cota stared me down. "It was you. You did this."

I kept my gaze steady while my mind spun. Yes, it was my fault. I'd stood in the way of the Arpex-led faction that had wanted Frique, but because of me, at least one, if not many of their kind had been blown to bits with the rest of the High and Mighties.

An Arpex had killed Sonia, who had been entirely innocent and even after all I'd done to keep her safe, she'd died because of me. Arpex had obliterated entire planets full of people for their dining enjoyment, took my hand, my memories, left me with scars so deep that even the best surgeons on Artor couldn't erase them. They were fucking evil. And here. And it was my fault.

"Because you had to be special," sneered Arin. *"I warned you. This is all your fault."*

Stassia's voice rang out, cutting through the accusation that hung in the air. "They've had their eyes on the Narvan long before he took over. This isn't about blame. It's about how we defend ourselves."

My brain snapped back into action. "We can assume there are Arpex on each world they attacked. As I said, they'll be targeting high-level people, whomever they can torture to cause the most havoc. We need some way to locate them and prevent them from eating memories. Our standard natural defenses are nothing to them. My defenses are nothing to them if that gives you any idea how help-less we all are here."

Helpless. I shuddered as the sensation of the Arpex rampaging through my brain again flooded through me. I'd prayed that feeling would never return. It had dulled slightly over the past couple years, but now I had a fresh reminder.

Arin laughed. *"You can't escape them. They're coming for you."*

The level of dread in my gut insisted he was right.

Concerned looks spread around the table, letting me know the board was beginning to fathom our situation. Once the memory share had made its rounds they'd understand even more.

"I'll let you get to work then. Let me know as soon as you have anything we can use," I said.

Stassia and I left them and Jumped to Karin.

We met privately with the Premier, his advisor, and his secretary. All three men stood as we entered the Premier's office and then returned to their seats. He remained focused on small talk until Stassia de-manded he state why he'd requested a private meeting.

"I'm resigning," he declared as he pulled the chain of office from around his neck and dropped it on the desk.

"Excuse me?" I glanced at Stassia to make sure I'd not misheard. She appeared just as confused as I was.

The middle-aged man sat there, looking at the chain forlornly before gathering himself into a more defiant state. After raising his glare from the chain to my chin, he turned his glare on Stassia.

"The position isn't working out as I'd expected," he said stiffly.

Though I'd told Stassia she could have the lead here, I decided to use his fear to get to the bottom of this odd turn of events. Thumping my grey fist on his desk, I called his attention back to me. He jumped in his seat.

"You were the one who swore to me that this was the job you were born for, that you had what it took and the drive to make my plans happen." I threw his words, spoken shortly after my return to the Narvan, back in his face.

His advisor took a step back. The secretary glanced toward the closed door.

The Premier stiffened, and with a thin but indignant tone said, "I changed my mind."

Since we'd disposed with the good terms, I leaned in close, pinning his hands to his chair. Stassia stayed beside me, keeping an eye on the other two.

"What exactly changed your mind?"

While he stalled in giving me an answer, I rampaged through his personal records and accounts but was unable to locate the payoff I'd expected to find there. With the Arpex wandering about, I couldn't take chances. I followed Stassia's earlier lead and dove into his mind.

He started to squirm, both inside and out. I could hear the other two shifting their weight.

"The secretary is looking at the door again." Stassia said.

"Don't let him leave. Either of them."

As it turned out, neither of them were leaving. The door flew open. Six men in armored coats rushed into the room with guns firing. At us.

There wasn't time to figure out who they were. I picked up the worthless Premier and threw him at the nearest attacker. The secretary took a shot in the neck as he finally darted for the door. The advisor stood against the wall, watching it all with wide eyes.

Stassia had two of them down in seconds. I stepped in front of her. The fact that she wore the same armor as I did and was perfectly able to defend herself didn't matter. Whipping out my pulse pistol, I thumbed the power to full and fired. The remaining four men collapsed. The office walls buckled, crumbling onto the floor and opening the large room to the hallway. A section of ceiling fell from above where the men had stood, filling the air with a cloud of debris.

Keeping one hand on Stassia, I searched the haze for any sign of the advisor. He lay under a section of the fallen ceiling.

"You all right?" I asked Stassia.

"Yeah." She coughed and waved at the dust. "See what you can get out of him."

I let go of her to lift the heavy tile off the advisor. Blood covered his face. Opening his eyes to see me looming over him, his arms flailed, searching for something to grab onto. His legs didn't move.

"Who's idea was this little encounter?"

"You're supposed to be dead." He sputtered, pushing at the wall, but getting nowhere. Blood seeped through his shirt. He'd caught a stray bullet. Maybe two, by the mess his shirt was quickly becoming. "Our people would be safe if you were dead."

The weight of Stassia's hand rested on my shoulder, letting me know she was on the lookout while I did what I had to do.

I dove into his mind, hard and fast, heedless of the damage my bluntness caused. The Premier had taken a meeting late yesterday. Resentment clouded his thoughts. He hadn't agreed with the plan, knowing he'd likely not live through it. He had served the previous Premier who had been in office when I'd run the Narvan, and he wanted to survive to serve the next, or perhaps take the position on himself. Now he was screwed.

He was pretty good defense-wise, shunting my probe toward information that pertained, but not giving me what I wanted.

"You're no better than they are," he said before his face went slack.

I scrambled to backtrack my way out of the twists and turns I'd taken in my effort to thwart his defenses. His heartbeat sputtered. I pulled out just as his pulse came to a stop, only then realizing the intense pressure of Stassia's grasp even through my armor.

He'd known I would kill him if he were caught. If he'd known that, then they had to have considered that six men with guns might not be successful. They had to have a backup plan.

"I don't like this. We need to go," Stassia said. From the urgency in her voice, I had no doubt if she could have Jumped herself, she would have taken us both out of there.

Unfortunately, my hasty exit on the heels of the adviser's death required me to take a breath and get my mental shit together before

I could manage that feat for both of us.

Footsteps rushed into the hallway and then into the room. None of the rapidly arriving office workers appeared hostile. They shrieked, gasped, and held their hands over their mouths. A couple wiped away tears. All of them settled their gazes upon us with heavy accusation.

I hadn't seen many of these people before, preferring to keep my meetings with the Premier quiet, as we always had when we worked for the High and Mighties. Primes and Premiers also preferred it that way, wanting to keep the appearance of power to their public. In cases like this, that particular policy didn't work in our favor.

We mercenary-looking types, dusty but unharmed, stood in the midst of a destroyed room filled with dead bodies, one of which was their bullet-riddled leader.

"They tried to kill us," I said quietly, knowing it sounded ludicrous given the visual evidence.

Now I was going to have to take the time to find a new Premier that I could work with, who could grasp how the Narvan really worked, and who would follow my lead without question. Preferably someone who didn't want me dead and wasn't willing to exchange my life for the very questionable safety of the general populace.

An inhuman voice cut through the muttering of the office workers. "Clear this floor. Immediately."

My lungs seized, refusing to take another breath.

"Wake up," screamed Arin.

The snap of jaw-wings filled the air. A scream, agonizingly long and then cut short with gagging, echoed in my ears. Panic again filled the hallway as the mourning accusers ran for the lifts.

The burning smell was wrong, different, not what I'd come to associate with the smells in my dreams of the Council's bases being destroyed. The lights weren't bright enough for the Arpex dome. Though I could hear Arin in my head, I couldn't feel him shaking me.

Stassia was here. Arpex were here. I prayed that this was a dream, one I would wake from any second.

Another set of jaw-wings snapped. Another scream.

Oh Geva, more than one. Blackness seeped into the edges of my vision.

Stassia tugged on my arm, yanking, her mouth moving, eyes frantic. All I could hear was my pulse-pounding, a heavy whooshing like the entire ocean beating against a brick wall.

And then it was there in front of me. Of us. Its blue shell glistened with red droplets. The black box about its upper shell cocked slightly, the only evidence of its last victim's fight.

This was all too real to be a dream. My nightmares had become reality.

Its presence wafted into my head, curling through my thoughts, caressing my terror like a lover. *"We've been looking for you."*

My legs gave way, dropping my ass on the floor and slamming the back of my head against the Premier's desk. I managed a tiny breath, and then another until they came in gasps that verged on hyperventilation.

I had to get Stassia away, to Jump, to yell at her to run, to pulse them both to the ninth hell, but I couldn't move. As if in slow motion, a second Arpex entered behind the first, surveying the bodies and then locking onto Stassia. It's jaw-wings opened wide, still dripping with gore from a recent meal. Stassia backed toward where I sat, one hand reaching out behind her to me, the other drawing a weapon.

My muscles finally responded to my desperate plea to fucking do something. On my feet, I sought out Stassia, knowing I was in no condition to Jump both of us, but intent on at least getting her behind me.

She was just out of reach.

Stassia pulled a pulse pistol from her coat and fired. The Arpex in front of her toppled over, its wings obliterated, box destroyed, its shell cracked.

The other Arpex hissed, its vice-like grip on my brain squeezed until intense burning heat flowed down the sides of my face. Then the pressure vanished, leaving me aware enough to see my bloody hands and for the pain I'd inflicted on myself to register now that my brain wasn't being fed through a grinder.

Stassia was screaming in my head. Her screaming was filled with shrill, panicked words, but my scrambled mind couldn't make sense of them. Tears ran down her face as she glanced over her shoulder at me, doing her best to keep her attention on the Arpex. The flood of words continued in my mind, a muddy slur of concern and fear that suddenly snapped into coherent focus.

"We have to get out of here," she said, her voice too shaken to carry the force she normally exuded.

The Arpex seemed to be watching us both, its wings held safely to its back. "You're the mate," it said through its box.

"Leave him alone," Stassia said. *"What do we do? There's not enough charge left to kill it."*

Think. I needed to form words. To breathe. Kill. I needed a weapon. My pulse pistol. Fuck. I'd drained mine to wipe out the gunmen. I lurched my way back to standing and forced air into my lungs.

I could almost feel the damned thing grinning, drooling, clacking its claws with anticipation of the sweet meal either of us would make as it drew out our fear of watching the other die.

"I'll distract it. Run," I said.

"I'm not leaving you here."

I couldn't leave her either, not alone with an Arpex. The only way out of this was to Jump us both with my throbbing and scrambled mind. I grabbed her wrist and focused on the most ingrained jump point I had, the tank room on the ship, pulling us both there with every ounce of strength I had.

My head split open, or at least it felt like it did. My focus had failed. Stassia stood beside me in the office littered with bodies, including one dead Arpex and one very live one.

"Tell me about this man," it said.

"Stassia, no! Remember what I told you. Remember—"

But the glazed look on her face told me she wasn't listening. I pulled her to me, grabbed whatever gun my hand found first, and shot the damned thing until the clip was empty. All it did was hiss.

Stassia squirmed in my grasp. Her protest quickly turned into full-fledged thrashing and kicking. The back of her head slammed into my throat. Coughing, I let her go and pulled whatever my hand grabbed next from my coat.

"Run," I begged her, praying that the jaws of the Arpex remained on its back until she was away.

Instead of listening to me, she spun back around to face me, a gun in her hand. "Holy shit."

The fear and horror I'd seen on too many other faces confirmed that the Arpex had taken her from me. My racing heart plummeted into my stomach where it turned cold and hollow.

"Anastassia, please, get out of here."

She looked from me to the Arpex and the bodies on the floor. She nodded uncertainly and then was gone a heartbeat later.

My life with Stassia was gone. I wanted to sink to the floor, to let Fa'yet have his truth, to allow the Arpex to put me out of my misery, but my legs weren't on board with that plan.

I needed to know she was safe. Even if she wasn't safe with me.

"Jey, we're in the Karinian Premier's office. Arpex are here. Anastassia doesn't know me."

"Fuck." And then he was gone. He'd find her. She might be hazy about his relationship with her, but she would know him.

"Do you have more mates?" I imagined the Arpex licking lips it didn't have as it dove back into my brain.

Oh Geva, it might find Ikeri or Daniel next. Not willing to chance that happening, I fingered the grenade I kept lodged in a secure pocket of my coat. The small metal orb easily fit in my hand. It was similar to the bombs Merkief had used when he'd blown the Council's bases to bits. Would I see him when I next opened my eyes?

I touched the trigger sequence, lobbed it at the Arpex, and dove behind the desk.

NINE

"Daddy?"

I cracked open my eyes. Flecks of tank gel fell from my lashes. Seeing Ikeri's face was far better than seeing Merkief's. Except that hers was pale and dark lines lay beneath her eyes. "What's wrong?"

"You were asleep a very long while."

I couldn't find it in me to joke about the severity of my injuries this time. "Your mother, is she all right?"

Ikeri sighed and rubbed her face. "Not really."

I sank into the pillow, wishing I could sink further but the solid surface of the bed refused to give way.

"She doesn't know me," I said, hating those words with all of my being.

"She's very angry." Ikeri glanced up at the ceiling and then down to her hands folded on her lap.

The old Kazan, the one without me, was up there. I hoped Jey was still with her or at least Fa'yet. Poor Neko didn't deserve to suffer her in that form.

"She used to be like that most of the time."

Her face scrunched up. "But you still loved her anyway?"

Lying wasn't going to make any of this better. I sighed and sat up, rubbing the gel off my face. "Not exactly."

"I don't understand."

"It's complicated." I pulled the sheet around me and got to the edge of the bed. "She's up in the house?"

Ikeri nodded. "Uncle Jey is with her."

"Good. I'll take a quick shower, and then we'll go see if we can make her less angry, all right?"

Ikeri's fingers twisted around one another, the only sign of her agitation while the rest of her sat perfectly composed. "Uncle Isnar wants to talk to you first. Now or after the shower?"

I wanted to use my shower time to figure out how to deal with Stassia, not wonder what Fa'yet's rant might be about. "Might as well make it now."

Fa'yet filled my doorway seconds later. Ikeri left us before I could say anything. Maybe he had asked her to leave.

He stormed toward me. "Did you not hear me when I said I was sick of scraping up your near-dead carcass in front of your daughter? Do you have any idea how hard it is for her to witness that? To feel you dying in her head? How much it takes out of her to hold onto you while she gets me a solid jump point?"

I wondered if he was going to hit me, but he seemed to think better of it and assumed a strangling grip on the end of the bed instead.

"You know what that does to a person if she holds on too long? Don't you tell me how special she is, I know. And I know she can't handle this. She's doing her best to put on a brave face, but she's only a kid."

"I'm well aware of that. Dammit, I didn't ask her to, and I certainly didn't tell her how."

And like the last time, I wasn't exactly grateful to be back among the living to deal with all this shit. But the kids needed me, especially now with Stassia full of memory holes and Arpex causing havoc in the Narvan. I grabbed a shirt off the shelf and was reaching for whatever pants were on the top of the pile beside it when Fa'yet surged forward and shoved me back onto the bed.

"Then quit getting yourself killed!"

"Wasn't that what you told me to do?" I sprang to my feet and shoved him back. "Why do you keep saving me if you think death is what I really want?"

His irate gaze fizzled and dropped to the floor. "Is it?"

While I knew no was the correct answer, the one I should have been adamantly proclaiming, silent seconds ticked by. I'd been ready in that office. Taking out the Arpex that stole Stassia from me had made ending the chaos in my head an easy decision.

Arpex had been looking for me, for Geva's sake. By taking out the Council, I'd all but invited them into the Narvan. They wouldn't have taken Stassia away if we hadn't been joined.

None of this would have happened if I had stayed silent instead of talking to Jey at that fucking meeting on Sere years ago. If I hadn't given Merkeif the jump points for the Council's bases. If I had listened to Arin and just done my job. The people I loved would be safe on Pentares regardless of Arpex wanting Frique or not.

This man who had been my friend for years would be safe, bored certainly, but blithely going about a normal day rather than openly dreading my long delayed answer.

Honesty would be cruel after all he'd given up for me, because of me.

"Of course not."

Fa'yet nodded, relief palpable. "Then use your link instead of having meetings in person. Relocate to a damned bunker somewhere or something."

"Advising a system doesn't work that way, at least not always or effectively. Intimidation works better in person."

"Yes, respect only gets you so far," he muttered.

"Respect would be preferable, but again, it's not always an immediate option."

From the determination taking hold in his gaze and stance, I knew we were heading for another argument. One I didn't have time for if Geva was determined to keep me among the living. He needed a distracting task.

"The Arpex, was it dead? Both of them?" I asked.

"Everything outside of your armor was dead. You're going to want to let your coat regenerate for a few days, by the way."

I nodded. "Get back in there, collect what's left of either Arpex and get it to the University."

Fa'yet took a step forward, fists curling at his sides. So much for buying into my distraction.

"Have you heard anything I've said? Ana's lost her mind, your daughter is a wreck, your son doesn't understand why his mother doesn't know him, and frankly neither do the rest of us."

I should have taken the shower first.

It was bad enough that Stassia had forgotten me, but now I also had to deal with the ripples of that memory loss. How was I supposed to defend the Narvan against Arpex without Stassia to keep me from imploding? As Fa'yet had pointed out, I didn't have a very good record of taking care of myself.

"You're lucky Geva hates you enough to keep kicking you out of the afterlife," Fa'yet continued his rant. "I'll admit Pentares was not my favorite place either, but let's leave the cursed Narvan behind and make a new home somewhere people aren't trying to kill us."

"I can deal with people. It's the Arpex we need to worry about. They're bent on devouring everyone in the Narvan while raising their young where the prantha roam."

I placed myself in his personal space until he started to look worried. It didn't take long.

"I did everything I could to keep the Narvan safe when I worked for the Council, and I will continue to do so now. If you don't want to stand beside me, I'll send you off with a nice retirement package."

He scowled and made a show of straightening his coat. "Knowing you, it will contain explosives."

"Give it some thought before you talk yourself into a less friendly conversation." I headed for the door. "Any advice on dealing with Anastassia?"

"The last time I saw her this messed up was when she was coming off a serious drug addiction," he said. His anger had vanished, leaving him sounding worn. "She's confused and volatile. Be careful."

"Get Ikeri up top. I'll be there shortly."

I left him and went to stand in the shower. Our bonded connection was sealed on Stassia's end. She'd done that before and just like then, the distraction tugged at the edge of every thought I tried to form. She'd closed off our natural connection too. Or maybe they'd both ceased to be when she'd forgotten me. Either way, I had no way of knowing her state of mind.

The last time Stassia had been mentally confused, she'd tried to kill me. I prayed that wasn't the case this time around, especially not in front of the kids. Hopefully having others in attendance that she did know would work in my favor.

The shower passed with no great revelations of how to approach her beyond doing everything possible to not be seen as a threat. Jey let me know he'd left and seconded Fa'yet's warning to be cautious. Nerves on high, I dressed, leaving my armor and weapons behind, and kept my hair down to cover the worst of the scars.

When I arrived in the foyer, Stassia was already pacing her usual route behind the couch, but this time, armed and wearing her coat. Daniel stood close by, his face blotchy like he'd been crying. Ikeri held his hand, appearing even more weary than she had on the ship. Fa'yet leaned against the wall by the window and Neko sat perched on the edge of his seat at the security station. They all turned to look at me.

Knowing Stassia would need time to assess my threat level, I addressed Ikeri first, kneeling and holding my arms out to her.

She came forward, feet dragging, and wrapped her arms around my neck. Her thin body felt so fragile in my arms.

"You need to rest," I said.

Stassia halted her pacing, her gaze darting to everyone in the room, the door, and following my every movement.

"Mother needs me." Then she added silently, *"but she won't let me inside."*

"I'm locked out too. It will take time."

I held her back so she had to look at me. "I appreciate what you did, getting me help, but please don't do that again. You're very strong and good at what you do, but I don't want you hurt because you helped me."

Her bottom lip trembled. "I couldn't let you die, Daddy."

Heart melting, I hugged her again. "Go get some sleep. You can help again tomorrow when you're up to it."

Ikeri started toward her bedroom but then turned back. "Can I sleep with Mother?"

Devious kid, and I knew right where she got it from. She'd wait until Stassia was asleep and then try every Seeker trick she knew.

"Not tonight. Go to bed." I shooed her off.

I got up, watching Stassia watching me. I struggled to grasp the fact that the entire history I shared with her had vanished. She looked the same, but the woman who had sat on my lap that morning, who had joked with me and knew every inch of me, was gone. I swallowed hard.

"Stassia?"

She stared at me. Despite not having gaping open wounds on my face this time, she didn't appear to be much more comfortable doing so than she had back in the Premier's office on Karin. "You were there, telling me to run. Did you kill those people?"

"We both did. They were trying to kill us. The Arpex, the blue shelled things, do you remember those?"

She nodded slowly. "I think so."

"You told me you'd dealt with one before when the Council forced you to test the restrictive field they were developing. That's what ruined your link."

"Yes," she said with more conviction this time. "I remember."

"One of them ate your memory of me."

Her stance tightened. She glanced at Fa'yet who nodded. She couldn't have looked more skeptical if she tried.

"Why would it do that?"

"Because the memories that taste best are the ones we cherish most."

The cold dismissive tone she'd used when I'd first been hired came from her lips. "Did you read that somewhere?"

I took a deep breath and then another. This was going to be impossible. We'd had a history before she'd hired me, it was the one thing that had drawn her closer to me than to Jey or Merkief. Now I was a stranger. A large, scarred, and repulsive stranger—if her cringing was anything to go by.

How the hells was I supposed to get her back?

"Daniel." Needing a moment to gather myself, I beckoned him over to me.

He walked warily past Anastassia. *"I don't think she knows me."*

"We'll sort this out." I patted his shoulder. "Can you go check on your sister? Make sure she's getting to bed. She wore herself out helping us."

"Yeah." But he stuck by my side. *"Mom shut me out."*

The waver in his voice reminded me that I wasn't the only one who had lost the woman standing nearby.

"Me too. We'll get her back." Though, even as I tried my best to sound confident, laughter bubbled up, the kind that told me I was on the verge of losing it. I choked it back down.

Daniel gave Anastassia a wide berth on his way to look after Ikeri. He left the door open, but at least both kids were safely out of the line of fire.

I found myself under Anastassia's scrutinizing gaze. I wished we were alone somewhere, without an audience, but she knew Neko and Fa'yet and maybe that would help.

"Stassia, can we sit down and talk about what happened?"

She cocked her head. "Why do you call me that?"

"I always have." That wasn't exactly the truth, but close enough.

"They tell me that we're joined, but I'd never do that." She shook her head, her braid slipping over her shoulder. "I only take Jalvian partners. I'm not stupid enough to get caught up in your bonding shit."

As insulted as I was, I had to appreciate the fact that she hadn't tried to kill me. Yet.

The sight of the bands that signified our joining on the floor made every muscle in my back and neck seize. I knew she'd be confused, and I understood how that felt, but that didn't make the fact that this wasn't the woman I loved easy to accept. She was standing right in front of me, albeit well out of arm's reach. If I made the slightest move toward her, she'd take it as an attack.

"For the record, neither of us were on board with the bonding shit initially, but we made it work."

In my peripheral vision, Fa'yet's brows rose.

"I don't know what game you're playing, but I'm done," Anastassia declared. "Undo whatever it is you did to my head."

"An Arpex did that. I tried to stop it."

The cruel twist of her lips told me she didn't believe a word I'd said. Her pacing resumed, but in a more contained four stride area.

"The kids, the girl might look like me, but not the boy. He's yours?"

I gritted my teeth and blocked out Fa'yet and Neko's reaction when I said, "No, but he is yours. Ikeri is ours."

She rubbed her fingernails with her thumbs, never stopping moving. "There was someone else. Someone," her eyes widened. "Like you."

She laughed ruefully, shaking her head. Every muscle in my body went on high alert.

"I couldn't be that stupid twice." Stassia backed away toward Fa'yet. "Isnar, get me out of here."

He looked to me.

"Is your house on Karin secure?" I asked past the lump in my throat.

He nodded.

The bond screamed at me to not let her go. I wouldn't know if she was all right if I couldn't see her, not with our connections severed.

She needed time to accept what had happened. And space, she'd always needed plenty of that. Both of those things meant I needed to let her leave if I wanted a chance at getting her back.

The look I gave Fa'yet must have been a particularly bad one because he cringed as he approached Anastassia.

"Don't think I've forgotten how this turned out the last time I trusted you with someone I cared about," I said. "If any harm comes to her, there will be no warning or escape."

Fa'yet offered a solemn nod.

Neko started for them. I shook my head.

"We'll be back tomorrow morning," Fa'yet said.

"I don't know what you're all on," Anastassia said, "but I'll decide whether I'm coming back at any time."

"What?" I managed to say as the floor opened up and threatened to swallow me whole.

"I'll talk to her." Fa'yet slapped a hand on her arm and then they were gone.

I wanted to follow them, to yell and punch something or lots of somethings, but I stood there, teetering on the edge of the abyss in front of me. A tiny voice reminded me that the kids were here. They needed me, even as defective as I was.

Neko cleared his throat. "You did the right thing, boss."

I hoped he was right.

"So it's just the two of us for a while then?" he asked.

I finally found my voice again. "Looks that way."

The whole house seemed too quiet. Empty, even though we were standing in it.

"What's the plan?" Neko asked quietly as if he could sense it too.

"I need you awake with me later. Take the couch. I'll sleep with the kids. Yell if you hear anything."

"Got it." He draped his lanky form over the couch and turned out the lights.

I picked up the bands Stassia had left behind and brought them into our bedroom, setting them carefully on the stand on her side of our bed. Then I went into the other bedroom to find both kids staring at me with wide eyes. "Overheard everything then?"

Their gazes dropped to the blankets.

"Move." I waved Daniel off so I could squeeze in. He climbed back in once I was settled. "I figured you two could use some company."

After I turned out the lights, Ikeri burrowed under my arm to lie against me. "She'll be all right, won't she?"

"Yes." I hoped. Maybe. Someday. It wasn't fucking fair, I had just gotten her back beside me.

They both fell silent, though only Ikeri may have been sleeping. Daniel kept squirming until I finally gave in. "You want answers, I take it?"

He hit me with an overwhelming burst of frustration through our connection. He showed me how absent I'd been, how uncertain every day had been lately, with me in the tank, and the attack on Frique and the Narvan. He'd been trying hard at the academy, and for all of our yelling at him before, none of us seemed to care now. His mother had often snapped at him, being too busy running things in my absence to offer much assurance. Fa'yet and Neko wouldn't give him answers either. What Ikeri had picked up through her connection with me and shared with him, had only brought up a hundred more questions.

And now his mother was acting like she didn't even know him, and I wasn't his father?

It was somehow easier to try to comfort him than to seek any for myself. "Can I show you?"

I could feel his question before he gave voice to it. As gently as I could manage, I slipped into his mind to show him how to open himself to share memories with me.

"This is an Arpex." I showed him the two that had come into the Karinian Premier's office while trying to avoid focusing on the bodies and destruction. "It eats memories and people. I served one when I was imprisoned while you were on Pentares."

He touched my grey hand hesitantly.

"Yes, and most of the other big scars. It also ate some of my memories, just like it did to your mother. When it eats the memories of a single person, every memory that touches that person is damaged. It makes many things blurry and confusing."

With my artificial eye, I could see him studying me in the dark. "She was friends with Uncle Isnar long before me, so it's good she's with him for now. He can help her understand what she forgot."

"You're not my father?"

"Yes and no."

I sighed, opening my mind to him again to show him my brother. I picked a memory where he was telling me what he could about the mission he'd been on. Though I didn't remember the details, it had been his excitement and the sense of adventure that had held my rapt attention. Seeing his face, focusing on it for Daniel, made me angry all over again over everything the Arpex had taken from me. I would have still looked like him, older than he'd ever been, but not deeply scarred, not streaked with grey—like my time in the Council's service had stained me.

"His name was Chesser. He was my brother."

Daniel remained silent. I searched my memories for others to share. Most were fragmented with time, glimpses of him in uniform, dinner with our parents around the table, him with Anastassia in her too long red dress before we'd all fought and she'd stormed out.

"That's mom?" he asked, his voice cracking.

"It is."

"She's so young."

I'd been so busy still shaking my head at that dress that I hadn't considered how much time had changed both of us.

"She was. Chesser had planned to join with her, but he was killed by Fragians during the war with Jal."

"That was a long time before I was born."

Ikeri's soft breathing against my other side offered a sense of normalcy. I savored it for a moment.

"You probably don't remember Ikeri's birth, but it was very difficult for your mother. Yours was too, and she was alone then. I didn't know you existed until many years later. A doctor friend of hers had put you in a stasis tube. You were only a few days old for a very long time."

"How old am I really?"

"As old as you were yesterday, twelve. Stasis years don't count."

"That's not fair." He elbowed me lightly. "When did the doctor get me out?"

"When I told him to. Your mother was very sick and in danger. I hid you both on Veria Minor where I could keep you both safe."

"Wait, the whole time we lived on Minor, we were hiding? Those weren't your real jobs? That wasn't our real—"

I wrapped my arm around him, stilling the unraveling of his reality. "It was all real enough. We hadn't planned on returning to the Narvan, but things changed."

His body eased back against mine. "So she doesn't remember me because of you."

"She will. Geva knows there was plenty of time when the two of you were together without me, but that might be hazy too. It will just take her time to sort through it all."

"How do you know?" he whispered.

"Because Arpex took people from me too, like my own mother, and your grandfather."

He went quiet for a few moments. "We should kill the Arpex."

His flat statement caught me off guard. It sounded exactly like me saying the same thing of Fragians or Jalvians to Chesser after him telling me about his missions.

"I'm working on it." I smiled, giving him the same answer Chesser had given me.

Daniel fell silent and eventually his unresisting weight assured me he'd fallen asleep. Held captive by my children, I sat there wondering what Stassia was doing and wishing it was her lying against me.

After a while, I relaxed enough to sink deep into my link. Hours passed as I checked on the trade deals I'd started with other systems and read the daily reports from the planetary heads and notes from my contacts. The invading Arpex had been busy. I spent hours passing along instructions to those dealing with business partners who had forgotten trade deals and to others who found themselves embroiled in feuds they'd had no part in reigniting.

Jey was concerned Arpex might have infiltrated Fragia. Kess had his own suspicions of Arpex problems from the way the Merchessian families were riled up.

Karin needed extra guidance without its Premier at the helm to bear the load for me. I'd need to find someone suitable very soon or spend several days there myself sorting out the mess the Arpex and I had left behind. Then there was the Friquen official who had been critically wounded during the initial attacks and the lack of progress from the University to deal with.

The sun was up before I'd made a suitable dent in my workload. The kids jostled me as they got out of bed, tearing my attention from everything I'd been doing through my link and plunging my full awareness back into my stiff and aching body. They watched with amused faces as I pried myself out of the position I'd been in all night.

I stretched before attempting to stand. "Someday, you won't be young either."

Ikeri snickered as they ran into the kitchen. With my schedule and frequent dips in the tank, I'd given up keeping track of which meal I was on and just ate whatever was there. Daniel slid a plate of sliced fruit at me and Ikeri. Neko joined us a few minutes later, looking comfortable and well-rested despite having slept on the couch. I hated him a little for that.

"So what's the plan for the day?" asked Neko.

With Arpex on the loose and Stassia's role uncertain, I thought it best to play things safe. "All training is called off until further notice. The three of you will be spending the day on the ship. Stay away from the tank and out of Uncle Jey's room. Got it?"

Both kids nodded.

Neko waited until they'd run off to get dressed before quietly asking, "I see you opted out of sleep. Is it wise to be running around alone out there like that?"

"It's not the first time."

Worry creased his otherwise smooth forehead. "You're supposed to be avoiding stims."

And taking better care of myself, which probably meant not working all night. I sighed. "I forgot I have two nagging mates."

Neko chuckled but then stopped abruptly. "Will she be all right?"

There was no easy answer to that, and I didn't make a habit of lying to my trusty shadow. "I don't know. I hope so."

"Me too, boss. Me too."

It was comforting to see that he looked as stricken over Stassia's absence as I felt. "I have a few things to do in person, and then I'll be joining you to work from the ship, all right?"

He nodded. "Let me know if you need me. Those two can stay out of trouble for a few minutes on their own."

"I will."

As Neko headed for Daniel's room, I contacted Fa'yet. *"Let's try this without the kids present. Give me five minutes."*

His reply took longer than I was comfortable with. *"She would prefer to meet here."*

Of course she would. She'd always preferred that I come to her. I'd forgotten how aggravating her control issues were.

"I'll be there shortly."

I left notices with Tomias and also with Daniel's instructors of their absences and then changed my clothes. Once Neko had left with the kids, I Jumped to Karin.

Fa'yet met me at the door, questioning my lack of armor with a raised eyebrow. I shoved past him, needing to see Stassia. She wasn't in his opulent common room.

He leapt in front of the door that opened to the rest of his home. "Wait here, and for the love of Geva, please don't break anything."

Anxiety and trepidation ran laps in my brain. Fa'yet's expansive liquor collection beckoned to me. Would a drink help me calm down or make my hold on the bond even less secure?

"Are we drinking?" Anastassia asked.

I turned around and started toward her, unable to help myself. Her annoyed gaze stopped me two steps later.

"Bit early for that," I said. "Can we sit this time, please?"

Since she didn't move, I did, picking one of the brown prantha hide chairs I'd often sat in. No artificial fire crackled in his fireplace today, and the weaving-lined walls and thickly carpeted floors lacked their usual warmth.

"Why are you here?" she asked.

I tried to keep my voice level in spite of her abrasive tone. "Because you didn't want to come home."

"It's my damn house, not yours."

"It's ours."

She muttered something under her breath and then took the chair across from me. "What do you want?"

"You?"

Honesty gained me an eye roll.

I tried a different angle. "The Arpex are causing absolute chaos out there, and I could really use you beside me."

"So you're in charge."

"No."

"Good." She sat up straight and pinned me in her best challenging glare. "Then I'm in charge."

"Anastassia, for once in your life, this is not about being in charge. I've got enough work for five of me, and until yesterday, we were working together to keep the chaos at a semi-manageable level."

Her gaze traveled from my face to my boots and back up again. "Why would I pick you?"

The cabinet full of liquor called to me again. It might help take the edge off her disdain, but I had an overwhelming list of things I needed to attend to.

I knew what she saw, but I made myself look her in the eye, the same eyes that had been full of playful mischief just a day ago. "I didn't always look like this."

Her gaze faltered and she clasped her hands together on her lap. "You were injured while taking out the Council with Merkief and Jey. Isnar told me."

"Yes."

"There are so many holes." She shook her head. "I can't imagine what filled them all."

"Me."

She rolled her eyes again. "You don't give up, do you?"

"No."

She shifted in her seat, and I thought she might spring up and start pacing, but instead, she leaned forward with her elbows on her knees and her work face firmly in place. "If you have so much work to do, why are you wasting your time here?"

"I wasn't aware I was wasting my time."

"Jey told me how much the two of you have going on. I handled it all," she said in her default condescending tone that I hadn't missed in the least. "So why, if he can handle his half of the load, can't you handle the other? If I was deranged enough to saddle myself with an Artorian, I prefer to think I'd at least pick a competent one."

This woman might inhabit the same body as the one I loved, but it wasn't her. I wanted to strangle this one. It was quickly becoming apparent to me that my favorable memories of Kazan had been somewhat idealized over the years.

Her failure to think fast enough, to heed my warning, had resulted in the loss of Stassia and left me with this insecure, patronizing shadow.

Talking to her now, being in the same room didn't bring any relief to the driving urges of the bond. She offered no peace, only aggravation. The woman I'd bonded with, joined with, lived with, and loved, was gone, and the moment I admitted that to myself the bond writhed, crackling with rage. I gripped the arms of the chair.

"The Narvan is much different than when you held it, and we're in the middle of a fucking crisis. If you don't want to help, then you can stay here, out of the way."

"Out of the way?" She scoffed, eyes narrowing. "Isnar said that you were bonded to me. Maybe I found that to be an advantage I could use?" She shook her head. "I never wanted kids or any of this relationship baggage. I certainly never wanted you."

The room blossomed red and every muscle in my body surged with endorphin infused energy. How dare this shadow deny her own children, the years we spent together, and everything we'd shared. How dare she throw that in my face like it was nothing?

I burst from the chair and over the table sitting between us to grab her arms and pin them to the chair. "Not another word."

Somewhere in the distance, a door opened.

She bucked and kicked, but I didn't move, warring with myself over the urge to beat senseless this person who had insulted Stassia and me.

Footsteps rushed closer.

"Let me go," she yelled in my face.

A body that wasn't hers entered my reach. I let Anastassia go and caught Fa'yet in the face with my grey hand. He flew back the way he'd come, slamming into the wall beside the open door and sliding down to lay limp on the floor.

"Isnar!" She dodged around me to run to him, watching me warily as blood ran from Fa'yet's nose and mouth. He didn't move.

I took one step toward her and then another. And then suddenly Jey stood between us.

"Fa'yet said there was some emergency with you two?" Jey glanced around. His gaze settled on my hand.

I looked down to see blood there just as Jey finished making sure it hadn't come from Anastassia.

"Vayen, listen to me, you've got to calm down. Do that breathing shit or whatever it is you do."

If he Jumped her away, I'd have to hunt him down too. "Don't touch her."

The red made it hard to concentrate. All I wanted to do was take out whatever or whoever had taken Stassia from me. Nothing else mattered.

"Get me out of here," Anastassia demanded.

"No." He kept his hands in front of him. "Where the hell is Fa'yet? This is his territory."

"Behind you," I said, stalking toward the woman who wasn't Stassia.

He glanced backward and then back to me. "I'm so glad I got you that new hand. He was trying to help, you know."

"He got in the way."

Anastassia scrambled to the wall behind Jey and drew a gun, but she seemed unsure where to aim with Jey standing between us.

"Put the gun down," I ordered.

Jey spun around. "Really, Anastassia? Put that away."

Confusion dampened her bravado. She tucked the gun back into her coat, keeping an eye on us both. "He tried to kill me."

"From the fact you don't look like poor Fa'yet here, I doubt it. What did you say to flip him into raging maniac mode?"

Her mouth fell open. "I didn't... It's not my..."

I tried to focus on Jey rather than her, to make the red go away so I could think clearly. Blinking didn't help. Shaking my head didn't either. I grabbed Jey's shoulder, needing something solid to hang onto. He would do his best to stop me if I did get my hands on her again. I couldn't hurt her. I'd never get her back if I did.

But she was already gone.

The red threatened to take over again. If this was how Merkief had lived after he'd lost his family, his anger and seemingly crazy choices made much more sense.

I had to get myself under control. With the way my pulse was pounding, it was likely my heart would give out again.

"Anastassia," he snapped. "Apologize. Now."

She looked at him as if he'd grown a second head. "I thought you were on my side. You said—"

"Your side contains two people. You and him, and that's the one I'm on. So quit deflecting the blame and get on with it."

She sputtered.

The vein over his right eye began to bulge and twitch.

Energy sang throughout my body. I wanted an outlet, but seeing Fa'yet filled me with guilt. It wasn't him I was angry with. Or Jey or Anastassia. Arpex were to blame, and if I could have gotten one within reach, I would have ripped it apart with my bare hands no matter how much acid it spewed on me.

"I'm sorry I spoke the truth," she said.

Jey twisted out of my hold to spin around and grab her by the arms. "Anastassia!"

"I said, don't touch her."

He spun back to me. "Neither of us should touch her. And for the record, I had no idea how much of a good influence you were on her until now."

The red finally began to fade. I took a few deep breaths and let them out slowly.

"Can you drop her on Frique?" I asked. "I should get Fa'yet to the tank."

"I'll drop her anywhere as long as it's not at my house."

Anastassia gaped. "I'm right here."

Jey sighed. "Sadly, you're not. Which is a shame, because we could really use you right now." Looking deflated, he lightly placed his hand on her shoulder, and then they were gone.

I contacted Neko, sending him up to the house to watch over Anastassia, then picked up Fa'yet and Jumped to the ship. The kids were busy talking somewhere beyond the tank room so I made quick work of stripping him down and getting his profile ready. His swollen and bloody face wasn't easy to look at. I'd likely shattered bones. Though I was grateful that he hadn't woken to see to extent of what I'd done, he knew how to access the tank's files. I had no doubt that I'd hear about it soon enough.

The kids were in the office, Ikeri in the chair by the terminal and Daniel standing behind her. They both looked up when I poked my head in.

"What are you doing in here?"

"Talking to Seeker Tomias," said Ikeri. "You said I couldn't go there, but you didn't say I couldn't talk to him."

"I'll have to have a talk with Neko about that."

Her curls bounced as she shook her head. "Don't be mad at him. I begged."

Poor man. She'd already perfected Stassia's manipulation skills.

"Sign off then. I have work to do."

She nodded, fingers dancing over the terminal.

"Can we help?" asked Daniel.

"No, but you can stay as long as you're quiet." Being near Ikeri offered me a degree of calm. I needed all of that I could get.

And so passed three hours of going over reports and sending out notices via the terminal and then sinking deep into my link to supervise trade deals, advise Kess, and diffuse as much Arpex chaos as possible through my contacts. When the tank was done, I transferred Fa'yet to a bed where he would sleep another three hours. At one point, Daniel pushed a meal bar at me while the two of them nibbled on their own without complaint.

They both managed to sit quietly, each with their own datapad, doing whatever was likely not schoolwork, the entire time. Maybe our kids weren't so difficult after all.

The long night and endless hours wrapped up in work left my reserves guttering. If I wasn't going to rely on stims, I needed to sleep. And to deal with Fa'yet, as well as get to Merchess to help Kess deal with the war the families had started in earnest. And I needed to figure out what to do with Anastassia. I sighed. There wasn't enough of me.

Arin smiled sadly. *"You should have stayed. You wouldn't have lost her."*

There was no energy left to shut him off. His words swirled around in my head. No matter what I did, I always lost her.

"Daddy?" Ikeri's voice begged for my attention.

"Yeah?"

"Are you all right?"

She was giving me that analyzing old woman stare again. While the answer was a definite not-all-right, I scraped up enough will to get my face and head back in control. I couldn't afford to fall apart again.

While I intended to voice a confident yes, I thought better of that plan and went with a nod. It made the lie easier.

I shut the terminal down. "Stay here, I mean it," I told both of them. "I'll be right back."

With the door closed behind me so I'd hear if they snuck out, I made my way to the room where I'd left Fa'yet. A single shake woke him.

"I'm sorry," I said before he could begin the tirade his pissed off look promised. "I shouldn't have hit you. It's just that..." I raked my hands through my hair, gripping it and clasping my hands over my head, trying to find the words.

"She's not herself?" he said.

"Not even close."

He sat up, picking at offending gel flakes on his arms. "I talked to her for hours last night, trying to make her understand. She twisted half of it and didn't believe the rest." He swung his legs over the side of the bed and wrapped the sheet around himself. "You said you'd been a victim of this too?"

I nodded.

"Then you know how best to deal with it. Now, if you'll excuse me, I'm going to go take a shower and then turn in my resignation to my bastard of a boss."

"About that—"

He held up his hand. "Later. Go deal with your mate. And get some sleep, you look like shit."

Fa'yet stalked out of the room. Chasing him down would mean being in earshot of the kids. They already had enough trauma to deal with. Losing Uncle Isnar was not a topic I looked forward to if he was serious.

He'd looked quite serious. I swore under my breath as I made my way back to the office where the kids waited.

"Come on," I said with a smile I hoped didn't look as forced as it felt. "You two can go outside and play with Neko while I take a nap."

"Is Mother there?" asked Ikeri.

No, but her shadow was. "Yes."

They tucked their datapads under their arms and came to stand beside me. I Jumped the three of us up inside the house.

"Hey boss," hailed Neko. "She's in there." He pointed to our bedroom. "She's been swearing up a storm for hours. I don't know as you want the kids around."

"I'll take care of it. Why don't you take them outside for now?"

"Will do. Isnar?"

"He's busy. If you need to sleep before I wake up, take the couch."

"Good luck." He nodded toward the bedroom and then motioned for the kids to follow him outside.

When I opened the door, Anastassia jumped up from where she was seated on the bed. I went in.

"What are you doing in here?" she asked.

She'd hung up her coat and set her weapons out neatly on the floor. The bands had moved since I'd last been in the room. She set the datapad she'd been using beside them and folded her arms over her chest.

"It's my bedroom too." I hung up my coat beside hers and started to remove my weapons.

"I'm sure you can find somewhere else. I don't want you in here."

"Honestly, I don't want you in here either, not like this, but I need someone to wake me up in two hours."

"I'll gladly leave." She started for the door.

"Until you get yourself under control, you're staying. I know you've got a lot of things to try to piece together. You lost sixteen-some years of me and that had to create a fucking mess. I get it."

She halted her retreat. "We were together that long?"

"On and off, and without killing each other, miracle that that is." I pulled off my boots and sat on my side of the bed.

"And we were joined that whole time?" She glanced at the bands on the table.

"No, but we lived together, worked together, eventually raised kids together. We were only technically joined for the last two years."

"Technically?" She edged closer.

"We're complicated."

Anastassia managed a tentative smile. "I see."

I pointed to the closed door. "Those kids have been through enough, so if you're going to check out of motherhood, at least do it without swearing."

"You can't be serious." She laughed weakly. "If they truly are our kids, they're used to it."

"I assure you, they are not. Their mother is quite protective in that regard."

Anastassia stared at the door. I crawled into bed.

"If you're inclined to kill me in my sleep, know that Jey will be extremely pissed and the Narvan will be screwed. I don't recommend it." Yanking the blanket around me, I turned my back to her.

She stood there beside the bed for several minutes before asking, "Do you want the lights out?"

After my time in the Arpex chamber, I never wanted the lights on again while I slept. "Yes."

"Why don't you have Neko wake you? You'll probably kill me if I touch you wrong."

"I won't."

The room went dark. Her feet shuffled on the wood floor.

"Really? Because it sure looked like it was on your mind earlier."

Fa'yet's bloody and swollen face hovered behind my eyelids. One more thing to haunt me. Just what I needed.

"It was. However, you inhabit the same body my mate did, and I'd prefer that body remained unharmed."

She stood there, not moving, her breathing even. I was about to roll over and use my artificial eye to see what she was doing when she spoke again.

"And what am I supposed to do while you're sleeping?"

"What were you doing before I interrupted you?"

She sighed and when she spoke again, the hostility had vanished from her voice. "Getting an earful from Jey and then looking at still frames I apparently saved to my own datapad, according to my extensive investigation." She let out a shaky breath. "I've been trying to put things together."

That sounded promising. Trying was definite progress from the woman I'd dealt with the day before.

"So you believe me then."

"Unless I'm the only sane one, and the Arpex threw the rest of you a wild hallucinogenic-infused party."

The datapad scraped across the table as she picked it up. "I also read a few reports."

I sat up to face her. "Did you reply to any of them?"

"Not yet."

Thank Geva. "If anything is hazy that influences how you might reply, ask me first. We can't let others know we've been affected. Arpex are causing enough chaos without those that rely on us doubting our ability to deal with the situation."

I patted her side of the bed. "Go ahead. Your endless finger tapping helps me sleep."

"Glad to know we have the sort of relationship where I work late while you sleep."

"Actually no, you give me shit about how little I sleep, but I need to right now, so if you don't mind..."

Her weight tentatively shifted onto the bed, and the soft light of the datapad lit the room. She must have been reading because her fingers were still. I settled back onto my pillow.

"What happened to you earlier?" she asked quietly.

"I'm tired, and you've pissed me off enough for one day. If you want to be useful, play nice with Kess and help him sort out the families on Merchess." I closed my eyes, and when her fingers eventually did start tapping, I drifted off to sleep.

I came awake with a gasp and sat up to find my shirt soaked with sweat. Anastassia hovered at the edge of the bed, perched like she was ready to bolt for the door. The light from the datapad reflected in her wide eyes.

A quick check of my link informed me I hadn't even been out for the two hours I'd allotted. I stripped off the wet shirt and flung it onto the floor beyond the bed. No matter how hard I rubbed my eyes, I couldn't erase the image of the Arpex merrily hissing as it enveloped Stassia in its wings, piercing her neck and back with its barbs. Her screams still filled my ears.

I dropped back down onto the moist sheet and squeezed my eyes shut. With my heart pounding as it was, there was no way I was going to fall back asleep.

"Well, fuck that then."

I activated the lights and slid off the end of the bed, far away from her, and grabbed a clean shirt from the closet. I felt her gaze taking in every scar as I pulled the shirt over my head.

"I thought we didn't swear."

"Volume. We swear quietly. At least at home."

She nodded. "That, I find more believable. I did talk to Kess. He still wants you to be there in person. And he said I sounded off."

"You do." I bound my hair back. "You want to sit in here until the kids go to bed?"

"Not really."

"Then after we eat something, Neko can stay with the kids on the ship. You up for coming with me to Merchess?"

"What about Isnar? Maybe you should take him instead."

"He...quit."

She stood over her weapons, probably taking an inventory. "You're letting him?"

Inspiration hit me. "Not exactly."

I contacted Fa'yet. *"Where are you?"*

"My house. About that resignation, you want that in writing or shall we skip to the part where you lay out your standard threats?"

"I'll meet you there in an hour. I have a retirement gift for you."

His anxiety leaked through our natural connection. I cut contact and let him sweat.

"Can you handle eating a meal with the children you didn't want?"

She winced. "Yes, and it's not that I... I'm piecing more together. About them anyway."

"Good. They need you, you've been the more reliable one since we came back to the Narvan."

I opened the bedroom door, fully expecting some new crisis to be thrown in my face. Instead, Neko sat at the station while the kids were on the couch watching the news highlights on the vid.

"Turn that off and go play like normal kids," I said.

Both of their guilty faces popped up over the couch.

"But we're watching the things happen that you ordered, Daddy," Ikeri said.

I shook my head. "Turn it off."

"They watch you work?" whispered Anastassia as she came to stand next to me.

"They did today. I was shorthanded with Isnar down. I'm not used to this single father thing."

Daniel turned off the vid feed. Both kids watched Anastassia nervously.

"What meal are we on around here?" I asked.

"Dinner," said Daniel.

"You cook," Anastassia said as though she were fitting those pieces together just then. "Could you make something quick?"

He grinned and dashed into the kitchen.

"They're very odd. Too old," she whispered to me.

"It's the mixed blood."

Ikeri kept her distance until we sat down at the table. I called her over. She sat in the chair next to me, rather than her usual seat next to Anastassia.

"Are you feeling better, Mother?" Ikeri asked in her old woman voice.

"A little." Anastassia watched her intently. "You helped me get my speech back."

Ikeri nodded. "Can I help you now?"

"I don't know." Anastassia glanced at me.

"You can let her in. She's already seen everything you have in there."

Anastassia blanched and seemed to wither. "Why would I let her see all of that?"

"Because you wanted to work with Daddy again," stated Ikeri.

Anastassia studied me as if the answers were written there in fine print. Her voice was thick when she finally spoke. "I would show her what I hid from everyone, all those terrible things, to a little girl, so I could work with you?"

Ikeri hopped off her chair and ran around me to hug Anastassia. "It's all right, I'd already seen most of it from before I learned not to look."

I must have gasped because Ikeri turned to me. "Don't worry, Daddy, I couldn't sneak into your memories as easily then."

Then. But what about now? I closed my mouth and tried not to let my panic show. She *was* just like Etara, like Tomias. We'd found the secret recipe for making Seekers.

"I need to get some fresh air. Let me know when dinner is ready." I made it out the door before anyone had a chance to respond.

The moist warm evening air did nothing to calm my nerves. In fact, it only reminded me of the Arpex's chamber and the sweat I'd woken up in. We needed to get back to Artor. The house there didn't hold so damn many memories of Stassia.

Maybe I could sleep on Artor. But there were so many things to take care of before I foresaw the opportunity to fall into a bed again.

Daniel interrupted the chirping of the bugs that lived in the fallen leaves to let me know dinner was ready. I wiped the dirt off my boots and went inside to find them all around the table, even Neko. The kids talked about their schoolwork with minimal prompting from Anastassia. Crunching on the heaping plate of crisp bean noodles before the tangy red sauce turned them soggy, I half-listened to their conversation while going over incoming reports through my link. Neko ate quietly, his face drawn and eyes sagging. I imagined mine looked just as bad, if not worse.

Once our stomachs were filled, I sent Neko off to the ship with the kids so they could all sleep. We returned to the bedroom to suit up.

"Did you know Ikeri saw everything before?" Anastassia asked. "You seemed upset."

I sat on the edge of the bed, sorting through the pile I'd made when I'd disarmed earlier. "She'd implied she didn't approve of us when I'd previously ventured to ask her about seeing us in your mind. So yes, I suspected, but I didn't know how much. Even as a baby, she knew things she shouldn't have."

"You two are very close."

I nodded.

"Were you angry with me then?"

"For polluting our daughter's mind, yes. But I did really want you beside me again."

She wore a soft smile that twisted my stomach in knots. "We must have been good together."

Words lodged in my throat. I managed a nod.

"How does this work, me going with you today? I mean, if we get separated or I need to contact you?"

"You'll have to let me in before we go."

Anastassia took her time loading up the last of her weapons and slipping into her coat. "If I do, will that do anything to your bond? I've been trying to read about that, but I can't find much that pertains to our situation."

"Our situation isn't standard. It never was."

She stood within arm's reach. All it would take was a step to pull her close.

"Well?" she asked

I sighed. "I don't know. If it flares up, you can seal it off. You've been able to do that before."

Her face was so open, so much like Stassia.

"And that doesn't bother you?"

"Terribly."

"Do I enjoy torturing you?" She studied my face, as much asking herself as me.

I couldn't tell if this was her old self taunting me or a legitimate question, but I was too tired not to be honest. "Yes, but never like that on purpose."

"You won't go all rage monster on me again, will you?"

"I'm exhausted and I'm missing the woman who keeps me sane. I can't make any promises on that front." I put my coat on.

She studied her hands for a moment before letting out a long breath. "If we're keeping this thing quiet, do I need to call you anything specific in front of Kess or anyone else?"

"No."

"Really? No sickening pet names I came up with for you?"

"Unless you count, idiot, no. And you'll have to re-earn the right to use that one."

Anastassia glanced up from loading her weapons to see if I was joking. I ignored her and finished getting my own arsenal in order.

"Glad to know I didn't completely lose my mind when we got together." She pulled out her stim tin and held one out to me. "Not trying to be a bitch here, but you look like you need this."

The tiny savior sat in her open palm, beckoning to me with promises of alertness and energy. "Put that away. I can't."

Confusion plain, she dropped the tiny tab back into the tin and returned it to her pocket.

"You made me promise not to take them anymore."

Anastassia shrugged. "If I don't remember making you promise, you might as well take it. Sounds like the Narvan may need you for a while."

"Yes, well, so do you."

She cocked an eyebrow. "And you'd put my needs in front of the entire system?"

"Always."

She laughed, the soft kind that tugged at my heart and made me smile. "That's not how being a good leader is supposed to work."

"I haven't been good since the day we started to work together."

Her eyes twinkled. "I'm sorry about what I said yesterday. I can see how you may have convinced me to change my mind about what I wanted."

"Is that so?"

"Yes." She laughed again. "Are you ready to try this?"

I couldn't wait another second. I nudged against her mind. She opened up slowly, hesitantly, but I was in. Praying, I begged for the bond to flare, to feel the peace she offered, to know that we would be all right. A minute passed, then another, and still nothing happened beyond the ordinary open channel of natural speech between us.

"Nothing?" she asked.

"No." But damn it all to the ninth hell and back, I wanted her back like she'd been before.

I froze when she placed her hand on my arm. "Give it time, we only just met yesterday."

The crazy laughter that I normally kept buried bubbled out of my mouth. "You make it sound like you're not opposed to this, but yesterday you—"

"As I said, I've only known you for a day, and an insane as hell one at that."

The sooner we got done on Karin and Merchess, the faster we could get back to this. "Well then, you're ready?"

She nodded. I Jumped us to Fa'yet's house on Karin. He let us in, casting nervous glances at my hands, my coat, and me in general.

"He's promised to behave," Anastassia said, taking a seat in the common room.

I sat next to her. "I said no such thing."

"Oh shush, get on with it before Isnar implodes."

I waved him to the open chair.

"You two made up in record time," he said, looking between us. "Memory come back?"

A rosy hue spread over her cheeks. "We had a little talk."

Fa'yet shook his head and chuckled. "You work fast. Wish you'd done that the first time around."

"Me too," I said. "About that retirement gift."

"I'm not going to like this am I?"

"You're being promoted."

He grimaced. "Nope, I'm not going to like this."

I held out my hands to him. "You're the new Premier of Karin. Congratulations."

Fa'yet stammered, looking to Anastassia.

"Don't look at me. I'm as surprised as you are."

"Neither of you are half as surprised as the hopeful candidates for the job are going to be when I push this through."

But having a man I trusted leading Karin was worth the political mess this sudden appointment was going to create. We didn't have time for the usual planting of a chosen candidate within the election campaign. Fa'yet was Kryon. He knew how to manipulate people. What he couldn't smooth over, I'd solve with favors, bribes, or more permanent solutions.

"You know," Anastassia said to me, "Neko is going to be expecting his own planet when he retires."

"Good thing he's young. We'll have time to find a suitable one, and hopefully the leisure to go about the appointment the right way."

She shook her head and grinned.

"Why are you doing this to me?" Fa'yet squirmed in his seat. "Why can't I just stay in my house and take up some mindless hobby in silence. I'd even invite you all to dinner once a month. Would that be so bad?"

"Isnar." Anastassia's amusement vanished into a motherly scowl. "Vayen just handed you control of Karin. Say thank you."

"You know I hate people," he muttered.

"So gather a board or assistants and make them face the public. That's worked for others before you. You've sat in on the meetings, you were Kryon for Geva's sake, you know how this works," I said. "Spend your sizeable fortune in a way that best benefits our people. Enjoy whatever company you want when you want it and any blood on your hands will be by choice. You might even consider hanging up your coat."

He snorted. "Damn well have to, wouldn't I?"

I let him sit for a few minutes, stewing in silence.

He heaved a heavy sigh. "Fine. Thank you. I'll get back to you two regarding dinner plans. Make sure you bring your troublesome spawn. I might need help in the kitchen."

"We will. Oh, and I'll make the announcement of your appointment to the appropriate sources shortly. Make sure you have an acknowledgment speech ready."

He stood. "You're a fucking terrible person, you know that?"

I shrugged and motioned for Anastassia to follow me. We let ourselves out. When I reached for her to ready the Jump to Merchess, she stepped away with an odd look on her face.

"What?"

"Can I try something?" she asked.

"Can you try it elsewhere? I'm not fond of standing out in the open."

"Of course." She stepped back within reach.

We arrived at the jump point Jey and I used when dealing with Kess on Merchess, a single room apartment in Ka'opul city near their family compound. One small window and the one entry door made it easy to secure when we needed a place to rest. The mattress on the floor boasted a soft blanket and the tiny kitchen featured one occupied cabinet containing a handful of meal bars and a med kit. Typical slave quarters, except that they were forced to live six in the same space.

"That was very generous of you," she said, taking in our sparse surroundings.

"Don't tell anyone."

She smiled. "I can see how it's to your advantage to have Isnar running Karin, but still, I wouldn't have taken that leap of faith with him."

"I trusted him with you and the kids for years without me around. If he can handle that without screwing me over—"

Anastassia reached up and ran her calloused fingers over the thickest of the scars on my face, causing what I'd been thinking to vacate my mind. Geva, if only I'd held my own system when we'd first met our relationship might have gone like this from the start.

Her fingers trailed down my neck but then she hesitated.

"Nothing?" I asked.

Not that I expected there would be. I'd tried the same thing with Gemmen with no results. However, I was elated that Anastassia was willing to try.

"No memories anyway."

The connection between us opened further, allowing very pleasant thoughts to flow from her mind into mine, tentatively caressing until I was tingling inside and out.

"You sure about this?" For just meeting, she was moving damned fast. Though there had always been rumors of Anastassia hopping into bed with various men, I'd come to learn they were just that. Experience had proven that it took plenty of time for her to allow anyone to get this close to her.

"If we were really together for as long as you say, you'd know me. Prove it."

Screw Kess and his mess of a planet. This might not have been the woman I'd loved, not exactly, but it was the same body, and mine was attuned to it whether the bond was there or not.

I expanded the connection we shared but I initially let her lead, not venturing forward until she'd explored first. The instant her lips touched mine, I took over, making quick work of removing her coat and all the weaponry underneath and then shedding mine.

"Clearly you've done this before," she said breathlessly as she worked to remove my pants.

"Once or twice." I lifted her shirt over her head and dropped it as we worked our way toward the mattress.

"Here?"

"Not yet."

She laughed as I pulled her down on top of me. The mattress cushioned our fall.

TEN

Fully sated and wishing I could sleep for a few days straight, I dragged myself off the mattress and started recovering my clothes from the trail we'd made. Anastassia watched my every move, making me self-conscious about the fine scars that covered every inch of my body. Nessa had done a good job of treating my injuries after the Council bases had been blown to bits, but the evidence of that day remained like a detailed report written on my skin in a language no one could read.

"We should get moving before Kess thinks we're blowing him off. I don't need him backing out of our deal," I said.

"You're not the lay around and cuddle type, I take it?"

"Neither are you."

She'd also never been fond of parading around naked, and I rather doubted her memory loss had changed that. I gathered up her clothes and handed them to her.

"Thanks."

She made quick work of getting dressed and went about sorting her weapons from mine. "Was that different? I mean, us, we're usually like that, or was it because of..."

Unsure of what she was trying to ask, I played back the past hour's events and found myself smiling. "No, that was pretty usual. We certainly have our issues, but this," I pointed to the mattress, "has never been one of them."

"Really. Even after kids." She let out a low whistle.

"We are usually quieter when they're around."

"Right. Volume." She laughed.

As I dressed, I heard her say to herself, "Interesting. I don't remember the Artorian angle making this so intense before."

While I was pleased that she'd enjoyed our interlude as much as I had, it seemed that this was an experiment and not the speedy reconnection I'd hoped for. I'd proven her hypothesis correct, that was all.

But at least she was making a serious effort to cope with our situation rather than spurning me as she'd done initially. With my enthusiasm in check, I rearmed.

Once we'd put ourselves back in working order, we made our way down the two flights of stairs to the gate. The Ka'opul guard on duty nodded us through.

I contacted Kess. "We're in place in Ka'opul. Let me know when you've got your people in position for the Nikera and Keefe."

"We've been in position, waiting for you to grace us with your presence."

"I was busy."

He sent a burst of annoyance that I cut off. I made contact with the men he'd assigned to me, giving them instructions and our location.

"So what exactly are we doing?" asked Anastassia.

"Because Merchess is so contained and the families have full access, we thought it would be our best chance at capturing an Arpex. Travel has been shut down between the city domes since yesterday and everyone is under lockdown.

"If Arpex are still on the planet, they're in one of the three domes. However, because the families are currently at war, none of them would cooperate unless they were given equal treatment. Jey's supervising the Keefes and Kess has the Nikeras."

A squad of Ka'opul guard made their way down the street toward us, their uniforms clean and pressed. At least Siro had taken the Arpex threat seriously enough to send a decent-sized force.

"Is it wise to have all of us contained in one place?"

"Unless they're taking the whole planet out, I think we're safe. We're not all in the same city. That, I would worry about."

"And what do you want me to do?" she asked.

"Stay with me, but that's not very efficient. So if you promise to contact me if anything, and I mean anything, feels off, I'd like you to take two teams and sweep the opposite side of the street."

"We're seriously going to search building by building?"

I nodded.

"The entire city," she said flatly.

"You have your stims?"

"Yes, but what about you?"

"I'll live." I signaled for half the men to follow Anastassia.

"I hope so." She more mouthed than said, but I was sure I hadn't imagined it.

Watching her head off with her search party, I was filled with regret. I wanted to go back to the morning when she'd sat on my lap with the promise of ten minutes of bliss and her gaze full of mischief. If I could have crammed my shitty mood down for a few minutes and enjoyed what she was offering, I might have blown off the meetings until later. If I had just made her happy by going to the damned massage appointment, she might still be here. If I hadn't fallen apart when the Arpex arrived on Karin, she'd still be herself. If I'd pulled out of that probe a few seconds sooner and jumped us away...

Arin didn't need any words. He just stood beside me and nodded.

Stassia's shadow disappeared into the building across the street. One of the milling armed men advanced, coming to stand halfway inside of Arin. I squeezed my eyes shut and took a deep breath. When I opened them, Arin was gone.

The men waited expectantly for me to move or say something. With a heavy sigh, I signaled for them to head inside.

Siro's men had the codes to every building. We went into every room, from top to bottom, down one street after another working from the outside ring of the dome inward. All of the searchers had been given a full briefing on dealing with the Arpex and were instructed to contact us first before engaging in any manner. Still, I kept a close eye on my two teams, watching for any signs of confusion as we moved from one building to the next.

Hours passed and the dome dimmed to its night cycle, filling the surface above with thousands of artificial stars. My attention began to waver and all my thoughts circled back to falling into any one of the hundreds of beds we passed. I didn't even care if I dreamed of Arpex all night, my eyes demanded to close.

I called my team to a halt and shuffled across and down the street to where Anastassia's people were working. Upon seeing me, she thrust her hand into her pocket and came out with a stim.

"One?" she asked.

I nodded. "No more than that."

The tiny tab ignited energy in my veins, clearing my head and prying my eyes open.

We parted ways and went back to work. Night turned to morning and our teams swapped out for fresh men and women. I took a few minutes to spread the news of Fa'yet's appointment and glanced over a couple of reports while the new shift settled into smaller units. When I came back to myself, my legs ached and my lack of sleep left me with a headache now that effects of the stim had faded.

Anastassia's voice broke the monotony. *"We might have something."* She flashed me a location.

I sent my teams off to work and Jumped to Anastassia's side. "What is it?"

"The lock's been altered. They couldn't get it open without force. It's the only one we've come across like this."

I put my ear to the door. Silence. Maybe it was empty. Everything seemed fairly normal except that the door was warm against my cheek. "Everybody back."

"You're exhausted. Let them go in first," Anastassia said, waving at the nearest members of her team. "One of you get that open."

A woman approached the door and went to work on the lock. Then she paused as if frozen mid-motion. When she snapped back, she turned around facing us, looking dazed. She raised her weapon as if to fend us all off.

Two of the men on her team surged forward, disarming the confused woman. They pulled her aside, trying to talk sense into her.

"Tell the others we've got one," I told Anastassia.

"What are you going to do?"

"Keep anyone else from getting killed or forgotten." I was already a mess inside and out and now the fucking Arpex had ripped Stassia away from me. My adrenaline-flooded brain assured me that it could hold my frayed nerves in check long enough to wound this bastard and hand it over to the University for slow and hopefully immensely painful dissection.

"Stay away from it," I said. "If you need an out, contact Jey. I don't trust Kess with you."

I kicked the door in.

"Vayen." She sounded concerned.

I was too tired to put much stock in her possibly emotional response. "Stay back. All of you."

Inside, an Arpex stood in the middle of the room, its barbed wing-jaws already arched open. It hissed, wings shimmering with acid. My body refused to move. Panic hit me, both at being near the Arpex and because I was freezing up again, even after only seconds ago being sure I could do this. Fucking hells.

Anastassia stood on the other side of the wall. I had to keep the

Arpex from her, no matter what degree of the woman I loved was inhabiting her body.

I couldn't fail again.

My hand finally acknowledged my brain and drew my pulse pistol. I hit it with a low pulse, enough to knock it back and tear loose the lower edges of the thin wing membranes. Its speech box fell to the floor.

The Arpex raced at me, hissing at an ear-piercing decibles, and tattered wings snapping forward.

My mind went blank except for repeating *fuck* at full volume.

Anastassia yelled, "Vayen?"

Her voice snapped me back in control enough to thumb the level up a notch on my pistol fire again.

"Stay back," I shouted.

The barbs drove into my back and neck. Digestive fluids stung my face. Self-preservation kicked in, despite my intention to deliver a live specimen to the University. I shot it a third time.

The Arpex let go and fell backward, its shell fractured all along the front. Green fluid leaked from the cracks. Without a second thought, I grabbed hold of it. My time in service to the Council had made me quite familiar with Arpex, enough so that Jumping this one to the Artorian University wasn't an issue.

The staff had prepared an isolated chamber when I told them the Jalvians were hunting down a test subject for them. They hadn't delivered one yet, but when I arrived at my usual jump point with a giant blue-shelled creature, staff swarmed around me in seconds. A woman stayed behind while the others raced off with the Arpex on a cart.

"We've created a solution that should render the Arpex inert while we examine it," she informed me.

"Do it quickly and then kill and dissect it. Keep your people safe. Remember, you have to be close for it to affect you. Use bots to do the exam if you can, and stay in the observation areas."

"That's what we have set up," she assured me.

"Good." Suddenly light-headed, I located the nearest seat and fell into it. My face burned. "You wouldn't happen to have any healing gel on you, would you?"

Something was dripping behind me. I turned to see drops of blood splashing onto the tile.

"Excuse me, Advisor Ta'set, you seem to be injured."

I reached back, only to find that lifting my arm made the

light-headedness worse. "What's back there?"

She peered over my shoulder. "Seems to be some sort of bone-like spike lodged in your neck."

"One of its barbs must have broken off when I pulsed it."

"I'll contact a medical team."

"No, I've got it. Concentrate on the Arpex. Let Advisor Te know as soon as possible if you need further samples. Otherwise, his men will be under orders to destroy any other Arpex they locate."

"Yes, sir."

I relayed those orders to both Kess and Jey and then contacted Anastassia.

"I'm going to use the tank. Destroy any other Arpex those teams find. Make sure they finish the sweep. Any problems or you need to get out, contact Neko for a Jump. Jey's wiped and needs to focus on wrapping up Nikera city. Oh, and grab that black box I left behind. We'll need to get that to the University."

"You're leaving me alone on this?" she asked.

"You can handle it just as well as I can."

Not that I liked leaving her alone out there with Arpex around, but the work did need to get finished. Siro would have a fit if he discovered we'd backed out.

"Make sure to keep both sets of teams moving so you can get out of there as soon as possible. I don't want you strung out on stims either."

"I hear you. Enjoy some sleep."

"Not likely, but thanks."

I Jumped to the ship and sat there for a moment while I tried to clear my thoughts enough to call for Neko. I hadn't overdone it with Jumps recently, but I was totally drained after this last one. Every-thing seemed to swirl around in my head. The edges of the room alternately blurred and came back into focus. Time slipped away as I listened to the quiet and steady beating of my heart. It was a beautiful piece of music, like raindrops or the kids' footsteps on the stairs.

I listed backwards until my head hit the floor, reminding me to contact Neko. Words were so much work. I settled for a nudge and the image of the tank glowing above me, the gel twinkling inside in the thick clearplaz.

Neko dashed into the tank room, the kids on his heels.

"Need a little help." The words came out slow and slurred.

He got an arm under one of mine, hauling me to a sitting position.

The room tilted violently and the contents of my stomach demanded to evacuate my body with great and sudden force. As I tried to wipe my face, I noticed red welts covering my shaking hands.

Neko shouted at Daniel, "Help me get him undressed. Now."

Ikeri stood aside. *"What's wrong, Daddy?"*

Jostled about, they yanked off my coat. Daniel's uncertain fingers bumbled their way through removing a couple weapons while Neko did the rest.

Ikeri seemed so far away, and try as I might to speak to her, our connection turned to mush, leaving me to flounder alone. It seemed as though water flooded into my head, washing away all the places where my connections should be.

"Boss, what happened?" Neko's face hovered over mine. "Talk to me." Over his shoulder, he yelled to Daniel, "Hurry, get his profile up. Just like we showed you."

I tried to answer him, but my tongue was too big for my mouth. All that came out were moans, that once they escaped, I couldn't stop. Inside, I was drowning.

Neko got my shirt off. "What the hell is this thing?"

He yanked on the barb. I knew because I could feel my flesh grabbing onto it, refusing to let go. I tried to help him, but the farthest my arm would move was near my face, as if the muscles on my back were no longer my own. White fluid oozed from the welts that I now saw covered my entire body.

He manhandled me face down onto the platform.

"I can't reach him," wailed Ikeri.

"I can't put him in with this thing stuck in his neck. Daniel, hand me the knife we took off him."

"Don't hurt him," Daniel said.

"He's already hurting plenty. I don't think he'll mind."

Neko drove the steel into my neck, slicing endlessly, digging deeper until the blade hit bone. I kept waiting for merciful blackness to descend upon me, but it stayed on the edges of my awareness, taunting me with promises of relief while it bared jagged, rotten teeth and smiled.

Warmth flowed down my neck and over my back, dripping red onto the floor below the platform. I focused on the kids to try to distract myself. Ikeri sat on the floor crying, arms wrapped around her knees. Daniel stood at the edge of the platform beside my face, one hand on my head, holding me steady while Neko worked. He had his eyes squeezed shut and begged Neko to hurry.

The welts on the hand beside my face turned a deep shade of purple. Something seemed to ripple below the surface of the rapidly swelling mounds.

Neko swore. The knife and something else clanged onto the floor.

"Daniel, get back. Get your sister into one of the rooms. Close the door and make sure it seals tight. Now. Now!"

When Daniel opened his eyes, he screamed. I wanted to too, but my throat was too small and my lips seemed to be sealed shut. I would have paid Neko everything I had to kill me if only I could have given voice to the offer.

Thousands of tiny teeth tore their way out of my flesh and spilled onto the platform. Blue larvae writhed as they plummeted onto the metal floor. Neko stomped manically, his boots grinding them into a blue slurry.

His dance drifted around me until he reached the terminal. And still, he didn't stop. The pounding went on and on with wet sucking noises accenting each lift of his foot.

The floor fell farther away. The gel sucked me down until the blackness devoured me whole.

Anastassia sat beside me, her fingers tapping over the datapad in her lap. Words ran through my mind, but I didn't want to speak for fear of discovering that I still couldn't. I didn't want to feel anything, not my body, not the helplessness, not my skin exploding with Arpex larvae.

But I *could* feel them.

They crawled under my skin, their soft bodies wiggling back and forth, their shiny white dagger teeth feasting on my flesh. Gnawing and tearing until there was nothing left but blood and bone.

As much as I didn't want to touch their sticky slime-slickened bodies, I had to wipe them off me. I had to get them off right now.

Why wasn't she helping me? She just sat there, and then I saw that it wasn't her fingers making the tapping noise, it was the larvae eating her too.

I woke with a scream. Bolting upright, I gasped for breath in the darkness. But it wasn't completely dark. The dim light of the terminal illuminated enough to bring the tank room into focus. I was still on the platform.

Once I got the lights on, I discovered the blue and red smeared mess, along with the knife and barb that were there beneath me. I called out, but no one answered. Slowly, I lowered myself to the floor, trying to avoid landing my feet in any of the larvae and failing. There were so many. I ran my hands over my body, loosening the dried gel and making sure no evidence of their birth remained. My joy was cut short when my hand encountered a dip on my neck, like someone had scooped out the muscle and put a thin patch over the hole.

The tank should have healed it no matter how much flesh had been removed, this wasn't like my ear. The wound was surrounded by flesh. It should have been able to regenerate, to fill in the gaps like the gel always did. Unless there had been residual Arpex matter that had interfered with the healing process? I'd have to check the log to confirm my conclusion.

Skirting the worst of the flattened larvae, I reached for the bloody knife and the barb, which was encased in a thick dried sheath of meat. No, not meat, me, my flesh.

I dropped the barb and knife and made a mad dash for the bathroom before the heaving came to a climax.

A hot shower didn't erase the gnawing sensations that hovered just under my skin. I threw on a shirt and pants, turned off the lights, and sat in the middle of the bed, trying to get myself together before I dared contact anyone.

"Boss?" Neko's voice called out from the hallway, interrupting my fourth replay of everything that had happened from the moment I'd confronted the Arpex to sinking into the gel.

"Go away." I wasn't in any semblance of together yet.

His footsteps came to a halt outside the door. "I found a few larvae that I missed on the floor but only one was still alive. I delivered it to the University. Figured you'd want that."

"Thanks." He was right, but I never wanted to see those things again. I didn't want to hear about them or talk about them, nothing. I needed that whole experience to go away, but it was all I could think about, all I could feel.

"The kids are with Seeker Tomias. I didn't know where else to take them until we got things contained and cleaned up here."

"All right."

They'd seen it, witnessed every horrifying minute. I prayed Tomias was working all his power on them, smoothing over the sharpest edges of terror with warmth and light.

"I'll get the thing that was in you to the University too. I meant to before I left, but Anastassia needed me."

"Is she—"

"She's fine and up top. Exhausted, but unharmed. I didn't tell her about you. She needed to sleep."

"Thanks."

His boots creaked outside the door. "May I come in?"

"No."

I forced myself off the bed, but with every step toward the door, a larva exploded under my foot, it's slime-filled body squishing between my toes, turning the floor into a slippery minefield. A sharp pain pierced my neck. I tried to reach up, to pull the barb out, but I couldn't reach it.

I couldn't breathe. I fell to the floor. The larvae closed in, crawling over me, trying to get into my mouth as I fought for another breath.

"Boss?"

The door opened, spilling light into the room, but I couldn't reach it. They were chewing on me, under my shirt, crawling up my pants. I couldn't get them off. I wiped and slapped and swatted, but they kept coming.

"Oh hells." He ran to my side, but he made no effort to get them off. Instead, he grabbed my hands. "Come on boss, don't do this to me."

I shook him off and tried to reach one of the knives I knew he kept in his coat. If I stabbed the little bastards, they couldn't eat me. They'd never grow blue shells or eat another of my memories. I'd kill them all. Every one of them. I just needed a knife.

Neko kept shifting away.

There was a knife in the tank room.

Gasping for air, I shoved Neko aside and launched myself out the door and down the hallway. I slipped through the congealed mess on the floor until I wrapped my hand around the bloody knife.

Puncturing their little bodies felt so good. They made such a satis-fying sucking sound as I slid the knife in. Each one exploding into a wet spot that soothed the wound they'd chewed their way out of. Breathing came easier. I worked my way down each leg and then up my chest until I couldn't find any more.

I realized Neko stood nearby, his face a mask of horror.

I held the knife out to him. "Help me. They're on my back."

"Sure, boss." His voice was thick and broken. He grabbed the knife and threw it.

"Get them off!"

His fist met my face and then again and again. The tank faded in and out of focus. Cool air whispered over my skin and then gel washed over me.

Anastassia sat beside me, her fingers tapping over the datapad on her lap. She glanced at me. Her fingers went silent. "Neko."

He came running in. She jumped up, the two of them standing on either side of me. The sheet over me moved, first over my chest, then my stomach, my arms, my legs. I whipped it away, throwing it at Neko, exposing the host of larvae feeding on me, fresh welts promised more would be here soon, their teeth pricked just under my skin.

"Get them off!" I tried to smash them with my grey hand, but they were unaffected.

Anastassia grabbed my other hand. "Vayen, stop. There's nothing there."

Neko made a grab for me too.

"Get away from me." I knocked him aside.

"Do it," said Anastassia. "Vayen, look at me. I remember you."

She remembered? For a second the larvae didn't matter. I tried to open our bonded connection, praying for the peace and comfort I so desperately needed.

But that connection was gone. The bond was no longer.

The snap of an injector registered a second later. A flood of heavy warmth rushed through me. Maybe if I closed my eyes and slept awhile, the larvae would be gone.

ELEVEN

"Daddy?" Ikeri's soft voice drifted into the blackness that surrounded me.

"Where am I?"

"We're all on Veria Minor together. At home. Remember home?"

Images of our home on Minor faded in and out, dinner together, tucking her into bed, building block towers with her and Daniel.

"Yes."

"Good." She smiled in my head. *"You're safe here."*

We were happy here living under our aliases as Isnar and Rhaine. We'd faked our deaths in the Narvan to escape the High Council. Now we lived a normal life together, tripping over toys, and sharing news about our colony we'd picked up from her clients or my warehouse.

"When you wake up, you'll be safe here with us. You can relax and be happy."

She made it sound so easy. Safe and happy sounded good.

"Yes."

"Now open your eyes."

I'd fallen asleep on the couch. The local vid feed droned about the viability of progressive farming technologies within some of Minor's currently inhabited climates. Daniel sat at the other end, playing a game on his datapad. Ikeri sat across from me in the chair Rhaine often used.

"Where is your mother? Did I sleep through dinner?"

"No." Ikeri giggled. "She's right behind you."

Rhaine ran her hands through my hair and leaned over to kiss my forehead. "We waited. You needed a nap. You've been working so hard lately."

"Sorry."

I couldn't remember exactly what I'd been working on, but I made a note to stop staying so late at Dugans. I didn't need to work at all, but I enjoyed it. Roshonomen could take over whatever deal it was.

Ikeri sat taller in the chair than I remembered. "Are you hungry?" she asked.

"Yes."

I followed the kids to the table. Rhaine handed out plates filled with hollowed baked fruit filled with steaming soft grains and tart black berries. Daniel set cups of water at each place and then took his seat. His hair was getting too long and he kept watching me like he expected me to yell at him any minute.

I sighed. "So what did you do this time?"

He looked to Rhaine.

"Nothing, he's fine," she said. "Eat, before it gets cold."

Of the few meals she made herself, this was my favorite, as far as Verian food went. I savored the first few bites, and upon discovering just how famished I was, devoured the rest. Daniel ate in record time, took care of his plate, and glanced at Ikeri. She shook her head ever so slightly. He sat back down. Rhaine picked at her food, not quite looking at me.

"Why is everyone so quiet?"

I picked up my empty plate and reached behind me to set it on the counter. My hair tickled my neck. I didn't normally have it this long here. I pulled it back and rubbed the spot that kept tingling no matter how hard I rubbed. The skin felt odd, thin and smooth, like a scar. I scratched at it and came away with blood under my fingernails.

"Vayen, leave it be," Rhaine said.

Ikeri shot her a withering look that vanished in a flash. I wondered if I'd imagined it.

"Daddy, can we play?" she asked.

"Sure." But there was blood on my nails and the itching was worse. I scratched at it again.

Rhaine took my hand, pulling me up from the chair. "You have a bug bite on your neck. Here, let me put something on that for you."

She handed me a towel to wipe my bloody fingers and rifled through the cupboard where she kept the medicines. When she came back, she wiped my skin with the towel and then applied an ointment and covered it with a bandage.

"I'll check on it again later. Go play." She smiled and gave me a gentle shove out of the kitchen.

I'd almost made it up the stairs when someone knocked at the door. "You expecting someone?"

"Yes, I'll get it," she said.

We were safe here. Knocks on the door shouldn't have made my heart pound, but it did. I turned around to make sure she was all right but Ikeri took my hand. She pulled me upward.

"Come on, Daddy."

"I should—"

"It's okay. It's a friend. Mommy will be up in a few minutes."

"How do you know who it is?"

She smiled and pulled me along to her room. Down below, I could hear Rhaine talking to a man. She sounded worried.

I dislodged my hand from Ikeri's.

"I'll be back in a minute."

"Daddy. We're safe here."

She'd told me that before. In a dream. Before I'd woken up on the couch. "What did you say?"

Ikeri looked so tired all of a sudden. "Mother, you need to hurry," she called out.

"What's going on?" I scooped her up. "What's wrong?" And what happened to calling Rhaine mommy?

She wrapped her arms around my neck and hugged me tightly. "You're safe here, she repeated.

I didn't feel safe. Something was wrong. Very wrong. The itch on my neck grew worse. I carried Ikeri to her room and sat on the edge of her bed while she gathered up her toys.

A few minutes later, Rhaine stood in the bedroom doorway with a tattooed man beside her. "Isnar, you remember Tomias?"

"Yes." And he wasn't supposed to be here. We weren't supposed to have any contact with anyone from our previous life. We'd agreed. I got to my feet.

"It's all right, Daddy." Ikeri was right beside me, her hand in mine. She stood taller than she'd been a few minutes ago. Taller than my waist. How was that possible? She was only three.

Tomias strode into the room, red robes swirling in his wake.

"You don't belong here." I looked past him to Rhaine. "We agreed not to do this. What are you doing?" And why were the lines around her eyes deeper than I remembered?

"Why don't you sit down?" Tomias said.

For all their smiles, this wasn't right. I didn't like Seekers and they didn't like me.

"Why are you here? You hate me. You disowned her. You don't belong here."

Rhaine came to my side. She put her hands on my shoulders and guided me down to the bed. "Sit down, you'll feel better."

I scratched at the bandage she'd put on my neck. They were all acting strangely and the room was too damned small for four people. I needed some fresh air. Out of the corner of my eye, I caught something moving under my sleeve.

"What the hells was that?" I asked Rhaine. "Did you see it?"

"No." She gestured for me to lie down. "Close your eyes. Tomias will help you feel better."

"I'm fine." Except for my body twitching and tingling and the shooting pain in my neck.

I grabbed her arms. "There's something crawling around inside me, it's under my skin. You have to help me get them out."

How could she not see them squirming under my shirt? They were everywhere. A fat blue larvae fell from my sleeve, tumbling to the floor where it wriggled and squirmed until it righted itself. I pointed at it.

"Look, right there. Don't you see it?"

"We have to begin now," Tomias said. "Ikeri can't hold him any longer."

A pale young woman came into the room. She had a plain face with long reddish hair and yellow-green eyes that seemed to look through me. She placed a hand on Ikeri's head. "Rest now, little sister. I'm ready. Hold him please, Seeker."

And then she was in my head, and we were alone in the room, yet I couldn't move.

"Etara."

"You remembered." She offered me a cold smile. "You look no better than the last time we met."

"Worse actually."

She nodded. "You were infected by a creature you call Arpex. Poisoned, so it could use your body as a host for offspring."

I saw it all again, the terror in Daniel's eyes and the revulsion in Neko's. Felt the agony of the larvae chewing their way out of my body and as Neko carved the boney barb from my neck. Larvae spilled from me and fell upon the floor covered with my blood. Through it all, Etara watched with me.

"We may not like one another, but I would not wish this torture upon any living soul."

She clapped her hands and the room was clean again.

"Ikeri tells me that these Arpex have taken memories from you by force."

"Many times."

She brushed her hand over my forehead in a manner almost tender. "I can take this memory from you if you wish."

"Is it painful?"

"No."

"Then please take it from my children. They shouldn't have seen what they did."

Warmth lit her smile for the first time and when it did, she wasn't plain at all.

"I will give them the same choice that I have offered you."

"Thank you."

Though I knew I was on the bed, it seemed as though I were floating. It was altogether quite pleasant. I didn't itch and the larvae were still.

"When you take a memory, will it leave a hole? I have so many already."

"I will leave a whisper so you know what was there, but not the terror of it."

"Is there a cost? What do you get from this?"

"Your daughter asked this of me, and for her, there is no cost. It is her you will owe, not me."

"Then yes, please take it."

She bowed her forehead to touch mine and clasped my shoulders. "Close your eyes."

When I opened them again, Tomias and Etara were gone and Ikeri was sound asleep beside me on her bed. I gently slid off and went to the stairs. Halfway down I realized we were in the house on Veria Minor. I hadn't imagined that. Daniel and Anastassia sat on the couch. They jumped to their feet when they spotted me.

"How are you feeling?" Anastassia asked.

"I have no idea. What's going on? Why are we here?"

"Ikeri needed a place where you felt safe to prepare you for Tomias and Etara."

I sat on the couch, trying to sort it all out. "Yes, I think I feel much better."

"Good." She sat down next to me. "You had us very worried."

One shining moment of that nightmare rose to the forefront. Three words that made it all worthwhile. She remembered me.

"How did you recover your memories?"

If she'd found a way, she could help me. I needed our bonded connection so badly. I needed her back beside me.

I shifted in the long tunic that fit too tightly. Isnar hadn't been as bulky as I was now.

Her face fell and she twisted the band on her arm back and forth. My heart leapt to see it there.

"I didn't." She sounded defeated, unable to look at me. "It was all I could come up with to distract you."

"Oh."

The warm glow Etara had left around me snapped like the clap of an energy field shutting off. There was no hope of recovering her, of all we had been. That was gone.

I needed to change. The stupid clothes were cutting into my arms. There was too much work to do.

"Where's Neko?" I asked.

"Having his session with Etara."

"Good. Daniel?"

He nodded. "Already did. Ikeri too."

"The Arpex hunt, how did that end?"

She pulled her legs up on the couch and faced me. With her hair down and dressed as a Verian, she was much like Rhaine had been when we'd first arrived on Veria Minor, struggling to find her place.

We'd recovered from that once, maybe we could again.

"We found two more," she said. "We pulsed the first one like you said. It went down quickly. The second took the memories of two and the lives of four others before we took it out. They forgot their own men. It was hard to watch."

Having seen Arpex feast countless times, I knew exactly what she'd witnessed. I wished I could have been there instead of her so she wouldn't have had to have those images engraved in her head.

"The other cities?"

"You'll need to get the reports on those yourself. I was a little occupied with all this."

"Right. Thanks for that."

She nodded. "I'm glad I got to see you here, how we were, even if it wasn't quite real. We were happy here away from the Narvan?"

"Mostly, yes. We've been happy in the Narvan too."

Anastassia moved closer. "I wish I could remember." Her hand found its way into mine. "Please don't ever do that thing that happened that we won't talk about ever again because it was damn scary, all right?"

The thing she spoke of was now a quiet memory, and in briefly touching it, I knew I didn't want to look closer. "Only because you said please."

She laughed quietly. So did Daniel.

I looked over to see him grinning. "What?"

"Nothing. I'm going to go…" He ran up the stairs.

"What was that all about?" I asked.

"Maybe he thought we needed some time alone." She smiled.

"Did you send him off?"

"I might have."

"Anastassia, with all that—"

She pressed a finger to my lips. "Ikeri and Tomias have been trying to find a way to put my memories back."

My mouth went dry. She didn't look like she was joking or trying to distract me with a lie this time. "How?"

"A process similar to what Etara did for you, I think. Ikeri had told them how your people can share memories. Some hybrid technique of two ideas." Her fingers idly toyed with her sleeve. "They'd have to copy memories and then give them to me. Some, Ikeri holds from our therapy sessions. Most would have to come from you."

I stilled her nervous fingers with my hand. "Copies of memories?"

"Sort of, yes. Etara called them whispers."

"Knowing without feeling."

Anastassia nodded. "But I would know. We can work on the feeling after."

"I'd like that."

She kissed my cheek. "I think I would too." Then she slid off the couch and pulled me with her. "Now, you owe me some sleep and you have work to do. Are we staying here until Ikeri wakes up?"

"Yes. I need to have a talk with her."

"Be nice. She worked very hard to keep you calm by making you see things as you would have before. It took a while for Tomias and Etara to travel here. Neko was in no shape to Jump them, and we didn't want to involve anyone else."

I nodded. "He's not going to quit too, is he?"

"You'd have to physically pry him off you first. I don't think I've ever seen anyone as devoted."

"That's only because you don't remember me."

She shook her head and grinned.

"Come on then," I said. "Sleep for you, work for me."

We settled onto the bed, space between us despite our encounter on Merchess. That didn't surprise me, but her behavior on other fronts had. She turned out the lights. A soft tink of metal on wood indicated she'd removed the band again.

"Mind if I ask you something?" I asked.

"Can't promise an answer, but sure."

Her retreat to her old self made me pause, but I needed to know. "How is it that you can go from being the woman I started working with who thrived on comments like that, to jumping into bed with me? Do you have any idea how long it took us to get to that point the first time around?"

"I would imagine you didn't have every single person around me wholeheartedly endorsing you and us."

"Hmm. No, can't say as I had that going for me." I'd known Jey and Fa'yet had spoken to her directly and perhaps Neko, but they all knew about her memory loss. "Do others know about our problem?"

"Other than a few comments about me not sounding like myself, I don't think so."

"Then what do you mean?"

"Anyone who can inspire loyalty from Kess has got to be pretty remarkable. Neko would follow you anywhere and the kids adore you. You've got your half of the Narvan tripping over itself to stay on your good side and most of the other half too, despite Jey claiming he's in charge."

She shifted, moving a little closer. "You might not be what I'd planned on, not that I recall having any long-term plans in that department, but as far as options go, you appear to be the best one."

Her reliance on her old way of thinking grated on me, though it did seem to now be tempered with bits of her more recent self. I knew how this worked, and thankfully she'd only lost one person and not many like I had. She was working around some of the gaps, making connections, remembering details in the memories where I'd been. But not me.

As much as I was glad that we'd come as far as we had so quickly, the frustration over losing all we'd shared was hard to swallow.

Anastassia sighed. "I said something wrong again, didn't I?"

"Why do you think that?"

"You're too quiet."

Part of me wanted to disagree, to put her at ease, but she was right and lying wasn't going to help either of us. If the Seekers were able to help her regain some of what she'd lost, maybe it would be enough. Enough to bring her close to Stassia. But was knowing a suitable substitute for feeling?

I leaned over, found her forehead, and kissed it. "I miss you."

Half expecting her to make a snide comment about being right there, I much preferred the silence she sank into. At least when she was quiet, I could pretend it was Stassia beside me instead of her shadow.

She remained still while I found a comfortable position and dove into my link. Fa'yet had given a short but on-point acceptance speech before sealing himself into a bare office and barraging me with requests for advice on handling the growing Arpex-induced crisis and inquiries on staff choices. I spent as much time as I could giving him my input before moving on to what the University had learned.

Their report was short, mostly a list of bullet points and a request for a personal visit to go over the details, which were many and yet aggravatingly vague.

Jey was making headway with the Jalvian Prime and they'd destroyed one of their Arpex. Kess sent his thanks for the purge of Merchess. Fragia was a mess but they were Jey's mess. He'd been dealing with them longer and he had a better working relationship. At least they hadn't come after us yet, but all it would take was one Arpex asking the right question of the right person.

I wanted to get to the University while it was still daytime there, but Neko was sound asleep. I left a message for him to contact me as soon as he woke, and instead, went over the trade reports on my Kryon route venture and checked in with the other planetary heads.

A familiar hand shook my shoulder, urging me back to my immediate reality. I wasn't exactly eager to get back to that.

Blinking away the flowing words and strings of numbers, Anastassia's concerned face lit by the Verian sun shining through the window came into focus. "What?"

She stared at me for a minute and then flopped back onto her pillow. "I didn't know what was going on in there. You've been a little unreliable that way lately, you know? You had me worried, being all vacant like that."

Her concern appeared genuine. That had to be a good sign of progress in our favor.

"Nothing to worry about, just working. I've got to get to the University. Neko will be joining you here shortly.

Anastassia rubbed her fingers together, her body shifting in faint degrees as if she couldn't find comfort. "Would you mind if I went to Prime? I'd like to talk to Tomias about their proposition."

"Only if you take a transport. I may need Neko later and don't want him drained."

She sat up and reached for clean clothes. "I'll be fine. You could take him with you now."

"This is not up for debate. If you're talking to Tomias, that means no weapons. Which then means you and the kids need Neko."

"No one has ever harmed us on Prime, or Minor for that matter."

"Merkief killed me on Minor."

She opened her mouth and then closed it as if she were waiting for me to turn that announcement into some sort of joke. When I didn't, she nodded slowly and seemed to be mulling it over instead.

Anastassia pulled off her shirt, leaving her back bare. Reaching over her head, she worked her way into her tight undershirt, offering tantalizing glimpses of the side of her she chose to keep from me now that her curiosity was sated. Hopefully, her visit to Tomias would be beneficial to both of us.

After pulling on a light green tunic over the undershirt, she turned around. "You don't look dead. Tired, but not dead."

"Thank the tank for that. Would you like me to show you?"

"Share your memories with me through our connection?" Her face took on a pinched look. "Will that unlock the bond? Letting you in further?"

"I don't know. We've done this before, long before we were bonded."

"Really? You must have worked your magic earlier than you thought. I don't make a habit of doing that."

"The only habits you had when I hired on were extreme paranoia and abrasiveness."

She scowled and got up to pull on a pair of loose-fitting pants. "Then how did we end up together?"

I couldn't help but notice she was slipping further from my reach, but it was hard to remain patient and put on a pleasant front. I needed her to get back to herself so we could deal with all the shit going on around us.

"Why don't you want to try this?" I asked, making every effort at keeping my frustration to myself but failing. "It's similar to what Tomias is proposing."

She shook her head. "I need to talk to him about the whole process first."

So it was fine for me to be in her head for sex, but when it came to sharing anything beyond that, minds were off-limits? Confusing messages were old Anastassia's specialty. They'd driven me mad then too.

"So you'd rather have Tomias in your head than me?"

Her green-eyed gaze darted away.

"You still don't trust me, do you?"

My aggravation rose from simmer to boil even as I repeated to myself that she needed space. I was pushing too hard.

I needed to get away from her before I made things worse. "I'll be at the University. Neko goes with you."

I grabbed my coat along with whatever weapons were within reach and Jumped.

The University was buzzing with activity when I stepped out of the void. Unsure whether that meant something good or bad, I hailed the first person I could catch.

A woman took me in with the unfocused gaze of someone doing a hundred things at once. "Can I help you, Advisor Ta'set?"

"What's going on?" I nodded toward the unusually high level of bustling action.

"Everyone is excited about the Arpex dissection. Please come with me." She reversed her direction, leading the way down a level and into a room lined with rows of counters, most of which were filled with various parts of what I guessed to be the Arpex. Sections of its shell filled a wide table in the middle of the room.

"Director Sa'cota has taken over this project herself." She indicated the annoying thorn of a woman bent over a magnifier. "Is there anything else at this time?"

"No. Thank you."

Dismissed, she hurried out of the room, leaving me with Sa'cota and several other white-suited workers. She probed the edge of whatever it was she was examining with a gloved finger, seemingly ignoring me.

"Well?"

Sa'cota jumped and upon realizing it was me, scowled. "I heard you were injured."

"I was. What do you have for me?"

"Their physiology is quite fascinating." She launched into an explanation that I understood every fifth word of. This had always been Merkief's arena far more than mine, and right then I missed him considerably. If he could have been there nodding and making interested noises at Sa'cota, I could have been putting together an extermination team on Syless, something I was much more suited for. Instead, I did my best to follow along, not wanting to admit that she was talking far over my head.

"The barb you encountered, what purpose did it serve? We've discovered that they inject toxins, either to paralyze or heighten the endorphin levels in their victims. However, the barb that was delivered to us and the surrounding tissue suggest that particular appendage also served a different purpose."

"Reproduction."

"Infecting a host body." She nodded thoughtfully. "And what did you experience?"

"Extreme unpleasantness."

She smiled. I imagined she was about to say 'good', but she wisely kept that to herself. "The single intact larva sample we received is no longer viable."

"Too cold here. They need humid conditions, like Frique."

"I see. And why did you choose not to impart this information when the sample was delivered?"

"I didn't deliver it and wasn't in a state conducive to imparting anything at the time."

That damned smile twitched on her lips again. "Was it painful?"

I stepped into her personal space. "How do we kill them?"

Sa'cota shrugged, ignoring the fact I was armed, aggravated, and only inches from her vulnerable body. "Blowing them up seems to be the best option. Their shell is exceptionally durable. The only obvious weakness is their jaws, though they can survive without them for a time."

"Plucked its wings off, did you?" I asked, wondering if she had been one of those children who enjoyed tormenting insects or small animals to see their reactions.

"You did request us to seek out weaknesses."

"Any others?" Since my presence next to her had no effect, I stepped aside to peer through the magnifier at the pinkish-grey mass she'd been looking at.

"They can only vocalize speech the way we understand it through the use of the translator box you provided to us. Their natural speech patterns are unfamiliar. We're still working on that."

"Good. Their ability to screw with people's heads is just as dangerous as their jaws. More so, actually. If we can destroy the boxes, might that make people safer? Though, Arpex I've dealt with can mimic Artorian natural speech just fine and their invasive skills are far more powerful than ours. They can still prompt us for memory feeding whether they vocalize the command or not."

The tissue she'd been working with offered me no obvious clues as to what purpose it had served for the Arpex. I started to turn to ask her what it was when a sharp jolt hit the back of my neck.

I spun around to face her. The room kept spinning even though I stopped. Sa'cota took two long steps backward.

"What are you doing?" My words slurred, a testament to the speed of whatever she'd injected me with.

"Changing the things I can. We don't need you, tyrant."

Four other shapes moved in, her assistants. My grip on the table behind me began to falter. Sa'cota's face slipped in and out of focus. As far as I could tell, her hands were empty. One knee buckled. The other gave out a second later, dropping me to the floor where I swayed on all fours, trying to form a Jump to the ship.

"He's going to Jump," said a man to my left.

"I doubt that will be possible," said Sa'cota, approaching slowly. "Disarm him and then use the restraints. Bring him to the isolation chamber."

I tried to reach out to Anastassia, to Neko, even to Ikeri, but all I could hear were my own slurred words echoing inside my head.

Sa'cota's assistants went to work, removing my coat and weapons. The few semi-focused glimpses I got of their faces gave me the impression they were worried, but none of them voiced their concerns.

They half-dragged half-carried me to an adjoining room. From the unmistakable puddles of gloppy Arpex ooze on the floor, I surmised it was the same room in which it had been kept prior to becoming hundreds of individual specimens for Sa'cota to study.

How many pieces would I end up in?

Dazed by the drug, I only managed a minimal physical protest when they dropped me in the middle of the room. Four posts sprang from the floor. After two of the assistants made quick work of undressing me, the other two attached restraints to my wrists and ankles and then secured them on the heavy metal rings at the top of the posts.

Cold from the floor leached into my back. Even though I was no longer moving, the room still spun. I pressed my eyes shut and tried again to form a Jump. Like a frustrating dream, every effort seemed to happen in slow motion and with only a fraction of intended force. I couldn't keep the effort together fast or long enough to get anywhere.

It occurred to me that Sa'cota, being a director at the University knew all the details of links, natural speech, and Jumping. She knew exactly how to prevent them. And she wasn't afraid of me. She had no intention letting me out of the room in anything but unidentifiable pieces.

"That's enough," Sa'cota said. "Back to work, all of you. Oh, and Wen, could you please permanently silence his helpful guide?"

"Yes, Director Sa'cota."

The four assistants left us alone.

"I know you're awake. We have all your physical information on file. I was very precise with the dose." She loomed over me.

Though I tried to reach up to strangle her, my arm barely left the floor. I began to seriously regret not taking Anastassia's advice. If I'd had Neko with me, this situation might have been avoided. Or it might not. Her assistants didn't seem to have any qualms about offing the woman who'd led me to them.

The University's employee standards weren't up to mine. Especially where Sa'cota was concerned.

"You may have damaged one of the Arpex's reproductive barbs, but the other one happens to be just fine. Upon examining the first barb and anticipating its purpose, I removed the other from the living Arpex and placed it in stasis."

Her footsteps faded and then returned. Sa'cota held a long curved barb in her hand. She leaned in close and pulled my hair aside. "It appears the natural injection point would be here. This will hurt."

Sa'cota drove the barb through the thin layer of skin covering the hole Neko had carved while removing the last one. That's when I discovered that Sa'cota had chosen her drugs carefully. I might not be able to move or speak, but I could feel everything. And it hurt like all nine hells. My back arched of its own accord, muscles spasming across my shoulders.

"Thank you for being so helpful to supply the information about the humidity." She stepped away. "I'll be right outside. I want to make sure we get all the data recorded properly."

The door sealed with a heavy whoosh. Pressure built in my ears and then leveled off. The room was now a contained environment. Within minutes, the air grew warmer and sweat beaded on my skin. A thick blanket of silence covered the world outside.

I carefully probed the quiet place in my memory that Etara had created. Though I didn't want to know what was going to happen to me, I found myself digging deeper anyway. The information was there, cold, analytical, as if it had happened to someone else. While I had no doubt this had been a terrible experience, I couldn't remember that terror. I didn't want to.

Maybe, having not been injected by the Arpex itself, the barb wouldn't work. I spent a good long while imagining Sa'cota's face when she discovered that her torture didn't play out like she'd planned. And sweating. It was too damn hot.

A puddle gathered under my bare back, making the floor slippery. Not that it worked to my benefit in any way. My muscles were still not cooperating.

A wavering feeling worked its way up from my stomach. My parched throat contracted. My head started to throb. Disheartened with the knowledge that the barb was in fact viable, I tried to sink into a deep link trance.

Nothing with my link was working right. My head filled with echoes of desperate pleas to escape what was about to happen. I tried to reach out to Neko but that didn't work either.

How damn long was her drug going to remain effective? She didn't know how long the process took. I didn't even know how long I'd sat there before Neko had found me the first time. No matter what her time estimate had been, the process was likely sped up considerably now that she'd applied the heat and humidity that I'd foolishly mentioned. My only hope was that I might be sweating out her drug faster than anticipated due to that mistake.

As I looked deeper into the whispers that Etara had left behind, I realized that escaping wouldn't gain me a damned thing. If the hole left behind by the first barb hadn't healed properly, then my odds of using the tank while filled with living foreign organic material were far worse. I was stuck hosting these vile things, restrained or not.

Anastassia and Neko knew where I was. How late would I need to be before they came looking for me? Not that I had much hope that they could do anything about my situation beyond killing Sa'cota, which I'd much rather do myself.

She'd make a wonderful first meal for the larva forming beneath my skin.

And they were forming. I knew because, despite the dazed effects the barb inflicted on me, what had transpired before was right there in my mind like an instruction manual. The welts rose all over my body. The exact timeline was blurred, but it sure seemed like the process was speeding along at an alarming rate.

Swallowing was too much of an effort, my throat was too dry, as though all the water in my body had gathered in the pool on the floor. Moisture filled the air, drops formed and ran down the walls until the entire room was weeping. Yet, I couldn't get any in my mouth. I needed a drink, of anything, just something wet to soothe the shriveled feeling growing inside me.

I tried to catch a glimpse of Sa'cota where she surely stood outside the window, watching, smiling, and taking notes, but the barb scraped across the floor with even the slightest movement of my head, triggering sharp spikes of pain up and down my spine. I settled for the view of the wet wall and between bouts of nausea and dread, plotted ways to make Sa'cota and her accomplices suffer.

Though I was doing my best not to look, I couldn't help but notice the welts on my arm getting larger and more vivid. Soon they would begin to ooze and show signs of movement beneath as the larva grew. A shiver ran through me, and despite the sweltering heat, I realized I was cold, yet still sweating. If I was lucky, dehydration might kill me before the larva did. That would make Sa'cota very lucky too because if I made it out of this room alive, I was going to make sure she didn't.

The more I thought about killing her, the faster my heart raced. It reminded me far too much of the same sensation I'd felt before collapsing at Jey's home with my memory of his wife eaten by an Arpex. I tried to slow my breathing, thinking of Ikeri and the cloud of calm that surrounded her. No matter what I did, the speeding beat remained. Sa'cota's drug and the dehydration were not working in my heart's favor. The terror of knowing what was to come settled around me.

TWELVE

The sharp plink of a stone hitting the window came from where Sa'cota was watching. If she was trying to get my attention, that was too fucking bad. She should have shoved the barb into the other side of my neck if she wanted me to look at her.

The silence inside the room shattered as the panel beside the door exploded. The door slid open. Anastassia ran in.

"Got him. Neko, get help in here."

Three of her grimacing faces loomed over me. She snapped a handful of fingers in front of my eyes.

"Hey, stay with me. We're going to get you out of here."

I tried to answer her but nothing more than incoherent mumbling came from my lips. Seconds stretched into hours before a blurry Neko appeared behind her with several other men who spilled around him to release me from the restraints. My arms and legs fell like heavy welt-covered weights. The jarring motion drove the barb deeper. My entire back spasmed, arching, and twitching.

Anastassia swore and yelled, "Be careful!"

The four of them carried me out of the sauna Sa'cota had created. Cool clean air rushed over my fevered flesh. They brought me to a table, or maybe it was a bed, I couldn't tell. Anastassia stayed by my face, filling my view most of the time. I caught glimpses of Neko and the others, shouting orders back and forth. Other people bustled in and out of wherever they'd brought me. They inserted all manner of tubes and needles into my body. Machines were wheeled in, filling the space with blinking lights, whirs, and beeps. One of the beeps, high and loud, rose above the others, pelting out a ridiculously frantic and erratic rhythm.

"Get his heart rate down," shouted one of the men.

"You're going to have to stand back," said another to Anastassia.

At least he'd been wise enough not to tell her to leave. She stood where I could see her blurred face as a rush of heavy warmth coursed through my veins. Try as I might to stay awake, my eyelids closed.

A distant beeping invaded my fragmented dream, dragging me away from the burning ruin of the Council base and throwing me into a brightly lit room. Equipment lined the walls. A tangled web of wires and tubes ending in needles were strung between them and me. The needles were buried in my skin.

A woman's face came into focus. It wasn't Anastassia. She smiled. "I see you've returned to us, Advisor Ta'set. Geva be praised."

"Where is she?" I rasped.

She held a glass of water to my lips, which I gratefully drank. "Your mate was called away yesterday. We've been keeping her apprised of your improving condition."

"How long have I been out?"

"Eight days. We had to make sure the larva had been completely neutralized."

"They didn't hatch?"

She shook her head. "Your assistant adamantly advised against letting that happen, and your physical condition did not allow for it. As valuable as the offspring of the Arpex might be to our research, we had to let the opportunity slip by."

I gritted my teeth. "Where's Sa'cota?

"I was informed that Director Sa'cota was permanently terminated by your mate."

Sitting up cautiously, I took in the room full of medical equipment. None of it made me feel secure about my situation. The University had always been a safe place in my mind. Sa'cota had ruined that.

"And the others with Sa'cota?"

"Also terminated," she said quietly. "You need to rest. Your body is still adjusting to the absorption of the Arpex."

My heart skipped. "Absorption?"

The woman stepped back. "Your condition did not allow us to complete the birthing cycle so we were forced to keep them and the barb inside. Dissolved, of course. We are aware you use a healing tank and so they have been fused, bonded, if you will, to your cells to avoid any further complications. Your body has been in a state of adjustment to the absorption of their chemistry."

"And you've been studying this for eight days."

Her head bobbed. "Of course."

"You've learned what, exactly?" I held up my hands and yanked the sheet aside to make sure I hadn't grown claws or turned blue.

"Your skin has become tougher, making it difficult to take additional blood for testing. Everything we currently have attached to you is from before we began treatment. Scans have shown changing brain wave patterns. Beyond that, we needed you awake."

One of the machines began to ping faster. "You couldn't just extract the larvae?"

"There were too many and their growth too advanced. Not to mention your physical state." She took another step back, hand extended to the door panel.

"And Anastassia and Neko, they know about this?"

Before I could rip enough of the tubes from my body to allow me to get out of the bed and physically make her answer the question, she hit the panel and slipped through the door.

Blood dripped from where I'd removed their greedy little probing tools. Uncaring, I tore out the rest, freeing myself from their web. After a few minutes free of their wash of semi-sedation, I could use my link again. I touched Neko's connection and found him with Anastassia on Syless.

Not willing to be a test subject any longer, I Jumped to the unoccupied house on Artor and made my way to the bedroom to find clothes. Before slipping into the shirt I held over my head, I paused and threw it onto the bed. I sat down on the edge and poked at my arm. The bleeding had already stopped. My skin didn't feel all that different, maybe a little less elastic, almost like it was drawn tighter over the hard muscle beneath. My legs and stomach reacted the same. I grabbed a knife from the open chest and held it up, making sure the blade was clean before I sliced lightly across the back of my arm. No pain, no blood. I tried again with a little more force. Still nothing.

Finding myself somewhere between elated and pissed off, I took a stab at my arm.

That still worked, I discovered with a grimace. Blood welled up around the tip that had sunk into my skin. With all the force I'd used, it should have gone straight through. Curious as I was, shooting myself was farther than I was willing to go. Besides, I had the wayward University to deal with.

They'd bonded me to those hideous things, with their skin-rending teeth and soft wriggling blue bodies. The nightmare, and that was a word I wasn't about to argue with in this case, was inside me. Part of me.

While blade-resistant skin could be useful, I hadn't been given a choice in the matter. The betrayal of trust with the University staff and the way the attendant had looked at me, like I was some grand experiment, fueled my anger. Sa'cota's hate after all I'd done for Artor, for the University, it all built up inside, burning with a single-minded focus that I hadn't attained since I'd buried the bond with Anastassia when she'd been serving her time with the High Council.

As I dressed, I pondered the most effective way to convey my displeasure with the University. Killing them all was a waste. Killing some would set an example, but Sa'cota had already been taken care of, and I didn't know how much further her line of thinking had traveled. The attendant seemed to share a similar view of research over my choice of care, so undoubtedly there were more.

Maybe all of their funding should be cut off. They certainly hadn't produced anything helpful in this particular matter so far.

Allowing myself a few minutes to lie down, and using my link, I pulled all funding for the University that I'd arranged. Not yet satisfied, I pressured many sources I held sway over to retract theirs as well. They thought I was a tyrant? They had no idea how damn benevolent I'd been. I cut their water, their access to the power grid, and changed the passcode on their backup power access so that only systems pertaining to the link implants remained powered. If they wanted the rest of it back, they could beg for it. I left a message for Artor's Premier, instructing him to ignore all University contacts or he could suffer the same.

That task taken care of, I gathered up my weapons and coat and contacted Neko for his location on Syless. I found him and Anastassia, along with a host of armed men and women, outside of a row of derelict homes, their faces half-covered with wraps to keep their mouths and noses free of the blowing orange sand.

"What are we doing here?" I asked.

"You sure you should be up and about, boss?"

Anastassia's gaze held the same doubtful cast, and while that might have concerned me at one time, I was disappointed that it didn't now. The place she'd occupied in my mind, the calm peaceful place that I'd loved was empty. It didn't bother me that she was standing in a crowd of men or that Neko had placed himself right next to her. The driving need to be with her had vanished. None of the distracting red rage made an appearance. She was there, the same as everyone else, no warmth, no attraction, nothing. Was this an effect of merging with the Arpex? Hells, maybe Geva had finally offered me an ounce of compassion. Maybe I'd finally suffered enough.

"I'm fine. Did you find an Arpex?"

He nodded and pulled his wrap down so he could speak clearly. "Anastassia explained how you did the sweep of Merchess. We thought this was the best place to try the same thing. The cooperation level has been less than optimal, but we came prepared." He indicated the milling and armed swarm of soldiers.

A corner of my brain itched. The itch became a quiet hiss as I surveyed the houses. "You have a verified sighting?"

"Third house." He pointed.

"So level it."

"Love to, boss. Except the locals here have informed us that there is a large pocket of natural gas beneath this area, hence the current unoccupied status of these particular homes." He shook his head. "No explosives."

"How big of an explosion are we talking about?"

Neko grabbed one of the men from the group and presented him to me.

The short man shifted nervously. "We've been pumping the gas out since this morning, but it's a large pocket. Ideally, we'd prefer months. It's hard to say how far the damage will spread if it were ignited now."

The hiss in my head continued, but the sound varied, like wavering static. I stopped focusing on it so I could consult the area maps through the local network. "I'm not seeing anything vital in this area."

He ducked his head, avoiding my gaze. "People live here, sir."

"So relocate them."

A burst of wind kicked up a shower of sand and whipped it against the crowd. They all raised their wraps. Some even wore goggles. The normally stinging grains didn't bother me other than to irritate my eyes. Closing them solved that little problem and allowed me to concentrate on the sound in my head. It grew stronger, and then, as if my ears had popped, suddenly became a loud string of Arpex hiss speak. Not the words that they drove into their victim's heads to feed from, but their own language.

As the wind blew, I hazarded a glance at the others, standing still, heads bowed against the wind, hands tucked under their arms or gloved and holding any loose clothing around their bodies.

The hissing divided into three distinct tones. Three Arpex, all in one house, as if offered up neatly to explode by the planet itself. While I wondered if they could hear me in the same way I could hear them, the wind died as quickly as it had sprung up.

I addressed Neko and his consultant. "Looks like this end of town could use a bit of remodeling anyway."

"Sir, we don't have funds for that. Unless you're offering?"

I laughed. "No."

"A pulse may not ignite the gas," he suggested.

Neko glanced at the house and the men around him. "I'd feel safer taking my chances with the pulse. That's what we were debating when you arrived."

"Debating who to send in?"

Neko nodded. "Can you believe no one volunteered?"

"Face the Arpex and lose our memories or chance getting blown up?" sputtered the other man. "This surprises you?"

"Not really," I said, checking the charge in my pulse pistol.

"Don't even think about it." Anastassia knocked the pistol out of my hand.

I hadn't noticed her sneaking around behind me. Since she wore goggles, I gathered it had been when I'd had my eyes closed.

"You're not going, and neither is Neko," she said.

"Then pick someone," I said as I retrieved the pistol before sand worked its way inside.

She grabbed my arm and dragged me away from the others. Lifting the goggles to reveal dark circles beneath her eyes, she glared at me. "You would really destroy the entire block?"

"It beats Arpex destroying the whole damn colony. They're doing a fine job so far. Or maybe you haven't noticed that a gang is currently acting as the sole ruling force, the Prime's head has been mounted on a stake outside the government hall, and the economy has come to a dead stop?"

"Of course I have. That's why we're here."

"How many Arpex have you killed?"

She shook her head. "None, yet.

"How much have you searched?"

"Half the colony. It hasn't been easy. Not like Merchess."

Neko approached us. "I hate to interrupt, boss, but there seems to be some urgent business on Artor that might require your attention."

"Sunk to bothering you, did they?" I shook my head. "Artor is under control. My control, specifically."

"If you say so." He didn't look convinced, but he returned to the others.

"Why don't you get some sleep," I told Anastassia. "I'll take over here."

She adjusted the goggles to rest on the top of her head over her wrap. "I don't think that's a good idea."

"You're exhausted."

"And you've spent more time in the tank or recovering in a bed in the past few months than Neko's ever seen. Maybe you need to back off a little."

"I can't. If you hadn't noticed, the Narvan is a fucking mess, and you don't even know who I am."

"You haven't even asked about the kids."

"Been a little busy."

She pulled her wrap down under her chin so I could see the scowl I knew would be there. "They're still with Tomias."

"They should probably stay there. Be the best thing for them."

"What the hell are you talking about? They're our kids."

"You barely talk to them, and I'm never there."

Her eyes narrowed. "I'm trying, dammit."

"And I've been trying since the day Merkief and Jey showed up on Minor, but I keep losing. Maybe it's time to just accept how things are and move forward."

In a very un-Anastassia show of public affection, she grabbed my hand and clutched it tightly. "What have you lost?"

"My hand, my eye."

"You have new ones."

"My face."

"I don't mind your face."

"I distinctly remember your recent first reaction was 'holy shit'. I lost Merkief."

"You have Neko."

"Not the same. My sanity."

"Kind of in the same boat on that front."

"You."

"I'm right here."

I dislodged my hand from her grasp to tap my head. "But you're not here where I need you. Me."

She shook her head, the wrap swaying free in the wind beside her face.

"You allowed them to bind the Arpex to me."

"I couldn't let you go through that again. It was killing you."

"I'm part Arpex now. Part of the thing that tortured me, that took you away, that's plunging the Narvan into chaos. There are three of them in that house." I pointed to it. "Do you know how I know that?"

She bit her lip, the gleam of unshed tears in her eyes.

"They're in my head. I used to hear you. Now I hear them."

"I'm sorry," she whispered. "I didn't know what else to do."

"Thanks for getting me out of Sa'cota's hands, but the ones you left me in weren't much better. Geva's been trying to tell me how to make the Narvan work for years, but I've been too selfish to listen. Go home, Anastassia."

"What are you going to do?" Her gaze darted from me to the crowd behind her as if she were searching for help.

"Kill a few Arpex. Neko," I waved him over. "Take her home, I don't care which one. Stay with her, them, you know the drill. You'll know if I need you."

"You sure, boss?"

"Don't question me."

Uncertainty flickered in his eyes as he reached for Anastassia.

She dodged aside. "I'm not leaving you here to deal with them alone."

Damned Neko looked almost grateful.

I grabbed her, lifted her, and set her directly in front of Neko in the time it took her to gasp. "I said, leave."

Trusting that the two of them understood the order this time, I approached Neko's consultant. "How far does the gas pocket go?"

Unclipping the pack that was strapped to his back, he swung it around to dig out a datapad. He brought up a map. "Beyond those rocks," he pointed to an outcropping a short way off, "should be safe. Are you going to try to Jump the Arpex over there?"

"Possibly." In reality, my plan was far too fluid to commit to anything, but I did appreciate the fact that he was thinking of a solution. "Stay back and out. If this thing blows. I'd rather not have all of you go up with me."

"Agreed."

He handed me an entry card and then got the others moving while I studied the rocks in case I was able to do as he suggested. Once I had that jump point solidly in my head, I went over the contents of my coat, affirming those options as well. Assured that if nothing else, I'd be meeting Geva soon to thank her for utterly ruining my life, I set off toward the house.

As I got closer, the hissing grew louder, more concentrated. Patterns became apparent, some I recognized from my time in the Arpex chamber. They were angry. Well hells, so was I.

Guess we had something in common after all.

Visions of the destroyed council complex grew more vivid with each step, but I kept going until I reached the door. I swiped the entry card. The hissing grew more frantic. None of them tried to invade my head with orders to think of anything. Finding this highly peculiar, I went in with my pulse pistol in hand to further assess the situation.

Three Arpex huddled in the common room, their claws clacking, black boxes silent. They turned to face me in unison. Still they didn't demand anything. Maybe I wasn't close enough yet. I halted just inside the foyer, leaving the door open in case I needed a quick exit.

A single voice hissed more insistently in my head.

"I don't speak Arpex. Yet, anyway."

"What are you?" asked the Arpex in the middle through its black box.

"Not sure anymore."

"What do you want?"

"You to leave."

A sudden pressure assaulted my brain, one I was all too familiar with. Curious and with nothing to lose, I reached out over our hiss-filled connection and conveyed my aggravation with the loudest mental yell I could manage.

The three Arpex scattered, running out the door. I followed them. One fell, landing on its back, legs and clawed arms flailing. It hissed louder than the others and emitted a single word through its box. "Poison."

The other two kept running. The crowd of armed men and women took off after them, herding the Arpex out past the rocks, where several pulse blasts brought the chase to a swift end.

"Impressive."

I looked up to see Jey standing nearby. He shot the floundering Arpex and returned his pulse pistol to a holster beneath his coat.

"Anastassia was concerned you were doing something reckless. Again."

"As you can see, the situation is under control. I'm sure you have your own issues to deal with."

"Our issues tend to overlap, including your anxious mate."

"Not anymore."

He turned from the spreading ooze flowing from the shattered shell of the Arpex to look me over. "Care to clarify?"

"Bond's gone."

All his interest in the Arpex seemed to vanish. "How's that possible?"

"Might have faded after her memory of me vanished. I thought we could fix it, get it back maybe, but now I'm part Arpex, and that's internally screwed with Geva knows what. I don't feel anything."

"What? When the hells did that happen?"

"Eight days ago."

"Anastassia said you weren't feeling well, and that you were at the University for testing. She asked me to let you rest until you were back on your feet."

"I was completely out, and the *testing* was more like experimenting after extreme torture. The University had me under observation and sedation, or trust me, you would have heard a head-full about it."

Jey maintained his distance and kept both eyes on me. "I take it this wasn't voluntary?"

"Not in the least."

"Hence the wailing and gnashing of teeth coming from the University."

"Don't fucking touch them."

He held up his hands. "Wouldn't dream of it."

"Good." I contemplated what fire to Jump into next, but he interrupted me.

"Mind if we take a moment to explain to Anastassia how not-bonded, ruthless, work-intensive Vayen operates? She's concerned you're suicidal."

"Tell her whatever the hells you want. I have work to do. And so do you."

I left the remains of the Arpex to the soldiers and Jumped to the government hall to deal with the gang that had taken over. Twenty-three bodies and two hours later, I contacted what loyal people I had left on Syless and got them started on cleaning up the mess the Arpex had left behind. Half of them didn't trust the other, their memories filled with gaps. I was going to have to do something about that. After a moment's consideration, I composed a message for Tomias and Etara, requesting their assistance.

With the help of gathered forces, we removed all the bodies, both those of the regime I'd originally put in place and the one who'd overthrown it. Then I spent the next few hours interviewing those who were left to find suitable replacements. None of them were ideal, but they could be trained. Or replaced again.

Remotely assured by hasty promises made by the newly appointed Prime and her assistants, I left them to the continued recovery of order. Eight days worth of insistent messages provided an abundant amount of alternate options for my attention. However, my strength was flagging. I'd been off my feet for a week and my body, altered or not, wasn't up to its usual stamina.

Anastassia's concern over my health had been real, and I'd heard the monitors myself. No matter the degree of mess the Narvan might be in, I would need to continue avoiding stims, which meant I needed to rest periodically.

Content to let Artor sweat for a few more hours, I Jumped to the little apartment on Merchess. Anastassia wouldn't be there.

The mattress conjured up memories of what we'd enjoyed, but it hadn't been Stassia. Just curiosity. Data gathered, she'd returned to her old self, keeping me at a distance, making me work for every tiny step forward. All those steps were a distraction.

Anastassia had been right, I'd never been a good leader. Since the opportunity had presented itself now, it was time to make up for my previous mistakes.

Once I'd made sure the door was secure, I stretched out on the mattress and contacted Fa'yet, letting him know I'd be there in a few hours to rid him of his Arpex problem. He, in turn, filled me in on all of his other problems, in great detail, and with much frustration at my lack of response over the past week.

"Enough. We'll deal with it when I get there."

"You'd better, or you can find yourself a new Premier."

Screw the thought of sleep. I got up and Jumped to my office on Karin, stormed down the hall, bypassed Fa'yet's secretary, and entered his office without so much as a knock. The gun I aimed at his head must have adequately served its purpose, as his hands dropped from the terminal where he'd been working. He offered me his full attention.

"I would suggest never taking that tone with me again or you'll find your retirement cut short."

"Rough day?" he asked in his usual dry humor.

Had he been wearing armor, I would have shot him at close range to make my point, but he wasn't, and I didn't really want to kill him. He was one of the few reliable men I had left. Instead, I put the gun away, grabbed him from his chair, and held him up against the wall with the grey hand he was well acquainted with.

"I'm not fond of that tone either."

"Apologies."

I dropped him. "How many Arpex have you located?"

"None." He got to his feet and straightened his shirt and chain of office. "But we know they're here. There have been numerous reports of memory-related conflicts."

"So you've suffered their effects, but haven't located a single one?"

The muscles along his jaw twitched. "No."

"I expected more from you."

"I'm trying. This whole running a government thing is new to me, you know. I was more in the business of stealing information and credits."

"We all have our jobs to do. Try harder."

"If you don't mind me asking, what happened—"

"I mind. Assemble a team to assist in the removal of the Arpex. I'll be back in four hours. I expect them ready and waiting."

"Where do you want them?"

"I'll let you know."

"So you want me to assemble a team, somewhere, soon, with no clue where on this blessed moon you'd like them?"

"Is that a problem?" Maybe assigning him this duty wasn't a good idea. I wasn't used to this level of flippancy with the officials under my command. It was his nature, and I knew that, but I didn't want this uncertain and tense level of camaraderie, not when there was work to do, and not in our new business relationship.

He ran his hands over his face. "No."

When he looked up at me again, something on his face had changed. He was wide open, his mind too, concern clear as it had been when I'd found him on Veria Minor years before. "How's Ana?"

"Don't know, don't care." I clapped my hands. "Focus. Get a team together. If you want to impress me, locate an Arpex by the time I return."

He offered me a shaky smile. "I'll try."

I stepped into the void and returned to my mattress at the apartment. Not knowing what crisis might pop up next, I kept my coat and weapons on and closed my eyes.

The familiar landscape of the destroyed council complex surrounded me, flames licking at the debris, the creaking of the compromised structure accompanied the crunching of my footsteps over shattered clearplaz. I reached out to push a twisted metal bar from my path only to see that my missing hand had been replaced by a blue claw. The skin surrounding the grafted area was also blue, the tinge running up my arm like a spreading infection. I searched the floor and came up with a shard of glass.

I had to cut the claw off before the blue spread, before I became one of them. I drove the glass into my forearm. It shattered, not even making a mark. A glint caught my attention, sharp metal. I grabbed the makeshift knife and sawed at my arm. No matter how much pressure I applied, all I got were red lines, not even a drop of blood. A further search yielded a gun loaded with a single bullet.

I stared at the single round, contemplating where to apply it. Clearly, my arm was affected by Arpex chemistry. Bullets bounced off their shells. Shooting my arm would only waste the bullet. Using the metal shard, I worked my way up, scraping, seeking any sign of blood that might indicate how far the infection had truly spread. I made it along my shoulder and across my chest up to my neck before blood finally erupted from the cut. My celebration was cut short when I noticed the liquid spilling down my chest wasn't red, but green and thick. Arpex blood. Pumping through my veins.

Throwing the metal into the shadows, I stared at the gun in my hands. I could end this. There was no going back, not with their blood in me.

Something skittered in the shadows. Jumping to my feet, I glanced around, seeking the cause of the noise.

There, by my bare foot stood a tiny Arpex, no taller than my ankle. Without a second thought, I stomped, crushing it. Then there were hundreds more, pouring out of the rubble, swarming around me, hissing and clacking their tiny claws. I danced over them as Neko had the larvae, grinding them into the ground until the floor was slick with their crushed bodies and there were no more.

A peel of laughter escaped my mouth as I woke with a racing heart that for once didn't leave me feeling dizzy or weak. Instead, bursting with energy, I grabbed a meal bar from the cupboard, ate it in four bites, and Jumped to Karin. The fact that Fa'yet hadn't produced any Arpex wasn't a surprise as I'd only been out for a couple hours. That left me time to locate the Arpex on my own without having to explain my methods to anyone else.

I hailed a single-passenger high-speed air transport and programmed it to cruise the streets one by one. Inside, I sat back and opened the channel the Arpex had used before. I'd hear them if I got close.

The first one made itself known half an hour later, its hissing becoming demanding as I did a second pass to verify the location. I commanded the transit to land in the yard of what appeared to be a factory. The lights were on in the windows, and from the hum and rhythmic thumps, I gathered the machinery was running. Private transports sat in the lot. I went to the nearest door and walked inside. My boot landed in crumbles of a dried-up puddle of something yellow. As I looked around, there were more. Here and there lay piles of discarded clothing and bone fragments. The Arpex here had fed well.

The hissing was loudest above me. I made my way around the equipment to find a stairway that led up to a supervisor's office. Another puddle decorated the floor outside the door.

An Arpex crouched inside, its wings outspread and trembling.

"Don't eat me," I thought at it, using the few words I was starting to put together from the Arpex I'd known before and now seeing inside their minds.

The Arpex shuffled away. *"You speak?"*

I pulled out my pulse pistol. *"How many Arpex here?"*

It didn't answer.

Curious as to how a probe would work, I followed our connection and dove in.

The Arpex wailed in my head. *"Out, out, get out,"* it repeated, inserting a hiss after each word.

Most of what I encountered made no sense, the words and images too foreign. But it did work. We were not powerless against them. They were just different.

Deep in the midst of thoughts and memories was a green world, a land filled with towering trees that rivaled the size of the plexes on Jal.

"Tell me about your home," I said in the same demanding tone they had used with me.

"No. No telling. No taking."

"No?"

Its thoughts scattered, pulling in details of its world, the location, the climate, its population, its feeding and breeding cycles, all the information I could have wanted. It drew it all in close as if it could horde the information and protect it. I saw then how the branching theft happened, how the very suggestion of thinking about something began a chain reaction through memories like the most efficient researcher going above and beyond their duties. And though I did try to suck that information away from the Arpex, that didn't seem to be a benefit of my transformation.

Or maybe I was doing it wrong. I was a mere fledgling playing with my food, fumbling about. However, I did note everything I saw, copying the details to memory so I could share them with Jey and thereby the Jalvian forces that could take the damned Arpex world from them. It might not be their homeworld, but it was a start.

Satisfied that I had all I needed from this Arpex, I fired a heavy focused pulse, ripping its wings to shreds and cracking its shell. The Arpex fell over, hissing and squealing. Its volume slowly faded into silence.

I'd made it outside before a wave of dizziness hit me. Rampaging probes on people often gave me a headache, but this was different and made me physically ill. It was still worth it.

I Jumped back to my apartment for a half hour of rest before I had to meet with Fa'yet again. Lying there on the mattress, I went over what I'd seen in the Arpex's mind, trying to fit more of the memories together. In the end, I sent what I had to Jey so his people could begin planning to deal with this threat more efficiently than my one-on-one method. Screw the University. I didn't need them.

By the time I returned to Fa'yet's office, I had a full-on throbbing headache. I wouldn't be probing any other Arpex today.

"Perhaps you should sit down?" Fa'yet suggested seconds after I'd entered.

I stayed on my feet. I wasn't here as his guest or his friend, and I didn't need his concern.

"Send a team here." I flashed him the factory where I'd found the Arpex. You will need to compensate the families, return the transports, notify the owner or the estate of the owner of the current status of their business.

"You took it out alone?"

He was beyond concerned, and he made no effort to hide it from his voice or face. I had the distinct impression that he was contacting Anastassia as we spoke.

"If she appears in this office, you'll be on your own." Him, I could brush off. It would be far more difficult with her, and I couldn't afford that distraction.

"What happened between you two?"

"Nothing." And that was the damned truth.

"That's strange because I'm supposed to tell you that she's sorry. Which is equally as odd, if you ask me."

"If you want my help, you'll shut up and do your job."

His gaze dropped to my grey hand. He nodded, shoulders sagging. "We haven't located any others."

"I'll find them. Get your team to that factory to start clean up, and dispose of the Arpex. You'll know when I have another."

"How are you finding them so quickly? Tell me and I'll get people on it. I'm sure you have other issues to deal with."

Dammit, I hated staring down his openly worried face. Appointing him as Premier had been a terrible idea. We were too close, too much history.

"I can hear them."

"How?"

"You should ask Anastassia about that." I turned around and left before I lost my focus completely.

Finding another empty high-speed air transport took longer than I wanted, but one finally arrived to fulfill my order. I climbed inside, grateful for the cushioned seat and headrest. With the lights dimmed to their minimum setting, I again set out across Karin's populated zones. The transport worked one grid at a time, flying back and forth in long lines before moving to the next area. My eyes closed and focused on listening, I nearly nodded off. Then a hiss caught my attention.

Another pass over the same area allowed me to hone in on where the Arpex was hiding. I sent Fa'yet the location and moved on. Several grids later, my stomach demanded more than the bar I'd eaten earlier. I couldn't remember when I'd last had an actual meal. There were likely more Arpex lurking on Karin, but they would have to wait. I let Fa'yet know that I'd return later and landed the transport..

A step into the void brought me to Merchess where I purchased a quick meal and jumped back to my apartment to eat it and catch a little sleep. A few hours later, I woke in a cold Arpex-dream-induced sweat and returned to Karin for another round of searching. I spent the next two days there, locating what I hoped to be the last two Arpex in residence and sleeping in three-hour bursts. After conveying the location of the last one to Fa'yet's team, I returned to the mattress for another round of sleep.

After waking a second time in five hours with a gasp and pounding heart, I gave up on and considered finding a stim. There was a backup stash in the med kit. All I had to do was walk to the cupboard and get one.

The frantic beeping of the monitors at the University came back to me. Stassia's panicked face. Jey's too. I put my hand on my chest, feeling the beat slow to a normal rhythm. No stims. I just needed to rest. But sleeping didn't appear to be an option.

I got up and went out for a quick walk to find something other than a bar to eat. After devouring a heaping container of pasta and shellfish, I returned to the mattress and got as comfortable as I could while fully armed and armored, as I'd perpetually been for several days now. Sinking into my link, I checked up on the trade agreements I'd established outside the system and managed some of the fallout from my actions against the University on Artor.

Those tasks updated to a point I could move them farther down my list for a little while, I Jumped to Frique and made my way to the newly constructed military base. It was far from any village and economically comprised of three buildings and a large plascrete pad. I entered the humble longhouse the city council had designated as the base of operations for planetary defense. The Artorian pilots sprang from their seats. As per the Friquen demands, none of them were in uniform and the only thing that set them apart from the locals was the fact that they were eight fully Artorian men and women in very clean local clothing.

"Sorry, nothing exciting," I said. "I just need one of you to covertly transport me around Frique while I scan for Arpex."

One of them ran off to grab her gear. The others crowded around me. "How are you scanning for them? We could do it for you."

Eagerness, or perhaps extreme boredom, turned them toward begging to be sent out, to take this task from me. They pledged to complete it in record time with no civilian casualties and no damage to Friquen structures.

The pilot who'd volunteered to take me approached cautiously, eyeing the others as if they were going to explode if they didn't get to join in.

I'd had enough. "Well then, you'll need to undergo a very painful and nightmarish process."

Silence replaced their boasting.

"Still interested?"

One of them looked like he might still volunteer.

I shook my head. "Go back to whatever you were doing. I'm well aware of how bland this place is, but your presence here is important. You're the only immediate defense they have."

They nodded and backed away. I gestured the female pilot toward the door and followed beside her to one of the six ships waiting on the pad. We got in, and she went about getting the compact craft ready. I settled into the rear-facing seat directly behind her.

"You have a name?"

"Tamara," she said quietly. Then her words gained speed and volume as they tumbled out. "I'm sorry, I don't know how I should address you. They didn't tell us that. We didn't know you'd be coming. Yourself, I mean. They said we might meet you personally at some point, that you lived here, but I didn't expect...I've heard stories, but—"

"Advisor is fine. Take a breath for Geva's sake."

She let out a nervous squeak of laughter.

The engines powered up, a barely perceivable vibration passing through the ship. I'd requested the most silent, unobtrusive vessels with the most effective defense capabilities from Artor. The defense part remained to be seen, but I was pleased with the rest.

"Thank you," she said.

"For what?"

"Where are we going?" she asked, suddenly distracted with the controls.

"Standard search grid. Stay out of sight as much as possible, but move slowly. I need to listen for Arpex."

The ship rose into the air, the clearing falling away below us. Trees gave way to open fields while Tamara went about clicking and shifting various knobs, pads, and levers. A herd of prantha raised their heads as though they could sense us overhead.

"I attended the same academy you did. Your still frame is on display, Advisor Ta'set. You brought us the link implants. I know we're not supposed to know that it was you who saved us from Fragia, but there were rumors. And it's clear you've suffered a great deal to keep us safe."

"You have no idea."

She didn't. It was my brother's image my homeworld displayed with pride, not mine. Jey had been the one to make the treaty with Fragia. Geva only knew what other twisted rumors were floating around.

I cut off whatever her deep intake of breath was going to throw at me next. "I need silence, if you don't mind."

"Of course, I'm sorry."

As we passed over villages and towns, I kept the place in my mind open where the Arpex spoke, listening. I also brushed over my natural connections with Ikeri and Daniel, making sure they were all right. I did the same with Anastassia, and finding her awake and well, relayed a list of tasks on Artor and Syless that she and Neko could manage for me. Not wanting to break concentration enough to carry on a conversation, I made sure to leave as quickly as I'd come.

The crinkle of a wrapper in my pocket as I shifted in my seat reminded me to eat. With my Arpex connection still open, I pulled a bar out and ate on autopilot. Working my way through some of Fa'yet's less involved requests took another couple hours.

Tamara's voice cut into my work. "We're going to need to recharge."

"All right."

She turned us around and we shot back toward the primitive base. I noticed the pattern she'd used put us back near this same path each time we switched to a new block. Whether she'd been waiting for me to call off our uneventful search or had been prepared to return to the base if a situation arose, I didn't know.

"How long do you need?" I asked.

"Me or the ship? If you need to continue, one of the others can take you as soon as we land."

"You." She knew how to keep quiet and let me work, and I had no complaints about her performance. Her gratitude, however misguided, was also appreciated. The downfall of operating behind the scenes was that hearing any thanks directed at me was a rare occurrence. Alone as I was, that brought me a slight amount of warmth with no obligations attached.

"Four to six hours if you'd like me alert."

"I expect you powered up and waiting in five."

We dropped into the clearing surrounding the base where she executed an effortless landing. She flipped the release latch on the door.

"You're welcome to stay here if you're planning to sleep. We'd be honored to have you." She stepped out onto the freshly cured plas-crete pad. "There's even a hot meal if you're interested. They might scorn us outwardly, but the Friquen people do make sure we're well-fed."

While a real meal did sound good, the thought of being surround-ed by seven others, who were even more eager for my attention than Tamara, turned my answer into a definite, "Thank you, but no. I have other matters to attend to in the meantime."

She appeared disappointed but accepted my answer with a nod. The others were waiting just outside the longhouse, doing their best to appear to be busy sorting gear.

One of them called out, "We saved you a steak, Mara."

Tamara turned back to me, raising her eyebrows. I shook my head.

"Five hours then," she said and then took off at a jog to join the others.

I Jumped back to the apartment on Merchess. The silence there rushed over me, pulling me down to sit on the edge of the mattress. The thought of a steak made my mouth water. I half-heartedly considered going back, then pondered getting up and finding a meal on Merchess. Both required too much effort. After taking a couple of bites of one of the bars I had left in my pocket, I let myself fall back and closed my eyes.

Utter exhaustion did me the favor of offering dreamless sleep. With only a couple minutes to spare, I returned to Frique to find Tamara waiting just outside her ship.

"Where to next, boss?"

"Don't call me that."

She stiffened, her gaze dropping to the ground. "I'm sorry. I didn't mean to offend you, Advisor. Could you settle a bet for us? Do you have a rank?"

"Ranks haven't applied to me for a long time." I didn't make a habit of explaining my place in the hierarchy of either military or government because I wasn't public knowledge. Those who needed to know me, did.

Seeing that I didn't intend on further conversation, Tamara offered a stiff nod. She opened the door and let me enter first. We flew for another couple hours before I located an Arpex.

We landed, and I entered the thick forest where the Arpex had hidden itself. The only casualties of my pulse pistol were the blue bastard and half a dozen trees.

We neared the end of another long search run before I found the second one. At first, I intended to pulse it and move on, but I needed more information. That required getting into its head. Tamara likely needed a full night's sleep in order to continue anyway. That would give me time to recover from what I was about to do.

"Stay on board. I might be a little longer than last time."

Tamara nodded, but when she watched me leave, I had a familiar feeling. "If you plan on following me, I will stun you now and save us both a lot of aggravation. You will not leave this ship. Do you understand?"

She nodded again, this time uncertain and serious. I closed the door behind me and approached the small farm.

The stench of dead livestock made my stomach churn. The remains of one of the original occupants lay near the house on the ground. Holes littered the decomposing body, making it impossible to determine the sex or age beyond being the size of an adult. This Arpex had created a nest. I shivered, gritting my teeth against the memories, both recent and whispers of the past.

My mind raced, wondering how many larvae had survived. Where were they now and what form were they in? I would need to look around and gather samples.

Fucking University. They could get their own damn samples and they could do a whole lot of nothing with them until I allowed their doors to reopen.

I took a moment to verify that the power and funds were still cut. The ongoing torrent of messages, some spewing curses, and others begging for forgiveness confirmed that things remained at a standstill. I'd need to deal with that soon. The Premier wasn't pleased about the shutdown either.

Breathing through my nose, I pushed the unlocked door open to discover that the inside of the house didn't smell any better. The lights were all off, but enough sunlight filtered in through the windows to allow me to make out two dried puddles on the bare kitchen floor. They had once been people.

The Arpex's low hiss remained constant in my head. Uncertain of what I might find, I made my way through the house with a pulse pistol in hand but found nothing beyond rotting food and another dried puddle by the back door.

I made my way to one of the two outbuildings. A fairly fresh prantha carcass lay just inside. Live ones hung back, thin and calling loudly upon seeing me. The whites of their eyes were exposed and they stamped their hooves. I had no wish to encounter the long sharp spiraling horns protruding from their heads so I stayed where I was, peering into the shadows, looking for any sign of Arpex. The prantha seemed far more perturbed by my presence than anything else.

The dead prantha moved. Its hide quivering and then bulging. I stepped back to the doorway as a boot-sized blue creature crawled out of the prantha's mouth. It was a giant version of the larvae, but with the front claws of the Arpex. It opened its round mouth lined with needle-like teeth and hissed—both out loud and in my head.

Paralyzed for a second by the thought of that being the thing that had grown in me and wondering how many more were tunneling through the carcass, I didn't catch the adult Arpex coming up behind me until one of its claws latched onto the back of my coat. It yanked me backward against its body, its wings snapping up and out.

"Don't," I thought at it. "Poison."

It drove words into my head as though it was just as unfamiliar speaking to my kind as I was to it. "Lies."

"I was a nest."

"Nests die."

Its wings snapped shut, sealing me in its acidic ooze. It took longer than before, but the tingle of the acid burn slowly blossomed on my exposed skin. Held so tight that my arms were pinned against my sides, I couldn't get my pulse pistol up. While firing it at the Arpex's feet might make it let go, I'd also lose my own feet. That wasn't a step I was ready to take yet.

Something sharp nicked my back. I realized it was using its claws to clip through my armor. Ooze ran down my coat and splashed onto my boots. If I didn't get out of here soon, it would start eating away my armor and then we'd both find out if my poison status only pertained to memory snacking or also my flesh. I preferred my flesh whole and uneaten.

I reached out through our connection and dove into a probe like I had with the other one. This one's thoughts were rougher and harder to decipher.

"Where do you get your ships?"

"Ships," it repeated to itself as if tasting the word, finding meaning for it.

I could feel it reaching out to my mind, invading, seeking answers. In the interest of possibly making this inquiry work as it had with finding the Arpex's green world, I let it roam my head for a moment.

Then suddenly, the meaning must have clicked. The Arpex's thoughts raced by in a blur that I had a hard time following. A grey world surrounded by a barricade of ship-building stations and ports in orbit. A massive host of ships of different sizes and models were docked there in various states of completion. I recognized the small ships that had invaded the Narvan. There were flashes of a strange looking race of people, short and thick with blue-tinted flesh or maybe very fine scales. The same world but seemingly long ago, spotted with blue and green and only two ports in orbit. Different ships in the docks. All of that was peppered with snippets of meetings with the same race of people, the taking of memories, eating of blue flesh, puddles of dark fluid on the floor.

"You took this world. You enslaved its people?"

It didn't seem to understand my question, again seeking meaning in my mind.

The effort of digging my way through the strangeness of the Arpex's mind drained me fast. I couldn't keep this up much longer.

"Arpex world," it said.

It was now, at least. If we could find this place, we might be able to hobble the Arpex. If it didn't have forty other similar worlds somewhere.

A tingle on my back distracted me from my attempts to learn more. The acid had worked its way into the holes the Arpex had carved into the back of my coat. Time to be done.

As I had with the Arpex on Syless, I screamed in its head. The wings surrounding me retracted, letting in a rush of fresh air. Wasting no time to appreciate the easier breathing conditions, I pulsed the damned thing.

I coughed as I wiped away the thick layer of slime from my hair and face and then both hands. Shrugging my way out of my coat was more challenging, but it was too covered in slime to be useful. Without its weight, I was too light, like someone had turned down the gravity.

Or maybe that was because I was lightheaded, I considered as I found myself on my ass in the dirt staring up at the fading light overhead. The thought of calling someone in to take me to the tank crossed my mind. But that would require significant downtime, and I didn't know what the tank would do with the alterations that had been set in motion. Standard gel would take care of the burns in a few hours, and I could bandage up the few cuts on my back.

I was out of energy and exhausted with being so damn exhausted. If there weren't still young Arpex running around and Tamara wasn't waiting on me, I would have Jumped to my mattress and hibernated there indefinitely—assuming nothing haunted my sleep, which was highly unlikely.

However, there *was* work to do and people were waiting on me. There always was and would be.

Working my way up to my hands and knees, I observed a young Arpex approaching me, half-slithering, half-pulling itself along with its claws. Was the livestock dead before these things hatched or had they died because of them? This was going to be a significant cleanup job, and I knew just the eager people to do it.

I managed to get my second pulse pistol free and set to low in case I needed it again. After I'd turned the blue nightmare into sludge, I staggered my way back inside the barn to give the dead prantha a few kicks. Three more young Arpex made their way out of the beast to meet their end. Considering how many had littered the floor when Neko had stomped them all flat, there were a whole lot more of these things lurking about.

They could lurk for a little while longer.

I stumbled my way back to the ship to find Tamara waiting with the door open. She ran out to meet me.

"Good Geva, where can I take you? Let me take that." She held her hand out for my coat.

"Don't touch it or you'll look like me." Though my skin was merely red and irritated thanks to the alterations, Tamara would suffer far worse.

She put her hand down, yet still reached out as if to help me inside even though I was covered in the same shit. I managed to evade her touch.

"You got a med kit with gel at the base?"

She nodded.

"How about an open bed?"

"Of course." Tamara handed me the straps and then sat in her seat. "We're over an hour out. I'll let you know when we arrive."

I had to look pretty rough if she figured I'd be out for the return trip. And she was right. I barely remembered taking off and then suddenly Tamara was telling me that we were back. By the worried look on her face, she'd probably told me that several times before I'd heard her.

"I'll be fine. I just need a shower."

Tamara looked me over. "And gel, and a meal, and a bed."

"In that order, yes."

"We're already on it. If you don't mind Friquen-wear, there's even a change of clothes waiting for you."

"Thank you."

Two of the male pilots were waiting outside the ship as we exited. I waved them away. I wasn't that bad off, dammit.

"The bathroom is all the way to the back, through the bunkroom," Tamara said as we went inside.

The others were waiting in the common room where I'd first met them. No one rushed at me with questions or promises this time. The two men came in behind me, the door closing hard and loud. One of the men seated on the far end of the room jumped up and ran over to open the bunkroom door for me. Like I couldn't have done that myself.

The bunkroom was empty except for Tamara, who nodded to the single bed that had been pushed away from the others to sit against the wall. A folded pile of clothes sat on top of the blanket.

"Sorry, we don't have anything more. I'm sure you're used to much better."

"It's a bed. That's all I asked for."

She offered me a nervous smile and then left the room.

The bathroom was what I expected for something built hurriedly by Friquens for a force they had demanded but didn't really want. Like the rest of the building they'd constructed, it served its purpose and nothing more.

A glance in the mirror revealed my face and neck matched my hands. The slime had plastered my hair to my scalp. Someone had left a tube of healing gel, a towel, and everything I might possibly need for a shower on the counter. I opened the door that led to three shower stalls and picked one. Keeping my hands and face out of the water as much as possible other than a quick painful rinse, I managed to get the worst of the mess down the drain. I'd barely gotten the towel around my waist before someone came in.

It was the man who had opened the door for me. His eyes went wide and his gaze dropped to the floor. "Excuse me, sir. I'm Allund. Tamara mentioned you'd left blood on the seat. Might I have a look at your injuries?"

"I can get it."

"With your hands like that?"

I glanced at my offending hands. I needed to wear gloves when dealing with Arpex. And a full face shield. Or just to never see another blue bastard. I asked Geva for that one small favor, knowing it was useless. I was the only one who could reliably locate them thanks to the fucking University.

"I could leave if you'd rather," he said quickly.

It seemed that I was too tired to keep what was in my head off my face. "It's nothing, but look if you want to." I turned around.

"Not intending to be disagreeable, sir, but that does definitely look like something."

Looking over my shoulder in the mirror, I could see his cause for alarm even though I didn't feel it. The Arpex's razor claws had managed to slice through my hardened skin, driving fibers from my armor deep into the multitude of narrow gashes. The fiery red burns didn't improve the view. At least it had stopped bleeding.

"Just clean it and put some gel on it."

"At least let me get you an injection for the pain and to prevent an infection."

"Do I have to repeat myself?"

Allund rifled through the bag on the counter that he must have brought in with him. When he found what he needed, he poked at my back. I wasn't sure whether to be alarmed or thankful that I really couldn't feel much of what he was doing. The sensitivity of my altered skin was much lower than before.

"Have you all had medical training?"

"Just me and Henson. There was some new rule a couple years ago that says any off-world team has to have their own medics."

"I'd forgotten about that stipulation. Be thankful I suggested it. You don't want to see what the locals call medicine."

His fingers faltered. Whatever he'd been using to remove the fibers clanged onto the tiled floor. He mumbled an apology and went on another search in his bag.

"Are you about done with that? I need to get something to eat and grab a few hours of sleep before getting back out there. I also have an assignment for all of you."

"Almost, yes." He resumed plucking out the fibers and then slathered on a layer of gel. "You'll need to let that dry before you get dressed."

"I'm very familiar with how gel works."

"I can see that." He cleared his throat. "Would you prefer to do your hands and face before or after you eat?"

"After." Gel flakes in my food did not appeal to me. Like the cuts, the burns didn't hurt as much as before either. My altered skin did have its benefits.

"I'll help you with the shirt. You should keep your arms down until the gel has done its work."

"I can dress myself."

"Of course." He ducked away, grabbed his bag, and hurried out of the bathroom.

I followed on his heels. We were alone in the bunkroom. "Allund."

He spun around, bag held tight to his chest.

"I'm not a very good patient. Thank you."

His grip on the bag loosened, and he cracked a tenuous smile. "I'll let them know you're ready to eat."

"Please tell me one of you does the cooking."

"We take turns."

"Thank Geva. I'm in no mood for local shit right now."

Allund backed away and let himself out. I wondered if he was going to tell the others to run for it. It had been so long since I'd been in the casual company of regular people who didn't know me, not since our years living on Minor, and even then, other than my family, I pretty much only spoke to my employees. I didn't have to be in charge here, not to the degree I was used to anyway, but even knowing that, I couldn't quite grasp how to proceed.

Getting dressed seemed like a good start. I imagined some of them would like to be sleeping now and out of courtesy, they were avoiding the bunkroom while I was in it. As soon as the gel was no longer tacky, I worked myself into the shirt, careful not to raise my arms over my head too much, mostly because I didn't want Allund to have to come back in. The rest went on quickly.

I made my way out into the chaos that was eight people sitting around a table with one open chair. They were doing their best not to act like they hadn't just been silently talking about me. They probably still were.

Without any options, I took the open seat between Tamara and Allund. They formed a neat barrier for the others who hadn't already been directly subjected to me. "So what's for dinner?"

"Prantha," they all said in unison. Then one of them got up and went into an adjoining room.

Tamara snickered. "It's almost always prantha. The locals seem to think that's all we want to eat."

"That's because prantha is their largest export to Artor and Karin. They don't taste the same when we grow them at home."

"So this is your fault." Tamara nodded to the thick steak and pile of steaming root vegetables that were slid in front of both of us.

"Maybe, but I'm not complaining. Get me a list of what alternatives you want, and I'll make sure you get it."

"Too much of a good thing," she said, spearing one of the small orange orbs. "Thanks."

One of them produced a datapad and the others offered suggestions while we ate. I had to remind them several times that Frique didn't import food from Artor and then offered alternatives that were produced on world. Once their discussion had wound down, I held out my hand for the tablet.

Allund took it and set it on the table in front of me instead. I scanned over the list, replacing a few more items and adding a couple others, and then submitted it to the Friquen council as my personal request for the base.

"Done."

"Really, just like that?" asked Allund.

I nodded. "Now, if you don't mind. I need to sleep, and I'm sure some of you do too." I made sure to include Tamara in my glance around the table.

"Five again?"

"Six. Give the gel time to work."

Allund followed us into the bunkroom and applied gel to my face, hands, and neck before leaving me, Tamara, and two others in the dark.

Sleep did not come easy. It had been a long time since I'd slept in a room with anyone other than my family, or Jey and Merkief. Or Arin, but I tried hard not to think about him. He'd been quiet of late and I wanted to keep it that way.

I didn't know these people. Could I trust them? Wavering between Jumping to the safety of my mattress and wanting to prove to myself that I wasn't a paranoid recluse, I wasted almost a full hour that I should have been sleeping. As a last resort, I opened my connection with Anastassia. She was awake and busy working with Neko. I didn't say anything and neither did she. I just held the familiar connection open, being with her until sleep finally took over.

I woke before the others, thankful that my usual gasp and cold sweat routine hadn't awakened anyone else. I held my hand up in the half-light, happy to see the gel had cleared most of the irritation.

After quietly getting dressed in my own clothes that someone had removed, cleaned, and returned while I'd slept, I got back in the bed. I enjoyed not having a coat and weapons between me and the mattress for a little while. Unwilling to subject myself to more socializing, I utilized my link to touch base with Jey, add to Anastassia's task list, and check up on the recovery efforts on Syless.

Tamara's voice intruded on my work, "Advisor Ta'set."

I opened my eyes to find her dressed and ready, standing a few feet away. "I'll be out in a moment."

She nodded and left. The others were still sleeping. With a sigh, I wrapped up what I was doing and armed myself. I checked both pulse pistols, verifying they'd had time to recharge. That reminded me that I would need to clean off my coat before we could head out. Damned Arpex.

I found Tamara and the others in the common room. My coat lay on the table, free of residue.

"Thought you might need that," said one of the pilots. One of his hands was red and raw under a layer of gel. "Should have worn gloves from the start, I guess."

"You and me both. Thanks."

He gave me a nod and a smile.

I explained about the young Arpex and how they needed to be exterminated. Tamara provided the coordinates. The pilots accepted the task with the same vigor they'd exhibited upon my initial arrival. Three of them dashed off to prepare for the mission while the others stayed behind to inform the rest when they woke.

It took another four days and two more dead Arpex to assure me that Frique was clear. The other Arpex had also begun nesting and their sites required extermination. The Artorian pilots were eager to take up the additional tasks.

Much to everyone's delight and surprise, the first batch of new supplies arrived as I was preparing to take my leave. I said my fare-wells to the pilots and noticed Tamara hanging back from the rest.

She smiled wearily. My schedule had taken a toll on the woman. Her face lacked the youthful luster I'd first seen, her eyes were sunken. She asked, "May I speak with you outside a moment?"

I led her out in the humid evening air. The fading sun lit the horizon with a dusky orange, the blue-grey of impending darkness taking hold overhead.

"You don't get out much, with others, like us, do you?"

I cringed a little. "That obvious?"

She shrugged. "You should come back. When you have time, I mean. If you do. I'm sure you're busy. I know you are. But, I think it would be good for you, to be around other people." Her hands constantly clasped and unclasped as she spoke.

"We won't expect anything, I promise. The guys like having you here. It gives us something to talk about. Gets boring as all hells here, you know?"

I shook my head at her babbling. "I do know, and I would like that."

Those words surprised me, spilling out as they did. It was true. They'd been grateful for the food supply change and even after seeing how quickly and easily their request had been granted, hadn't asked for a single favor, not even hinted at one. None of them. I wasn't one of them by any means, but their easygoing camaraderie reminded me of the days when I would relax with friends from school. It was refreshing to be among my people in a place where no one demanded anything of me. They didn't make me feel guilty for not being there, or not talking to them, or anything else for that matter.

"Would you, if you'd like, not that you need to, but if you do want us for anything, establish a connection?"

"Breathe."

She blushed. "Sorry, I'm not usually like this. You make me nervous."

"It's what I do." I opened a natural connection with her, just enough to allow a contact should the need arise.

Her eyes widened. "Oh. You're his brother. Why isn't there a still frame of you on display at the academy?"

"Should there be?"

Tamara smiled. "Yes, at least, I think so."

"You have no idea who I am."

"I've heard rumors. A *lot* of rumors." She gazed up at the first stars overhead. "Do you have a mate to go home to?"

"That's complicated and none of your business."

"But true."

Her disappointment caught me off guard. I couldn't recall the last time anyone had expressed that sort of interest. With Anastassia at my side, it just didn't happen. She made people nervous too, and with the bond, the sexual attention of others didn't appeal to me.

But now the bond was gone.

I opened my mind to her a fraction more, enough to get a good feel for who she was. Beyond being a good pilot and respected by the people she worked with, she'd been kind and had done every-thing I'd asked of her with only a preconceived notion of who I was. Several years younger, she was unjaded, eager, and even attractive, I supposed, now that I looked closer. Nothing in her mind jumped out at me as anything but genuine interest.

And yet, I had none.

Either the infusion of Arpex had really screwed me over, or some level of the bond was still intact. I'd have to take some time with Anastassia to find out.

Eventually. When I had time and inclination to speak to Anastas-sia again. I had neither at the moment.

"Thank you, Tamara."

She rested her hand lightly on mine. "I mean it, come back anytime. Even if I'm not what you need here."

I looked down at her hand on mine. While she mistook that as a sign that she'd done something wrong and quickly pulled away, I was more baffled by the fact that I could barely feel her there. If this level of loss of sensation continued, I didn't want to consider the implica-tions. Yet, that's all I could do. My mind spinning, I stepped into the void and returned to the apartment on Merchess.

THIRTEEN

There had to be a way to stop the progression of the mutation. And fast, before I lost all sensation. Before I couldn't
feel anything even if I wanted to.

I paced the length of the apartment for half an hour,
debating who at the University I needed and who I didn't,
who should be punished further, and how. Yet, I kept
coming back to the realization that I had no idea what was
happening to me or who could stop it, or even if it could be stopped
or reversed. I'd need them all until I had answers.

Resuming my place on the mattress, back in weapons and my
damaged coat, I got busy through my link. Reopening the University
took much longer than my steel-fisted closing of it. There were so
many people to notify, employees, officials, and trade partners. The
only person who sent his gratitude for all my exhausting hours of
effort was the Premier.

While the masses filtered back to work, I spent some time
contemplating what I'd learned about the Arpex shipbuilding world
and what I could do about it. Other than the knowledge that it existed,
I had nothing to give Jey that would allow him to send ships there
to destroy it. If I could ask another Arpex the right question I might
be able to glean enough details to create a jump point, but there was
only so much I could do on my own against a heavily guarded world.
Not to mention all the ports and shipbuilding stations surrounding it.
I needed coordinates.

I left it at informing Jey of the planet's existence in the hopes I'd
have more to go on later. Then I headed to Artor to hunt for Arpex
to steal those coordinates from. With so much area to cover, dense
population, and heavy traffic, the challenge was far more daunting
than the worlds I'd worked on so far. The day passed in a blur of

listening for the hiss that made my skin crawl. I also worked through my link as my transport wove its way across the skies of Artor. Half the night had also passed and I still had nothing to show for my effort. Before frustration drove me to do something stupid, I decided it would be wise to get some sleep.

I landed the transport and stood there on the street side, listening to my stomach loudly protesting the meals I'd missed. Hunger was there, but it wasn't the same. Food still tasted good on the scant occasions I'd taken the time to indulge in an actual meal, but again, the enjoyment of that simple experience wasn't the same. Was it the single-minded focus from my lack of a bond or was this a byproduct of the Arpex mutation? Like hells was I going to use memories and people for sustenance.

Before heading to my mattress on Merchess, I stopped at the nearest food vendor and methodically shoved a meal into my mouth while keeping an eye on everyone around me from the shadows. As I chewed, the urge to get answers overrode my need for sleep. I Jumped to the University.

Seeking out the woman who had attended to me earlier took some time, but I eventually hunted her down. The fact that she visibly cringed upon seeing me was rather gratifying.

Nan Ne'vet stepped outside the lab where she'd been working with a team of others and pressed her back against the wall. "Well?"

"I'm not killing you today, so relax."

"What do you need from me first?" She leaned her head against the wall, rolling her shoulders while letting out a deep exhale.

"We'll start with three things. Arpex eat people and I barely eat anymore. I'm not going to start craving people, am I?"

Nan chuckled. "Your chemistry may be changing, but I don't think you have to worry about the transformation going that far. Your body isn't set up that way." Her analytical gaze flicked over me. "Unless you've noticed any intense pains that might indicate your organs are altering?"

"No, but let's not chance things going that far. You need to halt or reverse what you did to me."

"And the last thing?"

"I want you to perform this alteration on a few of others."

"So you want me to take the Arpex out of you, and repeat the procedure on other people."

I brushed one hand over the other, noticing the grey hand was affected every bit as much as my natural one. The skin atop my hand now had the feel of the heaviest of calluses. My palms were like my damn coat.

"Not take it out, halt it or scale it back if possible."

Nan's lips drew into a smirk. "So, there are benefits."

"If you think I'm going to thank you, you're wrong."

"But you're not complaining either."

"I'd call putting the entire University on lockdown a fucking huge complaint."

"Oh, that was you? Not a budget freeze or a security measure?"

I grabbed her by the rounded shoulders and held her up against the wall. Her feet dangled in the air.

"I froze your damn funding. Taking the liberty to fuse me with a fucking Arpex was a huge violation of the trust I had in all of you. Any security at stake was your own. You're fortunate I took some time to cool off first."

Rather than being satisfactorily cowed, Nan poked at one of my hands while still dangling in the air. "It's like your skin is hardening."

"Yes, I've noticed. It needs to stop doing that."

"How about communication? Are you able to understand them?"

"You do realize your situation here, correct?"

"That you haven't killed me yet because you need me? Yes." She gave me a forced smile. "Mind letting me down? We're wasting time."

"If I sprout wings and turn blue, I'm leveling this entire lab with you in it."

"Well then, we better get to work on halting the progress."

"Seriously? That's a possibility?" I let her drop, but caught her at the last second before she fell at some awkward angle that might impede her from doing what I needed.

"I won't know until I can run some tests. Why don't you come inside?" She held the door open to the lab where she'd been working. It was similar to the one where Sa'cota had taken me.

"I'd rather not."

She raised an eyebrow and shrugged. "Then I can't help you."

"I don't like you," I said as I brushed past her.

"You've made that quite clear." Nan pointed to a stool next to one of the empty square tables. "Have a seat."

While she busied herself with gathering what she needed for her examination, I contacted Anastassia.

"I'm at the University again. If you don't hear from me in a while,

I'd appreciate another extraction."

Her sharp tone pierced my head. *"You didn't appreciate my last extraction."*

"I did. The intent of it anyway."

She fell silent. Perhaps I'd caught her in the middle of something or she was just that pissed over my absence. It was disconcerting to have a conversation, purely with natural speech without the enhancement of our bonded connection to fill in the blanks.

"Anastassia." I sensed that I still had her attention but she remained mute. *"What they did, what you authorized, I'm—"*

"Furious. Yeah, I got that from your rampaging actions against the University."

"Then you understand why it's better for us if I'm not around you until I get this situation under control."

If I did lash out at her, which was quite possible in my exhausted and unbonded state, it would only further damage our working relationship. Whether we were together or not, I needed her help keeping the Narvan under control. She was also the mother of my children. We needed to maintain some level of civility.

"So your plan is to avoid me indefinitely." Her annoyance was impossible to miss.

"Can we not do this right now? I don't know what exactly is going on with this mutation."

"You said you could hear them. Is there more?" she asked.

"Yes. I'll let you know if I need you."

"What room are you in?"

I flashed her my location and then cut contact. Enough with distractions. Nan had already begun her poking and was now attempting to jab me with extraction devices.

"You know," Nan said absently as she ran her hands over my neck and up my throat. "I was on Director Sa'cota's team, though thankfully, not involved that day."

That explained her lack of reserve in making me part Arpex. My neck and shoulders tensed while I watched for any sign she was about to nail me with an injector like Sa'cota had.

Nan set one device down and picked up another with a much thicker needle. My teeth ground together. I debated calling Neko in before anxiety sent my heart off-kilter again.

"Please take off your armor."

I stared her down as I stood and removed my coat.

"All of that too." She waved her hand at my arsenal.

"I don't think so."

Anastassia stepped out of the void with Neko beside her. "Go ahead. I've got this."

Though I was relieved to see Neko, the same could not be said for Anastassia.

"What part of not being around me did you not understand?"

She glared at Nan, her hand hovering over the slit in her coat. "You didn't say this would change him."

"You didn't ask." Nan again gestured dismissively at the weapons I wore. "You said save him, and I did."

As I disarmed, my gaze locked onto Anastassia's. She broke away first.

"Can you reverse it? Make him like he was?" she asked.

Nan chuckled. "He doesn't want that. Do you, Advisor Ta'set?"

"Not exactly." I despised her even more for making me admit it in front of them.

While enduring the stares of Neko and Anastassia, I removed my shirt and sat back on the stool. Nan poked up and down my arm, first one and then the other.

"Quite remarkable. Another few days and you won't need that armor anymore."

"I'll stick with the armor, thanks."

She must have finally located the spot she'd been searching for because she jabbed the thick needle into a vein. My blood surged into the attached vial. When that was filled, she inserted another and then a third. At least my blood wasn't green.

"You assigned us the task of finding the Arpex's weaknesses. To find a way to defend against them, to defeat them. Each direction we tried didn't yield any significant results. Director Sa'cota was convinced we were going about this all wrong. That it wasn't the Arpex we needed to deconstruct, but our own kind that we needed to reconstruct."

She removed the needle and handed me an adhesive bandage. "You asked for a weapon to use against the Arpex. I created one. You."

"What is she talking about?" Anastassia demanded.

Nan labeled the vials and set them aside with care. "Given the uncertainty of the results, I would have preferred to use standard soldiers for testing, but when the opportunity arose..." She shrugged.

A tiny voice in the back of my swirling thoughts told me I should be livid that she'd just shrugged off my current state, but with Anastassia's smothering concern and Neko still locked in a disconcerted stare, I couldn't muster the effort.

"We will need to monitor the healing rate." Nan pointed to my arm. "Arpex shell is tough to fracture, but since all our subjects have been dead or nearly so, we have no information on their healing process."

"As long as you're not suggesting any larger injuries to monitor," I said.

Nan shook her head and picked up a scanner. "If you could stand?"

While I got to my feet, she called over an assistant and rattled off instructions for testing my blood. If Anastassia understood the implications of those requests, she gave no indication. They meant little to me.

Nan ran the scanner from head to foot both in front and behind, pausing to make notes on her datapad as she worked. Once she finished she nodded toward Anastassia.

"We will need to assess your levels of sensitivity. Would you rather she touched you than me?"

I didn't really want the results of that test revealed in front of an audience, but maybe this was the safest place to find out. Nan's touch was clinical. I didn't want to feel her. Any results would be more accurate with a touch I did possibly want. At some point. Maybe. It was a relief to not crave her touch but equally disconcerting how little I was driven to want it, or anyone else's for that matter.

"Yes, her."

Nan beckoned Anastassia over to stand behind me. "I'm sure your guard can handle the unnecessary brooding glares on his own."

Neko's scowl darkened. *"Boss?"*

"I need her. Let it go."

"You do have natural speech?" Nan asked Anastassia. "Testing will be more effective if he doesn't hear my direction to you."

The two of them were quiet while I imagined Anastassia made it forcefully clear that she did utilize natural speech. I waited impatiently for the warmth of Anastassia's hand to assure me that if we ever got the Narvan back in order, I might enjoy a physical relationship with someone. Or her. If we were talking by then. But I didn't need a further level of distraction beyond burning off some steam with someone I knew and generally trusted. That was all.

If she ever fucking touched me. What the hells were they doing back there? I started to turn around.

"Please face forward," said Nan. "You need to indicate when you feel something."

I waited, listening to Anastassia's coat rustle, thinking that meant she was moving her arm, that she was getting ready to follow Nan's orders. Being hesitant to touch me wasn't a surprise, given how things had been between us lately. A glance at Neko revealed nothing of what was going on behind me.

A distant rasping sensation worked its way from my neck down to the middle of my back. I couldn't see either of them so I had no idea what they were trying to accomplish or what they were touching me with.

"That's something." I started to turn to see what Anastassia was doing, but Nan caught my head and held it facing forward.

"What do you mean? Describe it, please."

"Pressure by something mildly abrasive?"

"Don't be an ass. We're trying to help you," Anastassia snapped.

"I wasn't."

Nan's voice rose, her apathetic tone slipping. "From the level of pressure, can you estimate how many fingers she is using?"

"I couldn't even tell they were fingers, and it's more of a sensation than any pressure. I'm going to go with two since you indicated more than one."

"That was my entire hand, and not pushing lightly either, dammit. What the hell did you do to him?" Anastassia asked.

Nan's fingernails ticked atop the datapad. "This level of loss of sensation was unanticipated."

As though she were quite uncertain of my reaction, Anastassia said, "She wants me to hit you."

"Go ahead." It couldn't hurt more than the confirmation of my fears.

Like a feeble blow that I'd had ample time to brace against, the thud of her fist meeting my back had little effect.

"Anything?" Anastassia asked.

"It sounded like you meant it."

Warmth seeped into my shoulders where I could see Anastassia's hands resting, but I couldn't feel them beyond the heat.

"So no pain then?" asked Nan.

"No. But temperature seems to still work."

"You can feel her now?"

"Only the body heat."

"Arpex do seem particular about temperature. The ability to sense it would be important." She came around to stand before me. "I'd like to do a study of your brain and the changes going on there as well."

"Which would entail what?" Anastassia asked before I could.

"A more in-depth scan and some exercises so that we can map how reactions and information are being processed. Nothing invasive."

"Can you help him?"

A scowl settled on Nan's face. "I won't know until I get all the results together and have time to sit down with them. Your threats aren't going to make my work go any faster."

In the interest of getting answers, I allowed Nan and her assistants to run the tests with Anastassia at my side and Neko hovering close by. As irritated as I still was with Anastassia, I was glad she was there, glowering at the staff every bit as much as Neko. She might not remember the details of who we were to one another, but it was obvious that she did care about my wellbeing regardless of that fact.

When the testing concluded, Nan dismissed me as though I were any other subject and left with her assistants. Neko stepped out of the room to give us a moment of privacy. I almost called him back in. Or Jumped back to the apartment. Anything would have been preferable to the strained silence that stretched out between Anastassia and me.

"Where have you been staying?" she finally asked.

"Wherever I happen to be."

"You could come home."

"Wouldn't matter if I did. All I do is sleep and leave."

The green eyes I knew too well stared me down. "So do I."

"There's a lot to do. I can shift some items off your list if there's too much."

"I didn't say that." She stepped closer. "I understand your divide and conquer more method, but you don't have to avoid me."

I fought the urge to step back. She was going to touch me. I could see it in the way her muscles shifted, in the softening of her face. It was one thing to have her play along with Nan's research, but this was different, and in front of me, where I could see what she was doing yet barely feel it.

"I'm not avoiding you."

Anastassia smirked, her hand snaking up around my neck. "You're a terrible liar."

"Not the first time I've heard that from you."

"I'm sure it isn't." Her lips hovered a breath away from mine.

"You know I won't feel that. Not at any enjoyable level, at least."

"That does pose a problem." She pressed her body against mine. "Good thing we have alternatives." Anastassia's mind opened, expanding our connection until her suggestion to feel for both of us was plain.

"Here?"

She shrugged. "Does it matter which door Neko is on the other side of?"

Sex and affection were private, at least they always had been between us. Her comfort level around others had eased since we'd employed bodyguards of our own, but here, in a room likely under observation, where Nan or her assistants could walk in past Neko with no cause for alarm, struck me as an odd choice.

When she kissed me, I went through the motions, trying to gauge her reactions through our connection, but it was awkward. Like I was numb, doing what I knew I should be, but there was no enjoyment in it.

Anastassia pressed harder, one hand working its way down to my pants where there was nothing happening either. I grabbed her wayward hand before it reached its unenthused destination and stepped away. As I did, her efforts faltered, only for a second, but just enough that her thoughts were clear.

"Nan put you up to this."

Her back went stiff, eyes closing as she bowed her head.

I couldn't even be angry about it. Her thoughts had also revealed that the only reason she'd agreed was because she was concerned.

She must not have been sure about my reaction because Neko came running in, doing his best to not look like he was ready to try and stop me from doing whatever either of them expected me to do.

With Tamara, I'd hoped it was a lingering hint of the bond that kept me from being interested, but Anastassia had killed that whisper of optimism. The fucking Arpex had taken everything.

"I have to go."

"Vayen?"

"Goodbye, Anastassia." I Jumped to Jal where there were plenty of blue bastards to kill.

FOURTEEN

Darkness and light flowed into one another in an endless loop as I searched Jal. The vast population and heavy traffic made it even more difficult to work than Artor, but the challenge served to take my mind off of Anastassia and my lack of physical sensation or enthusiasm for anything beyond work. My presence on Jal also seemed to assure Jey that I was in fact working and not doing anything drastic or insane.

Little did he know. Nan wasn't the only one doing research.

By the time I encountered the first Arpex on Jal, I had formulated a few questions. It was more comfortable speaking than the last one, but even less cooperative.

"What is the location of your shipbuilding world?"

Instead of a flood of thoughts or images, its mind was on lockdown. It took me a moment, but I figured out how to press harder, to demand the answer. Its mind remained closed.

Maybe this one didn't have the answer. I tried a different direction. *"Where do your speech boxes come from?"*

Still nothing.

It had to know something useful. *"How long do Arpex live?"*

Images finally flitted from its mind to mine. Larvae, the creeping clawed young, young with feet, full-grown Arpex, and then the cycle started over. Not exactly useful.

"Seasons? Years? How do you track time?"

"Time?" It repeated the word but gave me nothing.

The Arpex's wing jaws snapped open. Question time was over. I switched to a different track of research.

It screamed in my head. I screamed right back. Then I took off my coat and stepped within range of its claws with a pulse pistol in hand.

The claws did little beyond shredding my shirt and scraping my skin. The Arpex hissed its frustration at an ear-splitting volume and intensity that would have dropped me to my knees and made me rip up my face in the past. Now it was like there was a filter between us, like my understanding its thoughts somehow lessened the volume to a tolerable level. Maybe they couldn't hurt each other this way, not like they punished those they fed upon. I gritted my teeth and tried one last question.

"Where is home?"

I caught a glimpse of the green world, or at least one like it, before my hold on the probing inquiry became impossible to maintain. It was like trying to stab a round stone with a knife.

My head hurt bad enough that I wondered if I'd be able to Jump. I gave up and pulsed it. After letting Jey know where to send a crew to remove the body of my victim and those that had fallen prey to it, I picked up my coat and managed to Jump to the apartment on Merchess.

Hours later, I woke to bright sunlight shining in the little window in the kitchen, shooting its perky beam right at my face. I got up, propped my coat over the window, and sank back down in the blessed darkness. But there was too much to do, too many contacts begging for my reply, accounts that needed monitoring and trade transactions to oversee.

The good news was that Stassia's trade suggestion was paying off. Big. Had we been speaking and still bonded, I would have been spinning her around and spending a long evening showing my appreciation for just how right she was. But we weren't.

Instead, I spent long hours funneling those much-needed funds into the recovery efforts on Syless and Frique. Fa'yet had plenty of his own credits, much of which were formerly mine, to assist with the immediate needs of Karin. Fucking Artor could rot for a while.

Once I'd finished relaying replies to the most urgent contact requests, my stomach demanded food. I Jumped to Jal to pick up a double-sized serving of a tangy orange vegetable-laden soup Jey had often bought when it was his turn to provide a meal. I didn't know what exactly was in it and I didn't care. My memory told me it tasted good and it made the rumbling stop so I could resume my search. It took another few days before I found the next Arpex.

How the Arpex had managed to make it inside one of the damned towering plexes, I wasn't sure. Maybe security wasn't what it should be. Or the security personnel were made to forget what the hells they were supposed to be doing. From the empty stations throughout the lobby, I had a feeling I was about to find several dried slime puddles with bits of blue uniform lining the edges.

The occupants of the plex noted my arrival with stares and wary avoidance of all physical contact. It was as if I'd formed a wide force-field about my person that no Jalvian dared test. I had little doubt the local authorities had been notified of my presence and that that news would work its way up the communication chain until Jey's measures took care of it. I did the same for him in my half of the system if he ran into trouble.

The hiss I'd detected remained faint as I took the lift up the central column floor by floor. I'd made it up and down the entire plex twice before I resigned myself to a full-floor search of each level.

Halfway through the midsection floors, going door to door, listening in each apartment for an increase in volume of the faint but steady hiss, Jey contacted me for my location within the plex. I relayed it to him.

He arrived a few minutes later with a steaming box which he thrust into my hands and stood there while I shoveled the noodles covered in brown sauce into my mouth, barely tasting them. It was fuel. I had work to do.

He shifted from foot to foot, watching up and down the arced hallway. Instead of his usual uniform, today he was outfitted as I was used to him, in armor. From the familiar lumps beneath his coat, I gathered he was also armed.

"She said you looked gaunt. I forgot how focused you can get."

So that's who he was doing this checkup for. "I'm fine."

I crammed the empty box in the nearest refuse chute and headed to the next door. It wasn't until I reached the fourth one that I realized Jey had followed me at a distance.

"Don't you have better things to do?"

"What happened to your coat?" He pointed to the holes in the back. The weave was slowly regenerating the sizable holes.

I shrugged and made my way down the hall. "Arpex. Armor's superfluous at this point."

"So she said. Have you checked back in with the University?"

"Doesn't matter anymore."

If Nan had managed to make some great breakthrough, she would have let me know. However, I was inclined to think she had little interest in reversing the Arpex effect. And she hadn't contacted me. She'd made the weapon I needed. The Arpex had made me able to use it by removing Stassia and the bond. Now if everyone would just leave me the fuck alone, I could continue making progress.

"Of course it matters," he said.

"I'm trying to work here."

"You know," he stared me down, "when you warned me about what you'd become without your bond, I thought you were exaggerating, but you've achieved a whole new level of crazy intense." He shook his head. "I wish there was even a little Merkief in you that we could reach."

Mention of Merkief ignited a haze of red, not the rage-filled kind, but the kind that filled my sleep. The fireball surged through my vision. The walls closed in and then disintegrated, turning black and charred. I wore the long bloody thin yellow robe, but my arms and chest were unmarred. It wasn't my blood. It was Merkief's. He lay at my feet, an unhinged glaze in his eyes. Everything but his face was a twisted mass of bleeding flesh and bone. Try as I might to put him back together, he kept falling further apart, his blood soaking my shirt. His lips moved. I leaned closer and realized he was saying, "I'm sorry", repeating it over and over until he went still.

"Vayen?" Jey had backed away.

The walls returned to the cold blue-grey of the plex. The harsh overhead lighting beat down on Jey where he stood two apartments from me. He held a stunner in his hand.

"Do you want to take care of the Arpex on your own?" I asked.

"I appreciate what you're doing. Really. But your family needs you too. How long has it been since you've seen your kids?"

His tone reminded me of Deep Voice, of how he would try to manipulate me. The walls flashed from charred to stark and back again. I shook my head, trying to clear my vision.

"He's lying," Arin said. *"They're better off without you. Safe."*

I nodded. "They're fine. Mind your own damned business, and let me work."

"Anastassia isn't dead, Vayen. She wants to make things work with you. You have to talk to her."

Arin stood between me and Jey, his burnt grey suit hanging in tatters off his bloody body. *"Focus on the work. Just do your job."*

Arin had been wrong. I *was* special. The fucking University had seen to that. But yes, I did need to do my job.

"The only thing I have to do is eliminate the Arpex. You're slowing me down."

My vision flickered, revealing Deep Voice in his cloak where Jey had just stood. The hood shadowed his face. He reached out to me. Then it was just Jey again, wearing his armor.

Vids lined the walls. Arin snored softly on his mat. One of the vids flipped to the view of Jey standing in our Kryon quarters. He was talking, but I couldn't hear him. I turned up the volume on the controls.

"Vayen."

The vids vanished. I stood in the hallway again. Jey's gaze flicked from my face to my hands every few seconds.

Sweat trickled down my back under my coat. My damp shirt clung to my skin. I ripped the heavy armor off. Why was it so damned hot in here?

This was different from my usual barrage of visual torture, less focused, too many, too fast. My legs felt heavy, my stomach swirling.

Jey aimed a stunner at me as I started toward him.

"What did you slip into your thoughtfully delivered meal?" I asked.

"Apparently not enough. You should be on the floor."

He fired, sending a mildly annoying prickle of electricity through my body. He kept firing until the stunner gave out. I kept walking. There was no need to hurry. He wasn't running yet. And what better way to continue my research?

Jey exchanged the stunner for a gun. He took aim at my leg and fired. We both watched as the bullet hit, puncturing my pants, and then sinking into my skin only enough to breach the surface before falling to the floor. The shallow wound dripped blood down my leg and into my boot. I kept walking.

With a grimace, he exchanged the gun for a pulse pistol. I shrugged and kept walking, almost closing the distance between us.

He hesitated. "I'd rather not do this. Come with me, we'll get you to the University where they can help you."

"They already helped me."

Deep Voice stood there, only an arm's length away. I could reach out and strangle his conniving ass once and for all.

I blinked the sweat from my eyes. It wasn't him. Jey had drugged me. Deep Voice was dead, just like Merkief.

A wall blasted into my chest, my arms, shoulders, face. It knocked the air from my lungs and my hold on remaining vertical wavered.

Blood ran from my nose. And then I could breathe again and my head was clear, endorphin-charged blood coursing through my veins.

I wiped the blood onto my sleeve. "Are you done yet?"

The resignation in the set of his jaw, the downturn of his lips, and his putting away of the pistol answered my question.

"Do you need help?" he asked quietly.

"No. Go home to your family."

"Only if you promise to see yours when you're finished here."

"You're not in a position of much leverage to be demanding promises of me."

Jey looked me in the eye, unflinching. "I wasn't demanding. I was asking, as your friend, your partner, for you and for them."

"When Jal is clear."

He nodded and then stepped into the void. No doubt, he'd be running to Anastassia to report our agreement and what he'd seen. Or maybe he wouldn't go that far. If he did, he'd have to tell her that he fired on me, and she wouldn't be happy about that, not if she was concerned enough to send Jey to check on me.

I took a moment to brush over the connections I shared with Daniel and Ikeri and found them both busy and well. If either of them noticed my touch, they didn't acknowledge it. That was fine. I didn't have time for idle chatter.

With my mind again open to Arpex, I continued around the outside arced hall and then worked my way around the inner ring with no favorable results. At least the endorphin boost from taking on the low pulse had knocked the heaviness and nausea from my system. I took the lift to the next floor.

Time slipped by in a slow halting walk through four more floors and countless hallucinations before my concentration wavered to a point I was either going to have to call Nexo in to watch my back or sleep. I marked my place and retreated to my mattress on the floor in the apartment on Merchess.

Thanks to Jey's drug, my efforts to rest were interrupted more than usual by vivid dreams of the observation room where I'd been enslaved, of insane Arin telling me I wasn't special and that I needed to accept my place, of Shoulders beating me, and of being pierced by shrapnel over every inch of my body as Merkief exploded. I got up and ran cold water over my face, but that just left me awake. What I needed was to sleep, the good kind and a full night of it, but since losing Stassia, I'd lost any hope of that.

After a hot shower and changing into some blood-free clothes, I decided I needed a change of scenery to help clear the shit from my brain.

I strapped on a few weapons and Jumped to the outpost on Frique. Allund and two others were returning to the longhouse from the pad where half of the ships sat. They hurried over.

"Good to see you back." Allund's smile faltered. "Unless there's a problem?"

"Just checking in on your progress."

"Are you hungry?" asked one of the other pilots. "We'll give you the full report."

An untainted meal didn't sound terrible. I nodded and followed them inside. Allund and the other pilot sat down at the table while the third veered toward the kitchen.

"Tamara is not going to be happy," said Kal, the thin young man who sat beside Allund.

Allund shot him a shut-the-hells-up look.

"I'm here for your report, not to make Tamara happy."

Kal shook his head. "Don't tell her that."

I sighed. Maybe coming here wasn't a good idea after all.

Allund, seemingly eager to erase Kal's comment from my mind, launched into an animated and enthusiastic recounting of their progress in hunting down and eliminating the young Arpex on the contaminated sites. Along with the third pilot, food arrived in the form of cubed prantha, long beans, and black rice. I interrupted with a few questions, but mostly listened and ate, enjoying his lively report complete with sound effects and hand motions. Kal piped in as did Gereld, who had prepared the meal, adding more detail, Kal with more gore-filled description and Gereld imitating the reactions of the others.

By the time they had wound down, restful sleep seemed a more likely possibility. "Mind if I borrow a bed?"

Allund stood and gathered up the plates. "Not at all. The one you used before is right where you left it."

"I won't be here long. Only a few hours."

I left them to their cleaning up, went into the bunkroom, disarmed, and crawled into the bed. From the floral scent on the pillow, I knew I hadn't been the last one to sleep in it. I'd sat back to back with that same smell for days. Tamara. I flipped the pillow over and listening to their muffled conversation in the other room, drifted off to sleep.

A warm hand on my shoulder brought me awake in an instant.

Tamara jumped back.

"They said you were only sleeping for a few hours. I didn't want you to be late for anything."

I checked my link to find my desired three hours had turned into six. While I'd needed that, I also had an unending list of things I needed to be doing. I swore under my breath and grabbed my weapons.

"Thanks."

She nodded, flashing a bright smile. "I'm glad you came back."

"And now I'm leaving." I'd thought she'd understood my stance on her tentative advances before, but the pillow proved I was wrong.

Her smile faded. "Don't take Kal seriously. He likes teasing me. Allund told me what he'd said."

"This isn't your bed, is it?"

She shook her head, gaze dropping to the floor.

"Then stay out of it. I came here to get away. If that's what I can expect, I won't be back."

"It won't happen again, and I'll talk to them. I promise."

She was so young, they all were, having annoyed someone ranking above them at some point, they'd found themselves shunted out here. And yet I did enjoy their company as long as it was clear there were no ties, implied or otherwise.

"Good. This bed is more comfortable than the one I've been using."

"It's yours anytime."

I glanced around the bunkroom and found us alone, yet even so, I didn't want to take any chances.

"You know I have a mate, a family, what makes you think a bonded man would want to get involved with you?"

"I never proposed anything involved." She straightened and looked me in the eye. *"And you don't act like any bonded man I've ever met."*

"I told you, it's complicated."

I gave her credit for facing me. It wasn't the demure reaction I'd expected.

"And for your own good, keep the speculation of your friends and any thoughts of your own under control. If my mate did suspect anything was going on between us, she wouldn't hesitate to eliminate you."

"She's like you then?"

"Yes and no."

Tamara nodded thoughtfully. *"I understand."* She squared her shoulders and issued a challenging stare. *"For the record, I can be discreet, should you change your mind."*

I acknowledged her with a skeptical nod and Jumped back to the apartment on Merchess. Returning to the outpost would have to wait a while, even though I enjoyed their company and their bed. The apartment was adequate, but I wasn't looking forward to the utter silence.

Jal still needed searching as did Artor, Karin and Moriek. Everyone needed my attention and now Nan had turned me into the one fucking weapon we had against the Arpex. And I couldn't figure out how to best take advantage of what I'd become. Or was becoming.

It was all too damned much.

There had to be something I could do that would make a difference. Something other than hearing Arpex and pulsing them.

While I tried to figure out what that might be, I checked my weapons and loaded up my coat with a few more from the chest I kept in the closet.

As I fingered a couple grenades in the chest, it occurred to me that I might not know where their ships were built or their speech boxes were manufactured, or even where their homeworld or a large population of Arpex might be, but I did have a jump point to one of their food source worlds. Or at least the Arpex in the Council had feasted there. Perhaps others did too. It was worth a try.

"Don't go back there," Arin pleaded. *"How could you face those people after how many of them we killed?"*

"We set them free from Arpex," I said firmly. "We kept them from being eaten."

Arin shook his head. *"We fed them to Arpex and when its feeding cycle was over, we shot the rest. Who pulled the trigger? Not Arpex."*

My hands shook at my sides and my gut twisted into a knot. Closing my eyes to block out Arin's accusing stare only brought on an endless stream of dirty defeated faces and weary eyes that didn't meet mine. I'd killed them. I'd pulled the trigger.

"But they didn't feed Arpex," I whispered, seeking any hint of absolution from the man who'd introduced me to the offering planet.

His hard stare dissolved my ambition. I put the extra weapons back in the chest. Rather than doing Jey any favors after drugging me, I instead Jumped to Karin to resume my search for Arpex.

FIFTEEN

I spent fifteen hours alone in a high speed transport, working my way across the cities of Karin. All the while, I listened for a hiss, and yet dreaded one in my head—praying that Arin stayed silent and out of sight. Though I tried to get work done through my link, my thoughts kept wandering back to the idea of using the Jump point Arin had given me years before. This time, I wouldn't be there in service to Arpex. I could maybe learn something useful, something that would help take them down. Something that might make up for the lives I'd taken there.

Yet, each time I considered abandoning my search of Karin, I saw that damned rock with its chains, the bodies in the dirt, and a gun in my hands. I heard countless pleas to be spared, bargains for the lives of others, cries and screams. And then there was the silence, those resolved to die, usually the last few people of each cycle of offerings. I'd tried make their end quick. Unlike Arpex, I took no joy in their terror at watching each other die. The silence after the killing was over and only bodies lay in the dirt settled over the transport, dulling the sounds of the engine, of my own breathing.

The need to escape the small enclosed space, to be among the living, escalated from a thought to a dire necessity in mere minutes. I entered the command to land the transport at the nearest safe location. As soon as it touched the ground and the seal on the door released, I leapt out and stood, gasping. I bent over with my hands on my knees to keep me upright until the deathly silence dissipated. The usual evening sounds of Karin seeped into my awareness, the hum of traffic overhead and on the street nearby, people talking on the patio of the restaurant just down the street, and the distant rumble of a ship entering the atmosphere from the orbiting spaceport. Familiar sounds. Normal. In spite of breathing easier, a chill settled over me, one that made me crave the safety and comfort of my mattress on Merchess.

I Jumped there and though my muscles were tight to a point that a long walk or a workout would have been a wiser move, I made myself lie down. Armor and all, I pulled the blanket over me. I lay there in the darkness, staring at the ceiling with my artificial eye, repeating to myself that I was safe, that I was here in the Narvan, that there would be no offerings to retrieve when I woke.

Somewhere in my mantra, I fell asleep. Four hours later, I woke with the sound of four gunshots and screams echoing in my head. The faceless bodies of four dead offerings in the dirt refused to go away no matter how hard I rubbed my eyes.

Arin sat on the mattress beside me. *"Don't go. You'll regret it."*

"There are hundreds of things I regret. Probably thousands by now." I rubbed my hands over my face. "Not seeing if there's anything I can do to help those people would be one more."

I stood up, shaking out my armor and pulling my hair back into a slightly more organized mess. "You're welcome to come along."

But when I turned to see Arin's reaction to my invitation, he was gone. I did my best to recapture my resolve from the day before as I again loaded extra weapons into my coat.

After a couple quick deep breaths, I concentrated on a jump point I never thought I'd use again. It had been beaten into my brain, and even though it had been years since I'd been there, the Jump worked flawlessly.

The rock with its sets of chains was as I'd last seen it. The cistern was dry and there were no signs of offerings either living or those I'd killed to 'set them free'.

When we'd taken out the Council, I hadn't given any thought to what that might mean for worlds like this, assuming there were others, where offerings might be left to starve slowly without a grey suit to release them in one manner or another. If anyone had suffered that cruel fate, they'd been properly disposed of since. That gave me hope that I might locate the rest of the population here.

I'd seen them once, in the memories of the first victim I'd sought to save from the Arpex I'd served. They were simple people, and if Arpex used them for food, they wouldn't be allowed much technology, certainly nothing that would allow them to escape, like advanced transportation. They had to live relatively close to the offering spot.

There were no networks to consult here, no maps. I tried to remember what I'd seen in the head of the first offering I'd damaged before serving it to Arpex, and then compared it to what I could see of the surrounding terrain. Mountains and trees had been in the distance behind the place where his people lived.

I spun around and headed through the flat plain toward the far away mountains, nearly lost in a haze of clouds. In the past, I might have complained about the heat, but my altered skin was comfortable here.

A shadow passed overhead. I first thought it might be a bird, but it was huge. I held up my hand to block the glaring sun. An Arpex circled overhead. My feet froze on the ground, muscles taut, mouth dry.

Arin stood beside me, peering upward. *"They know you're here. They'll kill you. Leave now."*

"I can Jump anytime," I assured him, heart racing.

I'd known Arpex could fly. The one I'd served had done so to travel to and from its high platform where it preferred to rest. But to see one in the sky, flying out in the open, was new fodder for the nightmares I'd surely be having later.

And then there were two. They circled above me, slowly drifting lower. For a brief moment, I considered pulling Jey in for this. He'd surely be armed and available in seconds for the chance to shoot Arpex. So would Neko. But they were both busy and whole and needed elsewhere. I could do this. Or maybe not, but I needed to try.

"You're not special," Arin said.

I tore my gaze from the circling Arpex to glare at him. "Maybe I wasn't, but I am now. Not in a good way, but a way that's needed. Needed by the people who live here, by everyone in the Narvan."

Arin gave me a dubious look, one that took me aback. In all our years together he'd never exhibited any shred of belief that I might be something more than just another slave like him. But here, now, there was doubt in his eyes rather than the absolute conviction that had always accompanied those words.

"Prove it," he whispered before fading away to leave me alone in enemy territory with Arpex circling overhead.

I cursed Arin under my breath as I pulled a pulse pistol from my coat and waited for them to get in range, all the while praying that they wouldn't fly off to warn others or that twenty more wouldn't show up.

One dove. The other stayed high. I fired. The lower Arpex plummeted from the sky, landing heavily on the ground with a thud that

I felt through my boots. Even at a distance, I could see that its shell had shattered on impact. Green blood flowed into the dirt around it.

The higher one let out a shrill cry that would no doubt warn any other Arpex in the area. It dropped a little lower, but stayed just out of range, circling tighter. Unwilling to wait for its reinforcements, I took off toward the trees I could now make out in the distance. They matched the memory I'd seen. I hoped people were still there. People I might be able to free from these damned things.

Keeping to an easy to maintain pace, I glanced overhead periodically to assess the threat level from above. It wasn't long before one Arpex became three.

"The fucking University made me special." I muttered to the empty space beside me as I ran. "Want to see how?" Opening my mind to the place Arpex used, I listened.

They chittered with a sense of urgency. I got the impression that they knew me, or of me, what I was. That confirmed my theory that all Arpex used this place in their minds to communicate with one another, a collective of sorts. But I still had no idea how organized they were, who was in charge, or the range of their communication.

By the time I spotted the first hint of civilization, five Arpex glided overhead and two hours had passed. I wasn't sure if I should be relieved that they hadn't attacked yet or if that meant they had prepared a defense and were simply waiting for me to walk into it. I listened harder, trying to remember more of the Arpex language I'd picked up when I'd been imprisoned. The two words that stood out were *more* and *danger*. The context of either was unclear, but I had a good guess.

They had more. I was the danger.

I was also prepared.

Without any guilt, I tossed a stim in my mouth to make up for the energy depletion from the run. If this went how I expected, my heart giving out would be the least of my problems, maybe even a blessing.

My skin crawled, knowing there were five Arpex above me and likely others ahead—a horde of terrors waiting for me, waiting to eat me alive in one way or another.

The stim rushed through my body, throttling my rising panic and replacing it with my favorite companions: adrenaline and focus. I'd placed myself in a hostile situation, one I needed to prove that I could survive. Training, that's what I was doing here. It was just a training exercise. Breathing in and out slowly, I relied on experience and self-preservation to face what lay ahead. Everything else, I crammed back into the tattered box deep inside me.

The buildings ahead gained more detail as I drew closer. A city, nothing as large or grand as anything on Artor or Jal, but more like Pentares—an isolated colony that had exploded in size, not sprawling, but contained by the landscape surrounding it.

Stone buildings crumbled at the corners. The city lacked the bustle and noise of traffic, its streets clean but empty. It was like the color and life of it all had been leeched away, but I could still see what it once had been. People peered out windows and doorways keeping their bodies safe behind walls.

One of my aerial tails dove at me, almost as if intending to drive me further into the vacant streets ahead. I pulsed it.

It fell, it's wings outstretched, spiraling downward, to land in a broken pile in the street in front of me. The Arpex channel went mad with chittering and a hum that set my nerves on edge. Whatever recognizable words might have been in the conversation rushed at me far too fast to decipher. Their hostility didn't require interpretation.

A scream began to build, the kind I knew all too well. I halted my approach just within the city's sprawl and screamed right back at them. The pressure shattered and the channel went silent.

The flying Arpex descended, closing in. A glimpse of blue scuttled between two buildings to my left. And then another to my right. Within seconds, a swarm of Arpex surrounded me, both on the ground and in the sky.

Panic pounded deep inside me, begging me to leave this place. I stared at the horde of blue, weighing my options, debating how committed to this training exercise I really was. Doors and windows slammed shut as the non-Arpex occupants of the city did the smart thing and hid.

I stood out in the open, making the split second decision to see, for better or worse, what this new altered body of mine could do.

Before the first Arpex could reach me, I exchanged my used pulse pistol for a fresh one and grabbed a second pistol in my other hand. Wings might have been handy, but Nan hadn't seen fit to equip me with those. Hearing Arpex had its uses but wasn't going to help with this. It wasn't as if I could ask them all to pause a moment for questioning, and even if I did, I wasn't able to suck memories from them.

Some weapon I was. Good thing, I had other instincts to draw upon.

I let loose a full blast from each hand, one high, one low, and then spun around and hit them with two more. Pistols on empty, I decided to try the grenades while my targets were all tucked in tight and rushing toward me. With explosives lobbed at the enemy and no clear route of retreat, I dropped to the street and took cover under my armor, covering my head with my arms and hoping for the best.

The blasts knocked the air from my lungs. My ears rang. I drew my last fully charged pistol and chanced a look around.

Pieces of blue shells littered the street. A claw dripping with green blood lay in front of my knees. Two buildings had collapsed, rubble crumbling everywhere. Dust filled the air along with screams and yelling from the occupants. It may have been people in the surrounding buildings, or those trapped in the fallen ones. I couldn't tell with my hearing still distorted from the explosions.

A sharp blue foot caught me in the back. I rolled away from a second kick and scrambled to my feet. It dove into my brain.

"Tell me of your mate."

"I don't have one anymore, thanks to you."

I could feel its demand faltering, the flavor of it changing, becoming uncertain. If I hadn't known better, I would have claimed it was scared.

"Poison!" it screeched to the others over the Arpex channel.

With our minds connected, I saw the mental paths to the other Arpex around me. They weren't doing any asking, but they were observing both me and my tormentor. It's connection to the path shriveled and cracked, falling away like dust on a breeze. Seeing the poisoning process from the inside, was far more interesting than the brief enjoyment of watching the Arpex fall, limbs flailing, like the one on Syless had when it had tried to feed from my memories after my alteration. Jey wasn't here to shoot this one, to end its suffering.

I gripped my pistol hard, instincts urging me to pulse the damned thing. But it deserved to suffer. They all did.

The Arpex channel lit with a new sort of energy, the chittering taking in a higher pitch, one I couldn't seem to tear my attention away from. None of them demanded anything of me, it was more like probing. They were probing as a group, a collective wandering through my head. The pulse pistol and my hand seemed far away, too much effort to connect with, to use.

Old aches I'd learned to live with overwhelmed my body. My wrist burned where it met with my grey hand. Searing yellow light burned into my eyes. The stench of acid and body fluids filled my nose.

"This one has served," said a distant clicking voice in my mind.

The yellow light dissipated, but the heat grew until sweat ran from every pore. Try as I might to peel off my armor, to find any sense of relief from the oppressive humidity, I could do nothing. My hands were numb. I couldn't move. But something under my skin did.

"This one was a nest," said another far off voice.

"Study it?" suggested another.

"Kill it," one urged.

"Get up," said Arin, suddenly standing beside me. *"Get up!"*

"I can't." I was too tired, too many welts, too many Arpex slithering under my skin.

"Get up!" Arin shouted in my face, his voice stronger and more demanding. He held my pulse pistol, gaze running over it as though he'd never seen a weapon in his life. "How do I use this? How do I kill them?"

Arin's face wavered, becoming a different face, a young man with sloping shoulders and a ragged shirt. Blood ran from a gash in his arm, dripping into the dirt.

"Hurry, they're coming," he said, tugging at my arm with his free hand.

An Arpex lay on its side nearby, unmoving. I was poison. I'd killed it. Killing Arpex, that's why I was here.

"It's awake," chittered an Arpex in my mind.

"Kill it," chanted the rest.

"Give me that." I grabbed the pistol from unresisting fingers. "Hide."

The young man nodded and ran.

With the Arpex chanting in my head, I could pinpoint each of their locations just as I'd been doing in the Narvan. But this didn't require flying anywhere. They were all close by on the ground, and now they were desperately trying to shut down the branching channel that bound all of us together. Just as they had been able to see into my mind through this connection, to see my past, they could also see my present.

"Kill him before he kills us all."

"Protect the food."

The Arpex scrambled to plan a defense, only to realize I was right there with them, observing every suggestion. This hive mind might have had benefits, but right then, I was overjoyed with its downfalls.

They didn't have weapons here, not anymore. Arpex didn't need them, their food was subdued to the point of hopelessness. But now I was here, fucking that up.

Their thoughts darted to their ships, long disused, power levels unknown. Arpex had lived here in their glory while their food stock had cycled many generations. Arpex had watched with glee as they stole key memories, getting these people to take cities from one another until their civilization crumbled like the wills of those who now inhabited them. They'd shared their plentiful food supply with other Arpex, especially those that had served the whole of Arpex. They harbored a good deal of pride over the chains on the rock and the process of offerings they'd developed to please Arpex like the one I'd served. There were other sites like that one near other cities on this world.

My head spun with all I'd learned. If Arpex took Frique, this could be the future of Artor, of Jal, of the rest of the Narvan, nothing more than a massive farm. We'd become prantha, living only to create another generation of food or be eaten.

People weren't prantha. Not my people, and not these.

I spotted an Arpex facing away from me in the narrow space between two crumbling buildings. Knowing my pulse charges were limited, I focused the wave to the narrowest beam and quickest burst. Normally a pulse wasn't a precision weapon, not what I would have chosen for an up-close and quiet assassination. But these Arpex were unarmed other than their razor claws and feet, and their memory eating tricks no longer worked on me. I didn't need destruction at a distance. A pulse was the one thing I knew would pierce their shells and kill them. Noise wasn't a problem, they already knew I was here and after them. The Arpex weren't getting far, not when we were all connected in our minds.

I made my thoughts as quiet as possible and crept up behind it. Pressing the pistol to the back of its topmost protrusion, I fired. It's wing jaws sprang open, knocking me into the building it had been hiding against. When I regained my footing a second later, I found the Arpex on the ground, its wings stilling and its head a pulpy green mess.

Hunting the rest took the better part of the day. The one good thing about the Arpex knowing I was there was that they'd all relatively congregated in one quarter of the city to try and hunt me down. Without weapons and having learned my poison status, their defense was limited to flying overhead to try to drop rubble on me as I sought out the ones on the ground. Two had managed to get me in their wings when the pistol in my hand had come up empty, but thankfully, I'd been able to wriggle my hand into my coat to grab another. Covered in digestive slime, I'd had to hide out for a few hours while my pistols each regained one last charge to take out the four Arpex that had been hurling rocks at me throughout the day. When at last the place where Arpex spoke in my head went quiet, I made my way back to the edge of the city where I'd first entered the Arpex arena.

My muscles ached, and varying degrees of drying green blood ran down my armor. There were entrails of some sort in my hair from the last airborne Arpex I'd pulsed. Cuts and bruises from the rock attacks along with the acid burns from the wing slime had to make me look downright hideous to the crowd that had gathered at the site where I'd first set off the grenades. I was tired, but it was a very satisfying level of exhaustion.

Arin stood beside the young man who had snapped me back to reality. He nodded toward the crowd and surveyed the destruction the grenade had caused. *"Maybe a little special."*

"Maybe."

Arin grinned and then faded as the young man walked through him.

"You're still alive?" the man asked in halting Trade.

"To the amazement of many, it would seem so. The Arpex are dead. You're free. All of you."

They let out a cheer.

Without Arpex lurking about, I took a moment to observe these people in their city rather than in chains waiting to die. They were of no particular ages, all with varying shades of the same muddy brown skin. Many held hands, one leading another, speaking quietly to them as if explaining what had happened. A couple had the vacant look of missing too many memories, but again, others seemed to be watching over them. Arpex had feasted here, but these people had known this life for so long that it was normal to care for those who had forgotten themselves, or each other, or too much. And now they were free and maybe, someday, that wouldn't have to be normal for them anymore.

Except there were other cities on this world that were still ruled by Arpex.

"The Arpex that were here are dead," I amended. "But there are more."

Their smiles faded.

As good as it did feel to take out the Arpex here, my own home had Arpex problems. I fingered a few weapons through the slits in my armor, contemplating what to do.

"They'll come for us," said the young man.

"Yes. It won't be easy, but if you're ready, you can kill them. There is far more to life than becoming food for Arpex."

"Ready how?"

"They'll punish us for this. You'll stay and protect us, won't you?" asked a woman with curly hair that hung to her waist.

"I can't stay." I ran through an inventory of what I had on me. "But if I leave you weapons, will you use them on Arpex and not each other?"

"Why would we want to hurt ourselves?" she asked.

"You shouldn't. Nevermind." I shook my head and began to pull weapons from my coat. "Those who want to defend yourselves against Arpex, form a line here." I pointed to the ground in front of me.

The young man stepped forward. The woman stood right behind him. Others rushed over and formed a line. This was going to take a while, but I didn't mind, not even as tired as I was.

"Who is in charge?" I asked.

Confusion plain on their faces, they all stared at me. This was like questioning Arpex. I had to remember that not all of them spoke Trade and those that did, might not know much. I had to find the right words.

"Who picks the offerings?"

The young man pondered this for a moment before cocking his head. "The chained?"

I nodded. "How are they chosen?"

"Arpex choose," he said. "They taste us." He tapped his forehead.

"There will be no more chained," I said.

At least I didn't have to worry about some governing body willing to give up the newfound independence of everyone here in the hopes of mollifying angry Arpex once others learned what had happened. These people would have a chance to fight for their continued freedom.

I spent the next few hours handing out pulse pistols and grenades and instructing the newly-liberated people how to use them. It took two Jumps back to the ship's armory to restock before I felt like they had a fighting chance at maintaining their freedom. I added a reminder to restock the armory to my list of things to do. Neither line of defense took a lot of training beyond the obvious: make sure to aim them only at the enemy and know that anything near your enemy may be destroyed as well.

They wanted to thank me, constantly, offering me all sorts of trinkets, asking my name, where I came from, and if they could come with me. I shrugged it all off.

As delicately as possible, I touched their minds, one by one, until I found the name of their world and what I hoped were actual coordinates. They were so used to Arpex in their heads that my small intrusion didn't seem to gather any notice. If I could get them on a trade route and maybe have Jey send a few ships to finish the extermination, the rest of the population might have a chance too.

"Be safe," I said, sharing the habitual version of farewell Stassia and I had used for years. I Jumped back to the apartment on Merchess and wondered if they understood what *safe* was. Geva willing, they'd learn.

When I removed my much too light coat, my conscience felt a little lighter too. I stripped off my green-stained clothes, took a hot shower, and then stretched out on the mattress, enjoying the lingering feeling of satisfaction. I hoped that once the Narvan was also free of Arpex, I'd feel like this again.

SIXTEEN

When I awoke six hours later with my heart pounding because flying Arpex were chasing me down the street where I'd grown up, I was mildly pleased to note that the one thing that hadn't haunted my sleep was the usual flood of faces I'd fed to the Arpex. If that progress hadn't come at the cost of introducing flying Arpex, I would have enjoyed it a bit more, but I had to admit that I still felt pretty good about what I'd done. It had been quite a while since I'd felt good about anything.

In fact, I was in a good enough mood, that I decided to overlook Jey's pulsing and drugging me and returned to Jal to continue my hunt in the plex.

I dressed in my one remaining clean change of clothes, wiped down my armor, and rearmed with what was left in my chest in the closet. After making a note to restock that too, I headed to Jal to see what the universe would throw at me to ruin my good mood.

Resuming my search of the plex, I worked through several of the higher floors before the hissing grew a fraction louder. This one was different than the rest. It didn't try to talk to me or question what I was. It was more like empty static flowing through the channel the Arpex used. I tried one floor above, but the volume again deceased except for a section of three rooms above where I'd heard it on the floor below.

A quick consult of the building map revealed that I'd reached the top levels of the plex. The service staff lived in the lowest levels. The elite lived at the top where occupants were free of the shadows of the buildings within the city and air traffic was light.

With the vast multitude of towering plexes dotting Jal, I was surprised Jey hadn't taken one of the elite top floor suites for himself. After all, he maintained a far more public presence on his homeworld than I did on mine. If nothing else, his socially prominent wife would have appreciated the prestigious living arrangements. Yet, he'd chosen a single-family home. I laughed to myself. It was nice to see that Anastassia had managed to twist him from his social norms too.

In the northwest section, the afternoon sun would be shining through the windows of the outward-facing apartments, creating the heat Arpex craved. I went up one more level. The hiss remained at a consistent volume. That left me going door to door in the potentially affected areas, seeking out the apartments where no one answered my insistent demands for entry.

Being the middle of the day, most of the apartments were unoccupied, which meant a lot of time spent gaining entry by manipulating the plex's control systems. It was many hours later, that I knew I'd found the right one. The door sluggishly opened, revealing a makeshift seal of slime-hardened clothing on the inside. The stench of rotting flesh made me gag. Eyes watering, I stepped inside and closed the door. Something squished underfoot.

A shiver ran down my spine as I lifted my boot, knowing what I would find. A flattened thumb-sized larvae stuck to the treads. I tried to scrape it off on the carpet, knowing the effort was probably futile because there would be a hundred more.

The fading sunlight and the large windows along the exterior wall turned the main room into a terrarium. Between the moisture from the decaying bodies strewn across the floor and the trickle from the kitchen sink, the heavy air clung to everything, including me. Mold had taken over the walls, staining the pale yellow surface with black and red patches like a blind artist's masterpiece.

From the body count, offspring stages, and level of decay, I estimated the Arpex had infested three people at different times, the last being very recent. The multitude of dried puddles boasted of its ability to draw food to it and feed in peace. There were far more than the occupants of one apartment would account for.

A young Arpex latched onto the toe of my boot, its teeth trying to penetrate the tough surface, claws holding on. I kicked the nearest wall, crushing the hungry creature. It let go and lay still on the floor.

The further inside I went, the more my skin crawled. Then I noticed the vent covers had been cut through, probably with claws by the looks of the haphazard slices. Geva knew how many more young Arpex were wandering in the ducts or had found meals in other apartments.

Keeping my breaths as shallow as possible, I crossed the vast open room filled with torn and mold-covered furniture, tattered plants in giant pots, creeping larvae, and dried puddles of the dead. Beyond the wide room that served as common, kitchen, and dining, were four doors. All of them were closed. Figuring nothing could be worse than the room I stood in, I opened the first door.

Inside, crouched in the corner, sat a gaunt little boy. A teen-aged female lay curled on the floor nearby. By the color of her skin, I gathered she'd been dead for a few days. The Arpex hadn't made it through all of its offerings. I motioned for the boy to remain where he was. His dull eyes regarded me without even a spark of relief.

The next room contained more puddles, but these were thinner and dried almost to a powder, suggesting that perhaps the boy had been attempting to keep the Arpex's plate clean for a time.

I activated the third door and stood back. In the middle of the room stood the Arpex, or perhaps, more accurately, it hunched. It didn't acknowledge me, and the hissing, though louder, didn't change. No words, threats, or anger.

It had eaten itself into a state of torpor. The Arpex I'd served had done the same thing many times, though it chose its platform high above to hide itself from my view.

Curious, I widened my connection with the inert Arpex, slipping into its mind. When it didn't wake in a fury to attack me, I took a cautious look around. It didn't appear to be connected to any other Arpex. Not fully understanding how the branching connection worked, I focused on what was available in front of me.

The Arpex appeared to be dreaming, though I couldn't discern emotions, the images dealt with an abundance of food. The plex was that for certain.

Working slowly to remain undetected, I more whispered into its mind than demanded to see memories of the past, of where it had come from. A world of grey skies and warm rain drifted into my mind. Rising waters had sent the Arpex into a frenzy, washing away its young, drowning the population that had been its food. Ships had come to take the Arpex away, ships like the ones that had invaded the Narvan, but larger, like I'd seen at the shipbuilding world. On those ships, it had fed upon the crews of other vessels they'd overpowered. The Arpex spread out from there, sending their smaller ships into new systems as they passed through, seeding as they traveled.

I began to get the uneasy feeling that there was no single

homeworld teaming with Arpex that we could bring to heel like the Fragians. They were more of a parasite, spreading throughout the known universe, snacking on civilizations until they drove them to ruin and their dwindling populations reverted into nothing but a food source. Little wonder that the Arpex within the Council hadn't seen the need for the Narvan's recovery or sustaining the needs of its people. All they wanted was to feed and reproduce. The conquering end of the spectrum was only about bringing the food source under control. They didn't need our knowledge or our resources, credits, ships, or information. All of the things we based our society on were superfluous to them.

In my time observing for the Council, I'd gathered Arpex were used to bring populations under control. But even the Council had used that asset with caution. Given too much of a foothold, I could easily see the Arpex getting out of control. No one was handing them anything anymore, but neither was the Council holding them in check.

The most we could hope for was to exterminate those we'd been infested with and be vigilant about watching for more. I couldn't play enforcer for the entire known universe. Hopefully there were other people like me out there, able to hear them, to be a weapon against them. Maybe they had enemies of their own that thinned their numbers. I prayed that was true.

"How long do you live?" I asked. The Arpex on the offering world had shown me that they'd lived through generations of their food source, but that could be relative to that enslaved population breeding and dying young.

This Arpex went back to memories of traveling in the ship. It watched as another Arpex just like itself, as they all appeared, staggered one step and then collapsed onto the floor. It fell with its small clawed arms pinned on the floor beneath it and ceased to move. Two others came to take the dead one away. This one took over adjusting the dials where the dead one had been working.

So they worked until they died? I wasn't the only one not bothering to plan on retirement.

Rather than asking an outright question, I pictured the boxes they spoke through, shoving the image into its mind.

The Arpex showed me a room on a ship with shelves full of the boxes I knew so well. Trying to get solid answers was proving to be utterly frustrating. Did they have leaders? Had they sent out operatives with no harmful knowledge of their greater civilization on purpose? They had to have some sort of organization. Perhaps I just hadn't asked the right questions or didn't understand how to properly use this ability Nan had given me.

For now, I had a young boy to save. That was something I *could* do.

After closing the connection, I set my pulse pistol to a tight heavy wave. The Arpex toppled, green ooze leaking from the fractures in its shell. I contacted Jey to send a team over to begin clean up and informed him of the possible infestation, along with my speculation on the uselessness of the Arpex homeworld annihilation plan. With that disappointing task out of the way, I made my way back to the first room.

The boy sat where I'd last seen him.

I held out my hand. "Come on, let's get out of here."

The closer I got, I realized just how long the boy had been here. The entire room reeked of bodily waste and the dead girl. He didn't react when I picked him up. With his limp body in my arms, I made my way out of the room and through the rest of the apartment.

When we stepped outside and the door closed behind us, he began to sob, but no tears fell from his eyes. I Jumped to one of my usual points on Jal. It wasn't until I stepped out of the void with a gagging boy in my arms that I realized I should have warned him about the Jump. My kids were so used to it that I'd not given it a second thought.

"Sorry about that."

I set him down until he'd stopped heaving, but he had nothing to lose. With him back in my arms, I found my way to the nearest medical facility where I intended to hand him over to the first staff member I could find.

"Please bring him in here," said a Jalvian woman, leading us to a curtained observation room. She wore her long blonde hair pulled back from her face by a bright green cloth band that matched her loose-fitting shirt and pants.

She pointed to the chair beside the examination table. "Have a seat."

I went to put him in the chair, but the kid grabbed hold of my arm and wouldn't let go.

She ignored me and focused on him. "What's your name?"

The boy shook his head. His fingers clutched my coat, arms shaking.

I shifted him around so I could sit on the chair instead and settled him into my lap.

"How old are you?" she asked.

"Could you get him some water?

"Of course." She left us.

"Did it make you forget?"

The boy looked at me as if seeing me for the first time. He nodded slowly.

"They've made me forget things too. It will be all right. They'll take care of you here."

He shook his head.

"I killed it. It can't get in your head anymore." I looked for the woman with the water, but she seemed to be in no hurry.

"Look, I know you're scared and you have every right to be, but we need some information so we can help you. Would you mind if I helped you give it to the doctor?"

His eyes darted from side to side, and his grip didn't lessen a single bit.

"It won't hurt. I promise."

The boy didn't offer any sign of acceptance, but neither was there resistance. Working as gently as I could, I sank into his mind. It was every bit of a mess as my own. The girl had been his older sister, and it had been his family's apartment. His name was Markus. He was six. The rest was full of holes and horror. I backed out of his mind. The Arpex might not have devoured his flesh, but that was about the only thing the kid had left intact.

I knew exactly how that felt.

Unlike the people I'd helped on the offering world, this kid had no one to hold his hand and patiently explain things he'd forgotten. I hadn't been able to stick around and help the whole city full of people, but maybe I could do something for this one kid.

"We'll figure it all out. Don't worry."

Markus nodded. His grip on my arms subsided.

What the hells was I going to do with him?

When the doctor returned, she handed Markus a covered cup of water with a straw protruding from the top. He sucked it dry.

I offered up what little information I had, explaining that his family had been killed and that he was alone and had witnessed traumatic events that had affected his memory.

After giving Markus a cursory once over, she turned to me. "And you are?"

"Well connected. Clean him up, check him over, and we'll be on our way."

"He doesn't appear to have any obvious injuries. I don't know where you found this child, but he stinks. If you're claiming to be responsible for him, clean him up over there. We'll examine him shortly."

She tapped away on her datapad. "Someone from family services will retrieve Markus. He's going to be tough to place being unresponsive as he is and with cognitive impairment." She glanced up at me. "I'll need a family name for billing purposes."

"Markus, do you remember your full name?"

He couldn't have gotten much closer to me except to crawl inside my chest. The shake of his head was barely perceivable.

"I'll cover it."

Whether it was because I was Artorian, or outfitted in armor, or the state of my face, a disapproving frown cracked through her otherwise impersonal demeanor. "I'll need a credit chip for pre-authorization."

I made sure to hand her one with my grey hand. She plucked it from my fingers like the chip would infect her and ran it through the reader attached to her datapad. Her eyes lit up and she licked her lips.

She handed the chip back to me with the very tips of two fingers. "Looks like a full round of testing is in order. You'll find temporary clothing in the bathroom. I'll be back shortly."

I managed to disengage Markus and get him into the compact shower. After peeling away his clothes, I ran warm water over him. Bruises covered his ribs, legs, and arms, some fading, some fresh.

"Arpex like to kick, don't they?"

Markus nodded. He took the soap I offered him and did as good of a job as Daniel would have at that age, missing well over half of his body.

"Mind if I help with that?"

He held out the soap. I washed his back, face, and hair and rinsed him off. His drying efforts were as effective as his washing. I took the towel from him and dried his hair, then handed him the pale blue shirt from the stack on the counter. It hung to his knees. His hands disappeared in the sleeves. We wouldn't be needing the pants.

I filled the cup for him twice before setting it aside. With my coat back in place and Markus cleaned up, we returned to our curtained space. I sat him in the chair.

"They'll take care of you now, find you a place to live. I'll check up on you, all right?"

Markus sprang from the chair and wrapped his arms around me. "Stay."

I had Arpex to hunt, the Narvan to run, and plenty of my own shit to deal with. But when I looked down into those blue eyes swirling with desperation, I couldn't walk away.

"For a little while."

Beneath his mop of half-dried wavy blonde hair, Markus smiled. He was perched on my lap, running his thin pale fingers over my grey ones when the doctor returned.

"Shall we get started then?" She held her hand out, but Markus refused to let go of mine.

"Seems we're attached." I got up and we followed her.

"That's unfortunate," she said. I didn't have to see her face to know there was a scowl lodged upon it.

Markus did let me go long enough to endure a full body scan and then a longer one of his brain. After he'd been thoroughly poked and prodded back in the curtained room, the doctor announced he was dehydrated, malnourished, bruised and battered, but she found no permanent damage. She'd not taken his psychological state into account during her assessment.

"I'll be back shortly with a summary of the charges along with supplements to get him back on track. The family services representative is ready for you. I'll send her right in." The doctor left the room and closed the curtain behind her.

"Markus, do you have somewhere to go? Anyone you know who will take care of you?"

Tears welled in his eyes again as he shook his head.

"You can't remember or you know there isn't anyone?"

He shrugged. The poor kid looked so lost.

"Tell you what, would you like to come with me? Just for tonight. I'll see if I can find anyone who might be looking for you."

He grabbed my grey hand and cast a worried glance at the curtain as it parted to reveal a sturdy woman. Half of her blonde hair had turned to white. She regarded me with open malice.

"We won't be needing your services. Markus is coming with me."

"I don't think so. He belongs with a Jalvian family."

"You don't want to push this matter. Let him go."

"With you." She scoffed. "And who are you to him?"

I had no right to this kid and asking a traumatized six-year-old to make this choice was likely ludicrous in her eyes, but no one knew what he'd suffered through like I did. "Markus, are you sure?"

He tugged on my hand and stood behind me, peeking out from

around my coat. The doctor returned with a handful of supplies that she handed off to the woman intent on taking Markus from me.

"If you'd hand those over, I'd appreciate it. Since I'm paying for them and all."

"That was your choice. The boy does not belong to you."

"I'd rather not hurt anyone. Just let us leave."

"I don't know what fringe world you just shipped in from, but you won't be taking the boy with you," said the doctor. She slammed her hand onto a button on the wall.

I could have left him there, left him with his people, and gone my way, but only Geva knew who they'd stick him with. They wouldn't understand why his head was full of holes or help him figure out how to live with them. I put my hand inside my coat, not quite drawing a weapon, but they got my intent in an instant. So did the two security guards who rushed through the curtains.

I yanked Markus up into one arm. He clung to my shoulder, holding on tight, scared but not crying.

Barreling forward with my unhindered shoulder, I knocked one of the guards and the doctor aside. The other guard had the where-withal to hit me with a stunner. Between my coat and Arpex skin, it was nothing more than an irritating jolt.

My grey hand caught the guard with the stunner and sent him flying into the curtain, tearing it off the bar from which it hung. The woman from family services rammed into me. I knocked her aside. She sprawled on the floor. The doctor backed away. The other guard pulled his stunner and took aim.

"If you hit me with another one of those, it will be the last thing you do."

He lowered his weapon.

I made my way out of the building with several other security officers trailing in my wake. None of them tried to stun me. I let them be.

"This may make you sick again, but we need to get out of here," I warned Markus.

The Jump to the apartment on Merchess went as I expected. He threw up seconds after we'd stepped out of the void, but it certainly wasn't the first time I'd cleaned vomit off the floor. I put him down by the sink in the kitchen and wiped his face clean. Drinking a glass of water brought him back to his usual level of wary silence.

"It's not much, but it's where I'm staying for now. No one will bother us here."

I took in the three remaining meal bars in the cupboard. "How about I get us something to eat and then we get some sleep?"

He nodded.

"You can look around if you want to, but there's not much to see. Keep the door locked. I'll be right back."

A quick Jump to the food merchant who kept his soups warm at all hours was the fastest meal I could think of. Remembering how a full meal had caused me massive discomfort when I'd been mostly starved during my imprisonment, I figured it would be wise to keep the kid from too much solid food for a while anyway. When I stepped back into the apartment, I found him only a few steps from where I'd left him.

I took off my coat and most of my weapons and then we sat on the floor and ate. Rather, I ate while he devoured. The voluminous sleeves got into his soup more than once.

"You want something to wear that's more your size?"

Markus tried to roll the sleeves out of his way yet again.

"Give me a minute."

I Jumped to Artor and raided Daniel's drawers for anything he'd grown out of. One of the benefits of keeping several houses was that Anastassia's fanatical organization couldn't always keep up with all of them. With a few changes of still too large, but a whole lot closer, clothing in hand, I returned to the apartment. Markus sat in the middle of the bed, arms wrapped around his knees.

I held the clothes out to him. "Take your pick."

While he examined my offerings, I went to the cupboard and pulled out the med kit. The bag of supplies the doctor had prepared would have been handy, but we were well stocked. "I'm going to put gel on our bruises and cuts, all right? Then you can change once it's dry."

He slowly unfurled and undressed. Markus stood patiently while I applied healing gel to far too much of his small body. He winced several times but didn't make a sound.

I motioned him to the edge of the mattress to sit beside his clothes while the gel dried and spent a while scouring the local network, locating the record of his family's name on the apartment rental, and then searching for anyone seeking information on the Nytuns.

Little Markus Nytun was right, he didn't have anyone. For Jalvians, the Nytuns were a small family, single wife, only three children. Most of the extended members had perished in the recent encounters with the Fragians or back in the war with Artor. Those that had survived, one aunt and a grandmother, had lived in the apartment as well. They were all gone.

However, his prominent family had left behind a tidy sum of credits. I set about establishing an account for Markus and initiated the process of declaring him the heir. If the unpleasant medical staff had known his family's status, I had a feeling he'd have been treated far differently. Fortunately for me, they hadn't or I would have encountered a whole lot more resistance during our exit. Jey wasn't going to be happy about this.

Once dressed, Markus appeared more at ease. He set the remaining clothes on the floor by the mattress.

"What are you doing?" he asked.

"Working. Taking care of your family's accounts for you." I pointed him toward the kitchen. "More water and then to bed."

He managed to take care of that on his own and then sat down beside me. "Can Artorians read minds?"

"Not exactly."

All the rehydrating seemed to have loosened his tongue. While I was glad he was feeling better, I had plenty to do and adding an inquisitive little mind to slow me down hadn't been on my agenda.

"Do you have one of those chips in your head?" he asked.

"An implant. Yes."

"Father didn't like those. He didn't like Artorians either."

"I take it you remember your father." I got up and repositioned my coat over the window, double-checked the lock on the door, and turned out all the lights. "Let's get some sleep."

"Do you remember yours?" he asked.

"Yes, but not my mother."

I settled onto the mattress and stretched out only to find Markus right next to me. The bed had seemed a lot bigger with just me in it.

"You're going to want to be over here." I pushed him toward the edge of the mattress. "I have bad dreams, and I don't want to hurt you when I wake up."

Like a magnet, Markus was back against me in an instant. "I have them too."

I sighed and let him have his comfort. At least he wasn't stuck in that horrific bedroom anymore.

As much as I needed to sleep, Markus apparently did not. He lay still against me, but his mouth kept moving as if it had saved up

weeks of conversation while he'd served the Arpex. He'd tried to keep
the plate clean, but the Arpex kicked him until he couldn't move. His
sister had pulled him into the room where I'd found him, but the
Arpex ate so many of her memories that she didn't know how to eat
or take care of herself anymore. She'd gone to sleep and had never
woken up. Others had come to try to help him, but the Arpex had
eaten them too.

He'd snuck out to find food and water in the kitchen. The larvae
had scared him. When they'd gotten bigger, he'd stopped leaving
the room where I'd found him until hunger drove him out, and then
terror drove him back in.

As he talked, I wished I had some of Ikeri's calming gift. All I
could do was listen and occasionally share some of what I'd endured
to show him that he wasn't alone. Talking to him was simply talking,
not emotionally draining like when I'd shared highlights of my nightmares with Stassia. Markus nodded his understanding against my
arm and occasionally held onto my grey hand as we talked. Mostly, I
provided a breathing wall to sleep against. Which, eventually, to my
weary mind's relief, he did.

When I did wake eight hours later, it wasn't because of a dream
or the fault of the restless kid next to me, it was because I was simply
awake, rested and ready to get back at the thousand tasks requiring
my attention. Not a single nightmare had plagued me. Even Arin's
whispering was gone.

Fa'yet had wanted me to find someone to talk to. I'd never anticipated finding someone who understood, whom I wasn't afraid of
infesting with nightmares if I shared any details of what had actually happened. Neither of us could have anticipated Markus being the
one I felt comfortable talking with. But I was.

Fa'yet and Stassia had been right, I did feel a little better after
talking about what I'd gone through. If I could help Markus the same
way, maybe we could both be better someday.

Light from the night sky on the dome high above the city filtered
around the edges of my coat, filling the room with twilight shadows.
Markus was still out and quiet, and I decided that as a reward for
helping me get the best rest I'd had in a long time, I'd leave him that
way until he woke up on his own. Working through my link would
suffice for a while.

I didn't realize how deep I'd sunk into my work until the shaking
on my shoulder registered. Coming out of the trade negotiations

I'd been in the middle of took me a couple minutes, but I didn't want to frighten Markus. I pushed him gently away. Or tried to. He didn't move.

Snapping my eyes open and blinking away the streams of numbers, I discovered Jey looming over me. Markus was still sound asleep.

Despite my annoyance at being dragged out of a deal, I kept my voice down. "What the hells do you need?"

He pointed to Markus. "Mind explaining this before I jump to my own conclusions?"

I rolled off the mattress and led Jey over toward the door, putting distance between us and the sleeping boy. I kept my voice low and jabbed a finger into his chest. "I'd love to hear your conclusions first."

"Have you lost your mind? I got up this morning to find that a deranged Artorian mercenary kidnapped a six-year-old boy, the sole surviving Nytun heir, no less, who was undergoing medical treatment. Security and staff were injured."

"And you assumed it was me?"

"Vayen, there's vid coverage. What the fuck is going on in that bulletproof head of yours?" His fists clenched and unclenched at his sides. "You leave Anastassia, desert your kids. You put Jal before Artor. This isn't you, not even manic working you."

"Pulsing me isn't like you either. How about you get the fuck out."

A fluffy blonde head appeared between us. Markus's bare foot connected with Jey's shin. "Leave him alone. He saved me. Go away."

Jey glanced from Markus to me. His eyebrows rose. "Is that so?"

Markus nodded.

"And you think kicking me is a good idea?"

The boy didn't flinch. "Our heads are the same. They wanted to take me away."

I put my hand on his shoulder and pulled him back beside me. "He served the Arpex."

"Vayen, he's six. He's not like you. You're confused, and we don't know the extent of your transformation. He's just a little kid, and he certainly doesn't deserve this. Let me bring him home."

Age didn't matter. Markus knew the same terrors I did, and after one night of talking with him, I'd slept. Really slept. There was no way in all nine hells I was going to give him up.

"No."

"Now who's six?" He let out a growling huff. "How am I supposed to make this media mess go away without bringing him home?

I looked down at the blonde head that stood just below my waist, his skin-and-bones shoulder under my hand. This little Jalvian boy had done for me what Stassia couldn't, not even after our long talk after my breakdown, what Ikeri couldn't calm away, what no balm of Etara's could accomplish. He'd survived serving the Arpex, with holes as plentiful as mine and traumatic memories just as vivid. I could help him and he could help me. Geva had brought us together.

"He's coming home with me."

Jey's mouth dropped open. "You haven't been *home* in weeks. You aren't even speaking to Anastassia, and you have two children of your own that you can't find time for. What makes you think anyone would allow this?"

"You will."

"I assure you, I won't." He reached for Markus.

I drew one of the two guns I'd fallen asleep with. "Don't touch him."

"You're going to shoot me over a kid?"

"You shot me over nothing."

Jey's face turned red and his jaw clenched. "We needed to know the extent of the effects of the Arpex transformation."

"So you can take me out if you need to?"

"No, of course not." But his gaze wavered as he spoke, revealing the real answer.

I sped through my list of jump points, searching for one safe enough to bring Markus, one that would give us somewhere to work out a plan for the future. Preferably one that didn't involve bullets or anything more extreme than that between Jey and me. Veria Prime was as safe of a place as any, and Jey wouldn't follow me there, at least not right away.

SEVENTEEN

Seconds after stepping from the void with Markus in hand, I contacted Anastassia. She was the only one who could call Jey off.

"Can you meet me on Prime?"

"Right now?"

"Soon, and tell Jey we're meeting. He needs to back off."

"What did you do? He was ranting that you kidnapped someone?"

"Anastassia, please. I'll meet you at Tomias's."

She sighed. *"Only because you said please."*

My heart skipped a beat. Stassia had uttered those same words. She was in there somewhere.

I needed to find her again so that I could continue helping Markus. And to keep Jey off my back. Even if it meant losing my new-found focus on the Narvan.

I really was a selfish bastard.

Markus didn't get sick this time, but he took a moment to recover from the Jump, looking around at the dirt-toned town where Tomias lived. It was a far cry from the Jalvian city Markus had come from. Trees and shrubbery dotted the town's landscape. Bright curtains and pots of flowers beside doorways and under windows brought color to the otherwise bland view.

"Where are we?" Markus asked.

"Outside the Narvan on Veria Prime. We're going to see my children."

"You live here?"

"No."

"Why are your children here?"

"Ikeri is training to be a Seeker. Daniel is staying here with her for now. No more questions for a while, all right? I need to think."

Markus held my grey hand and walked in silence as we made our way to the red door of Tomias's home. A Seeker answered my knock. She stood there, robes wavering around her sandaled feet, with a bemused smile on her thin lips. The tattoos on her bare head were raised as if they were very new, the colors extra vibrant.

Her yellow-green eyes were familiar. "Etara?"

She nodded. "Your children are here, you don't have to knock."

"I feel like I do." The few times I'd brought Ikeri here for her training, I always had. This wasn't my place. I certainly didn't belong here, nor was I usually welcome. And walking into another person's home uninvited felt just plain wrong. Then again, many things Verian felt that way to me.

"When did you become a full Seeker?" I asked.

"Your memory balm was my final test."

What did one say to that? I had no idea. While Ikeri might be training to be a Seeker, I'd not looked into it much further. This was Anastassia's realm. Not mine.

"Congratulations."

Etara bobbed her ornate head, dropping her gaze to Markus. "And who is this?"

"He's like me." I knew how absurd it sounded, but it was the truth. "Perhaps you could help him a little in the ways that you do."

Etara pondered Markus and his hand in mine. "I may. However, I won't take credits for my services, not from you. You will owe me."

Her gaze held no malice, yet I didn't know what to expect from her. We weren't quite enemies, but neither were we friends. "As long as your payment brings no harm to my family."

She nodded and led us through the home where Tomias lived and into the rest of the hodgepodge of connected buildings. "Your own peace was short-lived then?" she asked over her shoulder.

"The thing you did? That's fine. But me and peace don't seem to stay on good terms."

She turned to face me. "You could change that."

"That would be nice. Really, it would, but life has other demands."

"As you say," she said in her agree to disagree tone.

Etara opened a door. A yard covered in green grass and edged with a rainbow-like array of flowers lay before me. She pointed to a long white building with a rounded tiled roof. "They're living there with the other young acolytes."

"Thank you for letting them stay."

She smiled. "They are both welcome. Your son is quite gift-ed as well."

"Daniel? How so? He's never displayed anything beyond normal mind speech, certainly nothing like Ikeri."

"We all have our own gifts." With that annoyingly cryptic comment, she ducked back through the doorway and closed it.

I let go of Markus's hand. He walked beside me as we approached the white building. I was well aware I didn't belong in this calm and peaceful place, especially not armed as I was.

A petite bullet of glee raced toward me with a face-splitting smile. Ikeri wrapped her arms around my waist. She didn't say a word, just opened her mind, emanating calm as she always did. One by one, in well-orchestrated coordination, my muscles relaxed.

"What do you think you're doing?" I couldn't even manage much of a protest for the effort she extended on my behalf. Between the restful sleep and now being relaxed, all I wanted to do was sit down and enjoy her company for a couple hours.

She pulled away with a guilty little smirk and regarded Markus.

I introduced him and she paused, glancing from me to him a few times. Her whisper-light touch flitted through my head as she did so.

"Ikeri, stop it."

"I'm sorry. It's just that he's so lost." She took my hand. "Like you."

With my voice firmly lodged behind the lump in my throat, I could only nod.

She held her other hand out to Markus. "Come. Daniel is bringing you something to eat. You both could use it."

Her calm again surrounded me as we entered the acolyte's dorm. The door had no lock and a long single hallway ran from one end to the other. Windows in the door on either end lit the hall. Colorful curtains hung in narrow doorways along each side. Dirt crunched underfoot. It was the least secure place my children could have been living, but I couldn't find it within myself to raise a protest at the moment.

Ikeri brought me to a room with a lavender curtain. She pulled it aside to reveal a sleeping shelf mounted to one wall and a small desk on the other. A single wooden stool sat in the corner opposite the bed. Sunlight danced into the room through a long narrow window set at the height of my shoulders, well above the head of the average Verian. Enough to offer light without the distraction of a view.

She let go of my hand and sat on the bed.

"Your room?"

She nodded. "It's all I need."

"Are you happy here?"

"I belong here. But don't worry, I'll always be with you too." She smiled like the little girl she truly was and my heart melted.

At least I could still feel that, now that I was there beside her. It had been so long since I'd seen her in person. It felt like it had been, anyway. I'd been too deep into dealing with everything else to think about the passing time beyond work, eating, and sleep.

I sighed, mourning my clarity of focus. It may have been a lonely state, but the efficiency of it was amazing.

But Markus would need more than me if he was ever going to have a decent shot at a normal life. A family that included two Seekers would be very good for him. If Ikeri and Anastassia were so intent on helping me, surely they could make much more of a difference for him. That meant I was going to have to let them back in too. Even more than not wanting to let my focus go, I really didn't want to have to come to terms with how much this damned alteration had cost me.

A heavy exhale escaped before I could cover my dismal thoughts. Ikeri tore her old lady gaze from Markus to give me a worried glance.

"I'm fine," I assured her, half-knowing she was likely skimming my thoughts and could see that was a lie.

"You can sit down," Ikeri said.

I perched carefully on the stool, unsure if it would hold my weight. Markus stood beside me. I could almost feel the hundred questions that must be ready to burst from his mouth.

"Has your mother been here to visit you?" I asked.

Ikeri looked as if she was unsure if she should answer. "Many times."

"Good." At least one of us was still playing parent. "She'll be coming soon. I need to talk to her about Markus."

The shining grin reappeared on her face. "Oh, that's a splendid idea. She won't say no. Don't worry."

"Ikeri!"

Anastassia wasn't the only one who could turn a name into a curse. Both of them jumped. I clamped down all defenses, which would have locked anyone else out of my head. For Ikeri, it was the equivalent of shoving her out a screen door that bore no lock. But she got the hint.

"Did she just read your mind?" whispered Markus.

"Yes, which she has been explicitly and repeatedly told not to do."

Ikeri bowed her head. "I'm sorry." She looked up through her tangle of curls. "It was just right there like you were all but shouting it at me. I couldn't unhear it, not when it is so good for both of you. Markus is exactly what you need."

"What *I* need? I think you have that backward."

She gave me one of her agree to disagree looks. At least she spared me the 'as you say' line.

Daniel arrived with a heavily laden tray in hand. I made quick introductions before releasing Markus to attack his plate.

Daniel sat beside Ikeri on the bed. "I hope you're hungry."

In truth, I was, and even Verian food made my mouth water. I slid my plate out of Markus's range. It seemed the soup the night before had barely made a dent in his raging appetite.

Condensation slipped down the tall glass of crystal clear water. I downed half of it and then went to work on the nutty-flavored squash and mountain of seasoned white beans. A palm-sized portion of smoked fish served as dessert.

I realized as I shoved the last bite into my mouth, that they'd both been sitting there patiently while Markus and I ate with a single-minded purpose.

They really were good kids. Odd, but good.

"Etara tells me that you have gifts," I said to Daniel.

He shrugged. "They like it when I help in the kitchen."

I noticed Ikeri smiling at her brother and realized I couldn't recall the last time I'd seen them so companionable. If ever. He sat up straight, eyes bright. He'd even cut his hair. They both wore the simple long tunics and loose pants that were common fashion to Verians, the same clothing they'd worn when we'd all lived on Minor.

Oh Geva, how different our lives would have been if we'd never left Minor. Not that I'd had any choice in the matter. I cursed Jey and Merkief for taking away this life that should have belonged to my children all along.

"That's all then, you're helping in the kitchen?"

"Don't worry, Daddy, he's not like me," Ikeri said.

"Good, because Daniel would make for an ugly little girl."

She giggled and Daniel grinned. Markus watched them both in silence.

We spent a good while talking about Ikeri's lessons and what

Daniel had learned in the kitchen before Ikeri came up short mid-sentence. "Etara is ready for Markus. I could help him, Daddy. Just like she can, or better. Why did you ask her?"

"She's a Seeker now. It's what she does, isn't it?"

"Well, yes, but—"

"You're still learning, and you should spend your energy on that."

Ikeri had perfected Stassia's peeved glare. Even if I didn't have Stassia as herself, I had her face on our daughter to keep me in line. As if I had a clue where that line was anymore.

I shook my head, wondering what I'd said wrong. "Can you take him to Etara for me and let me know when your mother arrives? I need to talk to Daniel for a little while since he knows better than to read my mind."

"That's because I can't," Daniel said, mostly to Markus.

My little blonde shadow clung to my sleeve.

"Ikeri won't let anything harm you, and she will stay out of your head unless you invite her in," I said.

"I promise," said Ikeri.

I pried Markus from my arm. "Go on. I'll see you soon."

If he were Artorian I could have opened a connection to stay with him, but he wasn't. Holding a light contact with him over an extended period would drain me. I couldn't afford that.

His steps were halting, but he did go. The curtain fell behind them and their steps faded.

I'd barely opened my mouth when Daniel blurted, "Ikeri told me."

"How does she plan on being a Seeker when she can't keep her mouth shut for five minutes?"

"It's different here. They don't keep secrets." He shrugged. "She said it would be easier for you if I knew."

"I *can* use words. It's half of what I do."

He chuckled. "I know. She's been worried about you. So is mom, though she didn't use words."

"That sounds about right." I nudged the tray. "So working in the kitchen, is that all you're doing here?"

"I can't spend all day in there. They make me go outside and take classes. But it's not bad. I mean, I like it. It's better than the academy. No one yells at me and they like how I talk. Mind speech is special here, not something they can make fun of me for."

"So they're training you."

"A little," he said as if it were an admission of a dear secret.

I studied the much younger and flawless version of my own face. "Is this what you want? To grow up here with a bald head full of tattoos as your future?"

"Ikeri does."

"I'm asking you." He was my son. Anastassia's son. Even as Chesser's son he had a propensity toward going his own way at any cost and so many other traits that might get him into trouble. Especially here.

I'd seen him get in fights, hells I'd taught him how to defend himself much more effectively than any kid his age should know how to do. Should I be training him in leading the Narvan? I certainly couldn't keep up the position forever. Hells, at the near-death pace I was going, I'd be lucky to last a few more years.

If I could show Daniel what needed to be done without the need for open violence, just as an advisor, would I want to? I could hand him the position neatly with Jey and Anastassia to further mentor him. They could stand beside him so that when my damaged heart did give out once and for all, I'd know my family, as well as my people, were taken care of. Could I thrust that responsibility on my kid?

I studied the innocent younger version of myself, imagining him in armor, having personal meetings with planetary heads, with Neko or a bodyguard or two of his own standing just over his shoulder. He watched me too, gaze darting over my face and then down at my hands and back again.

"No, I don't want to be a Seeker. I don't think I could be." Daniel glanced at the still curtain. "When I would go to the academy, when Ikeri was studying here, I'd miss her. In my head, you know? I could still talk to her, but it wasn't the same."

I nodded. He had grown addicted to her calm too.

"But when I'm here, I'm close by and I can tell her to stop when she gets too tired. I can watch over her."

Anastassia and I certainly weren't doing a good job of it, so I was happy to hear Daniel had stepped up.

"I still have my knife. They didn't take it from me. I thought they would."

"Yes, I would think so too."

Though they didn't seem opposed to me or Neko being here fully armed, a kid with a weapon was quite another sort of danger. Let alone a kid who wasn't Verian. And my kid.

"They know I have it. Seeker Tomias went through our bags with us. He knows I keep it on me."

"Do you think Ikeri is in danger here?"

"She's different. Everywhere we've ever gone, different hasn't been a good thing."

Maybe he was more observant than I'd given him credit for. Had this been what Etara had been getting at? "Then you should stay and watch out for her."

"Like you used to do for mom?"

"Yes." But Geva permitting, without all the blood, bullets, and stress.

Hope shone in his eyes. "I don't have to go back to the academy then?"

"I think we've both burned that bridge by now."

He took a deep breath and stared at the dirt floor. "I'll contact Uncle Jey then to give him my resignation."

"You set up a meeting, and we'll go together."

"Really?"

"I'll even sit beside you."

Relief gushed out in a deep exhale. "All right."

"About Markus..."

"I'm not opposed," he said.

"But not for, either?"

"I don't know him." He stood up and started pacing the tiny room. His volume grew as words spilled out. "You show up here with a ragged little kid wearing my old clothes after I haven't seen you in a long time and wonder if I want a brother? I don't even know if *I* have parents anymore. All I have is Ikeri."

I grabbed him when he came close enough and gave him a hug. "Of course you do. They're just not very good parents."

He let out a garbled laugh.

"I'm meeting with your mother today. We'll figure something out. Something better, all right?"

He nodded against my chest. When he stepped back, he kept his hand on my arm, his fingers probing. "Why does your skin feel weird?"

"What does it feel like?" I really didn't know.

"Hard. Are you wearing a new kind of armor? Where's your coat?"

"I don't need it here." But even with my altered skin, I missed the weight and storage and that it hid everything underneath. I didn't plan to stop wearing it.

He scowled. "I hope you use more words than that with Mom."

I wasn't exactly looking forward to talking to her and Geva only knew what words might be the right ones to win her over.

"The University sort of merged me with an Arpex," I explained.

"You don't have wings though, do you? You can't fly? Tell me you can't fly."

"Would you be more excited if I could or couldn't fly?"

His mouth dropped open and his face flushed.

"I can't fly. No wings. I'm not turning blue and I don't eat people."

"Well that's good, I guess."

"I thought so."

He stroked my arm again. "Is it bulletproof? Like your coat?"

"Mostly, yes. Works against pulses too."

His eyes widened. "You tested it?"

"Uncle Jey did. On second thought, don't contact him just yet."

Daniel suddenly turned solemn. "Did he forget you too?"

"No. We're just in the middle of negotiations."

He shook his head. "If you say so."

Geva be damned, the Verians were infecting my kid with their conflict avoiding ways. He backed away and reached for the tray.

"Ikeri said I should let you sleep."

"I'm not tired." Then again, who knew when I'd get the chance to grab a couple more hours or what the conversation with Anastassia would bring. "But I might close my eyes just for a little while."

Without Markus around, I wondered how I would sleep. Perhaps Daniel could use some practice. "Are you in the middle of anything?"

"I did my training this morning. Kitchen duties are voluntary."

"Would you mind hanging out here while I sleep?"

He grinned. "I get to be your bodyguard?"

"For now."

His enthusiastic nod made me laugh. I climbed onto the bed. Its hinges groaned but the straps that held the bed extended from the wall remained intact.

Daniel settled onto the stool, producing a datapad from his pocket. "Is it okay if I use this?"

"Can you keep watch and play a game at the same time?"

He seemed to ponder the question for several minutes and then finally set the datapad on the desk beside him. "Probably not very well."

"Then you know the answer."

The thin mattress wasn't as uncomfortable as it looked. I settled in, still enjoying the loose feeling after Ikeri's relaxing touch, and closed my eyes.

"Can I ask you something?" Daniel whispered as if it was someone else he wasn't trying to wake.

"Maybe."

"What I feel around Ikeri, is that what a bond feels like?"

"A bond is more, but yes, I suppose it's similar."

"More how?"

"I'll explain when you're older."

He sighed. "Mom says I'm too old already."

"Her people grow up slower."

"I know." The stool creaked as he shifted around. "They didn't like me much."

The kid could never sit still when he had something on his mind. "What is it?"

"When I'm away from Ikeri, I get angry easier. Like when I was at school when we lived on Pentares or at the academy on Jal. Is that why you're angry all the time? Now that mom doesn't remember you like before?"

"I'm not angry all the time."

"Sorry. I'll be quiet now."

Did I really sound that angry? "Daniel, I'm not mad at you."

He nodded, but true to his word, he stayed quiet. I closed my eyes again and this time I drifted off. Ikeri's touch in my head, only an hour later, interrupted my conversation with a charred Merkief. I shuddered, thanking Geva for the reprieve.

Daniel still sat on the stool, datapad at arm's length as though he had to push it further away to avoid temptation.

"Markus or your Mother?"

Ikeri rested her hand on mine. "Seeker Tomias asked to speak to you. It sounded important."

"All right." I sat up.

"And Mother is here," she added quietly. "Markus is still with Etara."

"Where is your mother?"

"With Seeker Tomias. He asked me to join you."

Daniel sat there looking between Ikeri and me.

"Come on, you too. Unless you have somewhere else to be?"

"I'll hide out in the kitchen, if you don't mind."

"Wish I could go with you."

He gave me a quick hug, and then scampered off.

Ikeri and I made our way across the flower-lined lawn and into a different building from the one Etara had led me through. We went in and straight up a narrow wooden stairway to an open room that encompassed the entire second floor of the long narrow building. Tall windows afforded a view of the quiet street below and the distant green countryside beyond the city.

Tomias sat in the middle of the floor, his robes splayed out around him. Behind him sat three acolytes in their late teens. Anastassia sat before him, sipping from a cup. She didn't look up when we made our way over, my boots making a hellish racket on the smooth wooden floor in the open echoing room.

Ikeri sat beside Anastassia, allowing for us both to have space. I sat on the other side of her. Tomias poured a steaming cup of tea from a clay kettle and held it out to me. I'd never liked tea, but since he was housing my kids, I figured it would be best not to be rude. I took a sip of the bitter hot water and then set the cup on the floor. The steam drifted lazily into the air.

Tomias didn't seem to be in any particular hurry, but I had plenty to do. "You had something to discuss?"

"You asked for assistance with returning memories to those affected by the Arpex."

"Yes?"

"We've been working on a solution for you."

I fought to keep the aggravation off my face and out of my voice, but it was damned hard. "And?"

"We'd like to test what we've been working on with the two of you. I've been told it may be...beneficial." He aimed the last bit at Ikeri.

She sat, back straight, eyes forward, not seemingly bothered one bit. She was her mother's daughter.

Except that her mother was far less herself, shoulders slumped forward, head down, fingers clasping her cup as though it were her sole focus in the entire room. Her hair hung loosely around her shoulders rather than being confined in her usual tidy braid, and she wasn't wearing her coat or weapons.

"And what exactly have you been working on?" I prompted.

Tomias cleared his throat and took a deep gulp of tea. "Ikeri told me that your people can replay memories, share them with one another?"

I nodded.

"Instead of just showing what you know to Anastassia, we'd like to try inserting those memories into the holes left behind by the Arpex.

They wouldn't be from her point of view, but we think, that unlike the whisper, like what Etara did for you, feeling would also be conveyed. By melding your techniques with ours, these memories would be closer to what was missing."

"And you're all right with this?" I asked Anastassia. She'd certainly not been agreeable about me sharing memories with her when she'd previously mentioned meeting with Tomias about this exact thing.

She nodded, still staring at her cup.

"How much of what I'm sharing with her, would you see?"

Tomias set his cup gently on the floor. "Everything."

"Will it be painful?"

"We don't know."

"Then try it on me first. She's already got enough headaches to deal with."

Anastassia finally looked up, a faint smile on her lips. "What can I share with you?"

"Gemmen. Tell me about him."

Ikeri glanced at me, eyes wide. "You don't remember Grandfather?"

I shook my head. "The Arpex were hungry."

"I'm sorry," Ikeri said, tears welling in her eyes. She turned to Tomias. "May I try from me first?"

He nodded. "That may be the best place to start. Ease into it slowly."

Ikeri took a deep breath and focused on me. "Do you remember the room, your office, I think it was, where we first met Grandfather?"

"No, I lost that too."

She gave me a pity-filled look that made me uncomfortable. "They took too much."

I didn't acknowledge her statement, as though I could deny it by pretending the truth hadn't been spoken.

"Let me in, and then think about bringing us to Rok, to Cragtek, we were going on a vacation, at least that's what you told us."

I opened my mind to Ikeri and searched through the haze around the vast expanse of gaps, seeking out anything resembling what she spoke of. I remembered telling Anastassia to pack, that we were going somewhere safe. She'd been excited about seeing someone.

"Yes, there. Now relax," she said with a compelling suggestion accompanied by a mental nudge. Slowly, softly, images flickered to life in the void where I'd been looking.

I'd Jumped all three of them into a room. A beat-up prantha hide couch sat along one wall, a large weaving hung behind what had to be a damned expensive desk, and a thick rug lay under my small feet. Ikeri's feet...as I set her down to be sick into a trash bin that Anastassia shoved at me.

Her memory played on, revealing the utter surprise and joy on Gemmen's lively face as he greeted us. Daniel sat on his lap at the terminal on the desk. Ikeri was happy but confused, excited to be in a new place, yet safe in her mother's arms. And then, suddenly, I was back in the open room with Tomias and the others. Try as I might, I couldn't place the moment where I'd lost touch with my surroundings to be immersed in Ikeri's memory.

"Now, look again where we just were. Is the memory still there where it should be?"

I went back to the place where the hole had been, only to find it filled. One less gap. One tiny step forward.

"Yes, it's there."

She smiled proudly.

"Now, can you give the same moments to your mother?" I asked. I'd loved how she'd blushed when Gemmen had asked her about us, and I dearly wanted to see her reaction to remembering that again.

Ikeri turned to face Anastassia, and they began the same process.

What happened outside the mind wasn't near as eventful as I'd hoped. Her expression never changed and neither did Ikeri's. But perhaps that was for the best, considering many of the memories I hoped to return to Anastassia. Except they would have to go through one of the acolytes or Tomias himself.

I began to reassess what I wanted to share.

When they were finished, Ikeri sat proudly while Anastassia watched me as though she were deep in thought.

"Can you manage one more?" asked Tomias. "I'd like to see a full transfer."

Ikeri nodded.

"Are you sure?" I asked. "Remember what I told you before about straining yourself."

She scowled. "I can do this."

It was hard to watch her be the student wanting to please her teacher while also being the concerned parent. I didn't know if she was straining or not, or if Tomias was pushing her too hard, but it was clear she was annoyed that I'd questioned her in front of the group.

"Mother, what would you like to know?" she asked.

Anastassia studied me for a moment. "How did we meet?"

I ran through meeting Anastassia for the first time in my family home with my brother and overhearing the argument about her not wanting to have children. There was nothing there that I objected to Ikeri witnessing, so I again opened my mind to her.

The memory was short as she'd stormed off soon after we'd met, but I tried to slow down and relay all the details and what I'd been thinking upon meeting the woman who had taken all of my brother's attention from me. She had to remember him somewhat. I hoped it would give her something to better fill the gap with and maybe shore up a few other hazy edges.

Ikeri waited until I'd finished, shrinking our connection to our usual level, before again turning to Anastassia. They repeated the same process as before.

When Ikeri broke off, she addressed Tomias. "That was much harder, having to hold the unfamiliar memory together between the transfer."

"I suspected it would be." He glanced at me and nodded a fraction. "You should rest now, Ikeri. Give thought to what might make this process easier both in the holding and energy required."

She rose without complaint and hugged us both. Her bare feet silent on the floor as she headed to the stairs.

Tomias signaled the others who sat behind him. "Each of you will do a transfer. It will be more difficult for you than it was for our little sister, but you are able. You will practice and learn."

I reconsidered my assumption that Tomias was pushing Ikeri. It was the others he was prodding to learn, not her. Her ease of skills would create resentment from the other acolytes, no matter how much peace they preached. I hoped Daniel was up to the job of keeping her safe.

He was going to need more instruction. I added that to my already overflowing list of obligations.

Each of the older acolytes took a turn sitting between us. Their thoughts didn't flow as fluidly, as though they weren't as open to this experience as Ikeri was. For them it was merely a medical process, a procedure to learn.

Grasping how to hold a memory intact during the transfer became a challenge from the start, requiring me to begin in subsequently smaller sections before we found a length that the acolytes were able to contain and successfully transplant. The first one tired out before we'd gotten through me not exactly gifting Anastassia with the replacement neckband. The second fumbled more than the first, only lasting through the end of that exchange. I tried to take it easy on the third one by sharing one of the hundreds of simple family dinners we'd shared while living on Minor, specifically one of them where one of her headaches had crept up, and I'd taken care of her. One by one, they were dismissed until we were left alone with Tomias.

"Would you mind if I also gave this a try?"

"You didn't practice with the others?" Anastassia asked.

"We had no one to practice on, not with your specific situation. It was only a discussion of theory until today. However, if we can make this work, we should be able to not only help bring peace to your people with whom the Arpex have interfered, but also to our elderly with fading minds and those who've sustained head injuries. This was not an area of comfort I'd thought to provide until Ikeri brought it to my attention, and then you also asked for assistance."

"She was already on the problem," Anastassia said.

Tomias nodded. "Her mind doesn't seem to rest."

Anastassia shot me a look I couldn't decipher. "I have a feeling she gets that from her father."

A subject change seemed in order before tensions rose too high. "What do you want to know?"

"Show me our joining."

"It's not what you'd expect," I said hesitantly.

"I don't know what to expect from you."

A burst of calm filled the room, emanating from Tomias. "Let's concentrate together, shall we? Where should Anastassia look for the gap that corresponds to this memory?"

"Pentares. She'd just left her lab and sent Raphael away."

A scowl settled on her face. "I'd asked him to continue our research so I could take a short leave. Not away."

"Away would have been better."

Tomias held up one hand. "Perhaps we should start elsewhere?"

I shrugged and let him in, beginning with seeing her through the window in the door after being away for years. I let him have every feeling, as much as he could handle. Which turned out to be not very much. He pulled away before I'd even got to entering the room. He poured the memory into Anastassia and then returned to me. I continued with my anger at seeing her with Raphael and her taking in my altered state. Tomias again paused to transfer these thoughts to Anastassia before resuming. To conserve the energy involved, I skipped her smoothing over things with security regarding my injuring of the guard and went straight to picking up Daniel. I'd considered skipping that as well, but I did want her to see us interacting as a family to offset my outburst. We wore Tomias out by the time I'd hurried through a scant number of the ceremonial words. I cut him off after it was clear we were skipping straight to the consummation.

He shook his head before the last transfer to Anastassia. "Not exactly a romantic ceremony, was it?"

"I wouldn't even go so far as calling it a ceremony, but it worked for us."

Tomias snorted a little and then completed the last transfer.

Anastassia's cheeks reddened and she opened her mouth as if she were going to chastise me. Instead, she licked her lips and regarded the empty cup on the floor next to her feet until the blush faded.

"We'll need to continue learning this process. May we borrow you again tomorrow for a short while?"

"I'll try. If nothing else, you could practice between Daniel and Anastassia. That would also get you a full transfer."

Tomias nodded thoughtfully.

I stood, being careful not to knock over the cup. "Thank you for your help with this."

Anastassia also got to her feet, though she didn't quite look at me. "You wanted to talk?"

"Yes. Outside."

She headed down the steps so I followed. We ended up out on the lawn before she turned to face me. "Do you think we can fix this?"

"Which *this* are you referring to?"

"Us."

"Honestly, I don't know. My list of things to fix is pretty damned long right now."

She studied me, eyes narrowing. "You're different."

"That would be the Arpex."

"No, you. You've lost the side I liked, the funny one with all the corny comebacks. Now you're all just," she waved a hand in the air, "sharp edges."

"You merged me with a fucking Arpex, Anastassia. That has consequences."

Her gaze dropped to the grass. "I said I was sorry. You were dying. I didn't know what else to do."

"I know." Dammit, Daniel was right. I *was* angry all the time. At Anastassia. The one person I needed to find some middle ground with. I took in a slow deep breath, exhaled, and attempted to find a more civil tone.

"The bond we had together, it leveled me out. Without it, as you've noticed, my focus is singularly elsewhere."

"On work."

I nodded. "You didn't want this relationship the first time around, and the Council conned me into bonding to you. We don't have to do it again. With as screwed up as I am these days, it would probably be best if we didn't. But we do need to figure out some sort of arrangement so we can work together to a degree we're both comfortable with and for the kids."

"An arrangement." She snorted. "With you like this?" She waved a hand at me. "The next time someone pisses you off, are you going to lockdown an entire planet?"

So she didn't approve of my actions against the University. Too damned bad. She wasn't the one they'd experimented on.

"It's been weeks since you've even spoken to the kids," she continued her rant. "From what I hear, you're barely talking to Jey. All I've gotten from you is assignments." She started to walk away. "I'm sure I'm falling behind, standing here. Wouldn't want to end up on the wrong end of your wrath hammer."

Fuck. If I didn't fix this, I'd lose Markus. "Anastassia, wait."

She turned to face me, arms across her chest.

Be less angry, I repeated to myself. "Your memory loss couldn't have hit at a worse time. I needed you."

I sat down in the shade of a flowering tree that bordered the lawn and patted the grass. She glanced around and then settled down beside me.

"When I was gone those three years, when I served an Arpex. It screwed with my head, getting out of there was even worse. I haven't been able to sleep well since I came back, and then with the heart issues and all the stress of what I went through, and then dealing with Arpex in the Narvan, I wasn't in a good place. You were trying to help me, and then suddenly you weren't."

A scowl lodged itself on her face. "I don't know *how* to help you. You're not even talking to me."

I ran my hand over the grass, wishing I could feel the soft blades, or much of anything else for that matter. "Before, you tried everything you could think of, even drugging me. Ikeri couldn't help me either. Etara did a little, but there is so much more wrong inside. If she tried to fix it all, I'd be nothing more than holes and whispers." I made myself look at her. "But I found someone who can."

Her green-eyed glare was almost as deadly as a bullet between the eyes. "Your pretty young pilot on Frique?"

I knew I was gaping and Tamara's life might well depend on whatever words did manage to make their way out of my currently dysfunctional mouth. Self-preservation performed a quick reboot of my brain.

"No. Not at all. Really? You knew about her and didn't say anything? You didn't hurt her, I hope? We didn't. No, not at all that. I—"

"Good to see you are still capable of feeling something for someone."

"Anastassia, it's not me. The damned Arpex shit you and Nan did...I've got whole lots of nothing for anyone. I couldn't screw around even if I wanted to."

The glare dissipated. "So what were you doing there with her?"

"I needed someone to fly the ship while I sought out the Arpex. She didn't ask questions, well, not many, and she was good at keeping us out of view so we didn't upset the natives."

"And that's all?"

"We found a few hatching sites, and I had the pilots clean it up. I went back to check up on them."

"And you were sleeping there, why?"

"Because the mattress on Merchess wasn't all that comfortable. Anything you don't know about where I've been?"

"There a few gaps, but for the most part, no. And you might note that I didn't barge in and threaten your pretty little pilot even when I had every right to since we are still technically joined."

For all her *technically*, that sure sounded like jealousy.

"Why didn't you? You live to threaten people."

"Because she isn't your type," she said.

"I have a type?"

She nodded. "If I'm it, then she isn't. I'd hoped you would come back on your own."

That wasn't at all something old Anastassia would say. Rhaine definitely. But we'd only started the memory transfers, and she'd acted on it long before today. Maybe she'd worked her way around the gaps to put most of herself back together. And she'd been hoping I'd come back?

"So what's this arrangement you're proposing?" she asked.

It might have been my imagination, but I swore she sat closer than she had a moment ago.

"I need to come home."

She nodded.

"And maybe we could talk more."

"Maybe?" Stassia let out an irritated huff.

"Anything more than that is me being selfish again," I said. "It's not what's best for leading the Narvan, you said so yourself."

"Maybe I like it when you're selfish. At least when it comes to us."

She was definitely closer, her shoulder pressing against me, the warmth of her fingers inching over my hand. When they intertwined, her eyes met mine. "Can you feel anything?"

"You were there for the tests."

She got to her knees and faced me, one hand in mine and the other on my chest. "I mean here."

I'd given her an out. Her freedom. Instead of embracing my offer, the face of the woman I'd loved hovered only inches from mine, her hands on me, looking earnest as all hells.

"Yes."

While I didn't have the specific urges that my memories informed me I should be acting on right then, I did miss her voice, her smell. I missed having her beside me, even if we weren't on speaking terms. The peace she'd offered, I missed most, but that would require a bond. Geva only knew if I could manage one of those in my Arpex-infused state—assuming Anastassia would ever want one again.

"Good. Then you should get on with telling me about who this helpful person is before I decide whether to stab or kiss you."

"I wouldn't feel either one."

She chuckled ruefully. "Oh, don't worry, I'll make sure that you do."

I opened my connection with Ikeri, asking her to bring Markus to us.

"You're not moving," she said.

"Ikeri is bringing him."

She sat back down, searching the yard. "You haven't switched preferences, I hope?"

"Of what little preference I currently have, no."

"That's good to know, and yet not." She turned to me. "Does that mean that Arpex are asexual, you think?"

"I'm leaning toward yes. They impregnate their hosts with the barbs on their wing jaws. And as I'm missing wings, I'm rather at a loss."

"I don't know about that."

When the mental caresses started, I knew right where she was going with her efforts, but there was nothing there. I was neither frustrated nor intrigued. Just nothing—except annoyed for feeling nothing and that she again had brought that defect to light.

"Please stop."

She went stiff and pulled away, both mentally and physically. "Really, nothing?"

"Like I said."

"Damn."

"I know."

That she was still beside me and interested was a miracle. What had I done for Geva to earn that favor? Knowing how my life went, Anastassia's continued presence was probably more of a curse. I chuckled half to myself.

Anastassia settled beside me again and rested her head on my shoulder. When Ikeri approached with Markus in hand and a beaming smile on her face, Anastassia gave me a questioning glance. "Him?"

I nodded. Urging Markus closer.

He appeared well and maybe a little less frightened. This little kid had so much ahead of him. If I could help him find his way through this current mess in his head, give him a home with plenty of opportunities and safety, he just might make it out whole. Hells, he might even be happy someday, maybe start a little Jalvian dynasty of his own, one more accepting than others because he'd been raised by Artorians.

Maybe Nan was right, we needed to reconstruct ourselves rather than deconstructing others.

Markus rolled the sleeve of Daniel's shirt up once again only to have the other one fall loose over his hand.

Anastassia halted him on his path to me. "Come here. I'll fix it."

I wasn't half as surprised as I probably should have been to discover that she did in fact have a dagger in one hand. She made quick work of the sleeve issue.

"I'm going to assume, since you are wearing one of Daniel's shirts, that you arrived here with him?" She nodded toward me.

Markus glanced between us, keeping her knife in sight as well. Anastassia noted his discomfort and put it away.

"Did he kidnap you?"

Markus shook his head.

"Did he hurt you?"

Again he shook his head, his fingers fidgeting at his sides as he did his best to meet her gaze.

"Can you talk?"

"Yes," he all but whispered.

She placed her hands on his head, running them down his shoulders and arms, patting his stomach and back, her Seeker training coming to the forefront, assessing his health and putting him at ease. "Do you have magical healing powers?"

His lips quirked. "No."

"He says you do."

"Anastassia, leave him be." I held out my hand to the boy. Markus plopped down in my lap.

Her smile matched the one Ikeri wore. "I guess he was right."

EIGHTEEN

Jey sat across from us at the table in the kitchen of our house on Artor, dressed in his full uniform to further illustrate his role in the meeting. Markus and Daniel were off somewhere on the floor above making enough exuberant noise to almost guarantee one of them would get hurt in short order.

"Let me get this straight. In the matter of a day, you've moved back in, Anastassia has taken you back, and you want to formally adopt Markus Nytun."

"Yes," we said in unison.

"Anastassia, you don't even like kids. Not even your own kids."

"I do too. Sometimes. Most of the time." She shook her head, loose hair falling around her shoulders. "Listen to them, they're getting along just fine."

Jey glanced at the ceiling with a disbelieving glare. "It sounds like they're killing each other up there. Why are neither of you going to check on them?"

"They're fine. You're just not used to the sounds of siblings playing," I said.

Something heavy clanged on the floor. Footsteps scrambled in what seemed like all directions.

He shot to his feet. "They're not siblings, and if anything happens to that boy while he's with you..." He made a mad dash for the stairs.

We followed close behind.

Daniel and Markus stood side by side in the doorway, only further illustrating the possibility of injury as Daniel, at twice Markus's age, was far taller and broader. Together, they blocked our entry into his room.

Daniel, unprompted, said, "Nothing. It's nothing. We're fine.

Aren't we?"

Markus nodded.

Jey's voice thundered over the two of them, making them both cower. "What the hells was that?"

I inserted myself between him and the boys. "Did you break anything? Are either of you bleeding?"

They each answered no.

"All right then. Do whatever you were doing more quietly and pick up your mess when you're done."

We went back down the stairs. Jey followed after a couple backward glances. We resumed our places at the table.

"Really, that's it?" he asked, looking at Anastassia. "No exploding temper, threats, nothing?"

"I told you, he's better."

"I wouldn't go—"

She kicked me under the table.

"And you plan on handling the three of them how exactly?" Jey asked.

Anastassia answered before I could. "Training. All of them. Ikeri and Daniel are already set on Veria Prime. Markus will either join them or find his own place once he settles in."

"If you think I would allow him into any of our academies after Daniel's behavior, you're wrong. Not if he's living with you two."

"About that," I said. "Daniel has been wanting to meet with you. I told him to hold off due to, well, circumstances being what they were."

"He's not getting back in."

"We're both well aware of that."

Jey's scowl lessened a single degree.

"So I'm supposed to formally sign over the rights of the sole survivor of a well-known Jalvian family to an Artorian who may or may not legally exist depending on who's doing the asking."

"Our children have full Artorian rights," I offered.

"Neither of which are fully Artorian. Look, we both know you paid a hefty sum for those rights, but they hold no validity beyond Artor." He sighed. "Do you have any idea how much of a legal nightmare this would be?"

Stassia straightened and broke out her level-calm voice. "If he goes home with you, who takes him?"

"Family services."

"And where will they place him?"

"A kid with his issues? Seeing his family eaten, losing half his memories, and all the trauma of the publicized kidnapping? Probably no one long-term."

"I didn't kidnap him."

"Yes, yes, you rescued him from a horrific situation and stole him from the arms of the service worker."

"She never touched him, as your vids will show. I wanted to leave peacefully. Your clinic staff were the ones doing the attacking."

"Yeah, I know." He sighed again. "I watched the feed, several times, but that's not how the media is spinning this."

Frustration leaked through Anastassia's level demeanor. "Then why are you being such an ass?"

The two of them locked gazes, after which Jey's scowl remained the same. "I don't like it, and I don't think it will end well. However, his chances back home aren't much better." He shifted in his seat. "I expect every damned Arpex off Jal as payment."

Anastassia placed both hands on the table and leaned forward. "Did we not just discuss how we both wanted him working less?"

"You said he was better." The chair scraped along the floor as he stood, his stance less than friendly. "If that's the case, he doesn't need to back off. You can have Vayen, and he can have Markus when he's done with the job he started. Or maybe he isn't actually better at all?"

Whatever deal she'd struck with Jey was hers to handle. She'd gotten him agreeable to this point, and I wasn't about to screw it up. I kept quiet and let them talk.

I wasn't sure what Ikeri had meant about me needing Markus, but Anastassia had also said as much. It was probably something more profound than what was obvious to me, that Seeker shit usually was, but on one front for sure, I had to agree. For the first time in years, I actually looked forward to sleeping.

The night before, with the four of us in the giant house had seemed odd at first. Ikeri had begged to remain on Prime, wanting to work with the others on improving their transfer process. As much as I wanted her to come home with us, I also wanted the acolytes to improve so Anastassia and I could have another session.

Daniel had been hesitant to leave her, but the lure of showing Markus around the house and my assurances that Etara and Tomias would watch out for Ikeri had swayed him. Daniel and Markus had been fairly quiet all evening, awkward as they got to know one another. Then Markus had fallen silent, dark circles on the pale skin beneath his eyes.

I stood with him in my arms, wondering where to go. Stassia nudged me toward our bedroom. After we'd disarmed and changed, I settled in with Markus. Stassia slid in behind me, her warmth curling around my back. If she'd tossed or turned, I didn't know about it. Markus and I woke well-rested, and he'd been playing with Daniel with short breaks for meals ever since.

"Vayen." Stassia elbowed me. "Hello, in there."

"Got it, yes, eradicate all Arpex on Jal."

Feet scampered around above us. I brushed over Neko's link and found him sound asleep. He'd be of no immediate help.

"I'll be there shortly," I said to Jey. "I'll need to drop the boys off on Prime first."

"I am capable of watching them, despite what he thinks." Anastassia gave Jey an offended sniff.

"You're coming with me."

"Oh, yes." She nodded. "I like that plan much better. Dropping them off it is."

Jey shook his head. "Once I start this paperwork nightmare, I'm not going back on it. So, one last time, are you sure?"

"Have you not been sitting here?" Anastassia got up and cleared away the plate of snacks she'd set out. The conversation had been too intense for anyone to consider eating. Cleaning up gave her something to do to that covered the emotion that must have been playing out on her face because it was still clear in her voice. "One more rambunctious body to watch over is worth getting Vayen back. At least I think so. Maybe you don't."

"Anastassia, I didn't say that. What I don't understand is the correlation between this one random kid and Vayen."

"He helps me sleep."

"And you don't think that's odd? A grown man sleeping with a little boy like he's some sort of security blanket?"

Stassia came to stand behind me, her hands on my shoulders. "I slept with them too. Nothing inappropriate is going on here, I assure you. If your daughter has a nightmare, you don't let her in bed with you?"

"She doesn't have nightmares."

"Then she's a lucky girl to not have encountered the sort of trauma that Markus and Vayen have. We can help him. Will you let us?"

Doubt shadowed Jey's penetrating gaze, but he nodded. The

medals on his uniform clinked against one another as he leaned over the table. "Let me know when the Arpex are taken care of. We'll discuss the finer details of the adoption then."

The heat in Stassia's hands increased. I put mine over hers, keeping her in place. Pushing Jey at this point wasn't going to do us any favors.

Seeing that neither of us rose to his bait, Jey stepped into the void.

"Where did you leave your armor and weapons?" I asked her.

"Frique, with Neko. He needed a break."

"All right, Prime first. I believe we also have an appointment with Tomias." I got up and strapped on the few weapons I'd brought with me, making sure everything was charged and loaded.

"Could you possibly take Markus to the house on Minor?" she asked. "Daniel has smaller clothes there and they'll help him blend in better on Prime."

"Is that important right now? There are already too many Jumps in my near future."

"I suppose it can wait."

But as she walked up the stairs to retrieve the boys, her stiff posture said otherwise. Or maybe she was still pissed about Jey. Either way, it wouldn't bode well for me to allow her bad mood to fester. Jumping myself took a lot less energy than taking Markus with me, and I was back before they'd come down. She took in the stack of worn Verian clothing and smiled.

"I didn't remember that you were so rough on your clothes," she said to Daniel, picking through the stack and finally choosing a set. Stassia pointed Markus to the bathroom. "Go get changed. We're waiting on you."

He accepted the clothing in silence and made his way to the bathroom with uncertain steps. When the door closed, she turned to me.

"I don't think he likes me."

"He was the same with Ikeri. I don't think it's you so much as what happened to him. Give him time."

She knocked her hip into me. "Worked with you, I suppose."

I noticed Daniel watching us. "What?"

He grinned. "Nothing."

When Markus emerged, pant legs dragging around his feet, he looked to me. I rolled them up for him. "There, that's better. We're going to go back to the place we were yesterday. Would you like to see Etara again?"

He shrugged.

"Then how about you stay with Daniel until we get back?"

Markus grabbed my hand and held on tight, staring up at me like I could read his mind. I shook my head. "I have to work for a while. I promise I'll be back in time for bed."

"Don't promise him stuff like that," Daniel said, scowling. "He'll think you mean it."

"I do."

"Daniel is right," Anastassia said quietly. She said to Marcus, "We will try very hard to be back by bedtime, but if we're not, he will take care of you and keep you safe."

"You let me know if he has any problems," I told Daniel. "He can't contact me like you can."

Daniel nodded.

I looked them all over and formed the Jump to Veria Prime. Jumping the three of them drained me considerably, to the point I didn't even complain about Markus's short-legged pace as we made our way through the streets to Tomias's door.

Stassia walked right in. We followed along behind her. I disengaged Markus from my hand and sent him off with Daniel. Stassia must have let Tomias know we were coming because he was waiting in the upper room with Ikeri and the other acolytes we'd worked with. Several more sat nearby.

"They've come to observe today, perhaps to take part tomorrow," Tomias said, indicating we should take our places from the day before.

He asked the acolytes we'd worked with previously to go first. Each filling a hole in Stassia's mind. When it came to Ikeri's turn, I pondered what to share with her, settling on my poorly thought out plan to foster a Verian kid that had finally won Stassia over to the idea of having a second child. Several months of debate, a knife to my throat, and a couple bouts of days of silence had culminated in that long, horrible two-week-long experience. I hadn't even known of its success until a few months later when she'd confided that she was pregnant and what had changed her mind. When I'd finished reliving it with Ikeri, she rose and kissed my cheek before settling in front of Stassia.

Tomias, having explained the process to the new acolytes as we went, again took his turn last. With him I shared the two of us working together, choosing a political meeting rather than a bloody one.

"Would you mind giving us one more session tomorrow? The

acolytes we've been using should be ready enough to assist you in the Narvan as requested the day after. Then I'll start with these. I've borrowed them from another Seeker."

Anastassia rose. "Yes, of course. Thank you, Tomias."

I followed her down the stairs and back out into the yard where we'd sat the day before. She turned around to face me.

"You wanted another kid that badly?"

I nodded.

"Who would have figured you for a family man?" She chuckled. "But considering everything now, I'm glad you convinced me."

"I think it was more you convincing yourself, but yes, I'm glad too."

She smiled as she took my arm. "To Frique then?"

I formed the Jump and we stepped out of the void into the trees. The perpetual heat of Frique blanketed me. If it weren't for this damned planet, the Arpex wouldn't have cared half as much about the Narvan.

We went inside to find Neko sprawled across the couch, face down. He didn't even twitch.

"The poor man hasn't slept more than a few hours in a row since you left."

"Why? He can't work like that."

"He refused to resort to stims. If you can manage without them, he's convinced he can do the same."

I poked Neko in the ribs. He rolled onto his side. I poked him again. He mumbled something. His eyes fluttered and then sprang open as if he'd been shocked. He scrambled off the couch and stood before me, hair sticking every which way and a red crease across his face from the couch cushion.

"Tired?"

He glanced at Stassia before meeting my gaze. "Sorry, boss."

"Next time take a damned stim if you need to. I don't want to see you this ragged again. Go to bed."

He stumbled into his bedroom and dropped onto the bed, not even bothering with the door.

Stassia closed it for him and then went into our bedroom to change. I stayed just outside the door she left cracked open.

She came out dressed in her usual black and grey, hair in a braid, weapons on, and coat in hand. But it was the bands around her neck and arm that stole my breath. "What are you doing with those?"

"Wearing them," she said matter-of-factly. "You presented them to me. We *are* still joined, right?"

"Well yes, but you..."

She slipped into her coat. "Good. Then let's go."

Befuddled by her back to looking like I wanted her to, along with sounding like herself, I took her hand and Jumped to Jal.

"Not bothering with your armor anymore?" she asked.

"Left it on Merchess. Too many Jumps. I'll get by."

We located an air transport and began the sweep near the plex where I'd found Markus.

Anastassia sat across from me, looking out the window at the buildings below. "What are we searching for exactly?"

"I'll do the searching. I can hear them."

"What do you want me to do?"

"Whatever you want."

She scowled. "Don't be an ass. What can I help you with?"

"I wasn't trying to be." Dammit, I needed to find a fix for my perpetually terse tone. At least with her. I pasted a smile on my face. "Artor or Karin, both need attention. Take your pick.

She pulled her datapad from her coat pocket and started tapping away. I'd missed the sound of her fingers dancing. In the dim light of the transit, her face, illuminated by the datapad, intent on whichever world she picked to attend to, was the woman who had sat in bed beside me so many nights, trying to stay awake until she was sure I was sleeping.

Easing back in the seat, I let my eyes slip closed and listened for the now familiar hiss of the Arpex. Hours passed but there was only silence in my head and intermittent tapping in the transit. I was about to call off the search in favor of getting other things accomplished when I finally picked up a hiss. I signaled the transit to land.

Anastassia looked up. "Find one?"

"Stay here."

"I'll take that as a yes," she said dryly. "They can't get to me through you, right? If we're connected?"

"I've not had a connection open when facing them before, so I don't know. We're not taking that chance. Stay here."

"I planned on it. But if you run into trouble, let me know."

And what could she do if I did? Lob a grenade into the building? I'd be wounded too if she did, and she couldn't Jump me. Not to mention, I had no idea what the tank would do to me in my current state. I really needed to get to the ship and spend a couple hours setting a new baseline profile.

If she came racing in to pulse it, she'd be close enough to become a victim again. And now, instead of charging inside to take care of the problem, I was worried she'd come in after me and get hurt. Dammit, this wasn't going to work, no matter how much I wanted it to. But if I pushed her away again, I wouldn't get Markus. I wanted to punch something.

"Vayen." She grabbed my face, forcing me to look at her. "Don't shut me out again."

I could leave her in the transport and send it back up as soon as I exited so she couldn't follow me. Except that she knew how to manipulate the system just as well as I did, and even though using a datapad instead of a link might take her longer, she'd still land it again. And she'd be pissed, and that made her erratic. I couldn't deal with that right now.

"Promise me you're actually going to stay here. I don't want you to lose anything else."

"Then promise me you'll come back."

She'd made me promise that same thing when I'd sent them all off to Pentares. They would have all been better off if I hadn't kept my word. While I'd given voice to the vow last time, I only nodded now.

The hiss in my mind grew louder. It knew I was here. The hiss slowly became fragmented words, hints of meaning. This one wasn't waiting.

"It's coming for me. I have to go."

Palming the door, I leapt out of the transit and into the street. Relief rushed through me when I heard the door seal shut. She'd listened. This one time.

"You speak," said a hiss-filled voice off to my right.

I sought out the connection and dove into it, prying its mind open to find out what made this one different, to see if it had learned about me from the others.

It lashed out with its foot, but the razor edge did little more than scratch my leg through my sliced-open pants. Seeing its efforts had no effect, it backed away.

It tried to block my mental invasion but that had little effect either. I sank deeper into its mind and instead of using questions as they did, I searched it like I would a network, more like a probe. Now that I was more familiar with Arpex brains it was easier to sift through the foreign images and thoughts to try to piece together its intent and its origin.

The world it showed me was the same green tree place that I'd seen before. It pushed hard, thrusting walls at me, shunting me aside at every turn. I caught glimpses of nests teaming with young and rotting non-Arpex inhabitants. All the colors other than the vibrant green were washed out, as if they were sensed rather than seen.

It didn't appear to have any prior knowledge of me, at least not that I could find in the evade and dig game we were playing. This Arpex was better at multitasking. I could feel it darting around in my mind, seeking out a weakness.

Trying to work as quickly as possible, I sought out how the Arpex themselves communicated in the wider range, looking for the channel that flowed between them. It was quiet. I didn't sense that this one was connected to any others like the Arpex in the same city had been on the offering planet. Their channel hadn't reached to the next cluster of Arpex either. Whether that was by choice or an indication of their range of communication remained to be seen.

"Have you talked to other Arpex here?" I asked in the hopes that questions might get me farther.

Its mind scrambled to block its answer, but for a moment images and words clarified. The only conversation, and brief at that, was between this Arpex and another who had shared the ship to Jal. They had parted ways shortly after and had not spoken since.

"Did you all come from the same place to take the Narvan?"

An image of Frique. Coordinates. Plentiful food. The information had come from another Arpex, one who visited and then vanished, like it had Jumped.

My hold on the flow of information wavered as my thoughts raced. Had it been the same Arpex I'd served? That one had a link, I'd seen it Jump to the offering world. It could have Jumped to share information and then back to the Council base. It could have escaped our attack. It could still be alive. My mouth went dry as my breaths grew quick and shallow.

Calm, dammit, I needed to remain calm. I couldn't afford to break down now, not while I was in the middle of getting information that I needed to protect the Narvan. Not while Anastassia sat in a ship nearby, unable to Jump herself.

The memories came into focus again. This one stood facing a crowd of Arpex, others lined up beside it. The sky had an orange cast. Not the green world, somewhere else. They boarded ships in pairs.

The Arpex slammed into my mind with the force of a pulse to my brain. It was far different than the nerve twisting pain the others had used that didn't affect me now. This did, immensely, and seized every muscle in my body. Breathing became an impossible quest, as did keeping my eyes open. I became distantly aware that I was falling.

Giant wings beat the air, spraying me with pebbles and dirt, all of which seemed to end up in my mouth. The Arpex had lost all words, ringing out an unending scream in my head.

And then the wind stopped and all my gasping finally brought air to my lungs. However, the scream remained. As did the pain.

Merkief's charred face greeted me with a smile. He was saying something, but I couldn't hear him over the piercing tone of the Arpex. Deep Voice, in tattered robes, his scarred face torn open and bleeding, pointed down a hallway filled with flames. I got to my feet and turned to go the opposite direction, gathering my bloody shirt around me, but Shoulders stood in my way, his face a shadow, gloved hands in massive fists. The flames suddenly didn't seem like such a bad idea. I sprinted for them.

Warmth surrounded me, but the fire didn't burn. I paused to wonder how this was possible and saw that Shoulders stood just outside the flames. I couldn't go back. I had to go forward. But now I couldn't move.

Locked in place, the flames licked at my skin, unable to burn my hardened flesh, yet the heat still seared. The thin shirt burst into ash, drifting on a lazy breeze to sprinkle my immobile feet with grey flecks. The pungent odor of my hair burning made me nauseous.

Merkief came into the fire and stood beside me, reaching out. Metal flashed in his blackened hand, pricking my wrist. Green blood gushed from the cut. My armored skin dissolved in an instant. He laughed, a sound even more terrifying than the never-ending scream of the Arpex.

I burst into flames.

And then there was only darkness and blessed silence. I drifted there, floating in the nothing, being nothing, relieved beyond all other thought that it was finally over.

I was over.

NINETEEN

A faint whisper penetrated the silence. *"Daddy?"*

It was calm in the nothing, peaceful. No pain, no worries. I let the whisper echo and fade until there was only a comfortable blanket of silence.

Ikeri yelled, demanding and angry, filling the nothing, dissolving the blanket that held me. *"Answer me."*

My body was gone, but I could still form natural speech. *"Let me be."*

They would be fine. Ikeri had Tomias. Daniel knew to watch over Ikeri. Anastassia and Jey could handle the Narvan and Neko had her back. Nan knew how to make more Arpex hunters like myself. I could rest, stay here in the nothing, and just be.

"What about Markus?"

Those three words tumbled about, turning over, twisting, rolling until they brushed against me from all sides. Markus didn't have anyone to fill the holes in his memories. He needed to make new ones and someone who understood him to help make that happen. Even though I no longer had hands, I could somehow feel his warm fingers wiggle their way into mine.

The nothing grew lighter, like the morning sky. Birds chirped in the distance as if they were outside very thick walls or maybe I was far underground.

"Just a little closer," Ikeri said, the anger gone now.

I could sense her excitement. And exhaustion. That alone ripped away the last vestiges of the peaceful nothingness and plunged me into a room filled with bright light and beeping equipment. One of the machines was going crazy, its shrill pings every few seconds made me want to reach out and smash it.

"Turn that off," Ikeri demanded.

"I need it on," said a familiar voice. Nan. "You've done your part, now let me do mine."

They'd brought me to the fucking University. Again. I desperately sought out the nothing, scrambling for any remaining shred of the silent peace, but there was only blinding pain in my head and my chest, and I wanted none of it.

"Do we need the boy in here? He's in the way."

People. There were people moving all around me, their voices, shuffling footsteps, rustling hands and cloth. Their breathing. I wanted them gone. All of them.

"Markus stays," Anastassia said. "You just hold on, Ikeri, and do whatever you're doing."

I managed to get my eyes open enough to make out Anastassia holding Ikeri against her, trying to be as unobtrusive as possible, wedged between the banks of equipment against the wall. Neko sat in a chair at the far end of the room, head in his hands. When I caught him glancing at me, I recognized the pinched look of too many jumps in quick succession. His head had to be hurting almost as much as mine. Daniel was missing, but Markus hovered at my side, his hands clamped on my grey one. Eyes wide, he caught me looking at him.

"Please stay."

As much as I wanted to answer him, my tongue wouldn't cooperate. My muscles were no more obedient when I tried to squeeze his hand instead.

"Why is he still awake?" Nan shouted. "Figure out the damned sedation right now! Is the operating room open and prepped?"

I lost track of the voices. Too many of them were talking at once, blending into an overwhelming cacophony.

Ikeri's calm voice pushed them aside in my head. *"They are going to fix your heart and other things. Sorry, I didn't understand it all. Mother approved it."*

She'd approved fusing the Arpex to me too.

"Be calm. Let them fix you."

Either she was exerting her calm to a whole new level or someone had figured the sedation out because I found myself back floating in the nothingness. It wasn't as quiet or as dark this time. Ikeri was still with me, but far away. I settled onto a warm soft blanket and closed my eyes.

When they opened again, I was back in the room with Anastassia asleep in the chair. Markus and Ikeri sat on the floor on either side of her, leaning against the chair, eyes closed. Neko was gone.

"Anastassia," said a voice I'd not expected to hear beside me.

I turned to focus on Jey. "Why are you here?"

"Someone had to make sure the staff didn't screw you over in some new way. She couldn't keep her eyes open and Neko was running on empty after all the Jumping."

"Daniel?"

"Still on Minor. I can get him if you want, now that you're awake."

I nodded. Though I wanted to say more, I found my eyes slipping closed before Anastassia made it to my side. Her hand ran over my face, leaving a trail of warmth behind.

When I opened them again, it was to Daniel sitting next to me. He alerted the others that I was awake. Footsteps raced to the bed. Someone held a glass of water for me. I drained it and lay back.

"Advisor Ta'set, how are you feeling?" Nan asked.

"I don't know."

"Well, the good news is that we were able to repair your heart, and by repair, I mean replace it with a close match. You'll be happy to know, it's a much closer match than your hand was."

"Not a natural replacement, you mean?

"Correct."

"Isn't that against code?"

Nan chuckled. "You're against code in so many ways already, I don't think this one more artificial thing is going to tip the scales any further. The rest might help offset that a little."

"The rest?"

"I did what I could for the effects of the Arpex fusing," she shrugged, "you know this is a guessing game, but I'm hopeful it's closer to what you wanted."

She cleared her throat and took a few steps back. "I did also take the liberty of authorizing the modification of your eye and hand to better fit within natural parameters. We can't have you representing our world looking like some hacked-together fringe job."

"I liked my hand." I tried to lift it, but it was too damned heavy. No doubt they still had me significantly sedated.

Anastassia lifted the sheet that covered me and pulled out my hand so I could examine it. "Don't worry," she said. "I made sure they only changed out the skin. You can still happily pound and smash with it."

"Thanks. And my eye?" Looking around the room, I didn't notice anything different. Markus, Daniel, and Ikeri stood at the foot of the bed. Jey and Neko were both absent.

"Matches the other one," Stassia said, smiling. She looked to Markus and nodded.

He crept closer. I knew something was going on because both Daniel and Ikeri bore apprehensive smiles. Nan took another step closer to the door and Anastassia's hand tightened on my formerly grey one.

"What, did my wings finally sprout?"

Markus reached out and stroked the side of my face. He leaned close, his voice the softest whisper. "They took the Arpex away."

I turned to Anastassia, wondering what the hells that meant. My mind remained a pockmarked mess, and I still held every memory of my imprisonment and encounters with every Arpex since.

Nan quickly handed Anastassia a mirror and stepped back toward the door. Anastassia held it up, adjusting the angle until my gasp confirmed she had it right. They'd removed the scarring, the worst of it anyway. The skin was still more scar than anything else, but it was a definite improvement, smoother and more subtle. I no longer shared a face with Arin and Deep Voice.

When the lump in my throat had passed, I turned to Nan. "They told me it couldn't be fixed. That it was too deep. I consulted multiple sources."

"It's not fixed, as you can see, but we did what we could. Perhaps your other sources were hesitant to take the chance of incurring your wrath should you be displeased with their efforts."

"My wrath? Really?"

Anastassia patted my hand. "You do go a little heavy on the wrath from time to time."

"I don't think so."

"May I have a minute?" Ikeri asked.

Nan regarded her warily and made a quick exit. Daniel waved Markus to his side and went to the door. Stassia gave me a warning look and followed the boys out. I watched them leave, amused that they all deferred to the young girl now at my side.

"You have a revelation for me too?"

She closed her eyes, long lashes brushing her pale skin. Her warm hands rested on my arm. "I'm sorry I made you come back."

I searched my recent memory for what she was talking about. My dreams unfurled, replaying in my mind. She'd found me in the nothing, guilted me with Markus, dragged me back to this body, this room.

"Is this about the wrath comment?"

Her lips quirked at the corners and her eyes peeked open. "Maybe?"

She should be sorry. I'd told her before to stop saving me, to let me go rather than put herself at risk. I'd been happy where I was, relieved. At peace.

I didn't appreciate the guilt she'd used to tear me away or how far she'd strained herself to convey it. She was my daughter too—willing to go all in no matter what the consequences if the situation was dire enough. Apparently, my death had been for her.

Though I didn't give voice to my ungrateful thoughts, she could read them just fine if she wanted to. I left that up to her. She gave no indication one way or the other.

My conscience said I should say thank you, that I should be grateful, that she'd done an amazing thing. But I was done with lying to her.

"You're fortunate that I'm too medicated to give in to wrath at the moment."

"What about after the medication wears off?" she asked quietly.

I couldn't blame her for not letting her father die. I would have done anything to have kept my parents alive if I'd been given the opportunity. I imagined they would have appreciated my efforts a whole lot more than I did Ikeri's. I imagined a lot of things for a few seconds, wondering how different my life would have been if they'd still been alive, if I still knew my own mother beyond a stranger's face in a still frame.

"Daddy?"

"I might be compelled to let it go."

Her palms grew hot on my arm and the faint tremor in her voice was matched in her hands. A faint tremor I could feel.

"Compelled how exactly? You're not going to make me quit training are you?"

Excitement overpowered my irritation with her. I tried to sit up more but my body wouldn't cooperate. "Move your hand."

She pulled away.

"No, touch my arm again. Lightly."

Her fingers flitted over my skin from wrist to elbow, making me shiver. Nan had done it. I could feel again. If my legs would have cooperated, I would have jumped out of the bed and sought out Anastassia to explore just how much sensation had returned. The very fact that I had that inclination made me happier than I'd been in weeks.

"Get up here."

Ikeri sat on the bed beside me, looking at me like I'd lost my mind.

I wrapped one arm around her, enjoying the sensation of her clothes on my skin. She snuggled closer and rested her light-skinned hand on mine, reminding me of the contrast between us. Light and dark. And her hand was only half the size. She was still so young.

"You may continue training because I have the distinct feeling that you're doing just as much of instructing as Tomias is."

"You're not wrong," she said, smiling.

"Promise me you'll pick pretty tattoos when the time comes?"

"I'm not Verian, Daddy."

"They won't let you become a full Seeker? That's ludicrous. You know more than they do, and you're just a—"

"Don't say little girl."

"Well, you're my little girl. You can be whatever you want to the rest of the known universe."

She hugged me, her curls tickling my neck.

"That's your penance. A hug every time I see you. Got it?"

Sitting back, she grinned. "Otherwise it's wrath?"

"Yes."

"Got it."

"Now, about those tattoos..."

Anastassia poked her head inside. "Ikeri, let him rest. He's got a lot of recovering to do."

"I'll see you soon." Ikeri gave me a quick peck on the cheek before slipping off the bed and dodging out of the room.

Anastassia remained half in and half out, both hands on the door.

"You could come in."

"I could, but you do need to rest, and when you smile like that, resting is not what comes to mind."

"I might be all right with that."

She grinned. "Go to sleep. We'll discuss that at a later time. When you're sure you're up for it."

"I can assure you...that I'm highly medicated right now and have no idea, but I'm holding you to that discussion."

"I look forward to it."

Neko's head appeared next to Anastassia's. "Are you two about done with the moony-eyed face-making? The kids are back on Prime and Jey is waiting for you, Anastassia."

"Yes," I said, "take her away. She won't let me sleep."

She snorted. "Make sure he stays in bed."

"You know what would keep me here?"

From the speed at which she vanished from the doorway, I gathered Neko had yanked her out of the way. Once he entered, he closed the door behind him and sat in the chair at the foot of the bed.

"Sorry boss, you're stuck with me, and the only thing keeping you in bed is the medication. We all know that. That's why it's in your veins until Nan's people have decreed that you've recovered enough to return to full action. Yes," he raised his hand, "We all know you're at full speed or nothing. That's why you're on nothing until further notice."

"Perhaps you missed the wrath comment earlier."

Neko shared one of his patented apologetic smiles. "Keeping you in one piece is a thankless job. Good thing you pay well."

TWENTY

I spent two full weeks in bed. Neko brought one of the kids each day to visit with me for a couple hours, and Markus slept by my side when it was night on Minor. Stassia came when she could, but the Narvan kept her busy.

Medicated as I was, I couldn't hold onto a network or even a conversation for long. I wasn't much help to anyone, and it drove me crazy in my more alert moments. My only consolation to being in bed was having plenty of time for Neko and Nan to monitor the effects of the latest alteration adjustment. Knives and needles still had difficulty penetrating, but a heavy thrust did result in significant damage. Messy damage, that Nan was none too happy about.

That was enough to convince me I shouldn't get too cocky with Jey anymore and wearing my coat would be a good idea.

Though we didn't test bullets or pulses, simulations based on Nan's testing suggested that close range would be an issue. Shots at a distance would leave bruises and a good deal of soreness, but no critical damage, much like wearing my coat.

Being able to feel had its trade-offs.

Neko had been taking far too damn many stims to keep up with Jumping everyone and guarding me from Nan's staff. Most days he seemed to be fighting an internal war between falling asleep on his feet and bouncing off the walls. The day Nan cleared me to leave was no different.

As the medication slowly left my system, control of my body returned. There was so much to do, I flitted between one thought and the next, prioritizing, weighing my options while I waited for the last of the sluggishness to leave my muscles.

"Did you happen to bring my armor? Weapons? Anything?"

Neko shook his head. "Sorry boss, just clothes. I didn't know what you wanted. You'll be better off getting it yourself."

Nan entered with an assistant trailing behind her. "You're not leaving us quite yet. You'll want to meet your volunteers."

"I will?" I glanced at Neko, hoping for some clarification.

He avoided my inquiry by staring at the ceiling.

The assistant turned off the last of the monitoring equipment and disconnected me from the remaining sensors. Nan examined my eye and hand again and then ran a scanner over my chest. She finished her exam with a thorough once over.

"You did bring him some clothes?" she asked Neko.

He nodded, producing a folded stack from beside the chair.

"Good. Help him get changed. They don't know he's been here, and I think it would be best to keep it that way, considering. Any signs of discomfort, dizziness, or shortness of breath, call me immediately. I'll be right outside."

Nan and the assistant let themselves out. Neko set the clothes beside me and backed away.

"I'm assuming you can do that yourself?"

"We'll find out." Though I was more clearheaded than I'd been since my last run-in with the Arpex, I took my time getting dressed, not wanting to keel over in front of Neko if something went wrong. By the time I'd finished, I wanted to crawl back onto the bed.

"You've been on your back for a while. Give your muscles a chance to get back in the game," Neko said.

"I'm well aware of how this whole recovery thing works."

"Glad to see you're back in your usual spirits."

I glared at him and took a few tentative steps. "Where's Anastassia?"

"She'll be here shortly. Jey is bringing her."

"Good." I halted my progress four steps from the bed and held out my hand to him. "Then she won't see you helping me get to that chair so I can sit down."

He rushed to my side. "That bad? Dizzy?"

"Tired. Did she give me the heart of an obese elderly accountant?"

Neko took my arm and guided me over to the chair he'd vacated. "You do remember that Nan told you it was manufactured, right? You were pretty out of it most of the time."

"Yes, it's just...four steps. That's all I've got in me?" I settled into the chair and closed my eyes for a few minutes.

Nan returned with Anastassia in her wake. They both regarded me thoughtfully from a distance.

"We may have to rethink this," said Anastassia.

Nan called out, "Everyone will be seated, Arelia. Reset the room immediately."

Footsteps rushed away from the other side of the door.

Anastassia came closer. "Do you remember what happened, what brought you here?"

I hated being on the outside of whatever was going on, and the haze of the past two weeks only added to my annoyance with her darting conversation. "I was interrogating an Arpex, but it wasn't going well. You were supposed to stay in the transport. But I'm here, so I'm guessing you didn't, and somewhere in there my heart acted up again?"

"You went down hard and the Arpex didn't. When it was clear you weren't getting back up, I took a chance and pulsed it while it was distracted with you."

"I was still locked in its mind when you killed it."

She nodded. "I didn't realize that at the time, but pulsing it was the only option I had. Neko had just arrived to get you when you stopped breathing. We didn't know what the tank would do given your alterations, and with you unresponsive, we decided this was your best chance."

"I remember Ikeri."

Anastassia crouched down in front of me. "She brought you back. The staff here couldn't, but she did."

Nan coughed. "We did stabilize him and took over his care from there."

"You did," said Anastassia. "And we thank you."

"What's this mysterious meeting?" I asked.

"You asked Nan to create more like you." She stood and held out her hand to me. "Don't worry, they are volunteers with full disclosure of the process upfront. All Artorian. We chose only men since we had a better understanding of those results."

I took her hand and let her help me to my feet, enjoying her rough palm against mine. "Are they like me as I am now? Able to feel?"

Nan nodded. "I thought it best to keep you all uniform."

"And we're going to meet them now?" As much as my mind wanted to dive back into work, all my body wanted was a nap in my own bed. I didn't even care which one.

Anastassia slipped her arm around my waist, effectively propping me up as we started out of the room where I'd been confined. "You're going to sit and explain the process of finding Arpex to them. Jey brought in a wounded one from Moriek two days ago. It's being held, as per your instructions, in a room elsewhere within the University."

"And you're all right with this?" I asked Nan, who walked ahead of us. "Aren't you supposed to tell me to rest and not strain myself or something?"

"Why do you think we're doing this right now, Advisor? I've been told you can't be trusted to do either of those things unless you know the situation is being handled."

"I see." I pulled Anastassia a bit closer. "Remind me not to complain so much about your obsessive level of organization.

She poked me in the ribs. "I'm serious when I say explain. No interrogating the Arpex, just talking. They've already received their assignments. Once you're sure they've got this, they're on duty."

"And me?"

"To bed after you eat."

"Is it a bad sign if I don't argue?"

She chuckled. "No. You just know who you're up against and that it's pointless."

"There is that." Though, on a good day, I still would have tried.

The four of us entered a lift and went down two floors. Thank Geva the appointed room was only two doors away because my legs started to shake.

After making sure I'd gotten my feet solidly under me, Anastassia opened the door and went in first. Three empty chairs faced ten others. The ten were occupied by an array of Artorian men, all in their own clothing with nothing to mark them as altered. They bore both northern and southern coloring, hair of varying lengths, one quite tall, the rest average, all in decent shape.

I tried not to hurry to the center chair, but sitting before I fell on my face was all I could think about until my ass settled into it. Neko sat on my left and Anastassia on my right. Nan stood, making introductions that my swimming mind distantly noted for later review. To add to my distraction, I could hear the Arpex now that I was listening for it, and it was pissed.

As I explained the process of opening their minds to the foreign place the Arpex used, I heard it calling out, begging any others who might be nearby to help it.

"They can't save you." I said.

"My kind will feast upon yours. Our young will spring from the bodies of your children."

"If you could all please locate the Arpex in a timely manner, I'd like to kill it before another one answers its call for a rescue," I said to my attentive audience.

"You're not supposed to be talking to it." Anastassia hissed, her face still serene.

I tried explaining in multiple ways where they had to look and how the process worked, but they weren't catching on. They hadn't had an Arpex in their heads before to show them the place to open and hear. One by one, I wiggled myself into the minds of the men before me, guiding them until they heard for themselves.

"We will find it and kill it," the tall one assured me.

"A heavy pulse is the most effective method. If you find yourself without a weapon or in a situation where a pulse is not optimal, the process you endured has made you poisonous to them. Trick them into trying to eat memories from you. It will kill them, but not instantly. Be sure to disengage before they die."

"Boss, you might want to wrap this up. You're looking Jalvian."

After ten light probes, losing my coloring wasn't a surprise, in fact, I had the sweats and shakes to go along with it. I stood, hanging onto the back of my chair with both hands to deliver a one minute rousing speech and dismissed them.

The second the last volunteer had filed out, I closed my eyes and let my neck relax. "Artor house. I like that bed best."

Anastassia must have given Neko the jump point because he delivered me right to the bed rather than the foyer. That was just as well. I never would have made it from the foyer.

"Do you want Markus?" Neko asked.

I pulled off my boots and lay back, grateful for the soft blankets and two fresh-scented fluffy pillows beneath my head. "When it's time for him. I'll probably still be right here."

"Good to see you're taking care of yourself for once."

"Go away, Neko."

"Sure thing, boss." He stepped into the void.

Two minutes later, Anastassia's footsteps echoed on the tile down the hall. She burst into the room and sat down beside me. Her hand went to my forehead, brushing the hair out of my face.

"How are you feeling?"

"Not so great." Awful and somewhere around half-dead was more accurate, but from the look on her face, she knew the answer already.

"It will get better. You and your new heart need time to get better acquainted. And just so we're clear, you're still banned from stims."

"I have a new heart now, besides, you said that agreement didn't matter since you didn't remember your decree."

"Along with the kids, Neko and I had a couple of sessions with Tomias's memory menders. I even talked Jey into a session. I remember enough to hold you to that."

That explained why she was acting more like herself.

"Do you think we could get Daniel linked?" I asked. "All this Jumping isn't doing Neko any good."

"I hope that's the exhaustion talking and not you seriously suggesting we implant our twelve year old son for transportation convenience."

"I'll take that as a no."

"That would be wise." She sat back. "Are you hungry?"

"Maybe."

She left me for a little while and returned with a tiny plate of protein spread and crackers.

"Seriously? I've had barely anything to eat for weeks, and this is what you bring me?"

She cocked an eyebrow. "Prove me wrong. Eat it all."

After four crackers, I surrendered in silence and slept.

When I woke hours later, Markus was asleep beside me and Anastassia's face was lit by the glow of her datapad on the other side of the bed.

"Shouldn't you be sleeping?"

"No rest for the wicked," she said with a tired smile.

"I do appreciate your wicked side now and then." I carefully made my way to the edge of the bed and sat up.

She laughed quietly. "Do you need help?"

"I hope not." I made it to the bathroom and back without any misfortune. Feeling ambitious, I set out for the kitchen and reheated the smallest bag of leftovers I could find in the cold storage.

Anastassia, minus her datapad, joined me just as I sat down to eat. She brought a fork and picked at the edges of my plate. "Jey's been taking on extra duties to allow me more time to work with Tomias and the others during your recovery. He said it would help both of us."

"He's not quite as selfless as that," I said. "Getting you back to yourself helps him too. And I'm sure he'd love it if another bond were in place to dial me down a couple hundred notches."

"I don't know about that far, but I wouldn't mind if you mellowed just a little."

She sat there, bands on but not connected like we used to be. Reigning in my unbonded focus was one thing, and I certainly wasn't opposed to whatever pleasurable methods she might agree to in order to make that happen, but anything more... I cleared my throat. "How are the acolytes doing?"

"We're on our third batch. The first two have been dispatched throughout the Narvan as needed to restore memories for the affected."

Having only finished half the food before getting full, I pushed the plate toward her. "That's good news."

She moved the remaining noodles around on the plate before choosing a bite. After she'd chewed slowly and swallowed, she captured me in her open gaze. "I miss having sessions with you directly."

"Perhaps you could persuade a certain acolyte to come home for a private session or two."

She set her fork down and licked her lips. "If you're up for it in the Verian morning, Tomias has asked to speak to both of us regarding Ikeri."

My heart seemed to be working just fine as it pumped furiously. "Is everything all right? I told Daniel to contact me if there were any concerns about her safety. Did I miss something while I was out of it?"

"No. I'm sure Tomias would have said something if it was a matter of safety."

"If you say so."

Markus whimpered and started to yell. I shot to my feet and ran to the bedroom. Anastassia was right behind me.

He grabbed my hand as soon as I was within reach and held on tightly. "Where were you?"

"In the kitchen, getting something to eat. We're both right here."

His voice shook. "It was going to eat me like everyone else."

I settled back onto the bed next to him. Anastassia took up her post on the other side.

"Did I tell you we made Arpex hunters today?" I asked Markus.

"You did?"

The datapad in Stassia's lap lit her face with a warm glow. She gave me a quick smile and went back to work.

"We did. A whole team of them, and as we speak, they're traveling throughout the Narvan to hunt down the last of the Arpex so they can never hurt you again."

"You're not hunting them anymore, are you?" Markus asked as he snuggled against me.

"Not unless I have to. We have ten new hunters now."

"Good. I don't want you to leave like that again. It was scary."

"Sorry about that." I rubbed his back until his breathing slowed, but I don't know which one of us fell asleep first.

Anastassia poked my shoulder. "Morning on Prime, lazyass."

"We taking Markus with?"

She gave me one of those side-eyed looks that said I was being an idiot. "You want to leave him here alone all day?"

"Neko's here."

"Neko's sleeping, and he's going to stay that way until the stims are out of his system." She tossed clean clothes at me.

"So you want me to do a double jump? Aren't you supposed to be nagging me to ease into this slowly?"

She laughed. Damn, I'd missed that sound.

"I've seen enough memories to know you wouldn't listen."

"I might if you asked nicely." I woke Markus and sent him to the bathroom.

"Glad to see you're feeling more yourself," she said.

"I'd gladly be feeling—"

"Young boy. Bathroom. Right there." She pointed. "Show me you can handle a double jump and we'll talk later. Right now, I'm as anxious to find out what Tomias has to say as you were last night."

"Right. That." While Markus was out of the room, I quickly got dressed in the Verian clothes she'd handed to me.

Once he returned and Anastassia got him changed, they stood close by.

"You're sure you want me to do this?"

"Nan didn't touch your link, and I've seen you do more in far worse shape. You can handle it."

"It's your fault if I keel over." I laid a hand on each of them and formed a Jump to Veria Prime.

I hadn't realized I'd closed my eyes until I pried them open to discover we'd made it and my head wasn't throbbing.

Anastassia elbowed me. "Hey look, you're still standing. Now, let's go."

Nerves weren't something she normally exhibited, and her anxiousness to get to Tomias rubbed off on me. I tossed Markus on my shoulders so we could make better time through the streets. When we came to the red door, Anastassia paused, took a deep breath, and went in. In my rush to follow her, I almost forgot to dislodge Markus. His yelp saved him from a sore head.

I set him on his feet. "Can you go find Daniel? We have to speak to Tomias."

Marcus nodded and made his way through the house.

"He seems much more comfortable here now."

Anastassia nodded. "He follows Daniel everywhere, except when he's busy following you."

"I have a feeling he'd be better off following Daniel."

"Oh, I don't know. Having him around has been good for you. Before you found him..." She shook her head. "I had no idea that a dis-bonded male could get that manically intense. Jey assures me you're the only one affected that way, or else all of Artor would have imploded by now."

"Hazard of the lifestyle, I suppose."

Even without a bond, the laser focus I'd had in the wake of its dissipation had faded. Whether that was due to dialing back the Arpex in my system, Anastassia's open presence, or a combination of the two, I wasn't sure. But if she wanted me less intense, she was getting her way. At least for now.

She led the way out into the yard and around to the tall narrow building where we'd met with Tomias before.

"Has Jey said anything more about the adoption?" I asked. "I seem to have fallen through on my end of that deal."

"Not if your hunters do their job."

"Ah, I see what you did there."

She smiled. "Covered your ass yet again."

"Just which memories have people been sharing with you?"

She waved at me to be quiet as we reached the top of the stairs. Tomias and Ikeri sat alone on the floor in the middle of the room.

Her curls were gone.

My feet stuck to the floor and my throat sealed shut. Which was probably a good thing because I wanted to tear Tomias in two either with my hands or my tongue. Simultaneously would have been preferable.

"Daddy, please. Sit."

It was the tears welling in her eyes that convinced me to do as she asked. Anastassia, now gripping my hand tightly, sat with me across from them.

"Tomias?" Stassia asked, her voice near breaking.

"Thank you both for coming," he said, filling the room with a blanket of calm.

I didn't particularly want to be calm. I wanted to know what the fuck was going on. "One of you better start explaining this."

Ikeri gulped. "You said I could be whomever I wanted to be with everyone else."

Stassia glanced at me. I nodded.

"You said I should pick pretty tattoos."

"And you said it didn't matter because you weren't Verian. Not to mention, you're ten." I fought to keep my urge to swear loudly and profusely under control. "Don't you have to be eighteen or something to become a Seeker?"

Tomias rested his hand on Ikeri's shoulder. "There is no set age to pass from acolyte to Seeker. It is a matter of learning and teaching and the accomplishment of a significant task."

"A task like bringing someone back?" Stassia whispered.

Ikeri nodded, her bald head catching the morning rays shining in through the windows.

"But she's not Verian," I said through clenched teeth. "Your teacher wouldn't even give Anastassia the full training because she wasn't Verian. How is Ikeri any different?"

Tomias sent a look so full of apology to Anastassia that I wanted to cry for her. I knew how hurt she'd been over Res turning her away and the dangerous alternate path she'd chosen because of it.

"She's pure inside. Where her body was created doesn't matter, only what fills her mind."

"But she's ten," I repeated.

"Her body is young, but you know as well as I, that has no bearing on who she is."

"Is this what you want?" asked Anastassia. "Do you understand that it will mark you for as long as you live?"

"I see no harm in being marked a Seeker," Ikeri said.

"But you are so young, won't the others be angry?" I asked. "And you're *not* Verian. I've seen how some have treated your mother because of that. I don't want the same for you."

"Daddy, I won't always be young." She sat up straight, eyes clear of tears. "And I don't have to stay on Prime or Minor. I can be a Seeker anywhere."

Anastassia shot a look at Tomias. "She wouldn't be required to stay? I thought that was the law."

Tomias winked. "She's not Verian."

"And you took the time to train her anyway?" she asked.

"She's been teaching us since the day you first brought her to me. With Ikeri it has always been as much give as take. It has been an honor having her here with us, and I hope she will continue to do so." His upbeat demeanor faded. "However, your concerns do have merit."

"Is she in danger from the acolytes or Verians in general?" I asked.

He peered past us to the sun-drenched city outside the windows. "Both. Resentment is difficult to overcome and it clouds the minds of some, even here. It would, I think, be wise, once this matter is concluded, to find a secure place to practice elsewhere for a few years."

"Until she's more the age of a typical new Seeker," Anastassia clarified.

Tomias nodded. "You may also give thought to further training that boy of yours. Not that I advocate the path either of you have chosen, but Ikeri is unique and she may require the services of one like yourselves. Verians aren't the only ones who may not appreciate her abilities, or conversely, may appreciate them too much."

"Duly noted. Thank you." While I was glad that we'd reached some level of acceptance, knowing that he'd actually seen the necessity of people like us made me even more concerned for Ikeri's safety.

"Now then," Tomias said, placing his hands on Ikeri's shoulders, "because of her age, as much as she dislikes when I bring that up, I must request your consent before we continue."

Anastassia turned to me.

"This one's your call. You know this world and the ins and outs of Seekers far better than I do," I said.

"Will you be all right if I say yes?"

I nodded, relieved that her past hadn't placed a roadblock on Ikeri's future.

"You may continue," Anastassia said.

Ikeri's radiant smile competed with the sun. Though she remained under Tomias's hand, she hugged me on the inside.

"Wonderful. We will begin the marking, which will take a week or so. She will also undergo a fitting and robes will be made. That may take a day or two longer than usual as we don't have anything her size to begin with. After these are complete, she will have a formal presentation to the others and then be free to go."

I held up my hand, enjoying the trepidation that flashed over Tomias's face. "That sounds long and involved. We will need to borrow her for an hour first."

The indignant look I received from Ikeri wasn't quite as amusing. "Daddy, that's not how the ceremony goes."

Anastassia shook her head. "If you're old enough to become a Seeker, you're old enough to realize that no one in this family is good at ceremonies."

Ikeri brushed off Tomias's hand and shot to her feet, arms crossed over her chest. "But this is *mine*."

Stassia said, "Have you seen the memories of how many of my ceremonies your father has botched? Consider yourself lucky he's only asking for an hour."

"Hey, you didn't seem to mind at the time," I said.

Tomias stood, hands fidgeting at his sides. "It would be best if you all remain here. I will wait below. I'd prefer not to deviate from our rites any more than necessary for the reasons we've already discussed."

"Thank you, Tomias," said Anastassia. "We will endeavor to be timely."

Ikeri watched him descend the stairs and then turned to us, even more irritated than she'd been before. "What do you want from me?"

"First," I regarded her calmly, "penance."

She groaned. "You stopped everything for that?"

I held out my arms and she came into them. Her smooth head on my cheek felt very strange. I dearly missed the tickle of her curls.

"No," I held her at arm's length so she had to look at me. "I need you to prove that you can be objective with this Seeker business, and I want you to know what kind of people Tomias is talking about that might try to harm you before you go through with permanently marking yourself."

"And how do I prove that?"

"You're going to show your mother who I am."

Her face scrunched up. "I've done that."

"The other side that I've told you not to see."

"Oh." She sat down heavily, her mind expanding our usual connection. "Where should she look?"

"After hiring Jey but before Merkief, I'm missing something in there myself, but there was a hotel room and Jey was sitting alone at a table when we walked in."

Stassia nodded as I relayed my initial immediate hatred for Jey. I rampaged onward from here. We shared a contract job, both working to take down the targets in the linked synchronicity that I dearly missed. I took a little pleasure in recalling the attack on Kess after he'd shot Merkief when Stassia had refused to let me do my job of protecting her, how she hadn't talked to me for two days, and had remained livid far longer. The final entry in my over-sharing tirade was a short portion of the war with Fragia. I showed her my protecting her from an attack by inadvertently smashing her face into a control console, and then Stassia had wrapped things up in record time because she was finally listening to me as far as her well-being was concerned.

There was so much more I needed her to know, to remember, but Ikeri had seen enough for one day. I reduced our connection to our normal level.

Ikeri shut it entirely, leaving me devoid of any sense of her calm. It hurt, but I wasn't entirely surprised.

"You've been in her head," I nodded toward Anastassia. "You knew I was there too."

She stared at the floor. "It's different, seeing it, feeling it through you, how you enjoy those things."

"Remember that feeling. There a lot of people out there that feel the same way, and you need to watch out for them. Once you're marked, you'll be easy to recognize. People here already know you're special. Everywhere you go, others will know too, and while most will be grateful for your help, some will want you for themselves or for whoever is paying them to procure you."

"Vayen, that's enough." Anastassia rose and began pacing. Her unbound hair fluttered with each step.

"She has a right to know the truth."

"I know, but I don't want to hear it. You're ruining her special day."

"I can tell you how badly everyone's day would be ruined if anyone lays a hand on her. She needs to be aware of the consequences."

Ikeri clapped her hands, the loud sudden sound reverberating through the room. "I liked it better when you sent me outside to play while you argued."

I glanced at Anastassia. "You changing your mind?"

She shook her head. "Are you?"

"No."

"Good," said Ikeri. "Then we're all agreed. I'll let you know when I'm finished here." She ran down the stairs without another word. By the time I got over there, she was out of sight.

"I dare say you pissed her off," said Anastassia.

"Yes, well, I wasn't real happy to be brought back to life, but I let her off easy there. As you've told me before, she'll get over it."

Stassia stared, mouth hanging open.

"I take it that she didn't divulge that little detail while she was busy reveling in her lauded accomplishment?"

"She's your daughter, the one person you spoil to your ninth hell and back. She wanted you alive. We all did."

"It would have been nice if anyone had taken a minute to consider what I wanted."

Her pace turned into a full-blown stalk. "To be dead? Is that what you want?"

I left her there and went down to the lawn to find a quiet spot in the shade to sit before I exploded in one way or another. The breeze carried the sweet scent of blooming white flowers that grew in a mass against the building. The sky above was clear and blue, the sun warm but not yet hot, the grass soft beneath me. Birds chirped in the trees overhead. I had to admit, it was hard to be angry here even without anyone throwing calm my way.

Anastassia approached behind me with halting steps. "Should we have let you go?"

"It was so quiet there. No one needed me. I didn't need anyone. I was, and that's all I wanted."

"Sounds lonely."

"It wasn't." Try as I might to hold onto what I'd felt in the nothing-ness, the utter serenity had faded to a point I could no longer grasp or adequately explain.

She sat beside me, picking at the blades of grass. For once, the silence between us wasn't strained. I opened our natural connection to get a hint of her true mood, but her thoughts were darting in too many directions to be helpful.

"I could send you back," she said.

I reached out and took her hand. "After all the effort you put into cleaning me up?"

"That was Nan."

"Nan doesn't work for free, and she never once mentioned any form of payment."

A smile worked its way onto her lips. "I might have implied that I would appreciate those modifications and that she owed you."

I wrapped my arms around her, enjoying the weight of her against me, the softness of her hair under my chin, the clean smell of her skin that even the flowers couldn't compete with.

"What's your secret?" I asked. "She was as unresponsive as a strung out merc from Thirteen with nothing to lose when I tried that route."

She lifted my modified hand, holding it gently in hers while slowly stroking each finger in turn, sending tiny shivers through me. Then she flipped it over and kissed my palm. Geva bless it all, I could feel everything.

"If I told you, it wouldn't be a secret."

"Perhaps," I said, nipping at her ear. "I should take you somewhere else and convince you to talk."

Stassia turned to face me, her lips curled into a wickedly tempting smile. "I might be agreeable to that."

"Only might?" I kissed her, letting my hand roam freely until she squirmed against me and soft moans punctuated every other breath.

"Very agreeable," she said, working her way down my neck.

I Jumped us directly to our bedroom on Artor where we made quick work of our clothes. We fell onto the bed, her straddling me.

She paused, casting a glance at the closed door. "You think Neko is still sleeping?"

"I think it doesn't matter. I picked this house for a reason. This bedroom is isolated from all the others. Which is very good, because I do plan on making you talk."

She threw her head back and laughed, deep and throaty and full of challenge. Rolling her off me and pinning her down, I did my best to rise to it.

TWENTY-ONE

"Jey? He's your secret weapon?" I accessed the house systems through my link and lowered the temperature in the bedroom. She hadn't cracked easily. We'd both worked up a considerable sweat before collapsing onto the sheets.

"Nothing elicits terror like a hulking Jalvian."

"Really? Nothing?"

Stassia patted my shoulder. "You weren't up to the job at the time. I had to call in reinforcements."

"That's not what you just said."

"Shush."

"I don't take being shushed lightly. Especially not after that comment."

Her kiss mollified me to the point where the exhaustion from our strenuous activities took over. I tugged the sheet over me and closed my eyes.

"Would you be terribly offended if I got some work done?" she asked.

"Yes, but no."

"Good, because I'd like to stay on top of things while you're recuperating. Speaking of which, you need to rest. I'm pretty sure we just blew through several days worth of your easing-back-in exercise regimen."

"What about Markus?"

"Do you need him?"

When I'd been sedated, the nightmares had left me alone for the most part, but now I had to take my chances. I couldn't drag him to bed every time I needed a nap, even though I did sleep far better when he was there. At least I had a full night's rest to draw from energy-wise. That was more than I was used to.

"I don't want him to think we forgot about him," I said.

"I'll take care of it. Now, don't make me shush you again." She kissed my cheek, and seconds later, her fingertips began their dance.

When I woke again, I was alone in bed. As the clicking of Arpex claws faded, I held up both hands to find them free of the blood I'd been scrubbing off its plate. My blood. I took a deep breath through my nose and let it out slowly. Once my heart stopped pounding, I got dressed.

I missed having Marcus next to me. There was something about having to be there for him that switched off the shit in my head. But even when he wasn't right there, the nightmares hit less often than they had. Maybe my subconscious knew I had to be rested to help the kid when I was awake.

Arin seemed to be taking mercy on me too. I still caught glimpses of him out of the corner of my eye now and then, but he'd been silent.

Between being less haunted, the promise of memory mender sessions filling in more of the holes in my head, and things improving with Stassia, I was finally feeling more like myself. With a light step, I went to find something to eat.

Stassia, Neko, and Markus sat at the table, halfway through their meal. Without a word, Stassia got up and returned with a plate filled with browned flat grains and a slab of fish covered in a creamy white sauce. She set it in front of me. Neko and Stassia did their best to extract a conversation from Markus about his day on Minor while we ate. My stomach was much more cooperative this time around and my plate was empty shortly after theirs.

"Worked up an appetite?" Stassia smirked.

"It would seem so." I surveyed the dishes. "Markus, how are you with carrying plates?"

He shrugged, dismounted from his chair, and started to clear away the mess. Neko gave me an odd look.

I returned it and then turned to Stassia. "Is there anything pressing I need to attend to in person?"

"The Arpex hunters have located one on Artor. The rest are either still in transit to their stations or settling in. The Seeker acolytes are already at work undoing the mess the Arpex created of people's minds, and the funds you've funneled into the planetary governments are helping with the rest. I've been in contact with all the heads and no one has any immediate need of a visit. Jey and Kess have requested a formal advisory meeting, but we can do that here. Isnar has also been asking about you, but again, he can come here."

"So you're pretty much not letting me out of the house."

She laughed. "You're very perceptive."

I turned back to Neko. He'd aged since he'd started working for us. Still wiry and good-natured, but the faint lines around his eyes and perpetual look of gauntness on his face were probably my fault.

"How long has it been since you've seen your family?" I asked him.

By the way he stammered a moment, I gathered I'd caught him off guard. One of my favorite things about him was that he took most anything I did or said in stride. That I'd managed to stump him on such a trivial question, on something I probably should have known for as much time as we'd spent together, brought me a up a little short myself.

"I talk to them now and then," he said.

"In-person, seen them."

He pursed his lips and looked up to the ceiling. "Five years or so? Not since before we shipped off to Pentares."

Stassia watched us both, her gaze lingering on me, one brow arched. If she wondered what I was getting at, she wasn't the only one.

I sat back, pondering how much I could accomplish from home along with Jumping the kids and Stassia as needed. It occurred to me that I had no idea where Neko's family lived. I'd never taken the time to ask that either.

"How long do you need?"

"Only takes a breath or two to Jump, boss."

This wasn't the first time, nor would it be the last, that I wished Stassia could host another link, but that option was a dead end. If I wanted to do the right thing, the thing my gut was prodding me toward, I would have to suck it up and learn to stay home more.

"Pack a bag. You're taking some well-deserved time off."

Neko cringed. "Are you sure that's a good idea? Not that I don't appreciate it, but with the kids spread out and you recovering, and Anastassia on full Narvan duty..." He shook his head. "I don't want to see you back in that University bed."

"Neither do I. Just in case, show me where you're going."

He flashed me a jump point. A quaint home, reminiscent of the Friquen house, except constructed of manufactured materials, mostly plascrete. It stood alongside several others. The sturdy structures appeared able to withstand attack or adverse weather.

"Where is that?"

"Little mining colony on a tough chunk of rock called Tisa. Couldn't wait to get away when I was younger. I jumped on the first transport out I could afford and ended up with Gamnock a year later."

"Do you want to go back?" asked Stassia. "I mean if you want to take a pleasure cruise around Karin or something more entertaining, we do happen to have connections."

Neko chuckled. "No, I should go see for myself what all my credits have done there. They send me still frames, but it's not the same."

"Your credits?" I asked.

"Oh come on. You think I'm ever going to spend all you pay me? With my luck, you'll shove me into some government position like poor Isnar, and I'll have to use my small fortune to bail out whatever crisis we're facing. No, no, I'm spending mine as I go."

"Hold that thought." I went into the kitchen and grabbed a bottle of whatever Stassia had placed at the front on the liquor shelf along with three glasses. After pouring everyone a drink, I sat back down and sipped my own. Stassia's cautioning glance informed me that was the best course of action if I didn't want to get chastised in front of Neko.

"So, tell me about this spending," I said.

Neko shifted awkwardly in his seat, eyeing the glass and me, mouth opening and closing a few times before turning to Anastassia.

"Don't worry, I'm pretty sure this is him being friendly," Stassia tested my liquor choice and nodded. "He's just not very good at it."

Neko tossed back half of the dark liquor before returning his glass to the table. He shed a nervous smile.

"Tisa was a whole lot of nothing. Housing was shit. Supplies were shit. The corporation sponsoring the colony only cared that we were alive and mining."

He drank the rest and fiddled with the empty glass. Stassia kicked me under the table. I poured him a refill and did my best to appear more amicable. Truthfully, I had no idea what that was supposed to look like anymore.

"I've sent my sister to medical training, constructed a facility for her, and hired her two assistants. You saw the new housing. I've managed to persuade a couple ships to put them on the trade route, and now we're working on a school. Unfortunately, I'm having a hard time convincing instructors that the move to nowhere is worth their while."

"That's very impressive," Stassia said.

"I can find teachers for you," I said. "Why didn't you say anything?"

"I don't know, you've both been a little occupied? Like, since I met you." He took another deep swig. "How the hell do you do it?"

"Drinking," said Stassia, draining the rest of her glass. "Along with a good deal of cursing and very little sleep."

I held up the bottle. She nodded. I refilled her glass.

Markus crept back into the room. "The dishes are set for the bot. Can I go to bed now?"

"Of course," I said. "But I'm not quite ready yet."

"May I sleep in Daniel's room?" he asked.

Stassia nodded. "That sounds like a wonderful idea."

Markus inched closer until he stood beside me. He leaned close to my ear. "Can you do that thing where you're with me in my head?"

It would be draining, with him being Jalvian, and I wouldn't be able to utilize my link while lodged in his mind, but the promising look on Stassia's face convinced me it would be a worthwhile expenditure. "Yes."

Finding the right delicate level of probe to assure him I was there and yet allow me to pay attention to Stassia further asking Neko about the colony on Tisa, took a few minutes. By the time I returned to the conversation, Markus had vanished up the stairs and Neko and Stassia had fallen silent. They were both watching me.

"Were you like that with our kids, before, when we lived on Minor?"

"I suppose so. You could ask them."

Neko shrugged. "I still say it's the new heart."

I had a feeling I'd missed more of their conversation than I'd thought. "I could go back to yelling at both of you if that would be preferable."

"That's all right, boss." Neko grinned. "I'm good with this. It's weird but good."

He finished the contents of his glass. "I guess I have some packing to do. You want me at the station for a while or should I go, or—"

Stassia waved him off. "Pack and go. We've got this."

"How long do you want me gone?"

"It's not that I want you gone." I ran a hand over my face and paused to marvel at the relative smoothness along my temple and down my cheek. "You need a break. But don't get yourself killed. I expect you back in two weeks."

He offered me a half-assed salute and took a staggering step before righting himself and heading off to his room.

"So, you can still be nice."

"Shush."

She laughed. "I may have started something I'm going to regret."

"Wouldn't be the first time."

She laughed harder.

I picked up the bottle and made a show of reading the label.

"Hey, you were pouring," she said. "Deal with the consequences."

"I plan on it."

I went to the security station and verified that Neko had us on lockdown. With my paranoia assuaged, I returned to the kitchen to scoop up a very surprised Stassia.

"Are you supposed to be lifting heavy weights?"

"Probably not. Do you want me to put you down?"

She wrapped her arms around my neck. "I'll allow this one violation."

"I may violate a few other things in short order."

"I may allow those too if you ask nicely."

Why did the bedroom have to be so damned far away from everything else in the house? I did my best to avoid smacking her head on any corners but my arms were shaking by the time we made it into the bedroom. As I set her on the bed and then ungracefully plopped down next to her before I fell face-first on the floor, I considered that I might have overdone it a little.

Stassia readjusted herself to rest her head in my lap. "Are you all right up there?"

"Just need a minute."

I liked her there, open and next to me. It reminded me of how we'd been. I nudged our connection a little further in the place that had vanished from both of our minds, the place that truly drew us together.

She expanded our natural connection.

"Hold on. I'm going to need a few more minutes."

Rather than the burst of sexual energy I expected, she quietly caressed all the right places until I wanted to fall over backward, close my eyes, and drift off to sleep. This level of calm was different from what Ikeri offered, yet it was familiar, and I'd dearly missed it.

"Quit that before I start snoring. For the record, that is not at all what I intended to do in here with you."

"I know." She reached up to run her fingers along my jaw and down my neck.

"Was this what it was like? Before, with the bond?"

"Very similar, yes." I nudged against her mind. This time she didn't resist my effort to share memories directly with her.

I shared the utter peace of the bond without words or interlopers. It wasn't a memory she needed to have inserted, only to understand.

"And why did I not want to do this the first time?" she asked breathlessly.

"We both had our reasons."

She studied my face a moment before going still. "Could you form one again? With me, now?"

"What? Why? And for the love of Geva, do *not* say that you owe me."

She cringed a little. "All right then, apparently there are a few more memories that require sharing. But seriously, are you able to form another bond? After what Nan did?"

"I don't know."

"Try."

"Seriously? Right now?"

She nodded, giving me a challenging stare.

"You do understand that it's not something I can undo if you come to your senses in a few hours. Assuming it works."

"I've done my research, thank you very much. I wouldn't be asking otherwise."

"Research." I snorted.

"I worked with Isnar on this topic for a couple of sessions. He showed me how it went before." She snickered. "He wanted to make sure I took it better this time if we choose to try again."

"You've lost your mind. You have your freedom back, and while I'm not at all opposed to being in this or any other bed with you whenever you want, we don't have to bond again."

She sat up and kissed me. "Is it my freedom you're so concerned about, or yours?"

I'd really never considered what my own freedom from the bond might look like. The one thing I was sure of was that after having this tantalizing taste of the peace she offered, I would gladly toss the Narvan and everything else aside to get more. I was a Geva-forsaken addict at heart for sure.

If we were going to do this, we were doing it right. "I didn't have the luxury of asking last time, but do I have your consent to try initiating the bond?"

"Yes." She said, filling me with the warmth I'd tried to convince myself I didn't need.

She kissed me again. For a few moments I forgot what I was intending to do. Seeming to sense my utter distraction, she eased off.

Hoping to make my reprieve a short one, I sank into my mind, cautiously exploring the place where the bond had been before. It felt relatively the same, though it was hard to tell since I was no longer the same. Everything in my head had a shade of Arpex on it. I gathered my nerve and expanded the connection, branching out into Stassia's mind.

It was strange doing this intentionally. I'd waited for it to magically happen with Sonia because all my efforts to make it work like I was doing now had failed. It hadn't ever solidified.

With Anastassia, I'd been too high on Chandi's drug to notice my brain doing the process on its own. Now, as I paved the path again, with purpose this time, it felt right, natural. Like for once, just maybe, I might be doing the right thing.

"It will take weeks to fully form, but I think it worked," I whispered, not daring to give full voice to my hopes.

"Good."

"Good? You're taking this so much better than last time. Remind me to thank Fa'yet. I much prefer my internal organs remain internal for a while."

"Was I really that bad?" she asked.

"You do love a good threat."

"I do. And you." She slipped her shirt over her head, then tugged at mine.

"Really?"

"Yes, really." The kiss she gave me stamped out any doubt.

"Well then, I guess I have a few threats of my own to make good on."

"That you do."

We made quick work of our clothes but it was a good long while before we got any sleep.

TWENTY-TWO

Jey sat at our table, appearing only slightly less disgruntled than last time. He shuffled the documents in front of him and took a long look at Markus who sat between Stassia and me.

"Yes, I know, this is a bad idea and it won't end well. You've already made that quite clear," I said.

He shook his head and shifted in his seat, jangling the medals on his uniform. "Maybe with another Artorian family it would. But seriously, you two?" He grimaced. "I know you. Both of you."

He swayed to one side just as I heard Stassia's boot connect with his leg under the table.

Jey held up his hand. "Clearly it's what both of you needed, all three of you, I suppose, and I agree that it's the next logical step to better integrating our people, but Artorians don't adopt Jalvians. It hasn't happened in so long that I had to go back four generations to find a record of it."

"Sounds like it's long overdue then," said Stassia.

Jey snorted. "Given how well Vayen and I got along during the years that you don't remember, you have no idea how ironic this request is."

She kept her voice level, almost too level. "He showed me. A little of it anyway."

Jey's gaze dropped to the documents. "I wish Merkief were alive to see this. You'd never hear the end of it."

For once I didn't cringe at the mention of his name. Not a single nightmare image flashed before my eyes. "You're probably right."

"You realize," Jey said, "that when you sign this and submit your blood imprint, you'll both be alive and officially active in the system again. Is this worth all the headache that's going to cause?"

Stassia looked over Markus to me, Jey's question plain on her face. We'd discussed this since the all-clear had come from Jal's assigned Arpex hunters three days ago. While we both agreed to go ahead, we also both had reservations and they weren't even the same reservations.

"Improving my appearance to the public was your sole intention when assisting Anastassia with motivating the University toward my alterations, was it not?"

I was gratified to see him squirm a little. He nodded.

Stassia's affronted sniff confirmed she hadn't considered that Jey might have other motives beyond helping her, but she kept her temper in check.

"And if we're taking a more public role, wouldn't it benefit us all to show our support of good relations with Jal by adopting one of your children?" she asked.

"As long as we can quell the last of the kidnapping rumors, yes. However, you have to realize that the general public is more fond of the angle they find most believable."

"We'll deal with it," I said.

"He didn't kidnap me," Markus said flatly.

Jey finally cracked a smile. "I know."

He presented us with the papers, which we both signed, and then we submitted ourselves to the reader that both recorded palm prints and took a small blood sample. I went first, much preferring the genetic code readers we used on Artor, but the process was over in less than a minute. He slid the reader over to Stassia, who took a deep breath and slipped her hand inside. Once we were both confirmed in the system, Jey ran his hand to confirm the validity of identities and as a witness.

No going back now, we were both alive again. Or, as Jey's records had it, again registered as active within the Narvan after having been out of the system for several years. I couldn't wait for the questions from old untouched contacts to start rolling in, and even better, death threats from every little grudge-holder who thought I'd been taken care of. Good thing Neko was resting up.

The planetary heads were not going to be happy with this new public face arrangement, at least not until I convinced them to be happy. Thank Geva for Fa'yet. He at least would be grateful to have someone else to publicly blame for everything that didn't go quite right.

Oh to be feared and hated on a large scale. It was just the level of stress I'd been trying to avoid since returning from Pentares.

But if Jey could manage, so could I, and I had Stassia at my back. No excuses, I could do this.

"Congratulations, Markus. You're officially a Ta'set. Don't hate me for this later," Jey said.

Markus grinned. "I won't."

"I'll remember you said that." Jey slipped the documents into an envelope and placed the reader on top. "You're healing well?"

Stassia nodded. "He is."

There were times I didn't appreciate her overprotective side and this was one of them. I almost snapped at her for speaking for me, but the warmth flowing through our reforming bonded connection soothed me to the point that I let it go.

Jey smirked, seeming to sense my momentary annoyance. "How much longer will Neko be gone?"

"Two days," said Stassia.

"Might I suggest laying low until then? And while you're at it, set a baseline for the tank. A lot has changed since you were in it last."

"He won't be leaving the house," Stassia stated firmly.

"Ever?" Jey asked.

"Not for you. Every time he does, he ends up in the tank or in a bed at the University."

The barely veiled venom in her voice made me smile. While it went over Markus's head, Jey's momentary flinch told me he'd picked up on it just fine.

I cleared my throat. "We'll discuss this further when Kess arrives. In the meantime, are you hungry?"

Jey leaned toward me, casting Stassia a suspicious look. "Is she going to poison my lunch?"

"Stassia, no poisoning Jey. If I have to run the entire Narvan myself, I'll definitely have to leave the house more often."

She sighed. "I suppose I'll let him live then."

"I'll get it," offered Markus, jumping down from his chair. He scampered off into the kitchen where I'd prepared the meal before Jey arrived.

"Now I see why you wanted him around," said Jey.

"We already have a kid for that. Daniel even cooks," I said.

"How are those two? I gather they're not here?"

"I'm getting them tomorrow. Ikeri is finishing up with the final batch of memory menders."

"They've been working wonders." Jey accepted his plate from Markus. "Wait, do you mean Ikeri is training them?"

We spent lunch explaining Ikeri's new Seeker status and our concerns for her safety.

"I'm glad I only have one kid, and that she's normal." He held up a hand. "Not that yours aren't normal, but really, they're not and you know it."

Stassia, who had been fairly quiet, nodded. Seeing that everyone was finished, she gathered up the plates and sent Markus off to study the lesson she'd given him earlier. He was turning out to be a quiet kid, not near as prone to mischief as Daniel had been at that age. Then again, maybe he just hadn't warmed up to us enough for that to kick in yet.

Kess let me know he was about to arrive in the foyer using the jump point I'd provided. I went to meet him.

If anyone had told me a couple months ago that I'd be allowing Kess internal house access, I'd have laughed out loud and for a good long while, but both Jey and Stassia assured me I wasn't making a huge mistake. I had a feeling it was largely due to Jey wanting me to remain out of view for a couple more days and Stassia being convinced that I'd remain wholly intact as long as I never left the house.

Kess stepped out of the void and glanced around. "Nice place."

It wasn't that I hated all Jalvians. I now had one living in my house for Geva's sake, but this particular one embodied all the stereotypes I'd been raised to despise: cold, treacherous, and willing to kill anyone if it got him ahead.

His calculating gaze took in every detail of his surroundings, of me, noting advantages and any signs of weakness. His long pale fingers tapped his thighs, no doubt missing the weaponry he'd left behind before Jumping here. He'd also had the courtesy to leave his armor wherever he'd come from. Someone was keeping him in line and I guessed it was Jey. They'd been working closely together since my imprisonment. I, however, couldn't shake the memory of him laughing in my head the first time he'd seen me in the grey uniform of a Council zombie. Even after all the times we'd tried to kill one another, that moment of silent laughter goaded me the worst. Despite the fact we'd had previous deals, that he knew I was taking care of Stassia and both of our homeworlds by going to the Council, I'd been helpless and his first reaction had been to mock me.

Jey trusted him, and we needed him. But I didn't like him.

"Are you going to glare at me all day, or are we going to do business?" Kess asked.

"Don't touch anything."

"Hands to myself, no nabbing the children from their beds, or setting jump points to murder you in your sleep, yeah, I already got the speech from Jey, thanks."

I gritted my teeth and brought him into the spacious room off the entry hall that Stassia had set up as our meeting space. That at least kept him out of the main house, but I still didn't like it.

Jey sat at the oval table, hands empty and resting on the translucent clearplaz surface. There would be no weapons drawn under this table. Everyone's every movement was in view. I didn't know where Stassia had found such a thing on short notice. She had her own connections.

Kess sat toward the middle of the table and I took the other end. The remaining three chairs were empty. I looked at Jey. He shrugged.

I reached out to Stassia. *"Where are you?"*

"Getting some work done."

"Get some work done in here with the rest of us."

"Jey and Kess didn't bring assistants. It would look better if you hold your own in there," she said.

"I don't give a shit how it looks. We're partners in this, remember? That's what we agreed on when we left Pentares."

"About that. No, I don't remember."

"You'll just have to take my word for it then. Now, get in here."

Stassia strode in a moment later and sat in the chair across from Kess. Then she slid it over next to me and placed her well-worn datapad on the table before her.

Jey sighed, shaking his head. "And now you've got the bond back. Don't bother denying it."

"Look at them," Kess said, "all googly-eyed and contented smiles. Kind of makes you ill, doesn't it?"

I started to tense, but then Jey laughed.

"Much more thankful than ill. You didn't see them separated. It wasn't pretty. The entire Narvan is much better off with them together."

Jey nodded toward me. "Have you told Kess about your new handy pulse-resistant skin?"

"It had not come up until now, so no, can't say that I have."

Jey went on, making quite a show of regaling Kess with his weapons testing on my Arpex-altered self. I didn't bother informing either of them that my armor-like skin wasn't as impenetrable as when he'd tested me before. Instead, I rather enjoyed the disturbed expression that spread over Kess's face.

The same look on Stassia's face was not so enjoyable.

"Let it go. He's just keeping Kess in line," I said.

"He actually pulsed you? I'm going to—"

"Stassia. Shush."

She glared at me. *"We're banning that word. Starting now."*

Jey's story wound down quickly. Maybe he realized what she was glaring about.

We spent most of the day discussing business between the Narvan and the Rakon Nebula where Kess controlled Twelve, Merchess, and Thirteen. Jey spoke for Fragia, as they dealt with him directly. Hours droned by on trade agreements, political debates, and interplanetary requests before we turned to recovery efforts.

"These Arpex hunters, can we make more?" asked Jey. "I'd like to see some Jalvians involved."

Stassia said, "If you have any telepathic Jalvians, we can pitch your plea to the University. Otherwise, they won't work."

"What about using the process solely for the armor capacity?" asked Kess. "If it means being able to withstand a pulse, sign me up."

I tried not to think about what had been done to me. Twice. "It's not a pleasant process, to say the least. Not to mention, we don't know how the procedure will affect non-Artorians."

Jey gave me a level-eyed stare. "So you're saying it will require some testing."

"That's the tip of what I'm saying. Do we really want more bullet and pulse-proof people running around?"

"So you get to be altered, but not us?" Kess asked.

A heated debate ensued, neither of them entirely backing away from the idea of either using the process for themselves, or creating an elite force to protect their worlds or to send off with the intent to subdue others.

Sick of repeating myself and listening to Stassia trying to deflect both of their angles, I finally stood up. "Enough. I'll discuss this further with the University. Until then, be thankful for the hunters you have to keep your worlds free of the damned Arpex."

Jey stood as well. "We are thankful, but I think you're failing to see the potential large-scale benefits of this discovery. I look forward to hearing what the University has to say."

"I also eagerly await your findings," said Kess, getting to his feet.

Neither of them sounded eager or thankful. They wanted in and weren't going to be put off for long. I waited until the two of them had promptly Jumped before dropping back into my seat and resting my forehead in my hands.

Stassia stretched her arms over her head and then out to each side. "That went well."

"No one drew a weapon, and I don't recall any outright threats, so yes, I suppose it did."

She stood and twisted side to side. I wasn't the only one with a stiff back, and the last couple hours had turned my neck and shoulders into a solid knot. I started to get up, but she gently shoved me back into the chair, her strong fingers going to work on my neck. I leaned my head back against her stomach and let the calm of her hands and presence wash over me.

"Are you willing to share the Arpex alteration with them?" she asked.

"No. We don't need impervious Jalvians. Can you imagine how nervous that would make our people?"

"But we've already altered Artorians."

"A handful. For a purpose that benefits us all."

Her fingers worked their way up my neck and into my hair, working in circular motions along my scalp until my eyes closed.

"You do realize that it would only take one of the hunters telling them the process and then they could replicate it on their own?"

"Are you trying to help me relax or not?"

"Sorry." Her hands stilled and slipped away.

"That's not the direction I was hoping for."

"Vayen, this is serious."

I sighed. "I know. You think about it, and I'll think about it. Then we'll consult Nan in a couple days. Fa'yet's coming by tomorrow and the kids will be home. Can we enjoy that first?"

"Yes." She kissed the top of my head. "Go check on Markus. I'll find us something to eat and then it's back to bed with you."

"I don't think I've spent this much time in bed since we met."

"If I join you, will that keep your complaints to a minimum?"

I pulled her onto my lap. "It might."

"Good, because you're going to take care of yourself." She wrapped her arms around me. "If you're intent on me letting you go next time you're on Geva's doorstep, I'm going to make sure that time is a long way away."

With the bond working its way back to full strength, I wasn't quite as upset about the loss of the nothingness. The peace between us soothed the hazy memories of those black-fogged moments. "I might be persuaded to stick around indefinitely."

She kissed me, her heart beating against my chest until all thought of Markus, dinner, and alterations had vacated my mind. And then she pulled away.

"I'm still not letting you out of my sight," she declared.

"I'm not opposed to that, but we were standing side by side when I lost you to the Arpex so you may want to rethink your methods."

"You're going to have to give me some time to perfect them."

"I'll do my best."

She laughed, leading the way to the bedroom. "That's all I'm asking for."

THE NARVAN CONTINUES WITH:

BOOK 4

Since coming home from Veria Prime two weeks ago with her bald head covered in tattoos, my daughter had been avoiding me. The boys enjoyed having their very own Seeker at our Artorian estate and Ikeri didn't seem to mind using her relaxation gifts on them, or Stassia, Neko, or even Fa'yet when he'd visited. Everyone but me. Our once close relationship had been strained since I'd shown her what kind of man I really was.

After several failed attempts at starting a conversation that gained me no more than a glare or a mental brain jab, I'd taken to being busy elsewhere. There was plenty to do.

Consulting with Nan, who had done the Arpex alteration on me, ate up most of my time. We'd been over all sides of the possibility of sharing the procedure with non-Artorians. On top of that, I juggled Kess and Jey's demands to do the alteration regardless of its seeming impossibility of success. Stassia and I shared the task of advising our half of the Narvan, but we'd both been working from home, dividing our efforts so we could provide as personal attention as possible. It had only been a couple weeks since Jey and Kess had laid out their barely veiled demands for the alteration, and now all our efforts in our half of the Narvan had Jey, who controlled the other half, convinced we were up to something. Kess was even more sure of it. Stassia and I needed to keep our position in the Narvan strong in case the inner-system war Jey claimed he also didn't want, became a reality.

It felt like a war was brewing at home too. Not only was Ikeri driving me out of my mind, the strain of it all was starting to boil over to Stassia and my sons due to me missing every family meal, and generally not being present any other time. I needed to fix things with Ikeri before everyone else in the house started to hate me too.

Geva must have been laughing hysterically over the fact that a ten-year-old girl could make me so damned miserable.

In light of any god possibly laughing at me, I slipped on my moderately-loaded, armored coat before leaving the bedroom. It felt good. Normal. A few days ago, I'd started wearing it during vid meetings to give the illusion that I wasn't only working from home.

If Ikeri would just talk to me, home would be a more pleasant place. I snarled at the hallway walls as I left the safety of the bedroom. I'd been working there through my link all morning but I couldn't ignore the rumbling in my stomach any longer. How was I supposed to fix anything between us if we couldn't even be in the same room?

When I passed the dining room table, Ikeri's lit datapad caught my eye. Any insight as to what was going on with her would be a gift from Geva herself. It was likely a conversation between her and Seeker Tomias regarding a safe place for her to employ her Seeker skills or maybe she'd been venting to one of the acolytes she'd trained with. Hells, I'd take anything that would give me a hint at a legitimate conversation starter other than 'I'm sorry'. That wasn't getting me anywhere.

I glanced into the common room and the kitchen to see if Ikeri was lurking. No one was in sight. Unless she was sitting at the security station, I was clear to invade her privacy. The light on the screen dimmed. Only a minute left before it shut off, and I didn't have her log in. Not that I couldn't have cracked it, but my conscience informed me that was going a step too far.

To be safe, I checked in with Neko, who informed me that he was the one at the security station and all was well. A touch on the screen brought the backlight up to full brightness. I allowed myself a glimpse at what was definitely a message. My breath caught when I saw it was addressed to me.

Nothing Ikeri did was haphazard. Maybe she'd heard me leaving the bedroom and baited her trap. That had to be what it was. Did she want me to read it or was this a test to see if I would respect her privacy as any decent person would?

After the memories I'd shared to show the dangers of people like me who might now be after her, Ikeri knew without a doubt that I wasn't a decent person. And there were plenty of us in the known universe. A young girl, so obviously marked as a healer, a novelty being non-Verian, and the daughter of parents with many enemies, made a tempting target. Even on peaceful Veria Prime, she'd brought out resentment in the calm and loving acolytes and other Seekers due to attaining her rank at such a young age. Any one of them could talk to the wrong person about what she'd done to earn her new rank, igniting the ambition of any credit-hungry fool. I might be known as a heartless bastard, but they'd bank on me paying any sum to prevent her from being harmed. Assuming they didn't already have a buyer lined up. A Seeker who could bring back the dead was priceless. My hands formed fists at my sides.

I closed my eyes, blocking out the tempting message. Was I supposed to avoid reading it to prove that I could be the father she'd known before she'd begun her healing sessions with her mother and seen us for who we really were?

Our lives had been different prior to our return to the Narvan, quiet, peaceful—allowing her an idyllic first few years of her early childhood. Now that we were back, Ikeri had learned what the regen tank was, how grievous the injuries were that repeatedly put me in it, and seen enough of my memories to understand why so many people wanted me dead.

At only ten, she was as revered as any elder Seeker, powerful and able to see the truth and pain hidden in a mind with the deftest touch. She was far too perceptive to be considered a child. And I was the advisor of multiple planets, a scarred man with far too much blood on his hands, who had exterminated the powerful and manipulative High Council and purged the Narvan of the terrifying memory-eating Arpex. As special as all of that made both of us, our accomplishments had also torn us apart.

Maybe something in her message would help put us back together. Resolved to my choice, I began to read.

About the Author

Jean Davis writes an array of speculative fiction and plays with chickens. When not ruining fictional lives from the comfort of her writing chair, she can be found devouring books and sushi, weeding her flower garden, or picking up hundreds of sticks while attempting to avoid the abundant snake population that also shares her yard. She lives in West Michigan with her musical husband, an attention-craving terrier, and a small flock of chickens and ducks.

Read her blog, and sign up for her mailing list at www.jeandavisauthor.com. You'll also find her on Facebook and Instagram at JeanDavisAuthor, and on Goodreads and Amazon.

If you enjoyed this book, please consider leaving a review. They are much appreciated. Thank you!